MW01676315

Praise for *Emancipated Heart*

"Jan pens an intriguing women's fiction wrapped in a rich tapestry of a historical setting that few know much about. I was hooked from the start and found it hard to put the book down. I so appreciated her attention to detail and research and know the readers will as well."

***Tracie Peterson**, best-selling author of over 100 novels including the Brides of Seattle and Lone Star Brides series.*

Author Jan Cline has penned an exceptionally poignant novel, set at the end of World War II, in a Japanese internment camp in Wyoming. With historical accuracy, *Emancipated Heart* takes readers to another place and time, with three-dimensional characters who quickly become real and compelling. I loved this book and look forward to more from this talented author!

***Kathi Macias** (www.kathimacias.com) is an award-winning author of more than fifty books, including Red Ink, a 2011 Christy finalist and the Golden Scrolls 2011 Novel of the Year.*

EMANCIPATED *heart*

Jan Cline

Cherry Blossom Publishing

Emancipated Heart

Published by: Cherry Blossom Publishing.

Formatting by Polgarus Studio
Cover design by Lynnette Bonner of Indie Cover Design
images ©
www.bigstock.com, File: # 18498260
Nurse's Cap: © BrokenSphere / Wikimedia Commons
Internment camp photo: By Parker, Tom, Photographer (NARA record: 4682167) (U.S. National Archives and Records Administration) [Public domain], via Wikimedia Commons
www.freeimages.com, File: # 1365437
www.freeimages.com, File: # 1425331

Printed in the U.S.A.

Thank you

…to God for daily inspiration.

…to my sister, Leah…for going with me
…to my friend and editor, Mick… for making me dig deeper
…to my friend, Suzanne…for listening
…to my friend, Jim…for showing me how to jump
…to my husband, Jerry…for not complaining about
my whining.

Books by
Jan Cline

A Heart Out of Hiding
Simple Devotion
The Greatest of These is Love

Contributing author to:
The Fiction Lover's Devotional Series
Books 2 & 4

Preface

If you had 48 hours to pack up only what you could carry, what would you choose to take with you? Which of your most precious possessions would you slip into a small suitcase to go with you to an unknown place for an unknown amount of time?

What if you were taken to prison without due process or charges brought against you? Would you assume your home or land or belongings would still be there when you returned? How would you handle being treated like the enemy of your own country when you had done nothing wrong?

On December 7, 1941, the day of the Japanese attack on Pearl Harbor, there were more than 110,000 people of Japanese descent living on the West Coast of the United States. The Issei, Japanese immigrants who were first generation of families living on U.S. soil, had come to establish themselves in America and to raise their children in a country they now called their own. All children born in America to Japanese immigrants were American citizens. Most were living the life of any other American, embracing the culture and trying to fit in, despite their obvious ethnicity.

On February 19, 1942, President Franklin D. Roosevelt issued **Executive Order 9066**, which permitted the military to circumvent the constitutional rights of American citizens in the name of national defense. Out of unfounded fears of espionage and sabotage along the Pacific, the government removed Japanese American men, women, and children from their homes with little warning, and placed them in internment camps, under deplorable conditions, in the interior of the country. Two-thirds of the internees were U.S. citizens.

These Japanese Americans, half of whom were children, even orphans, were incarcerated for up to 4 years, without due process of law, in bleak, **remote camps** surrounded by barbed wire and armed guards. At the time, Executive Order 9066 was justified as a "military necessity". However, it was later documented that there was never any proof of disloyalty or espionage for the Japanese Americans who were interned. None of them was ever charged with a crime.

The cause of this unprecedented action in American history was racial prejudice, wartime hysteria, and a failure of political leadership. The effects traveled home with the Japanese Americans for decades after the war ended. Many of them returned to the West Coast with no homes left, no money, and no jobs. They were, for the most part, not welcomed back in the towns and neighborhoods where they lived in harmony before the war. The struggle to regain dignity, financial security, and the right to be called American citizens continued for another generation.

Emancipated Heart's setting is based on the real internment camp named Heart Mountain Internment Camp, near Cody, Wyoming. I changed the name to Grand Peak to afford me some leniency in historical accuracy. This book is a work of fiction and the author does not claim the events within the story or characters to be real, only inspired by actual people and happenings.

The true events of the Japanese American internment is in recent years being brought to light, but most of Americans today know little about the experience or the historical facts surrounding it. After studying it for over a year, I hope I have shared a piece of the story in a realistic representation of the time. Many will take sides, but I encourage readers to just enjoy the book, then learn the facts leading up to and including post-internment. Below is a list of other books that might be of interest.

Jan Cline
www.jancline.net

Glossary:

Issei: First generation Japanese Americans who immigrated from Japan to America

Nisei: Second generation Japanese Americans, born in America

Origami: The Japanese art of folding paper into decorative shapes and figures.

John 8:36

So if the Son sets you free, you will be free indeed.

Emancipated:

...to free from restraint or influence; release from bondage.

Chapter 1

May 1945, Grand Peak Internment Camp, Wyoming

As Hana Kato hurried to wrap the framed family picture in one of Papa's plain white hankies, she held the fabric to her nose to make sure it didn't smell of bluing. Papa hated that. He was safe—only the fragrance of Mama's special soap remained. A minor detail, but the little things would mean so much from now on, because today Papa was going to prison.

Never mind that he was already in a prison of sorts, confined to a 46,000 acre camp surrounded by a barbed wire fence. And never mind that he was an innocent man.

The howling wind grated against her frayed nerves. All night it had persisted, sifting dirt through the small cracks in the family's barrack cubicle. Any other day her mother would scold her brother, Martin, directing him where to stuff mud in the holes in the floor and walls to keep out the dust. Today it didn't seem important. Today none of them could even fill the holes in their hearts.

Mama folded two pairs of faded trousers, then laid them in the suitcase on top of two shirts she had pressed with a hot rock wrapped in newsprint. Hana counted the rolled up socks; only room for three pairs. She pulled from her pocket the tiny image of a frog folded from the whitest piece of paper she could find, and slipped it into a corner of the suitcase.

"Safe return, Papa."

She shut it and ran her fingers over the faded print of the Kato name and address in Japan. This case had traveled the seas so many years ago, only to end up in such a sad place. Before Hana could latch it, Mama held up one finger.

"Wait, Hana. He need one more thing." She shuffled over to their only cupboard and rummaged through her tins of homemade Japanese teas and store-bought tobacco.

Little sister, Chiko, whined something to Martin from the other side of the room. More of the same sibling bickering that had gone on all morning. Her twenty-five years of sisterly experience told her there would be no stopping it. Her concentration waned as she endured the banter.

Chiko rattled on about something childish for a fifteen year old. Martin snapped back. "That's a terrible thing to say."

Chiko crossed her arms over her chest. "I don't care. I won't go. I'm too embarrassed."

Hana longed to crawl into a hole alone for a week or two, but today she had to work through the pain and push Martin and Chiko to do the same. Mama would require patience, a fleeting luxury at the moment.

With her throat tightening, she couldn't bite back her irritation. "Do you two think you're the only ones feeling bad? How selfish can you be, especially in front of Mama?" She pressed a finger to Chiko's chest. "I don't ever want to hear you say you're embarrassed about Papa again. He did what was right—the only man in camp willing to stand up for our rights."

She turned to Martin. "And you, brother. He protested so you wouldn't have to be drafted when you turn eighteen."

Martin flopped onto his cot and leaned his back against the wall. "A lot of good that did. Nothing's changed. Besides, I just might want to join up. Better than sticking around here waiting for—for I don't know what."

Chiko glared at Hana and reached for her prized Life magazine. She had worn the cover to tatters, losing herself in its pages when life got too hard. "And my friends make fun of me. I hate being a Kato."

Mama broke her silence. "Chiko! Shi! Walls are thin. You want whole barrack to hear?"

Hana shook her head. How could they have lived with Papa in this camp for almost four years and not know how important it was for him to be a voice against the injustices here? She glared at the two, words of rebuke spinning in a whirlwind. "I don't feel sorry for either of you. Papa's the one who's suffering. You've seen how pale and thin he is."

Martin thumbed a deck of cards. He'd better not lock her gaze or she would give him one of her killer stares. At seventeen, he should know better than to make things harder for them today. He kept his eyes on the cards. "You don't have to be so mean, Hana. Chiko's right. Papa's made it hard for us."

"I'm sorry if you think I'm mean, but…" Hana glanced at her watch. What? It couldn't be 9:20! "We're going to be late if everyone doesn't hurry." She came close to Mama who teetered on her hands and knees, rifling through Papa's box of belongings. "Mama-san, what *are* you looking for?"

"I look for his pipe. He will want his pipe." She pulled socks and ties from the box and tossed them on the dusty floor.

Although Hana could hear the minutes ticking away, she wished she could give Mama the time she needed to prepare for Papa's departure. Her stomach ached to see her mother so fixated on his comfort, torturing herself by avoiding the inevitable.

Hana scooped up the socks and ties, and knelt beside Mama, swallowing hard to keep her words respectful. "Everything he needs is in the suitcase. Time to get dressed, Mama-san."

Mama shuffled past her and tugged on the curtain around her cot, but not before smoothing the blanket on Papa's bed. Her slender bony hand caressed his pillow with a tender sweep.

Chiko examined her white blouse and marched toward her bed. "If I have to go, I need to find something different to wear. This blouse is stained on the edge."

Hana caught her by the arm. "There…is…no…time."

Chiko's eyes widened. She slinked to a chair and eased into it, staring at Hana through tears. Hana closed her eyes and counted some slow breaths. Deeper. One, two, three, four.

Mama wiggled through the curtain in her best—her only—Japanese tunic. The one Papa bought for her in Japan for their wedding day twenty-six years ago. The tunic of quilted red and glistening gold tapestry complimented her straight black trousers and petite loafers.

Hana blinked to clear her blurry vision and glanced at her parent's faded wedding photo hanging on the wall. Mama hadn't changed much; her eyes still bright and her waist still narrow. She smiled at her mother. "Mama-san. You are lovely."

A tear escaped and rolled down Mama's flushed cheek. Hana reached for the suitcase and closed it, snapping the rusty latches. "We'll miss saying good-bye if we don't go now. Martin, take the suitcase. Sachiko, grab the umbrella to shade Mama from the sun."

"Don't call me Sachiko. It's Chiko."

Hana bit her lip. "Fine, just get moving. Come on, Mama-san. Let's go."

Martin slid his comb from his pocket and raked it through his slicked black hair. He grabbed the suitcase and stomped out the door. Chiko followed, leaving the umbrella leaning against the wall in the corner. Hana tucked it under her arm. She peered in the cracked mirror and grimaced at the reflection. Her once porcelain skin, parched by the hot summers, now bloomed with freckles. At least her raven hair still held a hint of shine. She would do her best to shine from the inside out for Papa's good-bye. First she would have to brush away the cobwebs of sadness sticking to her, binding her in a suffocating cocoon.

Catching up with Mama, she opened the umbrella, blocking the rays of sun streaming from a glaring white sky. "Hurry, everyone. We're going to be late." She forced her uncooperative feet to move, and tensed the rest of her body, willing it to function. This was not the day to succumb to the rolling in her gut, the pounding in her head. If Papa could live through today, so could she.

It seemed impossible this day had come. Over the previous weeks she and Mama had worn a shortcut path across the dry field of scrub brush to the internment camp detention room to visit Papa. Each time, Hana would wrap up her sorrow securely as they breached the doorway of the building, hoping Papa would believe her strong façade. She wasn't fooling him, but he never let on. After ten minutes of chatter about the weather and what they would do when they left this place, she and Mama would say good-bye and be on their way up the hill again, back to their living quarters where Papa's cot sat empty.

Now as they neared the administration building, she gazed across the field and wondered how long it would take for their path to grow over with weeds. She would have walked it forever if Papa could have stayed in camp. Wishing could never make it so. Not even prayers could.

Hana stopped at the top of the hill. Two buses lined up in front of the building where Papa had been held. Camp police paced back and forth between small crowds of men. It seemed as if—no! Were they already boarding?

"Mama-san, Chiko, Martin! We have to run or we'll miss him." She waved Martin over and grabbed the suitcase from him. "You help Mama. I'll run with the case."

Gravel crunched under her thin loafers as she sprinted toward the gate. What if they couldn't get there in time? Papa would think they had forgotten him. He would think they were ashamed. Perspiration mixed with tears soaked her face, destroying any chance to look nice for Papa.

She glanced behind her. "Hurry, Chiko!" Mama stumbled. Martin came along side to steady her, slipping his muscular arm around her waist. Hana's throat twitched as she sucked in enough hot air to keep her going another few steps.

Several women and children clung to the fencing, shouting tearful last minute endearments. The sounds of crying were muffled by the noises of busses and soldiers barking orders. The bitter smell of exhaust smoke intensified after the first small bus left the compound.

Hana burst past the end of the building, around the fence to the locked gate. She resisted the urge to shake it, lest she make a scene. Even that wouldn't be worse than the agony of a missed embrace. The hot metal penetrated her palms.

An officer stood near, guarding the gate. Tall, blonde, Caucasian. She tried not to think of him as the enemy. "Please, sir. I must give my father his bag."

She glanced past the officer, spotting a familiar figure at the end of the prisoner's line. His posture even more subdued than yesterday. "Papa!"

He turned, his eyes wide on her, showing the first hint of fear she had ever seen in him. The sight of the deep lines above his brows and his shallow cheeks chilled her.

Papa righted himself with calm resolve in his demeanor, his tone. "Where is Mama?"

With no such calm remaining in her, she screamed over the rumble of the bus engines. "They're right behind me, Papa-san. Come to the fence."

The officer opened the gate and reached his arm toward Hana. "Give it to me. I'll get it on the bus."

She caught the man's expression—compassion, not condemnation. With nothing to lose, she stood up straight and gazed into his eyes. "Might we have a moment with my father? We've come to see him off."

Just then, Mama, Martin, and Chiko reached her, crowding in along the fence like beggars. Their faces pleaded what she had to say out loud. "Please, let us see him."

He hesitated, looking back at the camp director waving his arms and yelling at the prisoners to hurry along. Then he glanced down the row at Mama and the others. He pursed his lips and waved Papa over. "You have one minute. But only through the fence."

Hana stepped back and let Mama inch closer. Papa hurried to them and clasped his fingers over Mama's through the fence wires. Martin held back, but Chiko clung to Mama, whimpering softly.

Chiko could break any minute.

Papa's eyes glistened as he whispered to Mama something secret. Then he turned to Hana. "You in charge. It's very important. Take care of Mama, and if I don't come back, you find way home."

Hana's chest ached at the heavy words of responsibility.

Chiko's whimper turned to wailing. "Papa-san!"

Oh, little sister, don't. Be strong for Papa.

He reached a few fingers through the fence and touched her cheek. "Sachiko. Everything will be fine. You help Mama too." His eyes pinned on Martin, dark and resolute. "You finish school. Then prove to me you can be man of house." Their eyes locked for a moment. Martin's face seemed to turn to stone. He turned and marched toward the barracks on the hill.

Papa called after him. "Good-bye, my son."

Martin halted and hesitated for a moment. Over his shoulder he mumbled. "Good-bye, Papa-san."

Hana's heart broke for both of them. This feud had gone on long enough.

The guard sauntered over and stood behind Papa. "Kato. Let's go."

Hana watched her parents embrace only with their eyes. As sweet a moment as she had ever seen them share. Mama reached into her tunic pocket and pulled out Papa's pipe. She slipped it through the fence and into Papa's hand. He winked, and the smile that made everything seem all right appeared. Maybe they would all live through this. Maybe they could get him freed to come back to them.

She closed her eyes. In her mind's eye they were a family again, away from the war, away from internment and back to trusting the America they'd pledged to honor and support. Could it be they would go back to their home on Bainbridge Island? Back to the farming Papa loved? Maybe they would feast at Mama's table again soon.

Papa stuffed the pipe in his pants pocket just as he backed away from the fence barrier.

Chiko stuck as many fingers as she could through the fence and waved them at him. "Good-bye, Papa-san. Good-bye."

The camp director screamed an obscenity at Papa, telling him to get aboard. Before he turned to board the bus, he smiled and waved. His chin dipped in a slow nod at Hana. She couldn't let him down. The vision of his gaunt face remained with her as the bus sputtered out of the yard and away from camp. Away from his family. Mama and Chiko walked arm in arm up the hill ahead of her. Chiko dragged the tip of the umbrella through the dirt.

Hana spoke to herself the words she should have shouted to Papa as he left. "I'll bring you home, Papa. Whatever it takes, I'll find a way, and I'll bring you home."

John Yamada glanced up at the tower and then punched the baseball into his worn leather glove. They could talk about the group's plans right under the guard's lazy nose. Like hiding in plain sight. Some of the soldiers had grown complacent with their duty, and this one, despite the raw fury in his eyes, most of all. Still, what was left of the resistance group had seen enough trouble, and John continued to monitor any activity. Mr. Kato's words of caution rang in his ears even now.

He longed to wind up and throw the ball as far as it would go, past the tower, beyond the fence, and out into the scrub brush. Instead he pitched it to Thomas who tossed it to Gene. They all knew there would be no way to retrieve a ball on the other side of the fence.

With 468 barracks to dodge in and out of, hiding wasn't a problem. Most of the boys in camp had acquired the skill of tracking shadows and hugging corners. Still, rebellion required risk. Which could mean time behind bars like some of the other resistors. The isolated detention room held no allure and he wouldn't chance it. Not unless he had to.

They talked just loud enough to be heard by each other. John had been careless with talk before and paid a price. Frank threw John the ball and it landed hard in his glove. He rubbed it in the soft leather.

"I'm telling you, we need to lay low. Sarge watches us like a hawk."

The guard they called Sarge lurked everywhere these days, looking for troublemakers in the confines of the camp. John wondered what kind of job the man had before the war. Likely a profession that fed his secret desire to bully people. His imposing broad shoulders still made John jumpy.

Thomas piped in. "But some of the guys feel like we should do something to keep the momentum." The ball smacked his glove. He passed it on.

John kept talking as the ball went around. "Things have changed too much. You know some of those younger guys want to bully their way to importance. They use the group Mr. Kato started as a way to cause trouble for no reason. That's not what the group is about. We have to watch them close."

Thomas answered. "Mr. Kato would be pretty upset to hear what some of the guys plan to do. They aren't interested in making slow progress through peaceful demonstrations."

Frank jumped to snag the ball. "It'll be tough to continue the group with Mr. Kato gone. Who'll be in charge now? I mean besides you, John."

Someone called out a distance away. "Maybe me."

John knew the voice. "Hey, Martin." He tossed the ball again. "Don't blame you for skipping school today. Sorry about your father. I know your family must be awfully upset."

Martin dropped his arms to his side and inched toward him, each step growing in stride. "Seems to me if you cared, you would have been there."

All eyes on John, the young men continued in silence to throw the ball in the circle.

He talked slow and without much volume. "I do care, Martin. You should know that by now. I stood by your father through building the resistance group and through his arrest. I just didn't think the family wanted me there." The guard would be watching even though he couldn't hear the conversations. John curled up his lips in a grand smile, despite his churning stomach.

Frank slipped off his glove. "I gotta go."

Thomas tucked the ball under his arm. "Ya, me too. See you later, John." He stopped in front of Martin. "Good thing for your family you're graduating soon. Sorry about your dad."

"Thanks." Martin patted Thomas on the shoulder and moved closer to John, his jaw locked and eyes full of confidence.

A confrontation would be undesirable here in the yard. A casual glance at the tower revealed an even more zealous officer now stood over them, leaning his elbows on the rail of the tower, his gaze fixed on them.

John held his smile. "Let's walk for a minute."

Martin sauntered ahead after returning an exaggerated grin—a willing player in the game of cat and mouse. They slipped between the barracks and took the path to the Block 15 mess hall. The pungent smell of boiled fish and rice floated from the open doors. The line for lunch already stretched beyond the recreation building. Children too young for school scampered between their parents, laughing and squealing in a genuine lack of care for their situation. How wonderful it would be to feel free-spirited again. The memories of that feeling had already faded for John.

"Look. So innocent and unaware they are." John pointed to the little ones. "Is what we're doing in the group going to help them, Martin?" The question had plagued him since the arrest of resistors a month ago.

"I think so, and I want to join you. Not because of my father, but because I need to be part of something important. My father wants me to keep busy with something that will grow me up, but I don't think he had the group in mind. That's my idea." His chest puffed ever so slightly. John recognized the same naïve arrogance that once consumed him and his friends.

John looked the other way. Martin would be the natural selection to lead the group, following in his father's footsteps, if he had the stomach for it. Hana wouldn't be pleased to see her brother involved. He could play it safe and say no to Martin for Hana's sake, or he could give him his chance to belong and to become a man.

He knew what that felt like. His father had charged him with manhood too early. At least Mr. Kato hadn't abandoned his children by choice like John's father. The pain of that day still lurked as an ache in his chest. He remembered the sight of mother and father boarding a ship to Japan, his mother waving from the deck as if they were going on some luxury vacation, leaving him to fend for himself.

John toed the ground. "I'll agree to that as long as you do exactly what I say. No rough stuff. We have to be careful from now on. The war has to end sometime and I don't want you in prison with your father when it does."

Martin stuck out his hand and John gave it a firm shake. "Fine by me. Just tell me when the next secret meeting is and I'll be there."

His enthusiasm told John he had no clue how hard it was to resist the government, especially in wartime and within the confines of camp.

As John shook Martin's hand he envisioned finally having a brother, maybe even belonging to a family like he had never known. The family he'd been dreaming of since he first set eyes on the Kato clan.

"And if my sister finds out, I'll blame you." Martin laughed and slapped John on the back.

John tensed. The sting reminded him of all the times his father had done the same. He smirked to make light of it.

"Don't you dare. I need all the help I can get with her." He wanted to inhale the words back into his mouth. Martin could misunderstand.

Martin looked to the ground. "A word of advice. Hana's got enough on her mind. She doesn't need any more problems, if you know what I mean. I like you, John, but my sister needs someone who doesn't follow trouble."

The words rang true, but stung just the same. Still, it wasn't Martin's place to keep him from her. She had his heart from the first moment he met her. Martin had no reason to fear, but he'd play along and be careful where Hana was concerned. Their friendship had suffered once he became involved in her father's group. Another blow might finish it.

"Sure. I just meant that I want to help your family and sometimes she's a bit resistant. She's a proud woman, your sister." He nudged Martin with his baseball glove. "Gotta go."

Martin called after him. "Okay, keep me informed."

John left him standing in the winding lunch line and jogged toward home. Eating tasteless fish heads and rice in a hot mess hall wasn't his idea of a good meal. He turned the corner to Block 22. Hana walked in his direction with her eyes fixed on the ground. Her hair shone in the sun, her pleated skirt flipped in the breeze. John waited for her to look up. Would she be glad to see him, or ignore him? These days he never knew what to expect.

She stopped short when she saw him, but he inched closer, words stuck in his throat.

"Hana. How are you?"

"Fine." She stepped to get around him but he blocked her, planting his feet firmly in her way, close enough to smell her rose water perfume. The same his mother wore.

He couldn't keep his eyes off her dark intense eyes. "I wanted to go to the station this morning. I didn't think I should intrude."

She looked away for a moment then shrugged. "You thought wrong. I…Papa could have used your support." She glanced at her watch. "I have to get to Mrs. Saito's. She doesn't like me to be late picking up her laundry."

He blurted out the only thing he thought would redeem him. "I want to help. I'll do whatever I can, I promise."

She stared at him. He didn't expect her to believe him. He would have to show her. She was just that kind of girl.

He hesitated, but moved aside to let her pass and ignored the opportunity to go after her. He spent too much of his time trying to please her, but now the compulsion to tell her he cared overwhelmed him.

"Hana?"

She turned and continued walking backwards, shielding her eyes from the sun.

He cleared his throat. "Your father will be okay. Everything will be okay." He would take her pain if he could. The thought of her suffering jabbed at his heart. How could he make her understand he wanted to help? Then again, he couldn't even help himself.

She shook her head. "Wrong again. It will never be okay, John." She dashed around the corner, leaving him feeling he had just been cut out of her life in one quick slice.

He couldn't move. Nothing made sense if Hana hated him. He had to regain her friendship, but that could mean leaving the resistance group she resented so much. Everything had changed since Mr. Kato's arrest. Especially Hana.

Making difficult choices wasn't his strong suit, but he had no family to counsel him. Michael. He needed to talk to Michael. When things got bad, his words of wisdom always helped. He resumed his jog, away from his barrack.

"Please be home, my friend."

Chapter 2

Hana wove her way past the last row in block 10, hurrying to move from John's view. Everything had changed, especially her ability to trust her feelings, and especially her feelings about John. One thing was for sure, she and Mama would have to keep earning what little money they could in Papa's absence.

She peeked in the small window of the one room sundries store. Women and children with packages in hand bustled through the door, their one little piece of shopping heaven. A reminder of the hometown freedoms they left behind.

Old man Hosokawa leaned out the door and smiled, peering over the top of his spectacles held together with tape. "Your Papa need tobacco for his pipe? We just get some today."

Visions of Mama slipping his pipe into Papa's hand tugged at her heart. If she had the money, she would take Mr. Hosokawa's suggestion and buy some to send Papa. Until Mrs. Saito paid them, considering such extravagances would be out of the question.

"No, Papa doesn't smoke his pipe anymore. But thank you." The first spoken words of confirmation. Papa was gone. The finality of it snaked through her stomach, leaving a sour taste in her mouth. She might never see him again.

She stepped away before he asked for an explanation. The simple shopkeeper didn't know about anything happening in camp. His life centered on the store, volunteering to keep the internees' enterprise going.

She checked her watch. One o'clock? Mrs. Saito would prickle and fuss if she were late. The uppity woman never missed an opportunity to flaunt her self-endowed superiority. Just because she and her husband had money, she scorned those who had to work hard to earn back what they had lost to the government.

She remembered Papa telling Mama about them. *Evacuation not hurt them much. Frozen bank accounts and stolen possessions not affect the Saitos. Their life savings somehow stay safe.* Mama had shook her head and refused to hear more, even knowing how unfair it was that Papa had been targeted, yet Mr. Saito wasn't. They were both prominent businessmen, yet Mr. Saito had other connections.

Hana would endure the woman only to keep the meager income doing her laundry brought. As she came close to the Saito's barrack, two older women passed her, turning away their faces. Hana's ears burned and she looked straight ahead. Best not to look around and see who else might be scorning her.

Before she could climb the barrack steps to enter, Mrs. Saito appeared with her hands plastered to her hips, her wrinkled face puckered in a scowl. "You don't come in. We won't need you for laundry anymore. Your family shame the rest here. You people no good. Don't come here." She slammed the door. The sound may as well have been the rolling of a stone over Hana's tomb. Heat crept up her neck.

Two men behind her clapped—slow and deliberate. Chills tingled her arms. She couldn't have anticipated or even dreamed this would happen. She hadn't committed any transgression against the Saito family, so why the hostility? Papa had done no wrong. He defended their rights when they wouldn't. His rallies and public speeches against the drafting of internees were done to inform the people of how wrong it was. Even the Saitos had agreed of the absurdity of drafting men to fight for the government who imprisoned them. Now, fear had overshadowed their sense of right and wrong. Papa represented trouble, which they wanted no part of.

With her insides quivering she backed off the step. What would she tell Mama? Pouring rejection like this on her now was inconceivable. She walked along the perimeter of the compound, taking the long way home. The view through the fence never changed. The mountain beyond the desolate stretch of dry land stood as a work of art to her when she first arrived. After three years it still towered over the camp—nothing more than a cold jagged interruption against billowing clouds.

Now more than ever she longed for their real home. For the tangy spray of sea air and the shade of tall green trees. How long had it been since she walked through Pikes Place Market or sat quietly on a bench in the little park down the street from her house? How long would God allow this humiliation? She never understood His silence. And now a new shame to bear. She dismissed it from her heart. She would leave faith to Mama until they could join the others who had left for home. They could go too, as soon as they knew Papa could come back and go with them.

"Mama. She'll be so hurt. How will we earn money now?" She stopped and let the tears come. She had been too busy, too focused on the family to cry all morning like Chiko. Now it erupted like a furious volcano, violent and unstoppable.

She stood still and let it spill until she emptied her storehouse of strength. She couldn't go on like this and still try to reorganize the family, and fulfill Papa's wishes.

She slogged passed the next barrack and breathed in the sweet bouquet of tobacco smoke coming from a window. Without Mrs. Saito's business, there wouldn't be money for the trip home, let alone tobacco for Papa. This was a challenge she hadn't anticipated. There had to be a way to earn money for a fresh start once they left this place.

Bless his heart, Papa had little time his odd jobs over the last few months, depleting their coffee can stash. She cringed to think of the few dollars left in the bottom of the can.

She had a profession if she had the courage to go back to it. She heard Papa's words from the past, urging her to go back. *You good nurse. You go back to what you love.* Her knees knocked just to think of it.

Off in the distance the power plant smoke stack next to the hospital stood like a sentinel. Grey plumes poured from it day and night. The hospital sprawled out several barracks long, all connected by a hallways and other barracks. She had never been inside, but heard about the 150 beds and all the Japanese American doctors and nurses working there for very little pay.

"Can I really do it now, Papa?" Not even the hot wind answered her. "What if I can't remember how?"

"What's that?" Martin called from behind her. "You talking to yourself again, sis? Where have you been?"

She spun around to face him. "I could ask you the same question. You should have been home with Mama this morning. What's wrong with you?"

"Hey. What's wrong with *you*?" He leaned close to her face. "You've been crying. Are you still upset about Papa?"

He put his hand on her shoulder but she brushed it away. What did he know of her misery? He had escaped most of the emotional scene this morning.

"I have bad news. Mrs. Saito fired me. We can't do her laundry anymore because of Papa's trouble." No tears now. They had all dried up.

He held his palm to his forehead and winced. "Oh, man. Mama will throw a fit."

Hana leaned in and whispered. "Yes, and what will we do for money now?"

He pulled at her elbow and they took a few steps. "We'll think of something. Besides, it's less time you and Mama will have to spend at the latrine laundry basin."

Although not having to stand in line at the latrine for a turn at the wash basin was appealing, it wasn't much of a tradeoff. She pulled her arm away. "I already thought of something. I'm going to get a job at the hospital until we can go home. It's time I went back to nursing." She wanted to scold him, but she just needed to know one thing. "What are *you* going to do?"

Martin cleared his throat. His silence made Hana's stomach knot.

No wonder Papa had put her in charge. Martin had given up too, like the old man she met the other day. Maybe it was story time for her brother, just like the old days back home. Papa would tell them stories before bed if they were good.

"Martin, I had a strange encounter a few days ago. I came across an old man in a tattered straw hat hobbling along the space between the barracks. He stared at me for a moment." She looked to the ground. "A haunting stare like you see on the Issei faces here."

"And?"

"He picked through the dirt with a stick, then stooped to brush off something near his feet. He dug with his finger around the shape and pulled up a round rock. He held it out to me and said how perfect it was for his rock garden." She laughed, remembering his face. "His smile had dark holes where teeth should have been."

"Where are you going with this story?" Martin cocked his head.

She ignored his sarcasm. "He explained to me about his treasure." She tried to imitate the old man's wavering voice. "See? It perfect shape." "He rubbed more dirt from the stone. I told him he must have a lovely rock garden and he said yes, but it wasn't as good as the one at his home in Oregon."

Martin sighed and rolled his eyes.

"The old man's smile faded and he turned to stare past the fence. His eyes were so sad. He hung his head and stared at the rock in his hand. It dropped on the ground, then he turned and shuffled away."

She couldn't speak for a moment, the memory of the pain in the old man's eyes thickened her throat.

Martin toed the ground. "What are you trying to tell me, Hana?"

"He was like so many others here, dropping their dreams like useless rocks. This must have been how Papa felt this morning. He once found strength in the land, joy in the rich soil and the first flower. You remember how much he loved the process. His dreams were tied up on the farm."

"I don't understand."

"We can't let Papa give up too. We have to do all we can to stay strong while he's gone and encourage him not to lose hope. We have to work to bring him home. Do you want him to end up like that old man? Do *you* want to end up like that?"

"No." He turned his head for a moment. His eyes filled with tears when he looked at her. "I know Papa was hurt. I'll do what I have to do, but it will be my way." He stuffed his hands in his pockets and left her standing there.

She relented and followed him as they weaved their way through the barracks. She surveyed the block that had been their home for too long. Even in the darkest monotony of the place, Papa had always courted light with his playful antics and gift of music. Their tiny room had often glowed with songs and hymns the missionaries had taught them. It would be lifeless and boring without Papa. She would begin right away to write letters and make contacts to secure his release—with or without Martin's help. She heard of one man from Camp Manzanar whose sentence had been commuted. Why not Papa?

First things first. She glanced back at the hospital and shivered with all the memories of why she gave up her nursing career in the first place. The sights and smells of Pearl Harbor blackened with smoke rolled over her, reminding her with a shudder. At least there she had worked in a modern hospital until that terrible day. What would she find in this primitive facility? It looked more like a tarpapered warehouse than a medical building.

She shook off her doubts and grasped for hope from deep down.

"It's time, Papa."

Part of her wanted to run home. The other part heard the siren call of caring for patients again. If she ran, she would be no stronger than the old man with the rock she had told Martin about. Running would mean giving up. No matter how scared she was, the time had come to face her demons from that day at Pearl, but the pain of it lay deep in her bones. She forced herself to stay.

She stood inside the bare walls of a hospital made of barracks, staring at the swinging light bulb hanging on a wire from the ceiling. The wind breached the doors and windows here as much as any other building in camp. Unpainted wood floors and walls made mockery of what should be a dignified sterile environment. She fought the urge to grab the broom propped up beside the doorway and start sweeping the dust out the door.

The same round-faced nurse who curtly greeted her appeared from around the corner. Her salt and pepper hair, scrunched in a bun, slouched to one side of the crown of her head. Her skirt waist bunched around her ample tummy. "Doctor Bennett will be with you soon. Just wait here." She pointed to a white wooden bench and lumbered through a doorway down the hall.

Hana pulled her papers to her chest and let out a slow breath, then nestled into the seat and wiped her sweaty palms on her white skirt. She bit her lip as she thought about working again, and with Caucasian doctors. Already, the bitter scent of disinfectant ignited her memory of better times in nurse's training. All her old friends must be working in doctor's offices all over the Northwest. Of all the girls in her class she would be the only one interned. The rest were white—and free. She could see each of their faces and prayed they were all untouched by the war.

A young man burst through the front doors and sauntered to the reception desk. His rugged unshaven face and faded slacks clashed with his air of confidence. He reached over the top of the counter and pulled up a clipboard as if he owned the place. Hana stilled.

Maybe he wouldn't notice her. She didn't need an overly zealous janitor smirking at her while she worked on her courage for the interview. She leaned forward to peer down the hall. *Where's that nurse?*

When she moved, her bundle of papers slid onto the floor. One sheet floated like a feather on the breeze from the open window, and then landed at the man's feet. She gasped quietly. If only she could be invisible. He reached down and picked up the paper and turned to her. His brows raised as he scanned the document.

"Miss, uh, Kato is it?"

Here it comes. A rude remark from a Caucasian.

He stepped closer and waved the paper at her. "I believe you dropped this." She snatched it from his grip. The glint in his blue eyes shone for only a second before he looked away.

"Thank you." She fussed with the papers to put them back in order. She had spent hours organizing her records and credentials, having kept them with her even when they evacuated.

Mama had teased her for being so fastidious. "You good at organizing. Make good wife."

Now her hands shook as she gathered them into order. She had no doubt these pages would impress Doctor Bennett.

The young man took a few steps backward toward the desk and then leaned against it. "So, you're a nurse?"

Her foot tapped nervously on the floor and she quickly crossed her ankles. How amateur she must look. This morning's cold oatmeal from the mess hall rolled around in her stomach.

She looked up. "Yes. I'm here to interview for a nursing position." Her cheeks heated just to talk to him. Conversations with strangers weren't her strong suit. His eyes danced as if she had told him a precious secret. "Great. I'm sure you won't have any trouble getting a job here. We need some replacement nurses." He slapped the clipboard onto the desk and traipsed down the hall, whistling a Benny Goodman tune.

She rehearsed her greeting to Doctor Bennett, imagining him to be a stodgy old Caucasian man with spectacles and a receding hairline.

She would treat him with respect, no matter what his attitude. She wanted this job and would exert the charm needed to get it. Wouldn't she?

She closed her eyes for a few minutes until a woman's voice jolted her.

"Doctor Bennett will see you now." The nurse pointed down the hall. "This way." Her tone snapped like a rubber band.

Following her down the hallway proved to be a challenge, but after running to keep up with the woman's thick legs, she stopped.

A sign hung crooked above a door to her right. DOCTOR NEIL BENNETT, CHIEF OF STAFF. The nurse knocked and placed her hand on the doorknob.

"Come." Hana's neck tensed. This was it—a real interview.

She followed the nurse into the office and stood beside her.

"Doctor Bennett, Hana Mato."

Hana jerked her head and forced a smile at the woman. "It's *Kato*."

She frowned back. "Sorry."

The doctor sat with his back to Hana, cranking the handle on a pencil sharpener.

"Thank you, Nurse Potter." He didn't sound older or look older from the back. In fact…

He spun his chair around. "Good morning again, Miss Kato."

Hana's heart leapt to her throat. Doctor Bennett? The young man she had just spoken to? She felt her mouth hang open and snapped it shut. Even though her throat closed up, void of moisture, her palms managed to be cold and wet.

He stood and reached out his hand. "I'm Doctor Neil Bennett."

Why hadn't he revealed his true identity out in the foyer? Was he trying to make her feel like a fool? She held back a rebuke. Then he warmed the room with his broad smile. She wiped her hand discretely on her skirt and shook his hand, feeling the warmth of it melt her icy skin.

He motioned toward the chair. "Please, sit down." Hana forced her wobbling legs to move.

He slid horn-rimmed glasses up on his nose, making him look more like a mad professor than a doctor. His flirty stare glued her to her seat even though she itched to flee. His sandy hair could use a comb and his lab coat the hot end of an iron, but his long eyelashes made up for that. Agnes and Shirley back home would like him. They were always on the hunt for a handsome doctor.

She fumbled with the small stack of precious information and handed it to him. "I think you'll see I'm very qualified. I—"

He held up his hand and studied the pages. Hana pursed her lips and glanced at the stacks of files and books on his desk. His flippant manner mimicked that of the young Caucasians she had met before and since the war, but none of the doctors she ever worked with were so casual.

He leaned his elbows on the desk. "Yes, qualified. I see you were at Pearl Harbor. I was on Oahu that day too. My parents were missionaries there."

"I would have been promoted the next day to head nurse in the trauma wing if the island hadn't been bombed. I've been told I have a natural aptitude." She regretted saying it. What if all that talent had faded? Besides, it sounded like bragging and she wasn't sure she still had skills to brag about.

Someone knocked and marched through the door. Now this was what a doctor should look like. Hana surveyed the gentleman's tall stout frame and thinning hair. Older than Doctor Bennett and more distinguished looking, with wire-rimmed glasses and a tie under his crisp white jacket.

His chin jutted forward. "I'd like to see you in the hall please, Doctor Bennett."

"I'm sort of busy right now, Doctor Davidson. Can it wait?"

"No, it can't." The man stepped back, hands in his pockets.

Doctor Bennett stood, his face knit in a scowl. "Please excuse me, Miss Kato. It appears I've been summoned."

She sighed hard. Not even a courteous introduction. She leaned back in her chair and tried to relax her tense muscles. The messy office brought a smile to her face. Two pots of dried up house plants rested on the window sill, drained of life like the tumbleweeds outside. What kind of doctor must he be if he couldn't keep a plant alive?

The voices outside the door raised in pitch and intensity. Hana heard every other phrase—enough to know the conversation centered on her.

"...enough Japanese..."

"...but qualified..."

"...don't hire..."

Hana clenched her jaw. Clearly the job wasn't a sure thing. She felt the blood drain from her hands as she grasped the wooden arms of the chair. Maybe she should leave. Yes. Make a quick exit and forget the whole thing. She scooped up her papers from the desk and stuffed them under her arm.

"Are you going somewhere?" Doctor Bennett nearly sang the words.

She stared straight ahead. "I thought it best considering the argument in the hall."

He strolled around his desk and motioned for her to sit. She did, after hesitating a moment.

The young doctor smirked. "About that conversation. Let me fill you in. I'm Chief of Staff. He's not. Enough said." He held out his hand. "Let's look at those papers again."

Just as Hana returned to her chair, Nurse Potter bolted through the door.

"Emergency, Doctor Bennett."

He jumped up from his chair. "I'm so sorry, I have to go. We can finish this conversation later, I hope." He threw his stethoscope around his neck and ran through the door, and then poked his head in again. "Oh, you're hired."

As his footsteps echoed down the hall, she slumped in the chair, afraid to breathe. Hired. A nurse once again and a weight lifted from her chest. Papa would be so proud. Even though Japanese American nurses earned a fraction of the Caucasian head nurse in the camps, she could still put Mama's mind at ease. Her tension gone, she found her way to the lobby and out the door, clipping along toward home.

"Hana!"

Chiko ran toward her, waving a piece of paper. She stopped, panting for breath. Hana grabbed Chiko's arm—something bad had happened.

Not now, Lord. She had the urge to throw her hands over her ears and sing to keep from hearing whatever Chiko had to say.

"I have permission to work in the produce fields. I'll go for four hours each morning with the rest of the girls as soon as school is out. Isn't that great?"

Great. Not terrible news, not good either. She studied her sister's flawless face, her shyly blossoming figure. Not a child anymore, but not a grown up yet. Chiko had to start making her own choices. Did it have to be now, and about this?

"Does Mama know?"

Chiko nodded and dropped her smile. "You don't want me to go, do you?"

"Guess it's done, isn't it?" Hana took Chiko's arm and pulled her in the direction of home. "Let's talk about it later. I'm hungry but I don't want to stand in line for lunch. And why aren't you in school?"

"Half day."

Chiko chattered on about the fields, and the bus, and the other girls. Her words floated away from Hana unheard. How would she keep track of Chiko, work at the hospital, keep Martin out of trouble and help Mama? The ache for their past simpler life filled her chest. Childhood memories rushed over her of evenings at the kitchen table with Papa teaching his children how to make origami. Hours would tick by as they laughed at each other's attempts to make frogs and swans. When they had stayed up too late, Mama would shoo them off to bed.

Those were the good years, the best years for the Kato family. Now they were a family torn apart by war and distance. What could she do to make sure they had happy times in their future? Papa counted on her.

The relief of a new job disappeared. Time to get back to the real issues of living in camp.

At last John caught Michael at home. He'd given up trying yesterday, but knocked on his door just after dinner this evening, hoping for an audience. His timing had been right and Michael invited him in for refreshments.

The tea cup rattled in the saucer as Michael handed it to John. The flowery green aroma of Sencha soothed his nerves. Michael always knew just which tea to serve him, counteracting or complimenting his mood. This was the mystery of his friend—a special knowing. Older and wiser, he welcomed John into his home not long after they both arrived at Grand Peak.

The fine drapes of colorful material hanging from Michael's ceiling that first day had intrigued John. "How did you get these?" He had asked. "After only one week at the camp you've managed to turn a bare cubicle into a shrine of Japanese culture."

Michael had never really answered him about the trinkets and pictures decorating the only piece of furniture, a makeshift table made of an old nail barrel. A black curtain covered the window at all times, despite the warning of such practice by the camp director.

"I don't want to see that world out there unless I have to," He had explained to John.

Now John took a sip of the brew and breathed in the calm of the room, waiting for Michael to open a conversation, the usual custom for their visits. The large pillows on the floor were quite comfortable to sit on, and somehow Michael managed to keep them free of much dust.

Michael held the delicate porcelain cup in both hands and slowly brought it to his lips. His dull gray shoulder length hair, wasn't pulled back in a braid as usual, but tucked behind his large ears. Despite the deep lines around his eyes and mouth, a youthful sparkle in his eyes left John guessing his age. It was as if he had lived beyond any age, beyond any physical restraints. This is what John liked best about him.

Michael took a sip and raised his bushy black brows. "What brings you here today? I sense something weighs heavy on your mind."

John eased into his request with his best finesse. "I haven't seen you in a while and thought I should check up on you. Plus, I need a friend. And advice."

Michael swirled the liquid in his cup like a connoisseur of fine wine. "I'm fine." He pointed around the room. "I have my stack of unread books, my unfinished letters to family in Japan, and my music." He pointed to a phonograph he'd ordered from Sears and Roebucks. They often sat by the hour together, just enjoying the soothing music of Japan.

"Sounds like the kind of lifestyle I need more of. Especially now when I feel conflicted about what I'm doing." John leaned back against the wall.

"What *are* you doing, John?"

"You know. The resistance group. Now that Mr. Kato and the others are gone, I don't seem to have the fight I need to lead the ones that are left. Some are counting on me, some are losing faith in me. I think some hate me." Now that he had poured out his heart in one gush, he dreaded Michael's advice. The statements he just made hung in the air, the whining reverberated in his ears.

Michael pushed a small dish full of tea cookies toward him. His spindly fingers picked up two for himself. "What else?"

His response fell hard at John's feet. What did he mean? "Nothing else. Just need to figure out how to do what I need to do and still stay out of trouble. Or maybe quit the group." He snatched up a cookie and popped it in his mouth. The sweet taste of almond reminded him of his mother's cookies. So long ago.

"What else?"

Really. John hated this game. "There is nothing else."

"Yes, there is." He paused for another sip of tea. "How is Hana these days?"

John flinched. Michael knew to read between the lines, hearing the questions in his voice, even without knowing the facts. Kind of spooky. Most of the time he felt relief someone knew him that well. He'd rather stuff this particular intimation, but he had come for help. He needed it.

"Okay. So I'm worried about Hana. I want to help her, not upset her or make life any worse for her. So do I quit the group and find something else to do, or do I risk losing her friendship or chance hurting her by taking over where her father left off? I know she doesn't want the group to get out of hand, but that's what's happened since Mr. Kato was arrested."

Michael drank down the last of his tea and placed the cup on a hand carved tray. He folded his hands in his lap and sat silent for a long cool moment. "Friend, you have a difficult decision to make. This is a test of your manhood, your belief system, and your loyalties. This time I can only help you by encouraging you to keep asking the questions."

Was that all? He had calmed himself thinking Michael would have an answer for him, especially now that his confusion had been unlocked.

Michael pushed himself up from the floor. "I'm at a crossroads myself, and many of my questions are indirectly about you, John."

John gulped. "Me? Have I done something wrong?"

"No. It's just that now you lead a group that goes against everything I stand for. Force instead of words, anger instead of understanding. I hoped you would stand up to it." He picked up the tray and set it on the table. "I've been warned not to associate with you."

"What? So you're going to give up on me because you were threatened?" Blood rushed to John's face. He stood, his hands balled into a fist. He would confront anyone that did harm to Michael, but he never thought his friend would end their relationship. The revelation hit hard.

Michael held up his hand. "That's not what I said. I wouldn't dissociate from you because of a threat, only because I need distance to maintain my way of life. If you're going to be more involved with a group that advocates violence, no matter how mild, I'll need to make a stand of my own."

Just as John gathered the words to respond voices hollered from outside the barrack. Michael moved toward the door. John ducked at the piercing sound of shattering glass. Something had crashed through the window. Footsteps of someone running away pounded the dirt outside. He darted through Michael's door and then burst through the outside barrack door. To his right, no one. To his left, only a swirl of dust remained.

"John." Michael called from inside.

Shards of glass crunched under his shoes as he entered the room. His heart stuttered. Michael held a cloth to his neck. A cloth covered in blood.

Michael pulled the cloth from his skin. "Proof of my warning, I suppose." Blood dripped down his neck and onto his shirt. "It's more than superficial. May need some stitches. I'd do it myself, except it's in a difficult place—"

Reaching for Michael's arm, John pulled him toward the door. "Stop kidding around. We're going to the hospital. Are you good to walk? Watch the glass on the floor."

Michael nodded and followed John. "I wasn't kidding. I've stitched up—well, never mind." He shoved glass out of the way and shut his door. Two older women crept out in the hall, faces pale and eyes wide. One took a step in their direction, but the other pulled her back into their cubicle. Voices rumbled through the walls of the other rooms.

John slammed the outer door. "Cowards."

"Not cowards, just trying to stay out of trouble, like me, and I hope you."

Michael wobbled a bit. John caught his arm and pulled him close. "Lean on me."

In the distance, the hospital seemed too far to walk to. The sun rested on the top of the mountain, waiting for them to reach their destination before setting.

"You know, I don't know much about you, Michael Okada. It seems like all we talk about is me. What did you do before coming to camp?" They took a few tentative steps, Michael's tall frame leaning into John's as he answered.

"Something I thought important at the time. Let's say I had a change of heart."

They hobbled past clusters of barracks before reaching the path to the hospital.

John thought the breath he held would leave him forever if he let it out. This was his fault. If only Michael had told him before. He would get to the bottom of this mess and find out who threw the rock. Michael had never hurt a soul. He had been threatened because of their association. The obvious outcome slashed at his perceived leadership of the group.

Michael slowed.

John hoisted him up. "Only fifty yards or so. You okay?"

"Yes, I'll make it. Thank you for assisting me." His voice strained to answer.

It was the least he could do for him, for now. "You're welcome, my friend."

Chapter 3

"You busy?"

Neil Bennett slumped to hear his solitude was about to vanish. The sound of Doctor Davidson's voice in his doorway shattered any chance for him to finish his project. For the second time today he stuffed the file of paperwork back in the desk. Reclaiming time to fill out the forms would be implausible considering the proverbial revolving door to his office. He had to finish them soon if he wanted to secure his missionary status. Interruptions seemed the order of the morning.

He tossed his pen on the desk and leaned back. "No, come in. I was just coming to do rounds." Only half true, but it might signal that he didn't have all day. He stood and buttoned his lab coat.

Doctor Davidson put to rest any excuse to leave. "No need. Not many patients today. I think it's all under control until tonight. Anyway with all these Japanese nurses around here, who needs us, right?" Doctor Davidson sat. His trick had failed.

The uncomfortable silence settled in, as usual, and Neil waited for the rebuttal comment on his hiring practices. He wouldn't defend his hiring Miss Kato if that's what this visit was about. Doctor Davidson sank into his chair and picked at his fingernail—the usual cue for Neil to inquire about his missing son. Someday perhaps Doctor Davidson would accept that his son had probably been killed, and lay on Japan's soil along with so many other young soldiers.

"I suppose there's been no news." Neil tired of asking the same question, but his heart broke for this man each time he witnessed the darkness covering him. Today Doctor Davidson's face drooped a little, his eyes tired and puffy. Maybe he did have bad news.

Doctor Davidson sighed hard. "No. Nothing."

The same answer to the same question. He wanted to understand this man as much as he wanted to understand the internees, but today's busyness had already consumed the caring he needed for this man. His parents taught him about compassion and reaching out. Instead, at this moment his heart echoed, empty of empathy. His father would have jumped to Doctor Davidson's side by now, arm around his shoulder, praying and weeping.

The despair on Doctor Davidson's face was almost enough to draw him in. "I'm sorry. Don't give up hope." Just words, but all he could manage. Did it sound trite? He pounded his fist on his thigh. He should be more sympathetic.

Doctor Davidson leaned forward and rested his elbows on his knees. "I've come to think of you like a son, Neil. I hope you will let me counsel you as I would have advised my son, Tom. You have lots to learn and young men need a strong example."

A good example. In Neil's mind that meant spiritual headship, teaching God's ways in a universal standard. Not bigotry and hatred for your fellow man. Doctor Davidson must be referring to Hana Kato—another Japanese thorn in the great doctor's side. He would never be a fatherly example until he relinquished his bitterness and stopped hiding from God. Neil prayed often for another opportunity to share God's love with Doctor Davidson. He sensed today wasn't the day.

Still he would put out the bait and maybe get a nibble. "In time I'm sure you'll find a way to live without a son. I won't be here forever and well, you know how I depend on my Heavenly Father. I value your friendship though. We've worked well together here." He bit his lip. Enough said.

Doctor Davidson squinted, smiled a half smile, and shook his head. Message received, but just as he suspected, today wouldn't be the day for a spiritual revelation. Doctor Davidson finished the banter.

"Well, I'll be there for you. You need someone here on earth, don't you think? I'm going to the mess hall for a bite. Haven't felt so good, and I think it's because I'm not eating right."

Not eating right? Neil suspected it was more about eating too much. The man's lab coat had not reached around his middle for months now.

Doctor Davidson stood and patted his belly. "Want to come?"

"No. Thanks though. I have work to do." Another partial truth. He didn't feel like entertaining more suggestions about joining a practice with Doctor Davidson after the war, or to meet that special young woman he knows back home. He understood his need to be a father figure, but it would have to be with someone else.

He fell against the hard back of his chair when Doctor Davidson left. He closed his eyes and imagined ducking and dodging to avoid Doctor Davidson in the hospital halls. Not a pleasant way to spend the rest of his time at Grand Peak, worrying about offending the chief medical officer. A relationship with the man, wanted or not, would mean dodging expectations he couldn't possibly meet.

If only he had his father's missionary talents. He would someday. It would all fall into place and his heart would learn to melt for people like the great Doctor Davidson. He just had to pray for more faith.

He shuffled the application paperwork again. His palms sweat as he scanned the page of personal questions about his past, his faith, and his vision.

Just as he took the top off his fountain pen the sound of metal crashing on the floor pierced his ears. By the time he leapt from his chair and raced to the hallway, loud voices echoed from several doors down. Nurses scurried around someone lying on the floor. He took three steps, and as the crowd parted, he could see Doctor Davidson flat on his back.

He knelt next to him and pulled his colleague's puffy eyelids back. "Doctor Davidson?" He felt for a pulse. "Get Nurse Potter, now. And bring a stretcher." He wasn't used to barking orders. Nothing this exciting had happened around here for some time.

"Doctor Davidson. Can you hear me? Do you have any pain?"

Doctor Davidson groaned and flailed his arms. Two male orderlies came with a stretcher and pushed nurse's aides jabbering in Japanese out of the way. A female voice uttered two words loud in the language and all onlookers backed away.

Hana crouched beside him. "I'm sorry, Doctor Bennett. Nurse Potter is at the mess hall. Can I help?"

There was no time to review her skills. She had only been here a few days and although he trusted her, his breath quickened to think of putting this man in her hands. Or worse yet, having Doctor Davidson wake up and see a Japanese nurse by his side. He slid his stethoscope under Doctor Davidson's shirt, resting it on his heaving chest. "Heart beat rapid, but steady."

He peered down the hall. "When will Alice—Nurse Potter be back?" Doctor Davidson groaned louder now. "Never mind. Get an IV set up in the exam room and bring in the code cart just in case. Can you manage that, Nurse Kato?" His question hung in the air between them.

Hana glared at him. "Yes, Doctor. Right away." She pushed herself up and hurried down the hall.

Doctor Davidson coughed as aides struggled to lift him. Time dragged as they rolled him, pushed him and pulled him until finally his entire body, except for one leg, was on the stretcher. Neil pulled it up and waved them on. He ran ahead and met Hana bounding out of Exam Room 2.

"Everything's ready, Doctor." She sped past him, obviously on a mission.

Inside the room, he stopped to look around. Indeed it was ready. She had competently prepared for every kind of emergency this hospital could handle. His clenched jaw relaxed. He could breathe now. As he turned around to complement her, Nurse Potter burst through the door.

"Sorry, Doctor. Just gone for a few minutes."

Hana rushed in with a tray of syringes and wove her way around

Nurse Potter. He glanced between the two women and made a hasty, dangerous decision. He puffed his chest with a big breath, ready for a confrontation.

"Actually, Nurse Potter, I think we have it under control. Miss Kato can assist." He didn't have the courage to watch the woman's expression. Hana moved right in, rolled up Doctor Davidson's sleeve, and swabbed the crook of his elbow with alcohol.

The room stilled for a moment, the air thick with competition. Then the echo of feet stomping out of the room made Neil wince inside. He eyed Hana when she looked up. He shrugged and she smiled. That smile. It was worth Nurse Potter's wrath to see it.

He gently shook his patient's shoulder, feeling the bulk of his body. "Doctor Davidson? How do you feel now? Any pain?"

Doctor Davidson's eyes popped open, and he jerked his head to meet Neil's face. He pushed Neil back and spewed some expletives. Hana smiled again, or was it a smirk? She continued her IV procedure, leaning on Doctor Davidson's arm to steady it.

"Ouch!" Doctor Davidson screamed like a child when she poked him. Without flinching she slapped tape around his arm, adjusted the bottle and tube, and then left his side. It happened so fast Neil could only stare. Very impressive, and he opened his mouth to share the sentiment.

Doctor Davidson roused. "Who was that? Where's Nurse Potter? Get that Jap out of here."

Hana spun around. He covered Doctor Davidson's mouth with his hand and shrugged to her. He should have let Nurse Potter take over. Hana's eyes welled with tears. He wanted to punch Doctor Davidson, and thought she might be coming over to do the job when she moved toward them.

She approached the bed and leaned in close to tuck in his bed sheet. As she fussed with it she made use of her juxtaposition. "My name is Miss Kato." She spoke softly to Doctor Davidson, who looked away. She straightened up and tipped her head. "Shall I send Nurse Potter in, Doctor Bennett?"

He hesitated. What should he do? He had to do the right thing for the patient.

"Yes, please. Thank you, Miss Kato for your proficient organization and assistance."

She stared at him and blinked away the moisture in her dark eyes. "You're very welcome. It's my job. I'll send her in right away." She turned again to Doctor Davidson. "I hope you're feeling better now that my IV is working."

Neil wanted to laugh, but he felt more like crying. Hana had summed it up quite nicely. Doctor Davidson must have thought so too because he held his sharp tongue for once.

"Here I am. What can I do?" Nurse Potter surveyed the room and chuckled. "Looks like she had things in hand here. Fine nurse, I'd say."

Neil's jaw fell open. What was this? A compliment to a Japanese American nurse?

"Somebody pinch me." He mumbled.

"What?" Nurse Potter's face puckered, then relaxed and flushed.

He shook his head. "Nothing."

Even Nurse Potter couldn't deny Hana was more than capable. As soon as Doctor Davidson stabilized, he would check on her and tell her so.

"It's my latest invention. Another attempt to keep the dust out."

Martin teetered on the wooden chair, stuffing cracks in the boards above the door of their barrack room with shreds of paper soaked with rice flour water. His fingers poked and smoothed the paper, forming it to the shape of the crack. Once filled he moved on to another breech, and then another.

He waved his arm over the wall. "They could have built these shacks better. Green wood, substandard materials. It's a miracle they're still standing after three years."

Mama shook her finger. "Better than horse stalls."

Chiko slapped shut the book her nose had been buried in. "Yeah, I remember those horrible places. They didn't even clean out all the horse manure before we got there."

The makeshift mini-prisons had only been their home for several weeks, but the humiliation stuck in Hana's craw much longer than that. The nights she spent sitting up to sleep haunted her dreams, waking her with the sights and smells lingering. Being treated as animals singed their dignity, if not burned it out altogether.

Mama shook her head. "Forget it. We fine now."

Hana slid off the edge of her cot and held the back of Martin's chair. He stopped his work and frowned down at her, his lips pursed as he glared at the mess in his hand. He jumped down and thrust the bowl of mushy paper at her, nearly spilling the milky mixture. She'd kill him if it splashed on her skirt.

"I hope this works, Mister Paper Man." She fingered some of the floating pieces.

"This is my final try at something to last more than one wind storm. I'll give up if this doesn't work. You'll have to take over for me anyway."

Hana stuck out her lower lip. He clenched his teeth and grabbed the bowl from her. "Funny. I'm not pouting, I'm stating facts."

Take over for him? Why would he say such a thing? Even though he complained, she knew he took pride in doing chores.

Mama peeked around Hana standing in her way. "Good job, Martin. It work. You see."

Hana backed up to her cot and sat. The space they called home felt warm tonight. Not from the heat of the day seeping into the drafty barrack walls. The banter of family conversation bonded them, rare moments since Papa was arrested. If she could only get a response from one of the letters she mailed last week. To have everyone together again would be the answer to her hopes and Mama's prayers. Separation would not be a permanent situation for the Kato family if she had any way to fix it.

Someone knocked at the door and Martin squinted at Hana. "You didn't invite the whole neighborhood over for my birthday, did you?"

"No. Just a few dozen." She held a straight face as she sauntered to the door. She couldn't count on two hands enough friends to invite to a party.

Martin followed her and laughed when two of his school chums and John charged through the door singing Happy Birthday. Chiko ran to the makeshift cupboard Papa made from a crate, and uncovered the paper bag over the three day old cake from the sundry store.

She beamed as she presented it to Martin. "Sorry. No candles."

Martin took it from her and turned the plate around in his hands. "It's okay. It's cake, anyway." He set the plate on the table. Mama pulled out her stash of plates and forks she'd pilfered from the mess hall and cut small pieces of the stale dessert.

John winked at Hana. She felt her face flush, and returned to the edge of her cot. The camera seized from her when they arrived would have come in handy right now. She could have sent a picture to Papa. A freeze frame reminiscent of better times.

The boys all stuffed down two pieces of cake. Mama collected everyone's empty plates as they stood in a circle telling stories about Martin's antics in camp. Martin met Hana's gaze and moved to the center of the room under the bulb hanging from the ceiling. Her pulse raced as he glanced around the room, wringing his hands. He wasn't himself.

"Mama, everyone. Thanks for the party. I have an announcement to make. As he pulled a folded piece of paper from his shirt pocket the room fell silent. He opened it, held it up, and cleared his throat. His shoulders straightened as if he were about to deliver an important message to a crowd of people.

"I received my draft notice the other day."

A small gasp escaped Mama's mouth. Her tone turned cold. "They cannot take you. You man of household since Papa gone. And you not graduate high school yet." Her shoulders dropped as she shuffled to Hana's cot to sit. Hana pulled her close and wrapped her arm around her waist.

"I'm going, Mama-san. I want to go." He took a few steps toward her. "I'm sorry if you're disappointed. I've thought hard over what is the right thing to do. Besides, I already talked to my teacher about graduating early. It's all set."

Hana held her breath waiting for Mama to scold Martin. Chiko sniffled over in the corner. She understood her misery. First the loss of their father to prison, and now big brother going off to war. The air in the room suddenly thinned, and the temperature seemed to rise. This couldn't be happening. After a long silence everyone relaxed and resumed chatting. Mama fussed with wiping the table. Her small arms moved slowly, collecting the crumbs.

At last she stood tall and squared her shoulders with Martin.

"Here is what I think." Her voice crooned calm and steady. "You do honorable thing and God will be with you." She pointed a finger at him. "Only you can decide which is honorable for you."

It was just like Mama to remind them of God's hand in their lives. Another example of her steadfast faith even through these last horrible years. Hana closed her eyes and tried to pray, but even empty words evaded her. God had too much explaining to do before she would believe as Mama did.

Chiko scooted up to Martin and hugged him. The other young men gathered around him and talked about uniforms and how the girls would be after him now. Their voices still jumped with pubescent instability. Eighteen year old boys trying to be men ready for war.

The churning in her stomach held her back from any congratulations for Martin. This was all wrong. She thought he would honor Papa's stand on the draft. When had Martin grown up enough to make this decision? Standing there he seemed to be a head taller than yesterday.

Another knock on the door and Hana motioned John to answer it. A Caucasian gentleman handed him a telegram and tipped his hat.

"For Mrs. Kato," was all he said. John looked back to Mama who nodded. He took the telegram and shut the door.

Hana closed her eyes, fearing the worst. John held out the yellow envelope to Mama, but she pointed to Hana. From inside welled a deep dread that radiated to her arms. He handed it to her and she snatched it to hide her shaking hands. Every eye was on her and the envelope. She could feel their energy draining her.

Please, God. No bad news tonight.

The envelope opened easily and she pulled out the crisp folded yellow paper.

Mama held Chiko's hand as they huddled close to Martin. "Read it."

Hana swallowed down the thickness in her throat. "To Mrs. Kato. From Doctor Green, Leavenworth Prison, Kansas. Mr. Kato had heart attack this morning. Stop. In serious but stable condition. Stop. Prognosis fair. Stop. Will keep you informed. Stop."

All eyes shifted to Mama. Chiko buried her head in Martin's chest, but Mama stood still. Hana held the back of a chair, fearing her knees would buckle.

"Hey, we'll see you later." Martin's friends patted him on the back and slipped out the door.

John moved a chair over for Mama and touched her arm to help her sit.

Hana knelt by Mama. "He'll be okay, Mama-san. The doctor said prognosis is fair. That's better than critical."

To her surprise Mama smiled and nodded. Her eyelids drooped, but no tears came. "Sure. He be all right. God is there with him. We just pray harder."

Hana blinked back the moisture filling her eyes. She stared at John until he looked her way. Her eyes pleaded with him for the help he promised. She needed it now more than ever.

Papa had to come home or he would surely die.

Hana arrived at the hospital early this morning. Today she would ask him. Doctor Bennett must have some connections he could call upon to get Papa a medical release. A heart attack is serious. There must be an official somewhere who had compassion for a sick, aging internee. One *yes* is all they needed. One expression of humanity in a time when it seemed to have disappeared for any Japanese, American or not.

She tucked her hair behind her ears and left the locker room with the box of almond cookies under her arm, made with Mama the night before on top their potbellied stove. The task had produced a mess of their living space, and she had used up the last of Mama's almond stash.

Mama didn't seem to mind cleaning up. "It fun to make cookies again. Just like home."

Only not like home. Scavenging the ingredients had been a monumental job, and Chiko found a way. Whether Doctor Davidson would appreciate the collaborative effort or not remained to be seen. Hana held in her doubts and her nervous stomach at the thought of presenting the cookies to him. One last gesture of courtesy for someone who went out of his way to demonstrate superiority.

She turned the corner to the wards. Nurse Potter stood at the end of the hall, arms folded across her chest. "Are you working today?"

Hana gritted her teeth. "Yes, but since I have a few minutes before shift, I wanted to deliver something to Doctor Davidson. What room is he in?"

"He isn't seeing visitors." She took a few steps around Hana and mumbled to her. "Room 22."

She forced a smile. "Thank you. I'll be right back." She'd find the chink in Nurse Potter's armor yet.

Standing in front of Room 22 she wiped her sweaty palms on her uniform. She closed her eyes and saw Mama's finger shaking at her. She would tell her to be nice, no matter what. The cookies would be good support.

His gruff voice bellowed when she knocked. "Come."

A few feet inside the doorway she hugged the wall, breathing deep. She could hear her heart pounding in her ears. She looked at the box, then at him. Perhaps it was a bad time and she should come back later. *Don't be silly.* One last remnant of courage ebbed. "Hello, Doctor Davidson. How are you feeling today?"

The newspaper in his hands rustled as he turned a page, his eyes focused intensely on it. "Better."

A few more wobbly steps brought her to his bedside. Willing her hands to still, she held out the box. "I thought you might like these.

It's my mother's best almond cookie recipe."

He turned his head and stared at her so deeply she nearly backed away. She held the box steady, waiting for him to acknowledge it. With a quick jerk his large hands snatched her offering.

"Thank you." He rested the box on the bed and returned his attention to the paper.

Her gut told her to leave. She waited another long minute, listening to his heavy breaths. The silence won over her benevolence. "Feel better soon. Good-bye."

He held his gaze steady on the paper. "Mm. Hmm."

She stormed to the hall. A cold response for a kind gesture. Had she not treated him with respect? After all she had done for him when he fainted."

"Lord, I'm done trying to be kind to this man. He isn't worth the effort."

She sighed deep, the bad taste of bitterness in her mouth. There had to be a way to work around his bigotry. Somewhere inside him there had to be a likable person, or at least tolerable. She didn't have time now to dig for it. She had just enough time to talk to Doctor Bennett before Nurse Potter came looking for her to crack her whip, which couldn't sting any more than the doctor's coldness.

She inched toward Doctor Bennett's office until a loud voice bellowed from the other room. More voices echoed. She scooted past the office door to peek into the first ward. Two Caucasian police stood with their backs to her, their hands clenched behind them. Hana recognized one of them from the evening she visited John in detention last year—the night she decided she wasn't going to let him have her heart. Not that he had ever asked for it.

An MP hovered over a patient's bed, shouting. "Just tell us."

The patient wiggled to sit up straight, but fell back onto the pillow. He barked out a scratchy reply. "I told you, I don't know anything." He blinked up at the ceiling and held one hand to his bandaged head. Didn't the MPs around here have anything better to do than bully sick old men too old and injured to be subjected to such an inquisition?

Japanese nurses scurried out the door, eyes lowered, faces pale. The thick tension pressed in on Hana as she listened in.

"Miss Kato."

Hana jumped and spun around, her heart in her throat. Nurse Potter stood behind her, breathing heavy with lips pursed to one side.

"What's going on in there?" Hana spit out the words before she thought to greet her.

"You'll find out later. Now please get out of the hallway. Doctor Bennett wants to see you before you come on shift." She took a few steps down the hall and turned to Hana. "Did you find Doctor Davidson's room?"

Hana nodded.

"Don't mind his bad mood." Her eyes softened. "He's always like that. You'll get used to it." With a single raised brow she flipped her wrist. "Now scoot."

Hana slipped her hands in her pockets and released her tightened stomach muscles. Nurse Potter was proving to be a complicated person. Standing at Doctor Bennett's office door, she raised her hand to knock. Before her hand touched it, he swung the door open, motioned her to come in, and disappeared around the other side.

Hana pushed the door open, cautiously inching her way in. She spied him kneeling on the floor in the corner holding a bedpan wrapped with bandage tape around the open end, hovering over something she couldn't see.

He held up his palm. "Shh."

She cocked her head to get a better vantage point. The object of his attention must have been behind the desk or under it. Her shoulders tensed.

Is he crazy?

Doctor Bennett raised up slightly, holding the bedpan with both hands. In a sudden swift move, he crashed the metal onto the floor. Hana slammed her hands to her ears. She had the urge to run, but she froze, not knowing what this lunatic doctor could be up to.

"Ha! Gotcha." He jumped up and grabbed a book from his desk, then ducked down for a moment and reappeared with the book covering the bedpan. He held it out like a trophy.

"Got him. Want to see?" He grinned like a boy who had just slain the giant.

"Got wh...what?" She stayed put just inside the office until it was safe to come in—until *he* was safe.

"The mouse. I've been chasing him for days and now I've outsmarted him. Come see."

"No, thank you." She let out a shaking breath. "I wonder if I may have a moment of your time. If you're finished, I mean. For a split second she wondered if she should forget her request. She found it difficult to take seriously a man holding a bedpan, claiming to have captured a rodent.

He lifted the book a crack and then slammed it down again. "Huh? Oh, yes. Sorry."

As he moved toward her with pan still in hand, she backed into the hall. Mice were her least favorite of all animals. She had her fill of them at the horse stalls. There would be no introduction if she could help it.

Doctor Bennett moved past her and looked down both ends of the hall. "Hey, orderly."

A stalky young man in white dungarees stopped in the hall. "Yes, Doctor?"

"Take this creature out back to the field and deposit him there." In a grand gesture he shoved the pan and book at the young man. "And don't let him escape on the way."

Hana held her stomach in to keep from laughing at the poor man as he held the pan at arm's length, grimacing. A brave soul and a grand gesture.

"Now, Miss Kato, come in." Doctor Bennett pulled out a chair.

She checked the floor beneath her before sitting. Suppose there were other mice in the room, like a family of baby mice waiting to skitter along the floor under her feet? Then again, how would she know he actually had a mouse in that pan? He could be delusional.

"Don't worry. He's a bachelor mouse." He laughed and plopped into his chair, seeming pleased with himself.

He chomped the last bite from an apple and threw the core in the garbage can. She could smell its sweetness. Her mouth watered, but she refused to look into the pail. She stared straight at him, ignoring his greedy inconsiderate manner. If he only knew how long it had been since she had a fresh apple from one of the grand eastern Washington State orchards.

She thought of how beautiful the rows of fruit trees were, hedged along the Columbia River. She momentarily relived the annual family trip to the middle of the state and the days spent picking apples for canning. Martin would do more eating than picking, ending up with a belly ache the first day.

Doctor Bennett's voice startled her. "I need to fill you in on a patient admitted last night. You might have seen the MPs questioning him this morning."

"Yes." Obviously her request would have to wait. She waited for details about the Issei man she saw with the police when she came in. Her curiosity about the incident peaked at the thought of hearing more.

He spoke casually about what sounded like a serious incident. "He was in a ruckus last night and got pretty badly beat up. Seems there is a group of rowdies in camp that are trying to persuade others to join their cause." He plucked a tissue from a box and wiped the apple juice from his hand.

Rowdies. She knew exactly who he referred to. It had to be what was left of Papa's group. She had heard through the camp grapevine that John cautioned the others in the bunch about laying low. So much for his ability to control the group, and so much for him giving up such nonsense. Papa was gone and the group should have dissolved. No one else could lead it properly—not even John.

"Anyway, you'll relieve nurse Sugata and care for him for this shift. Is that agreeable?"

As much as she would rather be in the children's ward, she had to agree. "Yes, of course." She would be careful not to get involved.

Doctor Bennett hesitated as he studied her face. Her flushed cheeks and fidgeting hands would surely give away her anxiety. The last thing she needed today was to be linked to John's activities. For her and for her family's sake.

His tone turned more professional. "I interviewed the patient when he came in last night. He told me a few names of young men that had been bothering him, forcing him to write letters to authorities and such. Some of them caught him just outside his barrack last night. He mentioned a familiar name. I can see on your face that you know who I'm referring to. I want you to know I won't repeat it. He told me only after I administered medication for his wounds."

The walls closed in to trap her. What did he want her to say? She could confirm his accusation by nodding and get John into more trouble. John obviously didn't care enough about her to stop his activities, so perhaps he should suffer the consequences. She folded her hands on her lap.

"Miss Kato, I will not break the patient's confidence. Please know that. I just wanted you to be aware in case there was a chance you could intervene."

"I understand. Thank you." Wait, how could she intervene? She shuddered to think he would believe she had influence over John or that there was something between them. Heat traveled from her neck to her face.

He stood, facing her, his brows knitted. "I hope I did the right thing by mentioning it. You look upset."

Hana met his gaze. "It's all right. But I don't—"

He moved to the edge of the desk. "I just don't want your family to suffer any more than you have already."

A shock wave pushed her. *My family? What is he talking about?* John wasn't family.

She realized he probably didn't know John and meant someone else. She had to choose her words carefully now. "I'm not sure what you mean."

He shrugged. "I mean your brother should take care to consider the ramifications of—"

She choked back angry tears. "My brother? Is that the name you heard?"

"Well, yes. Isn't that who you thought I meant?"

Hana looked to the floor and shook her head slowly. Not Martin. It couldn't have been Martin.

Doctor Bennett stood next to her. "I can see we weren't connecting. I'm so sorry. I only wanted to warn you in case the patient tried to talk about it."

Hana swallowed hard and nodded. She grasped the edge of the seat, unable to look at him. *Think, Hana. Think.* Martin had left the barrack after the party when everyone went to bed. She thought he went to the latrine. She had fallen asleep and never heard him return. He must not have realized how harmful this could be for himself, and for Papa. Or was he so angry at Papa that he would disgrace them?

Papa. It would devastate him to know Martin had participated in this terrible thing.

Doctor Bennett crouched beside her. "I feel awful that I've blundered this. I can get someone else to cover for you. I'm so sorry. What can I do?"

She sighed and leaned back. "It's all right. I'm glad you told me. I'll take care of it." *God help me.* "I'd like to take the shift with the patient, especially now." At least she knew; at least it was out in the open and she could handle it before Papa found out. Her mind searched for names of people who might write to Papa and tell him.

She stood and shuffled to the door, then glanced back at him, forcing her words. "Is that all?"

"Yes. You said you needed to talk about something? Would you like to come back later?"

His frown surprised her. Did he really care? She clutched the doorknob to shut the door and nodded. "Yes, thank you."

"Hana?" He grabbed another apple from his desk and tossed it to her. She reached up with one hand and snatched it from the air. A taste of home. Just what she needed at the moment.

Despite her heartache she couldn't stop the smile that erupted. "Thanks."

With the apple tucked safely in her pocket she took a few deep breaths. The favor about the letters could wait until later when her nerves reconnected. For now she would swallow her pride and ask God for help. Mama much never know.

Maybe God would listen to her if it were for Mama's sake.

Chapter 4

"...to the flag of the United States of America. And to the republic for which it stands..." Young children dressed in white short sleeved shirts and navy blue shorts repeated the pledge in unison as Neil neared the school. This was the last day he would hear that melodious rhythm of rhyme; the last day of school for the year. The circle around the flagpole would be empty from now on.

Freedom and justice for all didn't thrive here at Grand Peak. Images of the newspaper cartoons depicting Japanese American's as herded sheep, and magazine articles on the benefits of internment flashed in his mind. His hands balled into fists in his pockets.

"Touching isn't it?" Neil turned at the sound of a voice. A young Japanese man rested his hands on his hips and shook his head. "It's required for the children to stand here each morning to demonstrate their loyalty. I bet you didn't know that."

Neil wasn't sure if the words were a challenge or statement. Either way, if it were true, the young man's condescending tone was justified.

Neil looked him up and down. "You're the guy who brought in your injured friend a while back, aren't you?" He noted this person's posture, tensed and poised for an argument, just as it had that night at the hospital. He remembered treading lightly with both him and the patient.

"Yes. John Yamato, and my friend is doing fine, not that you want to know." John took a few steps in the direction of the Block 20 mess hall.

Neil's neck stiffened. "Wait. What's that supposed to mean?" Heat filled his face.

John strolled back to stand in front of him. Cigarette smoke permeated his clothes, but he appeared clean cut, good looking even, though his forehead creased with frown lines as he spoke.

"I mean, I doubt you care about an injured Japanese guy." His tone wasn't haughty or arrogant. Just factual. How telling that John would assume a Caucasian doctor wouldn't care about a patient. Any patient.

Neil shook his head and tucked his hand behind his back. "You don't know me. If you had a problem with a Caucasian doctor stitching up your friend, you should have said so that night. There were plenty of Japanese American doctors available who could have done a great job."

John nodded. "Maybe next time I will." He tipped his head and smirked.

Neil stuffed his hands back in his pockets. His jaw twitched, but then let the words come. "Sometimes I wonder who has more prejudice around here, your people or mine." He turned to the children filing into the school and huffed away the tension in his chest. "Anyway, I'm sure everything will be as it used to be once the war is over. Maybe better."

John's eyes also followed the children. "Typical Caucasian ideology." He stared into Neil's eyes. "It will never happen. Not in our lifetime."

The statement hit Neil in the heart. "You don't think your circumstance will improve even out of the camp, do you?" This was the very thing his parents had worried over for the Japanese in Hawaii. They knew. He should have believed them.

John chuckled. "You kidding? For an educated man you don't know much about what goes on in this world. You can go home and carry on like nothing happened. Back to your house with a white picket fence, to a job that pays more than I can only dream of. What are we supposed to do? Do you think people are just going to stop hating us once the war is over?"

Words of reassurance stuck in his dry throat. He dare not try and speak them. The children disappeared through the barrack door. John could be right. Life for these children could be more of a challenge than he realized. Public schools, new neighborhoods, and possible persecution waited for them on the outside. Kids could be just as cruel as adults.

John shifted next to him. "You're wondering about the kids' future, aren't you? It will be hard on them. They don't understand why they are here, and they won't understand when they go home why the other kids won't play with them, or worse. Some of them may even wish they looked just like the Caucasian kids, with round eyes and blonde curly hair." His voice trailed off as if chasing a memory.

He stared into John's eyes. "If I hadn't witnessed the hardships of these people first hand, I might still believe the government propaganda about how great life is in the camps. I want you to know there are those of us who will try to help your people after you leave here."

John crossed his muscular arms over his chest, his piercing eyes held steady. "You keep saying *your people*. Listen, Doctor. My people and your people are one in the same. I'm an American. I don't want the help of those who put me in here. I'll do fine on my own." He turned to leave again and called over his shoulder. "*Your people* better worry about the kids." He jogged away, his words still echoing against the tar-papered buildings.

Neil studied the frayed faded flag. The good old Stars and Stripes had taken a beating for so many years, and now flapped tired and powerless in the hot breeze, unable to protect its own citizens from imprisonment. Hiding away in the hospital had helped him avoid the revelations now slapping him in the face. It was time to pull his head out of the sand.

Children's voices singing "The Teddy Bears Picnic" floated through the open windows as he headed for his office. He hummed along until the voices faded. He met Nurse Potter standing inside the main entrance of the hospital. She rolled her eyes.

He held up a hand before she could speak. "Yes, I know. Doctor Davidson is anxiously waiting for me to release him."

She growled and handed him a clipboard. "Actually, it's the staff that's eager to have him back as a doctor and not a patient. Tell him to lighten up a bit, will you, Doctor Bennett?"

He stifled a laugh, resisting sarcasm about preferring the man remain bedridden. He had no choice but to release him.

Loud voices pulled him into the hall. At the far end the great Doctor Davidson stood waving one arm at a nurse, and holding the back of his hospital gown with the other arm. The nurse chattered away in Japanese, and shook her finger. The noise reminded him of the bands of Hawaiian jungle monkeys fighting. Other workers stood with their backs against the wall, eyes wide and mouths open, but not coming to the ranting doctor.

Doctor Bennett sickened at the scene resembling a propaganda cartoon. A large red-faced Caucasian towering over a small Japanese person wasn't funny, but it seemed the little ladies were holding their own, and once he reached them he burst into a nervous laugh. Doctor Davidson stopped his tirade with his arm still in the air. Seeing Neil, the little nurse put her hand over her mouth and stepped back. Those lining the hall chuckled softly.

He mustered his most authoritative voice. "What is going on here, Doctor Davidson? You look as though you're losing this battle." He glanced at the nurse, frozen in place, eyes locked on the still seething doctor in front of her.

Doctor Davidson waggled a finger at the woman. "Get this nurse out of my sight. She took my clothes and won't bring them back. I'm returning to duty."

Sauntering to his side, any humor he found in the situation now vaporized. "Is that so? You're off duty at the moment, so that makes me the decision maker, wouldn't you say?"

Doctor Davidson's glare was sharp enough to slice, but he stood still and smiled half-heartedly. "If you really want to be discharged, let's talk rationally about it in your room, shall we?"

"Fine. Let's take care of it then. I tell you I'm not sick." He stormed through the door, his bare feet slapping the floor and his gown flapping open behind him.

Neil turned and waved the others to leave. The nemesis nurse stood with her hands clasped in front of her and eyes to the floor. He had seen the man bully other nurses and knew in time one of them would take him on. This nurse won the distinction.

He leaned over and whispered to her. "I suggest you refrain from speaking Japanese. You know the rules, Miss."

She frowned back at him. "I'm sorry, Doctor Bennett. It's just that he can be so mean."

Nurse Potter stood ten feet away with her hands behind her back, her face scrunched in a frown. "Nurse Ito, come with me." Her tone resonated neutrality, however there would likely be a tongue lashing as soon as he was out of ear shot. He had to save the offender from the queen bee, who at the moment loomed like a menacing cloud in the hallway.

He came close enough to look in her eyes and whisper to her. "Nurse Potter, I think the nurse has learned her lesson, right?"

She dropped her hands to her side and huffed a sigh. He smiled and nudged her with his elbow. Her tough exterior cracked a little as she turned her head. He could see the corner of her mouth quiver, struggling not to curl into a smile. She nodded and sauntered away.

Color flushed back into the pale cheeks of the nurse. Her shoulders dropped and she walked in the opposite direction of Nurse Potter.

He called after her. "Go get Doctor Davidson's clothes before he explodes. Please."

Hana peered out the doorway of her patient's room, smiling. A small dimple appeared on each cheek highlighting her laughing eyes.

"Doctor Bennett!" Doctor Davidson called from inside his room, dashing Neil's hopes for a conversation with Hana. When she disappeared, he took one step in her direction, then back toward Doctor Davidson's room. Hana would have to take second place to the whining doctor.

Neil stared at the ceiling. "God, give me patience for this man."

He grabbed the clipboard off the peg on the wall and leaned through the open door. "All right. I'll sign your discharge papers if you promise to improve your mood. You have all the nurses around here riled up."

"Just sign them."

Neil glared at him with pen pressed to the clipboard. This battle would belong to him, even if he had to stand there all day poised to sign.

"Okay, okay. I'm sorry. I'll be nice." Doctor Davidson flopped onto the edge of the bed.

Neil scribbled his name and waved the papers in the air. "See you later. Your clothes will be delivered shortly."

He strolled past the room where Hana had been and peered in. She came toward him with tray in hand. No more smile or dimples, but no frown either. She scooted around him and set the tray on the cart in the hall. "Has Doctor Davidson settled down? I don't hear his bellows anymore."

He leaned against the wall and chuckled. "What a scene, huh? I especially liked the chewing out she gave him in Japanese." He shook his head. "What was she jabbering about anyway? You can tell me, it won't get her in trouble."

Her smile blossomed again, making heat radiate in his chest. "I don't speak Japanese."

He caught himself from losing his footing and sliding down the wall. Why didn't he know that? Then again, how could he know? He had assumed—a habit that left a bite this time.

He looked away so she wouldn't see the heat in his face. "I'm sorry, I didn't even stop to think—that is, I assumed—"

"Of course you did. Everyone does, but I only know a few Japanese words." She pushed the cart toward the supply room. "I'm as American as you are."

Her tone was pleasant. Perhaps he hadn't offended her. He followed her into the supply room. "I wondered if you would mind if I asked a few questions about your life before camp."

She tipped her head. "You mean as a nurse?"

His heart ratcheted up a few speeds. "No."

She shrugged and pushed the cart against the counter. "I suppose that means you're curious about Japanese Americans in general."

Now he had to jump out of the hole he had dug. She would think he was flirting with her if he asked about her personal life. He slowed his breathing. "Actually, I'm interested in your family and what's going to happen once you leave here." He wanted to know more, but this would be a start.

Hana looked to the floor and meandered to the door. She turned around and met his gaze. Still no sign from her that she resented his inquiry, but he didn't know her well enough to be sure she wouldn't suddenly fly off the handle. No, not Hana Kato. He had confidence in her self-control.

After a long few minutes of silence, she shrugged. "I can tell you what I think will happen to our family. You probably won't agree."

He smiled but held back his excitement that she would open up. "I might."

She pulled off her cap and tucked back strands of loose hair, then sighed. "I fear for my family. We have all heard stories from those who have already left and tried to go home. No jobs are open to them. No one wants to rent to them, and the children are ridiculed in school. Does that paint the picture well for you?"

Her eyes swirled with moisture. There were no words to answer her. He wiped his sweaty palms on his trousers. His heart had pushed and pulled over these people since he first stepped foot at Grand Peak. He had stayed in his comfort zone in engaging with them. Until now.

Her delicate hand hung at her side, balled into a fist. "I know firsthand how cruel people can be because of their attitudes. Small misunderstandings can be resolved. It's the big snowball effect of prejudice and arrogance that has me worried."

He swallowed down any pride he might have, and took a few steps toward her. Fighting his compulsion to put his hands on her shoulder, he slipped them safely in his pockets. "I'm sorry. I hadn't thought much about it until this morning. I saw the children at school and—"

As he glanced away from studying Hana's expression, a reflection of another face appeared in the window of the door behind her. Doctor Davidson had obviously been listening to their conversation.

"Yes? The children?" She tipped her head to catch his eye.

"Oh, never mind. Let's just say my eyes have been opened."

He stared at Doctor Davidson until he scowled and moved away. Neil's stomach twisted. He should go after him, but he still had to hear more from Hana Kato.

She moved into his line of sight. "Doctor Bennett?"

He tore his gaze from the window.

"I'm sorry. Go on, Miss Kato. I'm listening."

This business about the rebel group beating up an old man had to be settled. Yesterday had passed so quickly, and her intentions to confront Martin were hijacked by too many interruptions. Her stomach growled, grinding so deep it hurt. Skipping lunch wasn't a good idea, but she had to find her brother.

The aroma of coffee from the mess hall floated under her nose. She hadn't had any of the strong mixture brewed by the workers in the mess since the first sip three years ago. Today she might need the extra boost. Once inside she spied Martin behind the counter serving meals like a restaurant pro. She poured a cup of coffee from the urn and waved to him.

He called and raised a long serving spoon. "Be there in minute."

Although impressed he had been willing to take a menial job to help out before he left for basic training, it might not have been enough to keep him out of trouble. Wanting to know for sure had plagued her long enough.

She found a table void of breakfast dishes and sat. Sipping the coffee, she closed her eyes, thinking of the last cup she had with the girls—the day the bombs fell on the harbor and in her neighborhood.

She could still hear the shrill sirens and explosions in her mind.

"Hey." She flinched at Martin's voice. "I only have a few minutes. So, what's wrong? You look very serious. Hard morning at the hospital?"

"Funny you should ask. I took care of a patient the other day who was admitted after he was beat up. Know anything about that?" She stopped and studied his eyes. Growing up she could always tell when he was lying. He could never look her in the eye if he were hiding something, and he would usually bite his lower lip.

Martin looked away and her breath caught.

"Martin, tell me what you know." She tugged at his arm. He jerked it away. "This is serious. If you are involved in any way, you must tell me."

Martin faced his sister. His clenched jaw twitched his temples. She had struck a nerve and would stick with it until he confessed.

"Okay, I know something about it, but I wasn't there. I was supposed to be. John pulled me out of the job. When he heard some of the guys wanted to get rough he called a halt to the whole thing, but a couple of them went through with it. One of them turned coward and used my name when they were roughing up the man, to make sure I would get the blame instead of him, so the story goes." He shook his head and looked away again. "I don't suppose you believe me."

"You mean, you wanted to be there?" Her heart sank to her sickened stomach. This was not the brother she knew. What had happened to change him? He was no better than the older men—giving in to pride and anger. Except the young ones turned to violence while the old ones just slipped into apathy. She would never accept this for Martin.

"It wasn't supposed to go down that way. Some things are necessary. Sure, not to the extent of what happened, but we have to do something." He leaned in close to her face. "You don't understand. You and Mama just sit by and let everything happen to you. I'm not like that. I guess I'm more like Papa than I want to admit." He slapped his palm to his chest. "It doesn't matter. I'm leaving for a different kind of fight soon."

Tears choked her. "Mama would be devastated to hear you talk like this. And Papa…poor Papa. He would never have allowed that to happen." She had to take some blame, but how could she have seen this coming?

She lowered her quivering voice. "Rumors of your involvement are another blot on the Kato name. Martin, you must stop this activity. It's as Mama always says, God will make a way. He is our defender. Don't you believe that anymore?"

"Do you?" His words stabbed her.

He was right. She had failed to show him by her own faith—a faith that had floundered. "Yes. Sometimes I have doubts and sometimes I'm angry too, Martin. I hate it here. I hate it that the government abandoned us. It's too big for us to avenge. We'll move on as soon as Papa comes." She put her hand on his arm. "Please, don't get into any more trouble."

He threw his hands in the air. "I didn't do anything!"

She glanced around the room and held her finger to her lips. "You knew about it. That's the same thing."

Martin grunted and looked to the ceiling.

How could she reach him? "Maybe you could spend more of your time trying to find a way to get Papa home. Our future depends on it. It might take you mind off yourself for a change."

His face softened. "Like I said, I'll be out of here soon. You won't have to worry about any rebels except John. I'll take my chances on the real battlefield."

She had put off telling him her real thoughts. Perhaps now he should hear them.

"I don't want you risking your life in combat for a country that abandoned you. If you would resist in a non-violent way, like Papa, at least you would be safe." She moved her head, looking side to side, watching for listening ears.

"You're crazy if you think I'm going to go to jail. Besides, I don't believe the same as you and Papa. I think it's right to fight. I'm an American, not Japanese. I have no confusion about that. We are at war with Japan and I'll do my duty like hundreds of other of our men."

He stood and she reached to grab his hands. She felt them ball into a fist. "Martin, if you leave, who will take care of Mama and Chiko and me?" She had grasped the last straw to keep the family intact, but she could feel it blowing away on a wind of misunderstanding and pride.

Martin's voice hardened. "You will. Remember? Papa left you in charge, not me. You'll be fine."

John called from the other end of the table. "Or better yet, I will."

Martin yanked his head to his left. "This is a private conversation, John."

John hoisted his foot on the bench seat. "Doesn't have to be, unless Hana agrees. I don't want to intrude. I'd like to honor your father by helping his family while he's gone."

Hana jumped in before Martin could. "I appreciate it, but I'm not sure Papa would really want that." She turned away.

John moved closer and kept talking. "Actually your father and I discussed it. I don't suppose he ever told you, and I didn't want to hurt Martin's feelings by telling him. But if Martin is leaving, you will need an occasional helping hand, don't you think?"

She smirked at John and shook her head. Papa wouldn't do such a thing. Hana studied Martin's expression. His eyes cast a look she had seen far too often lately. Sharp and cold. A veil of pain slipped down over his face. She wished she could hold his hand as she had when they were children. He trusted her then.

Martin showed a strained smile. "Well, friend. So glad you are here to take over what should have been my place all along. I guess my father wanted to make sure I didn't have any say in this family. If he trusted you so much, go right ahead. I don't care."

He sauntered to the kitchen and gathered up trays of dirty dishes, then disappeared to the rear. Hana's appetite vanished, replaced with tension and sadness for her little brother. Little? Not anymore. She couldn't just take his hand and lead him home and she was done scolding.

She stood and shifted her uniform top. Nerves and humidity made her back wet and sticky.

She turned her attention to John. "The only thing I need from you is your support. You have your ear in the grapevine between camps. If you want to be helpful, find out how we can get Papa released."

They locked eyes. John leaned in. "I wish you would let me do more, but I understand. I'll see what I can find out."

She broke her gaze when she sensed that old pull. Each time she thought she had broken the spell, it came back. She let her gaze drop to the floor. She wanted to stomp her foot and scream. Things should be different. Instead of this ridiculous tug of war, they should be enjoying each other's company. If they were anywhere but here in this camp, their conversation would be like something she dare not even imagine.

"Thank you. We just need Papa home. Then everything will be okay."

John waited there as if hoping she would run into his arms. She couldn't. Not now. Maybe not ever.

"Bye," he said, and hustled to the door.

There were so many times he could have been there for her, but wasn't. With so many disappointments she had lost the ability to trust anyone. She had upset Martin, offended John, and stood alone with no one to left to care. Like a sweater thread, every relationship she held dear unraveled. Finding normal would be harder than she thought possible, but she would find a way.

There was one person left she thought might have connections to move the family towards wholeness. She had put off talking to him long enough.

"All right, Doctor Bennett. You might be my only hope."

❧

The familiar pain of rejection groveled in his stomach. Another attempt to unite with the Kato family had failed. If he couldn't find a place to belong here, what would his life be like on the outside? It didn't matter. He didn't need anyone.

All the way to his barrack he replayed the conversation with Hana. A proud woman, she would never accept his help. No matter how hard he tried to redeem himself, she couldn't see him as anything more than a rebel. She didn't want to believe he had been on her side all along, and at her father's side since the beginning. His head hurt from thinking about it. He slowed his pace to stop the tightness in his chest.

As he entered the barrack, there lurked George Saito, leaning on the wall by John's cubicle door. "Hey, John."

John's neck bristled at the sight of George dressed in linen slacks and shiny new shoes. His family had money. Too bad it wasn't enough to buy their son a better personality. Something about George made John want to push his face into the wall.

John made eye contact. "Waiting for me, Georgie?"

The squinting eyes and scowl proved he had hit a nerve with the name. George looked down and mumbled. "Yeah. Want to talk to you."

John stifled a chuckle and pushed open his door. "Let's go in. That is, if you don't mind a sparsely furnished room. I never bothered fixing up the place." No one ever came to see him and his roommate, Thomas. All they needed were their cots and a couple chairs. Now that Thomas and many of the other young men had taken advantage of the permission to go to college, he was long gone from the camp, leaving John alone in a barrack of families.

John perched on the edge of his cot. "What's on your mind?"

George sat on a turned over crate and leaned forward to brush the dust off his shoes. His black hair was slicked back with too much hair tonic. John wondered if he knew the other young men made fun of him.

George cleared his throat. "We need to hold a demonstration soon. There's been no show of resistance lately and we can't get complacent. Some of the other guys agree with me." His voice jumped up and down as he rambled on.

Even at seventeen George was too immature to be in the group, but his parents' money carried weight with the other men. John blinked away visions of himself at that age. He hadn't lived a privileged life like George. Still, a similarity between them nagged at him. Poor kid just wanted to belong.

"Well, George, what I heard is that a few of you beat up an old man and then blamed Martin for it. I don't agree with those tactics. Especially after I called off the whole thing." John pulled off his tattered sneakers and tossed them to the side. He looked into George's eyes. "I'm telling you for the last time, Georgie, we need to lay low. They're watching us closely now."

George jumped up and scratched his head. "I don't get it. And who said I was there when they beat the guy up?"

John's head ached. "You don't need to get it. I don't think you ever will." Time to get rid of Georgie and take a cool shower before the day got any worse. He stood and reached for a towel, a clean pair of jeans and short sleeved shirt hanging from nails on the wall. George paced like a caged animal. John knew he wanted to prove himself, but someone else would have to babysit him.

John stood close to his guest. "Why don't you go home to your mama and forget about the group?"

George's hands balled into fists. His jaw clenched as he glared at John.

The little clock on the window sill said 6:15.

John threw his towel over his shoulder and tucked his clothes under his arm. He still had time to make a call on someone to help Hana. "I'm sorry. I have to go." The door creaked when he opened it. George stomped into the hall and out the main door. He turned around just as John reached the bottom of the steps.

"We don't have to listen to you. Maybe we can do what we want." He took off running before John could respond.

Something in his gut twisted. A spoiled brat could do his share of harm, and blame John for all of it if he wanted revenge. Before he could turn and hurry to the showers, Martin stepped out from beside the barrack.

John guessed he was in for another energy drain. "You following me, or just playing hide and seek?"

Martin crossed his arms. "Didn't want to interrupt George's threats. Sounds like you might have an uprising in the group, fearless leader."

John cleared his tightening throat to stop a comeback. Martin would be gone soon, off to fight a war he couldn't. He would excuse just about any remark for that. "Why are you here, Martin?"

"I want to ask you a question."

"Shoot."

Martin blurted out what seemed to be boiling inside. "Why are you so determined to be part of my family? Are you trying to take my father's place, or mine? Or maybe you just want to be close to Hana."

Had he been so bad at communicating his concern that Martin felt threatened? It was as if emotions and assumptions were just snatched out of the air when it came to living in this camp. It was no wonder families and communities had been so easily severed, just when they should be cemented.

John pointed to the steps. "Sit down, Martin. Let's talk." Martin obliged.

If he were to earn the trust of this one-time friend, he would have to be more transparent. Going off to war worrying about someone taking over his family wouldn't do for Martin Kato—he owed it to Mr. Kato to straighten this out.

"When I first arrived at Grand Peak, I was an angry guy. My parents had abandoned me. They had to go back to Japan—well, anyway, that's not important. Let's just say I was looking for trouble and hated anyone who was a father figure. Like Mr. Kato."

Martin frowned. "You hated my father?"

"No, just the authority he represented. When I found out he was leading a group of men to stand up for the rights of Japanese Americans in this camp, I wanted to show him up. I did everything I could to undermine his rapport with the other men. I didn't trust anyone, most of all anyone who might tell me what to do."

Sweat dripped down Martin's neck. "Yeah, so what happened?"

"I gave him a bad time." John laughed. He could now, but it wasn't funny then. He had caused Mr. Kato aggravation at the least. "You know what he did?"

"Probably put you down and made fun of you in front of the other guys." Martin rubbed the back of his neck and wiped the sweat on his pants. "That's what he did for me."

John's chest tightened. It would be hard to keep his temper if Martin insisted on maintaining an attitude. He let out a slow quiet whistle. "Nope. You're wrong about that. And you're wrong about your father in general."

Martin squinted. He had intrigued him. Now he had to go in for the lesson. "Your father is a great man. One night at a meeting I heckled him and he just took it, ignoring me. It made me mad, so I hung around after the meeting, ready to have it out and put him in his place. I knew he would kick me out of the group. I was asking for it."

"So what did he do? Run before you had a chance to confront him?"

Martin's tone was like fingernails digging into John's skin. "Shut up, Martin. You don't know what you're talking about. Do you want an answer to your question about me or not?" He slowed his breathing, waiting for Martin to bolt.

Martin bit his lower lip. Then grumbled. "Go on."

"Okay." He took a deep breath. "After the meeting I strutted up to him like the big man I wanted to be. He saw me coming and held out his hand and grabbed mine to shake it. He told me how much he admired my spunk, and that I had obvious leadership potential." John shook his head slowly, tears choking at his throat. "He asked me to be his right hand man that night." He paused. Martin's head hung, his body still. "In time he asked me to watch over his family if something ever happened to him."

Martin leaned back and stared at the sky. John waited for his words to sink in. Around them the familiar sounds of early evening began. The lines to the latrines formed, children scuffed up dust in their haste to get home for the mess hall. Perhaps Martin needed more.

"He nailed me. He knew I needed someone to care, someone to believe in me. He did that for me and it changed me. He wants to do that for you too. He loves you." John repressed the urge to pat Martin on the shoulder. He wasn't sure what to expect. Martin was a man now, wasn't he? He should understand from a man's point of view, but could he?

Martin's silence split through the hot air rippling across the compound. John breathed in the arid oxygen and relaxed his tense stomach muscles. There was nothing left to say.

Martin finally spoke. "I'm sorry. I didn't know." He stood and faced John. "I've been feeling the same as you did about your father—abandoned. But if he could do that for you, he can't be all bad." He sighed hard and rubbed his palms on his jeans. "Truth is, I never gave him much of a chance to be my mentor. I'm sort of jealous you had that chance instead of me."

John stood. Now it felt right to encourage with a pat on the back. "It doesn't have to be that way. You still have time." He hoped it was true. "I just wanted you to see how important your family is to me. I won't do anything to hurt them while you and your father are gone."

Martin nodded. Friends again. Maybe the day hadn't been a waste after all.

As Martin turned to leave, a crash sounded behind them. John spun to see the door. The stomping of running feet drifted off into the area behind the barrack.

Martin rushed around the corner in pursuit. John knew not to bother. They would be gone just like at Michael's room that night.

He slipped through his door to see glass from his only window scattered on the floor, a fist-sized rock lying in the middle of it. It may as well have had George's signature written on it.

Martin panted in the doorway. "Oh, man. What a mess. I couldn't catch whoever it was. Hey, blood! You stepped on the glass with your bare feet? That wasn't too smart." He pointed to the floor.

Pain suddenly stabbed at John's big toe. He lifted his foot and checked the floor behind him before stepping back. Blood dripped as he moved. Martin shoved some of the glass with his shoe as John backed up to the wood crate. He propped his foot on his knee. A cut an inch long sliced diagonally across the bottom of his right big toe.

"Great. Just what I need." He wrapped the towel still in his hand around his foot.

Martin winced. "You need to go to the hospital?"

"Naw. It'll be fine. I'll just be sure to wear socks and shoes for a few days."

Martin shrugged. "You want me to get a broom? I'll help you—"

"Nope. Go on. I've kept you long enough. I got it."

"See you later." Martin left through the open door.

The throbbing in his foot worsened as he wrapped the towel tight to stop the bleeding. He breathed deep to slow the adrenaline from pumping out more blood. "Stupid!" He put his foot down and tried to stand. Pain shot up his ankle.

He wouldn't get his shower in today. Nor would he be able to make inquiries for Hana as he promised. He had to do it tomorrow.

The toe should be fine by then.

Chapter 5

Only nine o'clock and the temperatures already spiked into the mid-eighties, chasing away the cool breeze blowing off the mountain. Neil tapped the gauge of the thermometer over the door of his tiny bungalow and looked above the horizon. No clouds in the fierce blue sky for the last three days. He tramped through the dry weeds and dirt clods to take the shortcut to the hospital. The sun bore down on his head, but his Dodger's baseball cap shaded his nose from the burning rays. No one told him Wyoming would have such extreme weather. It was only the end of May and keeping the hospital cool for patients had been a challenge.

The heat from his office blasted him as he opened the door. He hooked the musty wool blankets over the windows and plopped into his chair. He wasn't sure what was worse—the smell of the blanket or the heat of the sun. At least the patients' rooms had roll-up blinds. Now if only they could get enough electric fans to thwart the stagnant air.

"Excuse me, Doctor Bennett."

He spun around. Hana's fresh face greeted him. Her uniform crisp, she wasn't the least bit wilted. How did she manage it in this heat? Her hair fell loose around her face, not tucked back as usual. She leaned through the doorway.

"May I speak with you before my shift starts?" Her voice lifted the heavy heat pressing in on him.

He stood and removed his already sweat-soaked lab coat. "Certainly, Miss Kato. Come in."

The morning had improved with her presence, better than any cool breeze on a parched day. He hurried to the door to usher her in and to peek in the hall. Doctor Davidson wasn't going to eavesdrop this time. "Amazing temperatures around here. I suppose you're used to a more humid climate on the coast." He leaned against the edge of his desk while she slid into the chair in front of him. She nodded and shrugged at the same time. As much as he liked the stillness to just study her face, her silence was awkward. "What can I do for you?"

She fidgeted with the hem of her skirt. "I was planning to talk to you yesterday, but the day was so busy with patients. I was wondering—well, hoping you could help my family with something." Her face turned crimson.

He moved around his desk to sit in his chair. His ears perked at hearing of a chance to help Hana. No matter what it was he would jump at it. "Of course, if I can." Curiosity tickled his thoughts.

She leaned back and grasped the arms of the chair. "As you know, my father has been sent to prison."

"Uh huh."

"Well, a few days ago we received word that he had a mild heart attack."

Neil's breath caught. "I'm so sorry. Does he have a history of coronary disease?"

She folded her hands neatly in her lap and blinked back the moisture in her eyes. "No. He hasn't been well since he was arrested and, well naturally, we are afraid of what prison life might do to his health."

"I agree. How can I help?" He tried to imagine her struggles. Living through Pearl Harbor's bombing, internment, and now this. For most people, such things would have broken their spirit. Not Hana.

She leaned forward and pleaded with her eyes. "Do you think, I mean, do you know of anyone in authority that could pull some strings to have him released on grounds of medical hardship?" Her face softened. His arms ached to reach out to her and tell her he had an answer for her.

His heart sank at the reality of her request. It must be hard for her to ask. "Is he in the prison infirmary? I could possibly contact them to learn more about his condition. I don't think I…" A name from the past suddenly came to mind. *Major Harmony.* He strained to see the man's face in his mind's eye while Hana talked.

"It's vital we get him back here where I can care for him. I thought you might know someone. I suppose it was wishful thinking." Defeat washed over her countenance while she tapped her fingernails on the arms of the chair.

He jumped to his feet. "Just a minute. I might know someone who could help."

Now Hana rose. "Really?"

"Before I came here I took care of a Major at a base hospital, and he was supposed to be heading up the POW health services or something like that. I don't remember exactly, but I would be willing to check into it for you. It's a long shot. I'll try." The possibility of rescuing Mr. Kato from probable death excited him. Saving lives, especially this one, is why he became a doctor.

Hana's eyes brightened. "Would you? I—we would be so grateful. I can try to get you the little bit of medical information we have on his current condition. The telegram we received was pretty vague." She chattered on at high speed.

He marveled at what hope could do for a person. That's what these people needed. Hope.

She reached over to shake his hand. He held hers tight as her smiling eyes looked into his. She pulled her hand away and backed up a few steps. She studied his face until Nurse Potter's voice broke the silence.

"Doctor Bennett?"

Their connection had been severed. For now. "Yes, Nurse Potter. What is it?"

Hana scooted past her after a whispered thank you to him.

Nurse Potter's apologetic tone surprised him. "I'm sorry to bother you. I think you should see the young man that just came in. Doctor Davidson is with another patient and this one needs attention. He's in considerable pain from an injury a couple days ago. Has been feverish for twenty-four hours he says."

He signed hard. "Of course. Thank you. I'll come at once. Miss Kato and I were finished anyway."

He thought he saw the ends of Nurse Potter's lips curl up. What could possibly amuse her? He wiped the perspiration from his temples with his sleeve and grabbed his white coat. Splatters of blood from yesterday remained on the front. He glanced at her. Her head swung side to side in a definite *no.*

He hung his head like he had when in trouble with his mother. "I don't have a clean jacket."

"Give it here." She yanked the jacket away from him and turned it wrong side out, then twirled him around by his shoulders and slipped it up his arms. Spinning him once more, she dusted the arms and stepped back.

He fumbled to find a pocket, but they were all on the inside now. "Um. Thanks."

She resumed the bossy voice he knew so well. "Welcome. Follow me."

He took long strides to keep up with his head nurse. She had many more years of practice hurrying down hospital hallways than he did. He tried to keep his eyes off her hefty swaying hips and swinging arms. He was afraid he would be tempted to imitate her like he did the doctors at medical school.

She burst through the door of the exam room and held it open for him to pass. Sitting on the exam table with one foot dangling and one foot propped up by a pillow was the young man he had met twice before.

What is his name? Don…no, John.

He stepped close to the foot on the pillow. "Hello again. What's happened?"

John winced and spoke through gritted teeth. "Stepped on some broken glass. It hurts real bad today."

Nurse Potter pulled back the bloody homemade bandage to reveal an angry red toe. John groaned as she unwrapped it completely. His face paled white against blotchy red cheeks.

Neil washed his hands in the sink and dried them. "Let's have a look." A red streak snaked its way up John's ankle. If any glass remained, it had to come out. He picked up a sterile probe from a basin and gently prodded the open wound.

"Doctor!" Nurse Potter made a flying leap to catch John's head as he fell back on the table. Neil reached to grab his arm and succeeded in holding him from falling onto the floor by locking his arm in John's.

She placed a pillow under his head. "He's out cold."

"John?" Hana appeared and hustled to the side of the bed. She stroked his forehead and turned to Neil. "What happened?"

He didn't have time to look up as he unattached himself from John and returned to the wound. "Cut by glass. Infected. Let me take a close look while he's out."

Nurse Potter stepped to the other side of the table, shaking a thermometer. She placed it under John's armpit. "He feels hot to me. You think so, Miss Kato?"

Hana rested the back of her hand on John's face. "Yes. It must be well over 100. I'll get some cold compresses." She whirled past them and out the door.

He looked up from the wound to peek at John's face. No sign of revival. "I'll need to clean this out. Nurse, will you get me what I need?" He moved up and placed his stethoscope on John's heaving chest. "Elevated heart rate."

Hana raced back into the room. He looked directly at her. "He's one sick boy. You seem to know him. Does he have family?"

"No." Hana's voice wavered as she arranged the compresses while watching John wiggle.

He took the basin from Nurse Potter. "I'll need an IV started."

"I'll do it." She already had the glass bottle and tubing in her hands. He inspected the label and nodded. If Hana knew this patient well, he would have to watch her closely. The last thing he needed was a nurse falling apart.

"Is he going to be all right?" Hana's brow furrowed as she tenderly sponged John's arms and neck, her touch noticeably more intimate than with other patients. He clicked off his speculations as soon as he felt them rising up.

"Don't know yet. Let's see how he reacts to the I.V." He returned to flushing the gaping hole, pushing the plunger to force fluid from the syringe as fast as it would flow. Pieces of tissue broke away from the wound as he cleaned it. He held back the bad news from Hana. The infection was at a dangerous level and moving fast.

As he pulled back a foul flap of skin, John screamed. Hana rushed to hold him down, throwing her body across his thrashing arms.

Nurse Potter moved quickly to adjust the fluid line. "Keep him still if you can. I'll help in a moment."

Hana shrieked. "He's too strong for me!"

John flailed his arm, flipping Hana to the floor as if she had jumped from a spring board. Neil's heart lurched. He dropped his instruments, letting the basin of contaminated fluid beneath John's wound splatter on the floor. He reached Hana and gingerly turned her face. Her eyes opened and she gasped for breath.

"Hana? Where are you hurt?"

She groaned a guttural sound and sat up. Blood dripped from her forearm as she reached to rub her shoulder. "Ow!"

He grabbed her arm and pulled her up. "Get some bandages and antiseptic. Be careful not to step in or touch that fluid."

"How am I supposed to leave the patient? He'll throw himself off the table if I let go." Nurse Potter wrestled with John's right arm, pinning it with her hip against the bed.

Neil grunted, sweat dripping from his temples. "I'll take care of it. I'm going in the hall first to call for an orderly." He grabbed a blanket and stuffed it under Hana's head. "Stay put and don't touch anything. I suspect John has sepsis and it's moving fast."

His eyes bore into hers to make sure she understood. He mentally inventoried the room as he guided her out. Did Nurse Potter have gloves on? Yes. He shook inside at the scene, and at seeing Hana bloodied. He should have controlled the situation better. The enormity of his mistake settled into his gut. Hana's open wound could have been contaminated.

He didn't have time to ponder the ramifications. He would have to make an assessment later. All he could do now was get Hana to another room and then rescue the nurse.

"Orderly!"

"I mean it, little sister. You can't do it." Ignoring the throbbing in her right elbow, Hana tugged on Chiko's ponytail with her one good hand. The sling Nurse Potter sent home with her yesterday wasn't helping the pain or her patience. Neither was lying around on her cot while she could be at work.

She had to talk Chiko out of this plan to work away from the safety of this ironic safe haven of camp. After all, she knew so much more than Mama or Chiko about the dangers. Someday she would have to tell them exactly how she knew.

Chiko frowned back at her. "You worry too much. Lots of the girls get passes to work in the produce fields. Besides, I already have my permit. Mama said she would agree to let me if you said okay." She sat on the edge of Hana's cot. "I just want to be with the other girls. Maybe if I work with them, they'll forget Papa is a criminal. Even white girls come to work out there and I could find new friends, white friends."

Hana winced, but sat beside Chiko and slipped her arm around her shoulders. "I know you feel hurt about Papa, but what would Mama think if she heard you say that? All of us have had confusing thoughts, even me. You're old enough to be more careful about what you say. I'm trying to be careful about what I believe to be true about what's going on." She reached over and tugged on Chiko's chin. "Since when do you need the approval of those girls?"

"You don't understand at all." Chiko pulled away from Hana's touch.

She stood. "Maybe not, but I have good reason to be cautious about you working outside." Done with the sling pulling at her shoulder she slipped it over her head and laid it over her lap.

"What good reason?" Mama called out from the open doorway. She stooped to pick up the basket of laundry and stepped inside. "You always say you have good reason Chiko not work outside camp, but you never tell. Maybe you tell now. And why you not wear sling?" She hoisted the basket onto the table and pulled out a chair. Her posture straightened as she glared at Hana.

She would be in for a tongue lashing if she didn't satisfy Mama's demands for an explanation. Was this the time and place?

"Mama-san, I know what I'm talking about. It's not safe for any Japanese American to work with Caucasians out there. And I hate that sling."

"Yes, so why it not safe out there? It time you tell us why you so afraid." Mama crossed her arms. "And you put sling on."

She would say just enough to convince Mama it would be a mistake to agree to Chiko's request. She grabbed the sling and pulled it over her aching arm. She always did what Mama said, and could never understand Martin's and Chiko's resistance to her leading. Her blood boiled each time they pressed Mama on an issue to get their own way.

She sat up and clumsily fluffed her pillow. "I nearly didn't get home to all of you after Pearl was bombed, and well, I had a hard time there. It doesn't matter now. Can't you please let me do what Papa asked me to—protect Chiko?"

Her stomach tightened when she heard Martin's voice by the door. "You can't do all the protecting, Hana. I don't think Papa meant for you to make all the decisions around here. We should go with what Mama-san says." He shut the door hard and dropped his backpack on his cot.

Sure, now he decides to go with Mama's decision. This time she had to disagree.

"I didn't mean that I had the final say. It's just that I know Papa. He said what he said and I do have an opinion. Of course Mama-san will decide." Her relent didn't sit well with her, but for now she would compromise.

Everyone fell silent for a moment. Mama's eyes shimmered a faraway look. Maybe if she knew the whole story, she would keep Chiko home. Or maybe it wouldn't make any difference to any of them. Hana rubbed the back of her stiff neck, her skin hot to the touch.

"I think she'll be okay." Martin flopped onto his cot and put his feet up. "Even if I'm not around to watch over her, my buddies working out there this summer will keep an eye out."

Chiko smiled and nodded as she slid into a chair next to Mama. "See?"

Mama chimed in. "I think maybe Martin right." She brightened and grabbed a shirt off the mending pile. It must have relieved her to have Martin on her side. Hana would be too, except that now wasn't the right time or the right issue for Martin to finally make a stand.

Hana leaned back and groaned. She could never win with three against her. "Is it me, or did the temperature suddenly rise in this room?" She wiped perspiration from her lip. Martin shrugged and Chiko shook her head.

"It's just as hot as it was an hour ago." Chiko pulled a towel from the basket and folded it.

Mama seemed to have missed a beat in the conversation. "I think more about it, Chiko. I let you know when I decide."

Chiko stood and crossed her arms. "Oh, Mama-san." Hana glared at her and put her finger to her lips. Mama would have the last say.

Martin bounced to his feet. "Come on, Chiko. You can come to the mess hall with me. A church group is there handing out candy bars. Course you'll have to take a Bible too."

Hana could still remember the excitement at holding a brand new Bible in her hands. The missionaries at the church down the street handed them out by the dozens. Soon after, her parents started going to church there. It seemed like a lifetime ago. Whatever happened to that little New Testament anyway?

"It do you both good to read it." Mama shook her finger at them the same playful way she had at Papa the day he left. "Don't be late."

Hana stood and shoved Chiko's chair under the table, but then held the back of it, her knees weak and wobbly. "See if they will let you have a dozen candy bars for the children at the hospital."

Martin nudged Chiko. "Chiko can talk them into it. They can't say no to a funny face like hers." He ducked away from her swinging arm and fled the room.

"Stop." Chiko ran out the door after him.

The room stilled with the teenagers gone. Hana listened to Mama's soft breaths as she threaded a needle to mend Martin's shirt. Even the relentless wind had ceased. She opened the small window to let in fresh air without dust. The heat of their room swirled, compounding her woozy head.

Closing her eyes, she thought of home. Just to lie on cool grass, raking her fingers through the soft blades of green would be like a dream. A dream she had grave doubts about coming true. She heard Mama praying each day for freedom. So far, God hadn't heard, or seen fit to answer, except for a small group of other families who had been able to leave. If Mama's prayers worked, the doors would open for all of them to go home soon, but home to what? And without Papa?

Her mind whirled. Nothing made sense anymore.

Why is it so hot in here?

"Martin not graduate with class, but we find something special to give him."

Hana shuffled to her cot and lay down. "He just had a birthday, Mama-san. It's hard to come up with another thing to give him. Especially when he's going off to war." The words slipped out before she could stop herself. They had all tried to avoid the subject war since Martin was drafted. She bolted up straight and swung her legs around. Mama stayed fixed on her sewing, her calm expression unfaltering. Hana blinked to focus on her, waiting for the room to stop spinning.

"I know. God will be with Martin." She rested her work in her lap and smiled.

She leaned back against her pillow. The only thing she wanted to do was go to sleep. All the debates could wait. She couldn't think past the ringing in her ears, except to wonder how John was doing. Doctor Bennett said he would take good care of him.

"Hana."

"Yes, Mama-san?" She turned over on her side, willing the room to stop spinning. The fresh air from the window seemed to be stale again.

"I think Chiko go work in the fields."

Hana sighed. "Okay, Mama-san." Mama had made the decision with her heart. Hana knew Chiko's desire to blend in and be with the white girls was a form of self-abandonment. She had made the same mistake once, trying hard to be more "white" with the other nurses. It only bred hatred in herself—*of* herself. And tomorrow Chiko would go…go where?

Where are Martin and Chiko? They should be home.

Her concentration fled—replaced by a pounding pain in her head. She pulled off the sling and touched her wounded arm. Her hand below the bandage was swollen and red. It tingled like pricking needles. As she tried to sit up, she felt the contents of her stomach rising up.

"Mama. Help me." She leaned over the edge of her cot.

She heard Mama's sewing fall to the floor, footsteps, then Mama was by her side.

"You sick?"

"Yes, Mama. Find Martin and have him bring Doctor Bennett." She swallowed hard to keep from vomiting. "Hurry."

Mama reached to touch the swelling arm.

Hana screamed. "Don't touch it!"

Mama recoiled and stood up straight. Hana couldn't see her face. She knew she must have startled her poor mother. It was for her safety that she not get too close. The door slammed and the room closed in on her. She shouldn't have insisted she come home. If she was as sick as John, she could endanger her family. Doctor Bennett tried to stand his ground, but she had been her usual stubborn self, always thinking she knew best. He should have made her stay at the hospital. But it was too quick to have John's infection…wasn't it?

Everyone trusted her judgment and now she had—

"Doctor Bennett, you were right." She called out to no one.

Just close your eyes. Hurry, Martin.

The colors of Japan flashed by her on waving flags. She had never been to her parents' native land. Still, she felt the essence of it running through her veins. The spirit of it was written on the wrinkled faces of the old Issei men in camp as they filed by her on their way to somewhere—she couldn't see where.

Their language, their dress and ceremony all foreign, yet so real to her. Where were they going?

She gazed at her reflection in an unknown window. She was American, but Japan leaned into her heart as a mother searching for her child. Through the window she saw Mama and Chiko. Mama was dressed in the colorful tunic she wore the day Papa left. She called out to them and Mama extended her hand, almost touching her.

"Hana? Are you awake?"

Her eyelids wouldn't open at first, then she squeezed them and tried again. Mama stood over her, stroking her cheek. The room slowly came into focus, then fuzzy again. She heard ticking. Another attempt to focus brought Chiko into the picture. Behind her was a round clock like the ones that hung on all the patient rooms at the hospital.

She coughed to clear her dry raw throat. "Where am I?" Her voice scratched, barely audible.

Mama smiled and leaned down to Hana's ear. "You in hospital. Very sick girl."

Chiko skirted around the end of the bed, moving to Hana's other side. "We were so worried. How do you feel? You've been asleep for two days."

Blink again. Why wouldn't the room stop spinning?

"I'm dizzy and tired. Why am I here?" She closed one eye to look at her sister. "Why are you in a gown and gloves?"

Chiko took Hana's good hand. "Doctor Bennett says you might have an infection. Like John."

"Oh, yes. I remember." She groaned and rested her wrist on her forehead.

Chiko tucked the sheet in around Hana's waist. "It's a good thing Martin ran home and carried you all the way to the hospital. Doctor Bennett says it saved time."

Some of this made sense to her, but right now her dream seemed more real. Mama would know what it meant.

She fought the overwhelming urge to touch her throbbing arm. She knew better. Someone had propped it up on a pillow—she could see it through the blurry film on her eyes. "Mama-san, I was dreaming."

Mama leaned in. Her tired face sporting a half smile. "Yes? You dream about home?"

"No. I'm not sure."

Chiko giggled and squeezed her hand. "Maybe if you tell us it will get you awake."

"First, in my dream, I danced with Papa in our parlor to the music of Japan. He smiled as I swayed back and forth with him. But when the music stopped, I was all alone in our empty tar papered barrack, back here at Grand Peak. There were colorful flags." She swallowed hard. "Then I saw you and Chiko through a window and—well, never mind. It was silly."

Sadness fell over her like a veil. Not in Japan, but not in America either. That's what her dream meant. She was just nowhere.

Blink a few more times. A tear rolled down Mama's cheek. Her eyes closed. She must be feeling the same. Abandoned by both countries.

She squinted through a blur to search the room. "Where's Martin?"

Mama patted her shoulder. "He meeting with other boys who go to shoe camp."

Chiko laughed. "Mama-san, it's boot camp. Not shoe camp."

Hana winced at the joke that wasn't funny and rolled to her side. The air in the room, hot and thin, wasn't helping her flushed face. She had to get up, even for a few minutes to clear her mind. Just as she tried to sit up Nurse Potter rushed into the room with her usual take charge posture.

"Don't even think about it." She barked as if ordering a troop of soldiers.

Hana would have saluted in jest had she not been overcome by a wave of nausea. She flopped down, moaning when she bumped her sore arm. Nurse Potter rushed to her side to take her pulse. She thrust a thermometer in Hana's mouth. It tasted of bitter alcohol.

Nurse Potter shook her head. "Don't talk either."

Hana glanced back and forth between Mama and Chiko. Mama eyed Nurse Potter, and Chiko pursed her lips, obviously subduing another laugh. The nurse lightly touched the white gauze wrapping around the wound, then pulled out the thermometer.

"100 even. Better, but not good enough. I'll get the doctor. He'll be glad to see you're awake." She winked at Chiko as she whisked passed her. A strange gesture for Nurse Potter to make. She had never seen her wink at anyone before.

"She's nice." Chiko grabbed a chair and pushed it behind Mama. "Here, Mama-san. Sit."

Nurse Potter? Nice? Chiko getting a chair for Mama? Nothing seemed right. She closed her eyes, supposing she was still dreaming, or hallucinating. As soon as she really woke up she would find her clothes and get out of this place.

"Feeling better?" Doctor Bennett touched her wrist and jolted her sense of time and space.

Her eyes popped open. The icy cold end of his stethoscope touched her chest, sending a shiver down her back. The rest of her skin palpated hot and achy. Mama perched herself on the chair and Chiko stood behind her.

"No. I mean yes. I feel fine. When can I get up?" She took a chance he would believe her. She had more important things to tend to than lying here like a sick person.

"Sure. Nice try. You'll be here at least for tonight. You have a bad virus on top or your trauma from yesterday."

Mama-san piped up. "She been working with children at school. She teach origami. She get germs?"

Doctor Bennett shrugged. "Could be." He glanced at Hana. "Although I bet the children love that. I'd stay clear of them for a while, and all of you wash your hands more often. No more germ spreading." He smiled at Chiko. He flipped the stethoscope around his neck. "We'll discontinue the antibiotics. They won't work against this and your wound looks fine. I wish the meds were working faster for John."

Hana's muscles tensed. "What do you mean? Is he still here in the hospital?"

"Afraid so. He's very sick from sepsis. High fever. He wakes up once in a while and asks to see you, though. I can't let that happen till you are out of danger. Any other visitors he gets will have to gown up and keep their distance. Not sure how infectious he is, but it's best to be cautious."

Chiko perked up. "Could I go see him? I'm all wrapped up like a cocoon." She held up her arms to show Doctor Bennett her gown and gloves.

He raised his brows at Hana. She would trust his judgment. Besides, John was all alone. "Are you sure it's safe?"

He nodded. "If she follows the precautions. I'll make sure she does, if you want her to see him." She followed his eyes, instead of looking at her while he talked, he busied himself writing on her chart.

Hana referred to her mother. "Mama-san? Would you mind? I'd like someone to go see him."

Mama looked to Doctor Bennett and then to Hana.

Nurse Potter fiddled with Hana's I.V. bottle, then broke the silence. "I'll go in with her, if the doctor can spare me."

He replaced the clipboard on the hook at the end of the bed. "Just don't stay too long. Is this all right with you, Mrs. Kato? The nurse knows how to control the situation."

Mama nodded and pointed to Chiko. "You no touch anything. Just talk."

Chiko inched toward the door. "I'll be okay, Mama-san."

Hana's eyelids wouldn't stay open. She longed to let them close so she could sleep. Doctor Bennett must have read her mind, or her face. Oh, her face. She must be the image of a prize beauty if she looked anything like she felt.

Doctor Bennett tapped on her foot. "We gave you something to help you sleep. I'll be back in a while." He waved for Mama to follow him.

Chiko took Nurse Potter's hand as if they were friends. The woman stopped, regarded the gesture and then pulled her along, back to her bossy self. "You mind the rules. I'll help you into a fresh gown. And you may call me Alice." She turned to Hana. "That goes for you too. At least when the other nurses aren't around."

Hana wanted to smile, but her vision fogged again. She hated feeling wretched and helpless. If only she could be there for John. She closed her eyes and let sweet stillness come over her. Soft voices in the hall lulled her like a lullaby.

"Administered another dose…"

"I'll take that call…"

She had forgotten to ask Doctor Bennett about his inquiry for Papa's release. She tried to wake up and call him back, but the voices sang her deeper into relaxation, like a late night serenade.

She would ask him when he came back.

Chapter 6

Neil gripped the arm of his chair to keep from raising his voice. "But I've been trying to reach his office and can't seem to get through. Can't you just tell me if he got my messages?" He was hopeful when the return call came through, only to find it wasn't the Major. The woman at the other end of the line repeated her droning mantra. He gripped the receiver harder.

"I'm sorry, sir. I can't give out any information at this time. If you like, I will transfer you to another office. I'm not sure you will be told anything different." Her voice sounded a bit like an excited Claudette Colbert, but judging by her attitude she lacked the image.

"Please transfer me anyway." A click sounded on the other end of the line and then a long ring followed by another, and another. Just as he pulled the receiver from his ear to hang up, a male voice boomed through.

"Major Harmony's office, Sargent Klein speaking."

"Uh, yes, hello?"

How did I get through to Harmony's office?

"This is Doctor Neil Bennett and I've been trying to reach Major Harmony. Is he available to speak with me?" He leaned his elbows on the desk. At last some progress. Marching into Hana's room with good news would spread revived spirits for the Katos.

"Look, Doctor. I don't know how you got this number. You can't speak to Major Harmony."

He grit his teeth, wondering why on earth his simple request had caused such a fuss. "Sir, he knows me. If you would just tell him his doctor from the base hospital at—"

"Doctor. Major Harmony is dead. Killed in action two days ago. Do not call this number again. Good-bye."

He froze, the telephone line buzzing in his ear. Dead. He didn't know the Major had gone back into active duty. His breath left him, his ears ringing so loud he didn't hear Nurse Potter enter the room with Chiko in tow. He rested the receiver on its cradle and stared at the phone, his heart beating hard.

"Doctor Bennett? Do you know where Mrs. Kato is? Chiko here is ready to leave and—Doctor Bennett?"

He jerked his head at the sound of his name. "What?"

"Are you all right?" Nurse Potter left Chiko in the doorway and inched toward him.

"Yes, of course." He brightened up to cover his disappointment. How could he tell Hana? She had counted on him to come through for her, and Major Harmony was his only hope. It seemed the Kato family was destined to jump over one roadblock after another.

He picked up a pencil from his desk and tapped it on a book. "I, uh, haven't seen Mrs. Kato. Perhaps she stepped out and is back in your sister's room."

Chiko's voice wavered. "We were just there a few minutes ago."

He mustered a smile and bounced around his desk. "Well, let's go look again. People come and go quickly, you know." He let Nurse Potter lead the way. Down the hall Mrs. Kato sat on the floor in front of Hana's room, Martin next to her.

Chiko ran ahead and crouched on the floor beside Martin. "Mama, where were you?"

"I get Martin. He want to see Hana when she awake. Okay, Doctor Bennett?"

The sound of breaking glass tore through her question. He bolted through Hana's door. Her bare legs dangled over the edge of the bed, and the I.V. bottle lay smashed on the floor. His insides jumbled to think she might be hurt again.

"Hana! Don't move." He slipped up to the other side of her bed and pulled her by the waist until she was square on the mattress again.

"I'll get a broom." Nurse Potter rushed away after telling the family to stay put.

He held onto Hana until she leaned back into the bed, then pulled the white blanket up over her legs and placed his hand on her arm. He could feel her shaking. He stroked her arm, wanting to comfort and scold at the same time.

Martin called, his voice panicked. "Is she okay?"

Neil's ears heated. "Yes, but stay out until we clean up." He rested his palms on the bed, staring her in the face. She kept her gaze down, no doubt expecting a lashing.

Nurse Potter waddled into the room holding another I.V. bottle, an orderly close behind her with a broom.

"And what were you trying to do?" His tone must have been sharp because Nurse Potter frowned at him.

Hana blinked and a tear rolled down her cheek. "I was—I don't know. I heard someone call to me." She shook her head, then scanned the room. "I must have been dreaming."

The redness in her cheeks spread to the rest of her face. She stared at him. "You about scared me to death when you yelled at me. Trying to use shock therapy?"

"I'm sorry. You frightened me—all of us. I think you should stay in bed until we check you over."

"We go now. Hana need rest." Mama nudged Martin who pulled on Chiko's sleeve and tipped his head toward the door.

"We'll be here first thing tomorrow, if that's okay." Martin's tone wasn't asking, it was telling. He wanted to commend him for taking charge.

"That should work, Martin. Thank you. We'll take good care of her—and John."

Mama and Chiko waved to Hana.

"Good-bye, Mama-san. I'll be all right, don't worry. Martin, would you peek in on John tomorrow too?" She turned to Neil. "If that's allowed."

Before he could answer, Martin piped in. "I will." He pulled Mama and Chiko out the door, his eyes steady on Neil.

Even though the urge to over-rule Martin was strong, he would let him have his moment of authority. He had often wondered about the relationship between the Katos and the patient down the hall. It was obvious Hana thought of John as a good friend. He had hoped to be her friend too. Now he had to let her down.

The room quieted except for the ticking of the clock. She smiled, her eyes closed. "Thanks for sending them home." Peace settled over her face. He hesitated to interrupt it with bad news, but he stepped closer. He had no other choice but to get it over with.

"I have some news to share."

Her eyelids fluttered open. Anticipation sparkled in them as she turned her head on the pillow. He hid his sweaty palms behind his back.

She wiggled in the bed to face him. "Is your friend going to help Papa?"

He scooted a chair with his foot until it was near the head of her bed. "I'm sorry. I just found out that he passed away the other day. I had no idea. I wish I could say I knew someone else. I'll do some digging, but I have no one else to turn to right now."

Her eyes closed again. He stomach knotted, watching her lower lip quiver. He hated disappointing her. If only this plan had begun much earlier, Major Harmony might have been able to help. They just needed one phone call. One letter from the right person. One small miracle from God.

Her eyes remained shut. "I know you tried. Thank you. I'd like to sleep now, unless you need to take vitals or something." A tear slipped from the corner of one and dripped onto the white pillowcase.

He reached out to place a trembling hand on her shoulder, but pulled back. "I'm so sorry."

The room darkened once he pulled the chain on the hanging light bulb. The moonlight filtering through the window above her bed cast a sorrowful shadow. He pulled the door closed and peered through the small window. She should be better tomorrow, at least physically. No one could mend her broken enthusiasm, except her.

What was it his mother used to say? Something about God closing a door and then opening a window. He should have enough faith to believe it. He straggled down the hall to his office.

"Think, Bennett, think. There must be someone else you know who could help."

Yet, he knew there wasn't. He hadn't made many relationships outside of whatever mission hospital he worked at. Following his parents around had been a full time job, not conducive to a social life. As soon as this God forsaken camp closed down, he would change all that.

First, he had to look in his notebook of contacts and see if there wasn't someone to help Mr. Kato.

Notebook first. Then God.

Hana had never seen his face so pale and his eyes so dark. The last time they spoke outside the hospital, he was strong and defiant—ready to take on the world. Ready to help her get Papa home. She looked around the room. This was not the sanctuary of his barrack room, but a stark white prison that kept him from the mission he tried to execute daily in the camp. He lay silent—between frustration and weakness. His foot, wrapped in layers of gauze, rested on a stack of pillows. She secured her mask and tugged at her rubber gloves.

She had to know if he was all right. Worrying about him had taken over her thought life. She had been instructed to go home and stay there for a few days. This would be her only chance to check on him. Besides, she felt so much better, rest could wait.

"John?"

He jerked and opened his eyes to stare at her.

She smiled her most assuring smile. "How are you feeling?"

"Hana. I should ask you the same question. Did they discharge you? Are you better?" He struggled to prop himself up on the head of the bed, his eyes dull and frantic. She rushed over to help him.

"I shouldn't have disturbed you." She stammered. "I'm sorry. Don't exert yourself. I'll only stay a minute. I'm going home to lay low for a few days under doctor's orders." She pulled a pillow up for him to rest his head. "Doctor Bennett is overly cautious I think." She knew it wasn't true, but it might put John at ease. "He worries too much."

John ran his finger over the I.V. needle in his arm, focusing intently on it. His tone changed to a childlike accusation. "I think that's what anyone does when they care about someone as much as he cares for you, right?"

Hana swallowed hard. Was he talking about Doctor Bennett? John wouldn't look at her. Her face flushed at the very hint of any affection on the doctor's part. Her mind darted off to think of any time when he might have given that indication. No. John was dead wrong. It was a preposterous thought. But John's firm jaw told her he believed it. She stifled a smile.

"That's ridiculous. He's a doctor, I'm a patient and nurse. That's all." She tugged at the sheet to tuck it in on the side. "So you haven't answered my question. How are you feeling?"

"Just fine. I wish he would let me leave too. I have things to tend to—like helping you get your father home."

Hana sighed quietly, torn between caring about John's well-being at this moment, and taking an opportunity to talk about Papa. She glanced at his hands resting on his chest. They trembled, and she knew what she had to do.

"John, don't you worry about that right now. Please just get better and we'll work on that when you're out of here and back on both feet." Her tense muscles in her back relaxed. Somehow Papa's dilemma didn't seem urgent. Life presented itself to her in bits of trauma and she had to deal with one thing at a time.

John winced, pulled himself up, and reached for his bandaged foot. She grabbed his hand before he could touch it. His face contorted with pain, then he threw himself back on the bed. His arm muscles knotted like rocks. Hana placed her gloved hand on is right arm and stroked it until he breathed easier.

Perspiration dotted his forehead. She pulled the basin close to the edge of the bed and squeezed out the sponge soaked in room temperature alcohol and water. He stilled as she wiped his brow and temples with her softest touch.

He opened his eyes. "It happens once in a while—like a knife carving away on my foot. It'll ease in a minute." He pulled in a deep breath and let it out slowly. "Thanks. That feels good."

He turned to look into her eyes. She couldn't discern the emotion behind his stare. She knew so little about this man. Her arms-length policy had done the trick, but now she wondered if it had been right to be so distant. He truly did have a kind heart.

She brushed against her pocket and felt the rustle of paper. She smiled and reached in to retrieve the gift she had almost forgotten. Her hand shook as she held out her palm. On it perched her latest prize origami fish. "Here, strength, courage, and determination. For you."

He blinked several times and took it from her. He held it close to his face and examined it. "Thanks. Good work." He nearly dropped it as he coiled and grit his teeth.

She held her breath and leaned in. He relaxed again.

"Let's get your mind off the foot. Tell me about your life before Grand Peak. Why don't you ever talk about your parents?" Her back ached and her elbow stiffened. John needed a friend. She could stand the growing discomfort as long as it didn't show.

"You don't want to hear about it. You should go home and rest." His arm tightened again.

She pulled a chair close and sat on the edge. "No, really. I want to hear it. Talking is a good way to pass the time. I used to sit and chat with soldiers at Pearl before—"

He huffed and closed his eyes. "Okay. Here goes."

She leaned on the side of the bed without disturbing his posture. She would stay no matter how long the story and soothe his shaking and wincing.

"Even before the war my father was falsely accused of espionage.

We had never been very close, but I knew him well enough to know he would never have done what the FBI said he did. My mother feared they would take him away like so many of the other men in the neighborhood. Some of them were sent to prison and their families haven't seen them since."

She broke in. "Yes, I knew some of my classmates' fathers went to prison just like Papa."

John smirked. "Instead of sending my father to prison, this fine government of ours decided to deport all of us back to Japan. I've never been there. I was born in America. I'm an American. President Roosevelt didn't care. We had to go, so we packed what would fit in two suitcases and headed for the train station."

Hana thought about the day they sent Papa off with one suitcase. Tears welled up to remember it and to know that John had experienced the same thing. She knew now the reason he didn't stick around the day Papa left.

"My father didn't speak the entire trip to the station, and Mother kept dabbing her eyes with her handkerchief—glancing at me in the back seat. When we got out of the car, my father's best friend and co-worker waved to us from just a few spots down in the parking lot."

Another slight wince. He moved his hands under the sheets.

"Are you cold?" The room had warmed with the sun. Was he feverish? She touched his brow.

He blinked hard. "No, I'm fine."

"Okay, keep going with your story."

"When we got to the station, I picked up the small canvas bag stuffed with my meager belongings and then picked up one of the other suitcases. I remember Father touched my hand and pushed the case back down to the ground. I'll never forget the look on his face at that moment." John lifted one hand and pulled his pillow tight behind his neck. He stared at the ceiling and continued almost in monotone. "Red circled his dark brown eyes. His chin quivered for a second, then he cleared his throat. I could tell something was coming."

Hana shifted in her chair. She had to hang on until he finished reliving the moments, but she could feel herself losing the battle with fatigue. If she concentrated hard enough she could make it a while longer.

"Father told me I couldn't go with them. They had arranged for me to live with friends, and I would keep my job at the packing plant. My heart jumped from my chest to my throat and back again. It was a crazy plan. How could they decide for me? Sure, I didn't want to go to Japan, but separation from my parents was not the solution I had in mind." He turned to look at her. "They needed me—or so I thought."

Anger pushed adrenalin through her veins and her strength suddenly returned when she pictured John at the station—a young man, boy really, abandoned by his parents. How terrible to grow up wondering why.

"I can't believe they would leave without you. I'm so sorry." She gripped the sides of the chair.

"I pleaded with Father. He just grabbed my arm and shook my hand. He said good-bye and they would return as soon as they could. Mother threw her arms around me, telling me this was best for me. She reminded me to carry my asthma medicine at all times. She hung her head and sobbed as she walked away. That's my last recollection of her."

Hana's heart wrenched at the thought of being in John's place. "I can see now how you must have been looking for a people to belong to, like the group. I guess I might have done the same."

"How could my own father do such a thing to his son? What had I done to deserve abandonment? Each night I cursed my father and the government that ruined my life. I never saw them again. Never even a letter. I can't forgive them." He paused.

Silence built a bridge between them.

"Sorry, I've never rambled on like this before, but you asked…didn't you? Funny, it was your father who helped me regain my pride in being an American. Like I told Martin, Mr. Kato is a great man."

"John, your parents probably didn't know where to find you once you were interned. If they were deported they couldn't…"

He closed his eyes. It looked for a moment that he would drift off to sleep. She wished she could do the same. After several moments his chest rose and fell in sleep-filled breaths. He had to be relieved to talk about the events of that terrible day.

"Hana." Someone whispered from the doorway. Chiko waved her over.

Hana took the origami from John's side and set it on the table next to him. She hesitated, taking one step back and then forward again. He shouldn't be alone now, as he had these last years, with no one to care. Yet, she did, and never really told him.

"I've come to walk you home. Doctor Bennett said so. You need to leave before he comes back and sees you're still here." Chiko reached to help pull off Hana's protective gown. Hana jumped away.

"Don't touch me. I'll do it. Don't want to contaminate you too."

Chiko leaned in and stared at John. "Is he okay? He looks worse than yesterday." Her face crinkled with worry lines.

"He's okay for now. You need to pray he gets better soon." She threw the gown in the hamper and tossed the gloves in a special waste can. "Let's go."

"Won't you pray too?" Chiko's eyes questioned Hana so profoundly, she had to fight tears welling up. Her answer would be a resounding *maybe*. She wanted to be a better example for her little sister, but complacency was the best she could do. God remained silent. Until He could present her with some solid answers, her prayers would only be words.

"Let me hang onto your arm and we can go. That is if we can get past Alice."

"I like her."

"Yes, I know."

He tossed and turned all night, wishing he hadn't told her. She must have thought he complained and whined. Still the mist of compassion and caring glistened in her eyes as he finished the story. He worried about her. Even olive skin can be pale, and though she tried to cover it in front of him, she was still feeling sick. He'd never met such a brave determined woman.

Someday he would tell her another story, the one about how much he cared for her and her family, and that he planned to stay out of trouble from now on. She didn't need any more burdens right now. And then there was Doctor Bennett. A pang shot through his stomach like electricity. Jealousy? Or just more effects of the medicine? It didn't matter.

The air in the room thickened with an unusual heat and the smell of disinfectant. It nauseated him. If not for the small electric fan's attempt to circulate a slight breeze, he would have fainted.

Suddenly Martin was by his bedside. "You up to a visitor?"

He always wore the same thing, rolled up jeans and white tee shirt, but today he sported khaki slacks and a button up shirt. Surely Nurse Potter hadn't let him in. They would both be in trouble if she happened by.

John rubbed his eyes. "Sure. My door has been revolving all morning. Just don't stick me with any needles."

"Sorry. I needed to see you about something." He shuffled back to the door and peeked down the hall before shutting it. His eyes darted around the room and then settled on the I.V. bottle. "Are you in bad shape?"

John shrugged. He would try to be strong, but he felt hot and weak. "That's what the doctor says, but you know those doctors. Just want to keep me here, even though I'm not contagious anymore. I think Nurse Potter has a crush on me." His head throbbed as he chuckled.

Martin leaned on the rail of the bed. "I don't have much time. Someone's bound to come in and check on you. The sign outside your door says no visitors. Too bad you got sick. What's really too bad is that Hana caught this—"

John held his hand up, disappointed that Martin wasn't here just for a friendly visit. "Look, is this lecture going somewhere? Cause I would like to get some shut-eye." He clenched his fists instead of wincing. Martin didn't need to know about his pain.

"Okay, here it is. I overheard George Saito talking to some of the guys in the recreation hall. They are planning a demonstration in the mess hall tomorrow night during dinner. I'm leaving at noon tomorrow, so I can't do much about it."

The news couldn't be any worse. If only he had his strength back. He frowned at Martin. "Where are you going?"

"Boot camp. The fast track version. They don't have time to give us the full—"

"So tell me what you heard."

"Well, George was just telling them that since you were laid up he was in charge, and that it was time to make a statement." His eyes shifted to the door and back. "I was on my way to meet Mama and couldn't stop to talk them out of it. I know there isn't anything you can do from here, but isn't there someone who can stop this?"

The room spun when he shook his head. Who else would stand up to the young bullies trying to be big men? He should have stopped George when he had the chance.

Martin tipped his head. "What about your friend Michael?"

"They've already threatened him. That's how I landed in here." The room continued its wild ride. He closed his eyes tight. "Don't worry about it, Martin. I'll take care of it somehow."

He reached over and held out his hand. "Best of luck and take care of yourself. You better go before—"

Doctor Bennett's voice boomed from beyond the bed. "Before he gets booted out of here? And don't shake his hand, Martin. I don't think he's contagious now, but we want to be sure."

John hadn't noticed him slip in the room. His face was red and fire shone in his eyes. Martin bolted up. The realization that he could have exposed Martin to the same germ made his head buzz. His tongue felt thick and hot.

"Better leave." Doctor Bennett held the door open for Martin.

Martin pointed his fingers to his forehead in a mock salute. "See you, John."

"Yeah. Bye."

A thick silence covered the room. Doctor Bennett moved to the counter and grabbed a gown and gloves from the drawer. He took his time pulling on the gloves, punching his thumb between each finger to push down the rubber. John breathed the stale air deep into his lungs, then let it out in a slow blow. Appearing calm and well was the only way the great doctor would let him out of here.

Doctor Bennett turned. "I'm sorry to be so abrupt, John. Our testing supplies are low and I want to conserve. I'll test you tomorrow to make absolutely sure you can't pass this thing along anymore."

"It's okay. I should have known better than to let Martin stay. I was just under the impression I was safe to be around."

John followed Doctor Bennett's eyes as he checked the I.V. bottle. He was an attractive man for a Caucasian. He could see why Hana might like him. A kind of man she would do well with, except that he wasn't Japanese American. He helped create part of the problem of internment, a captor in John's eyes.

"I heard you talking. What is it you think you will take care of for Martin? I hope you understand you won't be leaving the hospital for several days. You had a close call."

Several days. That wasn't good enough. George's little group would be out causing trouble tomorrow night and he had to be there before anything happened. It would be his way of showing Hana he could stop the violence of the past.

Doctor Bennett thumped the mattress. "Did you hear me?"

"Yes, Doc." Would it do any good to tell him? He might use it to his advantage with Hana, making her doubt what little trust had reemerged in her. But George had to be stopped.

He cleared his throat. "I need to get out of here tomorrow afternoon. You have to make that happen. All I can say is that it's very important." His head buzzed like a plane engine and his mouth felt stuffed with cotton.

Doctor Bennett pulled up a chair and sat next to his head. "There is no chance I will do that. Tell me what is so important and maybe

I can help. Does it have to do with the Kato family?"

"No."

"What then? I'll do my best to help if you tell me what it is."

"Never mind."

"What's going to happen tomorrow night, John? I heard that much." Doctor Bennett leaned in close to the edge of the bed and then pulled away.

Martin closed his eyes, hoping he would give up his inquisition. "Don't get too close, Doc. You don't have a mask. And I can't tell you."

Doctor Bennett stood and edged toward the counter. "Then I'll ask Martin." His gown hit the waste basket when he tossed it. He took off his gloves and dropped them on top.

John's muscles ached, but he pulled himself up enough to look him in the eyes. With the heat about to suffocate him, he struggled to hold a steady tone. "I can handle it. Don't meddle where you don't belong."

Doctor Bennett's face reddened. "I thought you said this had nothing to do with the Kato family."

"I'm not saying any more. Please stay out of it."

The room swirled faster with each breath. He had to close his eyes to make it stop. His eyelids felt as though they were filled with lead. He couldn't keep them open one more second. If he could get a good night's sleep he would leave on his own steam tomorrow.

He heard Doctor Bennett pick up the clipboard, then Nurse Potter's voice in a whisper.

"Is he sleeping? Do you need me for anything?" He could feel her touch on his arm as she spoke.

John willed his eyes to stay shut, wanting them to go away. But their chatter continued as if he weren't there.

He heard Doctor Bennett sigh. "No, he's not sleeping. Please increase the morphine in the drip."

She whispered back to him. "I brought it with me. You already have orders on the chart, Doctor."

"Right."

John opened one eye a sliver. Doctor Bennett handed Nurse Potter the chart and stuffed his hands in his white coat pockets, perspiration dripping from his forehead. "And make sure that fan is close enough to cool him."

"I'll bring in some cold wet towels later on. Chiko is helping me tear up sheets to make more compresses."

John turned his slightly opened eye to peek at her. She smiled as she talked about Chiko.

Doctor Bennett raised his voice, he must have known John was faking sleep. "We'll talk in the morning, John. Get some rest."

He refused to respond. Rest. Some sleep and then make an escape plan. Such bad luck that the doctor overheard, and more so that he was about to get medicated.

Nurse Potter pulled his chin toward her. "Before you drift off, put this under your tongue." The taste of alcohol certainly didn't quench his growing thirst. What he really wanted was a nice tall glass of cool lemonade…

The room swayed, the bitter taste of the thermometer gagged him. His eyelids stuck shut, heavy and dry. The concoction must have made its way through the tubing to his body. Relief from pain was a good thing, but he couldn't let them drug him tomorrow.

I'm coming George Saito. I'll stop you if it's the last thing I do.

Chapter 7

The train bound for Billings would come any minute and take away another member of the Kato family. Martin and Chiko huddled together while Hana nuzzled close to Mama, whispering words of comfort which she desperately wanted to believe for herself.

"He'll be all right. He's a strong boy and, like you always say, God will take care of him."

Mama only nodded, her eyes lowered, no doubt remembering the day they sent Papa off. Sending a son off to war could finish most mothers. This could be the very thing that would tackle Mama's faith to the ground.

Hana shook her head at the angst in Mama's eyes, canvasing the yard. "Don't worry so much. We have permission to be at the train station." She pointed at other internees standing with their sons, waiting to bid farewell. "We have a right to be here." Her mother had grown too accustomed to the limitations of imprisonment. For many Issei, living in camp now felt more comfortable than freedom. She took Mama's hand. "It's all right. *We'll* be all right, won't we?"

Mama returned her smile. "Sure, I know. God take care of us."

Hana let go of her hand. "I've been trying to do that too, Mama-san. I'll be glad when God takes over completely."

Mama frowned.

Chiko flung her arms around her brother. "Your train is coming."

He rubbed the top of her head. "You behave, young lady. Have a fun summer now that school is out."

Mama straightened her posture, and when Martin came to her she shook her finger at him, the loving gesture her family had come to expect. "You be careful. You write letters, okay?"

Martin gently took her in his arms. "Yes, Mama-san. I will miss you. And I will write."

Hana had never seen Mama linger in an embrace before. She imagined the pain racing through her heart to relinquish her son to a war that might bring him face to face with an enemy that looked just like him. Papa and Mama had often talked about how strange it would be for young Japanese American men to fight against distant relatives.

When she finally got her turn, Hana hugged him tight and straightened his collar. "We will write too." The thought of never seeing him again melted her recent aggravation about him. He was braver than she ever knew. For any eighteen-year-old to have to give up his youth for war was unfair, yet so many did it willingly. Nothing else mattered now, except that Martin know he was loved. It's what she would want to know if she were facing danger or death.

She grasped his hands in hers. "Papa will be so sorry he missed seeing you off. Please take care of yourself and don't worry about us. I love you, brother."

"I know. I love you too. I'm sorry to worry you. I hope someday you understand why I had to do this. I'm not like Papa."

She wanted to tell him he was wrong. He had Papa's courage and self-respect. She couldn't stop the tears now. "It's all right. You are your own man. You've done what you felt was right. Mama always knew. I just now realized how proud I am of you." Her heart ached to see him go, and she knew she would learn to pray again just for him.

He reached into his satchel and rummaged around. She was about to ask him what he forgot when he handed her an envelope. "This is for you. A sort of truce, and for good luck." She slid it from his hand and pulled it close.

He turned and waved before walking away. His steps at first slow and uncertain, then he straightened his shoulders and picked up his pace. Mama continued to wave until he was on the train, and then stood very still. She spoke loud and clear. "God be with Martin."

Chiko chimed in. "Amen." Hana felt the sibling thread that always held them together snap. She shivered, even though it was at least ninety degrees outside.

Martin boarded and disappeared into the train that would escort him into manhood. In a moment he jerked open a stubborn window. Smiling his biggest smile, he waved wildly through a sea of other waving arms down the row of train car windows. "Good-bye! Tell Papa I'll be a good soldier."

Hana's heart rippled. He might not return to them. Many sons and brothers had already died; their names written on the role of honor in the library. The war had to end soon, or America would run out of sons.

After watching the train slip out of sight, they boarded a bus already half filled with families who had just said good-bye to loved ones. Resignation formed on their faces. They were all ready to go back to camp as if life hadn't just changed dramatically, but camp wasn't a refuge for Hana. It was still a prison she wanted desperately to leave. Until she could, writing letters to get Papa home would be her pastime. The last report for the prison doctor had not been encouraging. His condition remained the same. She knew what that meant. He was probably weaker and thinner than ever.

Papa. With no man in the house to lean on, they needed him back now more than ever. *She* needed him back.

"Hana, did you hear me?"

At the sound of Mama's voice, she jerked her head from the dusty bus window. "What?"

"I ask did you see how handsome Martin look." Mama opened and re-folded her paperwork, still clutching it to her. The corners of her mouth drooped, but she sat up straight and held her head high.

"Yes, he sure did look handsome." The image of his broad shoulders and new hair cut lingered in her mind too. She opened the envelope with care, revealing a colorful origami crane. Her heart flipped as a tear rolled down her cheek and dropped onto her blouse. He had remembered how to craft the animals Papa had taught them to make. A treasure she would hold dear.

Chiko stared into a magazine, obviously recovered from her grief. "Mama? Do you think it would be all right for me to wear a little makeup?" Mama looked up from studying the papers and scowled.

"No."

Chiko opened her mouth, then shut it tight after a sharp glare from Hana. This was no time to pester Mama about anything so trivial. Although everything seemed trivial after seeing Martin off.

The bus bumped along and passed through the main gates of camp. Dirt and gravel spit up from the tires of another bus in front of them, swirling silt past the window. The brakes screeched to a stop in front of the administration building. Hana took Mama's arm and walked through the aisle and down the steps onto the hard dry ground. Chiko stomped off the bus and hurried to the check in line where a man in uniform examined paperwork and counted heads.

"Keep moving, please." One short, stout guard waved them on. Hana noted his flat expression—the same emotionless affect on all the guards around here. She wondered how they could blind their eyes to the suffering of others, like Doctor Davidson had done, his pain and bitterness his excuse to treat the nurses as though they were the enemy.

With all of them checked in, Chiko walked ahead of them, magazine tucked under her arm. Hana knew she wanted to be accepted and feel like she looked as pretty as any other teen girl. Her resolve to keep Chiko a child was waning. After all, she was becoming a young woman despite Hana's possessiveness.

Perhaps she would talk to Mama about a compromise. It might make Chiko feel better about being Japanese instead of wishing she weren't. Mama had let Martin make choices for himself and it had turned out all right. *He* had turned out all right.

The image of Mama's face as she embraced Martin etched in Hana's mind. It was the same look she had when Papa boarded his train. But this was a son, barely a man. Now Mama would go back to the barrack and tenderly pack away Martin's civilian clothes, praying for her son to return. There would be no stopping this woman's faith. For Mama, the more hardships, the harder she prayed. Hana envied her conviction.

"I get laundry from you and Chiko, then go to the latrine to do wash," Mama said as they entered their tiny abode. Chiko pulled a sack from under her bed and shoved it along the floor toward Mama. They all hated doing laundry—hauling clothes to the latrine basin only to find a line of other women waiting. At least they didn't have Mrs. Saito's fine delicates to wash anymore.

"Chiko, help Mama-san take the laundry to the latrine, then come back here and help me straighten up Martin's things. He left his cot in a mess."

"There isn't much. Can you carry it, Mama-san?" Chiko barely looked up from her magazine as she sat cross-legged on her bed.

"Chiko!" Hana propped her hands on her hips. "Do as I say and help her."

Chiko threw the magazine down and huffed. Mama stuffed her clothes in another sack, along with Hana's and crooked her finger to motion Chiko over. "You take big sack. I take your little one." She smiled and opened the door, letting her daughter trudge through ahead of her.

Mama looked at Hana and shrugged. "She good girl. Just upset."

The door shut and Hana sat on Martin's bed, filing through magazines, papers, and scattered socks. Her emotional wall caved in as she breathed in his scent on the tee shirt she picked up off the floor. She wept until her knotted stomach released its clenching, then pulled out the origami crane he gave her and perched it on the window above his bed. Without Martin and Papa the room took on an emptiness she never felt before—at least not since just after the bombing.

She shook her head hard and grabbed one of his hankies from the stash under his cot. She just finished blowing her nose when Chiko bounded through the door and flopped onto her cot to continue perusing the magazine. Swallowing hard, she pretended to be busy de-cluttering the area around his bed, determined to get it done before Mama had to do it. She stole a glance at Chiko, who seemed engrossed in the pages.

Hana covered her shaky voice by clearing her throat. "Thanks for helping Mama. We need to be sure to support her as much as possible."

"Sure. I'll try harder, but I'll be busy in the fields starting tomorrow." Chiko flipped through another page. "Hana?"

"Hmm?"

"Don't you ever wish you could look different? I mean, less Japanese?"

"Less Japanese? Of course not. There's nothing wrong with the way we look." She stood up straight. "I think we are two very cute girls." She giggled and watched her sister's reaction. Her heart jumped a little when Chiko pursed her lips.

"I wish I was white."

The mumbled words struck like a fist in Hana's chest. She had suspected it. Hearing her speak it out loud pulled her breath away. At least Mama wasn't here. Her heart would be broken. Hana's mind raced with what to say to her misguided sister. She resisted the compulsion to scold until she dodged the shock waves.

She sighed loud. "Oh, I don't think you're cut out to be Caucasian. You don't mean that, really." She resumed her chore, waiting for Chiko to recant. If she didn't, there would be a serious conflict. One more obstacle to overcome before Papa returned. She listened for Chiko to speak.

"Yes, I mean it."

Neil plodded through the dirt clods, cutting across the field between his cottage and the hospital. Staying awake half the night thinking of John's unknown problem wasn't helping his concentration this morning. His six o'clock alarm seemed to ring just as he visited deep sleep. The same old questions about right and wrong, prejudice and understanding, had rattled around in his brain for hours. At least he had come to his own conclusion about the internment of these Japanese Americans. John had spent his three plus years here pushing for freedom. An admirable undertaking, but it had been a waste of energy because of attitudes that put them here in the first place.

Clouds hung over the mountain and slinked their way down to the fields just beyond the camp. Three days of parching sunshine had drained everyone, and now the moods had dropped even more, along with the temperatures.

The short walk to the hospital might be enough to clear his fuzzy head. He stopped to look back at the whitewashed exterior and small paned windows of his quarters. He slept on a bed in a comfortable little house last night. Hana and all the other internees slept on straw-filled mattresses in a small room.

He stopped and stared down at his nice new shoes. "You're a spoiled brat, Neil Bennett. You've taken everything you had for granted." He didn't care who heard him, although the likelihood was slim that anyone but a rattlesnake had been near enough to listen.

"Doctor Bennett?"

His head jerked up from his fix on the ground. Hana stood not thirty feet away, her hair blowing in the fresh morning breeze. How long had she been there? A few more minutes of day dreaming and he would have bumped into her, which would have been a pleasant start to his morning.

"Hana…Nurse Kato. I didn't see you there." He smiled and regained his stride, emerging from the field onto Avenue C. "What brings you out so early? Surely, you're not on duty at this hour?"

Her pensive smile didn't quite disguise her wrinkled forehead. She wasn't facing the sun, so she couldn't be squinting. No, something had Miss Kato distracted.

"I just saw Chiko off on her first day of farm labor." She glanced back to the administration building where the last of the farm buses bounced through the gate. Her hand trembled as she fidgeted with the collar on her uniform. "I'm early for work, but I don't suppose Nurse Potter will mind the extra help." She tucked her hair behind her ear.

He tried not to search her face, but she wasn't herself. "I see. We've been short-handed. She'll will be grateful." He stopped when he reached her. The dark circles under her eyes made his heart sink. Obviously her sleep had been fitful as well. "Since you have a minute or two, would you join me for some tea in my office?"

She checked her watch. "I suppose so. Tea sounds good."

He mentally scanned the contents of the tea drawer in his office. He should have checked to see if he had some before he offered. She would think he had made an excuse to spend time with her, which would be true.

"Well, then let's see if someone can rustle up some hot water from the mess." He tried to match her gait as she walked. Her small steps kept up with his two to one.

The side door to his office stuck tight as he pulled on it. Harsh weather had peeled paint, warped the siding, and cracked some windows. If the war didn't end soon, the hospital would need repair. It *had* to end soon. These people needed to go home.

"Here we are. Please, sit." He moved behind the desk and held his breath before pulling out the drawer where he kept a small collection of tea. He kept a straight face through his surprise at a drawer full of little white bags. Someone else had made him look good by restocking his stash.

"Nurse Potter."

"Hmm?"

"Uh, I'll see if she'll fetch some hot water."

"Hot water?" Nurse Potter sang from the doorway. "Like this?"

Her smirk left him speechless. How had she known he would invite someone to tea and need tea bags and hot water?

"Good morning. How long have you been a mind reader?" He winked at Hana, who to his delight, smiled wide.

She also winked as she strolled by. "I have been reading your mind for months, Doctor Bennett."

He shook his head. "I'm an open book."

Steam rolled from the tip of the spout as she poured water into one cup. She held the pot in her hand and scowled at him. "That's the clean cup. You'll have to use the dirty one."

Another smile from Hana and he suddenly felt as though he had slept all night. Nurse Potter waited for him to wipe the second cup with his handkerchief. She filled it and nodded at Hana before scooting out the door, then poked her head in.

"And when you're ready, there's a new patient you may need to see. We're getting her ready for an exam now."

"What about Doctor Davidson? Can he see her?"

"He said there's no point bothering. Quote: "She's not long for this world. Let her be." She bit her lip before disappearing.

Neil cringed to think the patient might have heard him. Another reason for a chat soon. Doctor Davidson had been shirking his duty when it came to the patients, staying out of sight doing who knew what. He shrugged. "Amazing woman. What would I do without her?"

Hana shrugged back. "She's been pretty kind to me lately. When I first met her, I thought she hated me." She leaned in and whispered. "A bit grumpy."

"Nurse Potter? Grumpy?" He flashed back to the day he first arrived. The woman had scared him to death.

Hana's hands wrapped around the cup as she lost her smile and stared into the tea. It dawned on him. Chiko's first day on her own.

"You're worried about your sister." He blew on the top of the hot liquid and sipped in the sweet taste of rich black tea.

She held the cup close to her face. "Yes. She's too young to be out there where it's not safe."

"Why isn't it safe?"

She glanced up from her steaming tea. "It's hard to explain to a Caucasian."

He had never thought of her as prejudiced. "Really?"

She leaned forward. "I don't mean to offend, but I have experienced the effects of intolerance and hatred. You may not know how easily people can turn on you, even when you're vulnerable. Chiko doesn't know either. She's just a kid."

Her eyes flamed with passion as she spoke. He knew now that

something must have happened in her life to make her this fearful. If only she would tell him.

She sipped more tea. "Well, I should go examine the new patient. Would you like to come?"

"Yes, of course. Thanks for the tea." She looked around his desk, moving her empty cup back and forth.

He waved an arm around the room. "Just leave it anywhere." He took one last sip and teetered his on top of a stack of papers. She winced and lifted it up, staring at the ring of brown it left. She put his cup in hers.

"I'll take them to the mess hall." She smiled that condescending smile Nurse Potter used when she wanted to straighten him out. He nodded in agreement.

The hallway was still. One or two wings of the hospital had been closed off for lack of use. Hana strolled ahead in the direction of the mess, her hair bouncing on her shoulders.

Neil looked away when he heard Nurse Potter talking in a room two doors down. He entered the cool dim exam room. She stood on a chair, yanking on the curtain to close it. The bed held the small frame of an elderly woman covered in a white fluffy blanket—one of Nurse Potter's special covers she saved for special patients. In the corner, tucked into the back of a wooden chair sat a little girl with large dark eyes, her slender legs crossed in front of her. She too was draped in one of the blankets.

He approached the bed, ignoring the urge to greet the little girl first. The old woman's eyes followed him as he leaned in to listen to her heart. Her bluish lips quivered. He winked at her and she winked back.

He leaned in to whisper to her. "What can we do to make you more comfortable?"

"She doesn't speak English, Doctor. The little girl does, but she doesn't know what's wrong with her Grandmother. She only knows a little Japanese." Nurse Potter shook her head. "How on earth do you suppose they communicate? Poor thing." She gazed at the girl, who twirled a strand of her long and snarled black hair.

The old woman touched his arm and pointed to her head. He stroked her brow, feeling the fever heat his palm. She coughed from deep down in her chest. The barking sound alarmed him almost as much as the rattling in her lungs.

"Temp is 103. Labored, shallow breaths as you can see." Nurse Potter tucked in the blanket.

Neil turned at the sound of Hana's voice. She knelt next to the little girl, stroking her hair and telling her how pretty she was. His heart warmed to catch the interaction.

Nurse Potter jumped toward the bed. "Doctor."

The old woman convulsed, head tossing side to side, her back arched in an agonizing position.

"Obaasan!" The child screamed and lurched forward.

Hana scooped her up in her arms and disappeared into the hall, the girl clinging to her. Nurse Potter took Neil's unspoken command and ran out of the room while he held the frail arms and legs from thrashing.

Time stood still for him during most emergencies. It seemed like hours before Nurse Potter returned with the I.V. bottle and medicine. She knew what he used in cases like this. He glanced toward the partly open door. Through the door he could see Hana crouched, speaking softly to the little girl. Thank God she was there to distract the little one with words of comfort.

Nurse Potter burst through the door and went to work administering what he hoped would be life giving fluids. Both turned at the sound of crying. The little girl ran through the door opening with Hana right behind her. She caught the edge of her skirt to stop her.

"Obaasan!" The crying child ran through the door. Hana snatched her arm and pulled her out of the room.

Neil whispered. "She's calm now, but I don't like her look." The stethoscope echoed a faint beat. Slow, then slower.

"We're losing her."

"Obaasan!" The pounding of his heart was drowned out by the cries of the little girl in the hall.

He slapped the wrinkled hands of the woman and peeled back her eyelid. "Come on, grandmother!" He stepped back and grabbed the oxygen tank. Nurse Potter pulled a mask from the drawer and unwrapped it, her hands seemed to fly through the effort to bring air to their frail patient.

He massaged the old woman's extremities while Nurse Potter checked vitals. After what seemed an eternity, she tapped him on the shoulder. "She's gone. You tried, but it's over."

His face wet with sweat, he backed away from the old woman. He shuffled to the hall where Hana and the little girl sat against the wall, clutching each other. The sobs of the child swelled his heart. Hana looked up. He shook his head.

Hana's eyes pleaded. "What will become of her now? Nurse Potter says the grandmother is her only kin." She rested her head on the wall. She closed her eyes and sighed long.

He pulled off his rubber gloves. "She'll go to the orphanage at Manzanar. That's the way it is."

The ravages of internment had escaped his reasoning until this moment. Hana knew it, John knew it. He had resisted it. Internment was America's big mistake. Was he going to be part of the answer or continue to be part of the problem?

Nurse Potter wrung her hands. "I'll get the orderly to take the woman." She slogged a few steps and turned to look at Hana. "Then I'd like to take the little one home, if we can get permission. Just temporarily."

Hana shrugged. "She says her name is Charlie. She's six. Do you think they will let her go?"

"All we can do is ask." He flopped down beside Charlie and gave her his stethoscope. Perhaps a distraction would stop her cries. She took it but continued to whimper as she twirled it in her hands. It shouldn't be this tough for the little ones in camp. He thought back to the day he and John stood by the flagpole, watching the children recite the pledge of allegiance. There had to be a way to make things better, or at least stop the endless tragedies.

He thought of John, lying in the bed, wanting to be part of the solution to injustice. But he was sick, and someone else would have to help. Should he be the one?

He stood and straightened his shirt. "I'm going to make a call to see about Charlie going with Nurse Potter. Can you wait here with her?"

Hana cocked her head as if she sensed his struggle between confusion and determination. "Sure."

He hurried down the hall. As soon as Charlie was taken care of, he would see John. The young man would have to tell him what was going on if he was to jump in this mess.

Chapter 8

The nurse tidied up his bed and jotted notes on the clipboard. He pretended to be asleep. It wasn't far from the truth. Every muscle in his body ached and twitched, as if he had just run a marathon. She pulled the door closed behind her, apparently never suspecting his plan. Some plan. Get up and limp to Block 15's mess hall. The busiest mess in the compound would be where George Saito and his clan would make themselves known. Unless he could stop them.

The clock said half past four. He would have to give maximum effort in order to get there before the clan arrived. Who knows how far they intended to go with their little demonstration. At least Mr. Kato's demonstrations had been peaceful and safe, until the last one. He saw in his mind's eye the picture of the arrest of Mr. Kato and the others. He would never forget the look on Hana's face as she watched them take him away.

He had tried to take over the group, but the only men he could trust to help him had left with their families right after the first round of releases. The rest were loose cannons.

"I just can't trust you Georgie." He whispered into the air, remembering why he had to do this.

It was time to get rid of the lingering strife in camp. The government had lifted their internment and freedom for everyone was just around the corner. Trouble would only serve to jeopardize that. Men like George Saito only wanted to be seen as big shots. Mr.

Kato never advocated bullying, only peaceful demonstrations.

"Time to go."

He lifted his arm, now free from the I.V. after two days. The blanket and sheet seemed to weigh ten pounds as he threw them off his body. *Easy. Take it slow.* One leg over the edge wasn't too difficult, but stepping down on his injured foot would be the challenge. He eyed the banged up metal locker used as a closet. With his blurred vision, it seemed so far away. Inside hung his jeans, shirt and shoes, just waiting for him to slip them on.

"Shoes on? If I can get over there." He groaned, keeping an eye on the door.

He eased the bandaged foot down onto the shellacked wood floor. Pain shot up his calf and he bit his tongue to keep from cursing. Keeping the door in his peripheral vision, he slid along toward the locker. Each time he stepped, the pain became more unbearable, taking his breath at times. He could make it, if he concentrated.

"You can do it, Yamada."

At last his hand touched the cold metal handle on the locker. He pulled it open, breathing deep to stay steady. The room had warmed like a sauna since he got out of bed, warm enough to cause salty perspiration on his upper lip. He pushed beyond the wooziness to reach for his clothes, his hands shaking like an old man. He would have to sit down to get his pants on. Beside the bed he rested in a whitewashed wicker chair and tugged one leg of jeans over his foot and up his leg. Would he be able to stand something touching his sore spot?

"One more leg." He stopped to catch his breath and stole a glance at the window in the door. "Stay away everyone."

The next foot found its way to the end of the trouser leg. He panted as he pushed himself up off the chair and buttoned the jeans with numbing fingers. The shirt slid over his arms smoothly. At the bottom of the locker lay his shoes. Thank goodness for loafers—no shoestrings to tie. Forget the socks—they would be tight enough on his foot.

Something caught his eye. Two figures passed by the window. He paused and then crafted each step, engineering his way toward the door. Leaning on the door knob, he made an opening in the doorway large enough to poke his swimming head out. All clear. And the side door at the end of the hall was also cracked. He could feel the breeze it created, inviting him to pass through. This would be his escape hatch.

The throbbing in his foot threatened to take him down. He would have to clench his teeth all the way to the mess hall. So far the gauze remained white. No blood soaking through. After one more look right and then left, he pushed himself, hobbling down the hall mostly on his good foot. Sparks flashed through his eyesight. *Don't faint.*

"Go, Yamada, go." One last lunge and he landed outside on the stoop. He gazed into the distance, judging at least a hundred yards between him and the mess hall. Could he walk the length of a football field? Could he do it without being seen or passing out?

"It doesn't matter, man. You have to do this."

He eased himself down the three wood steps onto the hard ground. The sun warmed his face. He reached up to close the door tight, but heard voices down the hallway. It wasn't worth risking someone seeing him. Sharp daggers stabbing his foot persisted through the walk across the dry field. Each step landed at least one foot on a rock. He kept his eyes roaming. No one must spot him limping his way to the edge of the first barrack row. Sweat dripped off his temples and forehead. He pressed on with no time to stop and think of his foot. A soggy sensation in his shoe signaled blood seeping through the bandage. He didn't dare look. Instead he filled his mind with the image of George standing outside his barrack, spouting threats.

"Georgie, you're a pain. I'll stop you with one foot tied behind my back." He had to keep talking, keep pushing through the torture. Someone could be watching him, but he couldn't stop to look around.

He stood in the shade between the Block 15 mess hall and another barrack. Only a few internees straggled in. He would wait for

George and jump him.

Unless he was already in there.

Nurse Potter hovered over Neil as he hung up the waiting room desk phone. Her mouth twitched when he smiled at her, like she was waiting to win a prize. He stifled a chuckle at her nervous scowl. Tempted to play a game with her, he decided not to toy with her high emotions.

He leaned on the counter and locked into her gaze. "You can take her for one day."

Tears brimmed in her eyes. He had never seen this before. The strong stern exterior of Nurse Potter cracked all because of an orphaned little girl.

Hana patted her on the arm. "Don't worry about anything tomorrow. I will handle the few patients we have with the other nurses. Doctor Bennett and Doctor Davidson will be here too. You just take care of Charlie."

They all watched the little girl who sat on the waiting room bench. Her sweet face void of happiness, she stared straight ahead. Neil's heart ached, knowing she must feel lost and alone without her Grandmother. His own dear Grandmother had passed away when he was about Charlie's age. He had parents to care for him then. Charlie had no one—except this nurse named Alice Potter. This could be a match made in heaven.

She sniffled—a new sparkle in her eyes. "I'll bring her back day after tomorrow and see if there's any news about where she will go."

Charlie gingerly took the woman's hand, tears rolling down her little cheeks. Nurse Potter glanced over her shoulder and hesitated. She raised her brows and Neil knew she only needed a nod. He gave it.

"Tell everyone good-bye." Her voice softer than he had ever heard, he suspected life would never be the same for his head nurse.

The child managed a short wave. "Good-bye."

Hana waved back. "See you soon, Charlie."

The door closed and Hana stood staring at it. She wiped her nose with a hankie.

"They'll be fine. I should hear something tomorrow. The woman I spoke to said Manzanar might not be an option now. I'll let you know what I find out."

Hana headed for the door. "Thanks, I'll make final rounds. Then I have to meet Chiko at her friend's mess hall. Have to hear all about her day in the fields." She rolled her eyes. "See you tomorrow."

Doctor Davidson waltzed toward Neil and tipped his head in the direction where Nurse Potter was headed. "Where is she going with that child?"

"Home. She's taking little Charlie home."

"She should be turned over to the authorities and handled through the system. It's not her place." Davidson crossed his arms.

Neil glared at the doctor. "She's being handled by the best system there is. Compassion and caring. Nurse Potter is what she needs, not the authorities. Can you understand that?"

Doctor Davidson let his arms fall to his side. Red-faced, he stormed away.

Neil checked his watch. Already past four thirty. He had to go see John now if he was going to make it to the right place at the right time. That is if John would come clean with what he knew. As he turned to get out from behind the desk, something grabbed his attention out the side window. He rubbed dust off the inside of the pane to peek through. His stomach jerked.

"John? What in the world?"

He pushed himself around the corner of the front desk and ran to John's room. Empty, but the door at the end of the hall was wide open. He scurried to the opening. The hobbling form of a person could only be the young man he knew should be bedridden. He watched him slink toward Block 15. He pulled off his jacket, throwing it over the railing. By the time he stumbled through powdery dry dirt, dodging sage brush and rocks, he lost sight of his prey.

This couldn't be happening. "You were headed in this direction. Where are you, John?"

He followed the smell of chicken broth and the sounds of silverware clanging a strange song. The mess hall was only twenty yards away. He had to see if John was there. He took one step, but before he could take another, John appeared from the between buildings.

"Hey!" Neil hollered and waved his hand.

John backed his way into the shadows again. Several couples with children neared the building. What was John waiting for? What was going to happen? After two more excruciating minutes, John didn't reappear. Getting closer was his only option.

"Hello, Doctor Bennett!" A woman called from somewhere on his right. He searched her face. A patient from last week. He smiled and nodded. When he looked back to the mess hall, John was on the stoop holding the door for an elderly man. Then he disappeared through the door.

Don't be conspicuous. As if a Caucasian man in the midst of a building full of Japanese Americans wouldn't be noticed. He would take the chance to get an opportunity to engage John.

"Get out of my way." Just inside the door John and another young man wearing jeans and a black tee shirt stood locking arms. He couldn't tell if they were friendly, until he studied the other boy's face—young, but cold and angry. The clenched jaw and wild eyes struck fear in Neil. He was caught in an unfamiliar world.

John stood firm, despite an occasional wobble. "I'm not going to let you do this, George." Some internees standing in the chow line turned to stare.

George's tone intensified, his voice growling. "The others are just outside the back door waiting for my signal. They'll take care of you so we can get on with it."

John leaned into him. "Why don't you take care of me yourself, Georgie?"

The urge to flee grabbed him. He sucked up a breath and walked four steps to stand next to John. "Hello, John." He nodded to

George. "Uh, George is it? Why don't you go outside with this discussion?"

George smirked. "Stay out of this. Who are you anyway? This doesn't concern you." With the hand that wasn't locked with John's, he gave Neil a slight push.

John jerked his arm free from George's grip and turned to Neil. "You should leave. I'll handle this."

Neil could feel his heartbeat thumping in his neck. He glanced back at George. The kid had guts, but getting shoved made his blood boil. "Doesn't look like you're handling it very well. There are better ways to make your point. Whatever that is."

George's face flushed bright red. His lips pressed into a thin line. No one moved a muscle, except for John, whose eyes widened as he looked past George. Neil turned. Hana, Chiko, and another young girl stood just inside the door. Hana's stared in their direction, as if analyzing the situation.

"John, you don't want to start something right here, do you? George, please call this thing off." Neil spoke in a low voice. It was no use. Hana must have heard at least part of his pleading. She waved Chiko away and marched over.

"What's going on here? John, you're supposed to be in the hospital." She frowned as her eyes darted back and forth between the three of them. "Doctor Bennett, what are you doing here?"

George straightened up. "*Doctor* Bennett?" He snickered and stuffed his hands in his back jeans pockets. "Well now. That's interesting." He leaned into John's face. "Your personal physician? Are you scared sick?" He threw back his head and laughed loud, drawing more stares from the growing crowd in the room.

Hana seethed. "Stop it, George. Just because you're from a wealthy family doesn't mean you should act like a brat."

George's face fell dark again. He grabbed Hana's wrist. "Shut up and go away."

The bitter taste of hate and rage simmered inside Neil. He reached for George the same time John did. George released his grip on Hana, throwing her off balance. The seconds ticked off in Neil's head, watching Hana fall back against the wall in slow motion. John grabbed George in a head lock, his sweat spattering off his arm. He knew John was too weak to hold him long.

Chiko ran from across the room and pulled on John's arm. "Stop it! You'll get hurt!"

John and George struggled, one to hold on, the other to break free. John faltered for a split second and George flailed his arms to break loose. Chiko stood in his way. His arm struck her in the chest and she catapulted sideways toward a table filled with mortified onlookers. Neil could only watch it happen as he jumped, but couldn't reach her.

"Chiko!" Hana wailed and pushed herself away from the wall.

George and John stumbled as Neil shoved them aside. "Get back!" He met Hana at Chiko's side where she lay face down on the floor.

Hana turned Chiko over and gasped at the blood covering her face. Neil gently pulled her hands from Chiko's shoulders and straightened the limp girl to lie flat on the floor. Blood gushed from a gash on her face.

"We need to keep her head up." He rested Chiko's head on Hana's lap. "Someone get me a clean cloth from the kitchen!" He shouted out into the crowd.

A young woman darted to the kitchen and emerged with a folded white linen cloth. "These just came from laundry."

Hana stroked Chiko's arm as Neil pressed the cloth to the gash.

"Press this to her wound." He took her hand and placed it on the compress. She looked up at him and nodded. Her demeanor turned from stricken sister to nurse right before his eyes. This was the Hana he knew.

John leaned on the table near Chiko. "What can I do?"

Neil didn't have to examine his face to know John must be near collapse. He could see a blood soaked the gauze peeking above his loafer not far from Chico's head.

"You can get your bloody foot away from Chiko." He didn't have time to be polite. John stood and backed away. "George. I need your help to get Chiko to the hospital." Neil waved him over.

George stood frozen, shaking his head. The angry young man of five minutes ago had transformed into a sniveling child.

John took a step forward and then glanced down at his foot. "I'll do it."

"You'd never make it with that foot. Is there someone who can help me?" Neil's tone had intensified. Chiko still lay silent—they had to move now.

A familiar face emerged and knelt by Hana. "I'll help."

John flopped onto the nearest bench. "Michael, thank God."

Neil bobbed his head and positioned himself to lift Chiko. "Evenly distribute your arms to support her. Hana you stay by her head and keep pressing on the wound."

Michael moved to Chiko's right side, and Hana switched hands to stay at her head. The scenario unfolding sent shivers up Neil's spine. Carrying an unconscious bleeding young girl all the way to the hospital spelled disaster in his mind. He had no choice.

He watched Chiko's face, her breathing shallow and rapid. He tensed his arm muscles ready to do what must be done.

"Everyone out of the way—keep the door open." John shouted orders as he limped to the doorway. He winced with every step.

"Michael, we have a ways to go, we need to keep her as still as we can, but we have to run. Can you do it?"

Michael nodded and looking into his calm face, Neil's heavy chest relaxed.

"Hana, don't worry about holding the compress if you think it's hindering us from moving. Just try to keep up."

Her voice fluttered. "I'll keep up. Just go."

"Ready? Together, go."

The first few steps jolted poor Chiko, then he quickly found a rhythm with Michael's stride. Down the steps and onto the dirt path, soon the hospital was in view. Chiko whimpered and coughed. Her coloring faded into a gray hue.

Hana's voice cracked as she plodded each step. "Hang on, Chiko. You'll be okay. I'm here with you."

Pain shot up Neil's back each time he took a twisted stride. "Hana." His voice shook from the jiggling. "Go ahead of us. Prepare a room and find Doctor Davidson." He struggled to breathe and talk. Michael's expression hadn't changed from the calm affect he had from the start.

She hesitated, then left the compress on Chiko's head and ran. She took the front steps two at a time, nearly stumbling before racing through the doors. He knew adrenalin would keep her going—for a while.

"Take it slow up the steps, Michael." Their eyes met for a second. No worry in this man's face.

In total agreement, they synced each move. It was if Michael knew how to anticipate each need. If only he felt so calm and sure of himself. Now his emotions played against his confidence. He should never have come to the mess hall. Maybe John could have handled George without him. Then Chiko wouldn't be in this shape; manhandled, bleeding, and bounced down the hospital corridor.

Hana stood at the exam room door. Her blood stained shirt peeked out from beneath a fresh white apron. Any terror she might be feeling wasn't reflected on her face. He'd never seen her so strong.

"Doctor Davidson isn't here. I don't know where he is," Hana blurted out.

Neil's heart sank. He would need help with the gash on Chiko's face if she was to come through without disfigurement. He could sew it up, but was not skillful enough to deal with facial scaring.

"Help us get the wound clean. I'll worry about Doctor Davidson. Everyone in the room glove up."

Michael pulled his hands out from under Chiko just as her eyelids fluttered open. She stared at the ceiling and screamed over and over. Neil had hoped she would sleep just a little longer. The shock set in too soon.

Hana threw herself on Chiko, holding down her arms.

"Chiko, Chiko. Shh. Be still, sweetie. Be still." She chanted in Chiko's ear until the screaming stopped.

Where was Doctor Davidson? He was the best they had with

head wounds. Anything Neil could do wouldn't be good enough. Sweat trickled down his temples.

He had to try. Chiko deserved his best, and Hana counted on him. He closed his eyes. The noise of the room muted.

God help me.

The screams tore at Hana's heart. She had seen this reaction many times at Pearl. Navy soldiers with head wounds often broke out of semi-consciousness wailing and screaming in confusion, unaware of their surroundings. But this was her little Chiko. She promised Papa she would watch over her. She had failed, and had to do whatever it took to get her well—right now.

Hana heard Doctor Bennett's voice. "We're taking her to x-ray now. Why don't you stay here and collect yourself before you collapse too?" She couldn't respond. Every limb shook with fatigue as she fell into the chair.

Someone placed their hand on her shoulder. "Are you all right?"

John moved to kneel in front of her. She gazed into his intense stare. He really did care. So why was he there making trouble at the mess? Chiko might not be hurt if he had just stayed in his hospital bed. She saw him wince and glanced at his leg, then back at his face.

"What happened, John? Why did you leave the hospital and fight with George? I don't understand." She trembled so hard she had to grab the edges of her chair.

He let out a long breath. "I came to keep George from causing a scene. He was going to try to get the resistance ramped up again. I thought I could stop him. I...I'm so sorry. I would never want Chiko hurt. You know that."

She knew it, and yet it didn't ease the burning in her chest, or the terror of what might happen to Chiko now. She couldn't look at him anymore. She scanned the room wondering what to do next. The only person there was a stranger standing in the dark corner by the door. She squinted to see his warm smile. What was there to smile about?

John pulled himself up, hanging on to the arm of the chair. "Oh, Hana. This is Michael Okada. He's a friend of mine."

Hana nodded. "Thank you for helping my sister, Mr. Okada. I appreciate it more than you know." She choked back the thickness in her throat and leaned into the chair, waiting for the trembling to stop. "I didn't see you after we got here. I thought you left before I could thank you."

He stepped from the shadows. "Call me Michael, and I did leave for a few minutes. Your sister is young and healthy. She'll pull through."

She almost believed him. His essence of peace and his soothing voice wilted her anxiety enough to stop the trembling. "But you saw her face. The gash is so long. What will her face look like and who is going to fix it in this so called hospital?" She hung her head, too tired to hold it up.

John scooted to the corner near Michael and slid down the wall to sit on the floor.

The silent room amplified the ringing in her ears. What should she do now? How could she make this right with Chiko? Mama would—

She sprung to her feet. "Mama. We have to get Mama here. She doesn't know."

Michael stepped to the side and blocked the doorway. "She's here. I went for her. She's all right and waiting for you in the outer room."

"You…you brought her here?" She sat hard on the chair. "That was kind of you."

He smiled. "Just necessary. I would have brought her to the room, but I wasn't sure you were ready."

"Would you go and get her now?"

"Of course." He turned. "Hana, take courage. You're a strong woman. You have not failed your sister." He talked as though he knew her thoughts. He left the room without a sound, almost as if he wore soft slippers. Who was this strange man?

An orderly poked his head inside the door. "They'll bring your sister back in a minute. X-ray's done and the nurse said she's awake."

Michael followed him out into the hall.

Hana crouched near John. Her anger melted as she looked at the pain and tears in his eyes. "Who is this Michael person? What do you know about him?"

John shrugged and rested his head against the wall. He reached down to rub his leg. "Not much. Only that he's been a good friend and is very wise. He doesn't talk about himself. Why do you ask?"

"Just curious. Mama will be here any second. How do I look? I don't want to frighten her."

He leaned in and whispered. "You look fine. Don't worry."

Something banged against the doorway. Doctor Bennett and a nurse pushed Chiko's bed through the opening, Mama right behind them.

"Mama-san." Hana ran to her side. She had to look in her eyes to make sure she was handling this all right. As usual, Mama's strength spilled over to her. Her shaking arms calmed as she slipped her hand into her mother's. Of course Mama was holding up. Hana had never seen her fall apart.

Mama patted Hana's hand firmly. "Chiko be fine. You see. God take care of her."

Hana patted back. "Sure. She's strong and healthy." She scanned the room, looking for Michael. He had resumed his position in the shadow. He nodded to her.

"I'll have to ask all of you to leave for a few moments. We need to get her cleaned up." Doctor Bennett's voice commanded. His frown sparked a new worry. "Just for a few minutes, please."

Michael and John led the way out the door into the hall. Hana and Mama followed Doctor Bennett several doors down. He turned and waved them into a huddle.

"I don't want to alarm you, but her wound is quite serious and should have a facial surgeon's hand to fix her. Doctor Davidson would do better than me, although he's not a specialist in this area. Doctor Watanabe would have been my choice. He and his family left the camp a few weeks ago. I don't know that the nearby hospital would have anyone qualified to help her. I can make a call."

He paused when Hana held up her hand. "You're telling us she won't have the proper surgery and could end up badly scarred."

He hung his head. "Yes. I'm sorry. This is not the place to get care for this type of injury. Like I said, I can make a call into town, but there are no guarantees they would take her for what they would consider cosmetic."

Hana's heart pounded against her chest. "They would take her in a heartbeat if she were Caucasian."

Mama grabbed her arm. "It will work. We pray. Doctor Bennett, you do surgery, okay?"

"No, I can't. I have no special skills to—"

A voice from down the hall commanded everyone's attention. "I do."

Hana let go of Mama's hand and turned. Michael stood behind her.

John stepped beside him. "What are you talking about, Michael? You aren't a Doctor. Let these people work it out."

"I *am* a Doctor."

Hana's knees weakened as she stared into his eyes. He spoke the truth, she could feel it.

Doctor Bennett parted Hana and Mama to stand in front of Michael. "Who are you? Maybe you should stop joking around."

"My name is Michael Okada. I'm a surgeon. At least I was not long ago."

"Doctor Michael Okada? Honolulu's premier maxillofacial surgeon?" Doctor Bennett stood his ground. "I don't believe you. I know of his work. You can't be him."

"I will provide all the proof you need." He turned to John. "Will you go to my apartment and bring the brown case from under my mattress?" John hesitated, scratching his head. "Please, John, there is no time to lose."

John hobbled away. Hana took note of his limp and bloody ankle. She couldn't worry about him now, it was Chiko's turn. Still, she hated that he was in pain.

A light breeze blew by Hana, refreshing her aching head. "I believe him."

Mama shuffled straight up to Michael and craned to look into his face. She grunted. "I too believe."

Doctor Bennett shook his head. "Okay, this is crazy. Chiko needs the best. He can't be Doctor Okada." He turned to Hana. "Why is he not practicing if he's a doctor?"

Michael's steady voice interrupted Doctor Bennett's tirade. "I will explain as soon as John returns. I suggest you have your best nurse prep her for surgery in case you find me truthful."

Mama's eyes brimmed with tears. "Hana, you decide. Papa say you take charge. I need you to say. I sorry. I need you to decide."

Decide Chiko's future. This is the ultimate test for Papa's faith in her. The burden should have been overwhelming—crushing. Then the peace that rushed over her settled the matter.

"Doctor Bennett. If John brings proof, I want Doctor Okada to operate."

"Hana, are you sure?"

She locked into his gaze and nodded, but was she really sure?

Yes she was. Really.

Chapter 9

Hana's nerves shredded to watch her mother pace back and forth across the room, flitting with no place to land. "Mama-san, won't you sit down? You will wear yourself out."

"Yes, you right. You go check on her." Mama sat hard on a chair, her face contorted in a glower.

"Mama-san, I just checked five minutes ago. They were barely getting started."

John hoisted his leg up on a chair in front of where he sat. "I'm sorry it took so long for me to get Michael's credentials. They weren't exactly where he said." He shook his head. "I still can't believe he's a surgeon." He adjusted his position and grimaced.

Hana stood and marched over to him. "Let me see your foot."

"I'm fine."

She used her strongest voice. "Take off that shoe and—actually, hop up on the counter so I can get a good look at it." She knew he was hurting more than he showed. His arm tensed as she pulled on it to get him out of the chair. He leaned on her shoulder and hobbled on his good foot to get to the counter.

She reached for his foot. "Do you want help with your shoe?"

"No."

John gingerly pulled off his shoe to reveal a partly shredded blood-soaked bandage. She had seen messy wounds before, but this made her stomach flip.

She helped him swivel his leg over the counter top. "I'm going to go grab some gloves and supplies. I know this counter isn't comfortable. I don't want you on the bed Chiko will be on. Stay put."

"Check on Chiko." Mama called after Hana as she dashed out the door. Chiko was in good hands. It was John who needed attention now, his foot in danger of reinfection. He had spent the whole afternoon in pain without complaining. Her heart fluttered to think how selfless he had been. Just when she thought she had him figured out, he changed on her. Or maybe he was this way all along.

She grabbed boxes of gauze and sterile saline to flush the wound and stacked them against her chest. Balancing her goods, she ran all the way back to the room. Someone shouted, echoing from her destination. She rounded the doorway and stopped so short, her supplies scattered on the floor. Doctor Davidson stood with his back to her, his hands on his hips, yelling at John.

"What's going on here? Get off that counter, mister."

Hana's blood boiled. This was not the day for this man to press her.

She retrieved her boxes as she scolded. "Doctor Davidson. I'm in charge here."

He spun around, his eyes glaring. "I beg your pardon. Miss Kato, you will never be in charge. Get this man out. Isn't he supposed to have his own room, anyway?" He pointed to Mama. "You and this woman don't have any business here, unless you are on duty."

Hana picked up the last of her boxes of gauze. She stood up straight and fired a sharp look at the doctor. Her hands twitched, ready to shove the bigot out of the room.

She threw the boxes on the counter next to John. "That *woman* is my mother. We will not leave. My sister is in surgery at this moment and we're waiting here. John's wound has opened up and I'm going to lavage and bandage it. You may rant all you like, but we're staying."

He glared at her. "Where's Doctor Bennett? Is he doing the surgery?"

"No. He is assisting Doctor Okada, a visiting maxillofacial surgeon." Stretching the truth seemed the only thing to do at the moment. Michael wasn't a visitor, unless he was an angel sent by God.

"I've never heard of him. I'll see for myself what's going on. When I come back, he'd better be off that counter and in his own room. Is that clear?" He straightened the collar of his white coat.

Hana stepped closer and lowered her voice. "Perhaps if we had been able to reach you, the situation would be different. But no one could find you. Aren't you on duty?"

His face beamed red, he opened his mouth to speak. Mama stood up to face him.

John broke in. "Don't worry, I'll be gone." His tone was hard. Hana wished he would have let her handle it. This bigot bully wasn't going to push her around anymore. She had thought maybe her efforts over the weeks would win him over, but her time had been wasted.

Doctor Davidson huffed out the door. Hana snatched up one of the boxes. Her hands shook and she struggled to open it.

"Stupid man." She sniffed back the urge to cry and tried to concentrate on John's foot.

Mama sat and then spun on her chair and shook her finger at Hana. "He angry in his heart. Not stupid."

John swung his leg over the side of the counter. "I'd better go back to my room. I don't want you to lose your job over me."

Hana gripped his arm. "You're not going anywhere until I've fixed your bandage." She pulled on rubber gloves and snapped one of them against her wrist. "Sit back."

"Yes, Ma'am. You're pretty bossy today."

"Sorry." She leaned in and flashed a fake smile.

John rested back on his elbows. "It's okay. I know you're worried about Chiko."

"You not worry. God with Chiko." Mama stood and wandered out into the hall. Even though she hid it well, she knew Mama worried too.

"She'll be praying up and down the hall. It's her way." Hana squirted fluid into the wound. John sucked in a loud gasp. Hana stopped for a moment. "It doesn't look as bad as I thought it would."

"What, praying in the hall or my gash?"

Hana stopped and scowled at him.

"I'm sorry. I shouldn't joke right now. I know this surgery is serious business. I have great faith in Michael. If he says he can do right by her, he will."

Hana could only nod, her throat clogged with tears. There was a time when she would trust God with this sort of thing. Now she found herself trusting man. Mama wouldn't approve. The wrapping finished, she secured the new bandage.

John groaned and wiggled. "Done yet?"

"Done. You can go back to your room. That is if the orderlies haven't stripped the bed."

John eased to the floor and turned to smile at Hana. "Thanks." His eyes fixed on hers so long she felt her face flush. Cleaning up the blood with antiseptic was an excuse to turn away. Then she would corral Mama back into the room and sit with her until the surgery ended.

John limped through the doorway. Doctor Davidson bumped into him, storming his way into the room. Hana braced herself for a barrage of nasty words, yet reminding herself of Mama's rebuke about the state of the man's heart. Submission wasn't her cup of tea at the moment, but keeping peace was priority.

"None of you have heard the last of this. If Doctor Bennett thinks he can take over and let a stranger, a Jap, do surgery here, he has another thought coming. You and your mother stay here and out of my way." He spoke softly, but the anger in his voice made her skin crawl.

"We won't be in your way, Doctor. Can you tell me how much longer the surgery will last?" Dare she hope he would tell her?

He looked down at her, seeming to enjoy the posture. "He's nearly done. Don't expect much."

He spun around and marched away, his coat flapping behind him. Her heart skipped, wondering what he meant by his remark. Surely Doctor Bennett would come and tell them if it weren't going well.

Doctor Davidson was only trying to torture her.

The knot in her stomach squeezed tight enough to strangle her. Everywhere she turned, her life changed from solid to liquid, with nothing to hang onto. A break in the emotional rollercoaster would be like a refreshing rain right now.

Mama was back in her chair before Hana realized. "You far away."

"Yes, Mama-san, I wish we were all far away from here." The chair next to Mama looked inviting. Perhaps sitting would alleviate the aching in her bones.

Mama folded her hands in her laps. "We should think of future. Papa will come back and we will be together again. You see. All will be fine." Mama leaned into her chair and stared at the ceiling. "You see. It all be over soon."

Hana sighed long and hard, but the knot in her stomach remained. Optimism fled, even at Mama's encouraging words. Nothing comforted her. The clock ticked off more minutes. Even though the room temperature must have reached 80 degrees by now, shivers ran up her back when she heard Doctor Bennett clear his throat.

She jumped to her feet. "What's wrong? Is the surgery over? How's Chiko?"

He pulled off the mask hanging around his neck and tossed it in the waste container. "I'll let Doctor Okada speak with you about it."

"Why can't you tell us? Did something go wrong?" Her limbs trembled to think of all the possible catastrophes—unbearable possibilities.

"You know it's best if the surgeon explains everything. I wasn't the one working on Chiko. Just wait a moment and he'll be here."

He sighed and then smiled a crooked smile. "I'm going to go check on John and then see if I can calm Doctor Davidson down. I'll be back in a few minutes. Wait here."

Wait. There was nothing else to do. She glanced at Mama who hadn't moved from her chair, looking completely calm.

Michael stepped in the room just after Doctor Bennett left. The circles under his eyes and his lack of enthusiastic demeanor made her heart sink. All her fears collided and tears burst forth. Mama stood to speak in her stead. "Doctor, how is Chiko?"

Michael held out his palm toward the chairs.

"Sit down, both of you and let me explain."

Neil's guts churned as he leaned against the wall by the door, listening, not sure how Michael would explain the surgery to Chiko's family. When the man was finished, he would take over and help the Katos through this terrible time. It was all he could do besides pray.

Michael's modulated voice floated through the crack in the door. This was a man he could learn from. His skill was one thing. His inner strength even more impressive, though Neil suspected it was from a source he couldn't accept for himself. He turned an ear to his words.

"Your daughter is doing well, Mrs. Kato. The surgery accomplished more than I had even hoped for. There was a hairline fracture on her cheekbone, but no displacement so it should heal on its own without any complications."

Hana sniffled, but as far as he could hear, Mama was silent. The urge to go into the room overwhelmed him.

Mama's voice finally quivered. "Thank you, Doctor Okada." He imagined Michael reaching over to take her hand.

Hana chimed in sounding hopeful at last. "Yes, we are so grateful. Will she be scarred very badly?"

"Her scar will be noticeable, but in time it will fade somewhat. She'll be as beautiful as ever, even with a scar. I have confidence she will overcome any self-consciousness with support from you and your family." He turned his attention to Mama. "I have seen some good results with a touch of makeup, if you're not opposed to such things."

As beautiful as ever. Neil believed it and knew Hana and Mama would too. Michael's confident tone consistently reassured everyone who came in contact with this mysterious man. If Hana could have seen his steady hand at work in the O.R., she would be as pleased as he was at this moment.

Doctor Davidson stormed out of a room down the hall and squared his feet to face Neil. Now would be a good time to settle this fiasco once and for all. Bursting into the operating room not only startled Michael, it was a display of brute force by a bully, not a sign of respect for another physician.

Doctor Davidson's stance remained solid, so Neil took two steps in his direction. "We need to talk."

He smirked. "Not really. I've done all the talking I need to do. I've just spoken with someone at the WRA head office. Specifically, the head of ethics enforcement. You have gone too far with the Kato family and now this supposed surgeon. I also have a call in to check him out." He blinked hard and his face turned pale.

"What happened to the man who wanted to treat me like a son? Is this what a father figure would do?" Was the man bluffing? "Just what is it I've done that you should talk to the authorities?"

"Fraternization with the enemy." Doctor Davidson turned to walk away, then stopped. "And I don't need a son like you. I received word this morning that my real son is alive. He's coming here to see me."

He ran to catch up with Doctor Davidson who had scurried down the hall. He grabbed his arm and spun him around, wanting to confront him, wanting him to know how much trouble he could have caused for Hana too. Yet, it was a time for rejoicing, not strife.

"Your son is alive? That's wonderful. You must be overjoyed."

Doctor Davidson dropped his gaze to the floor. He paused before he nodded and walked away, leaving Neil scratching his head. If a son raised from the dead didn't change this man's heart, nothing could.

If the man was truthful about turning him in, he should consider what might happen. His mind wandered to the unfinished missionary application sitting in his desk drawer. He could accept not practicing medicine anymore, he had decided to give it up anyway to follow in his parent's footsteps, but it was too soon to be without a profession.

He checked his watch. A quick chat with John and then back to the Katos. He rounded the corner and stepped inside John's room. His patient sat on the edge of the bed, fully clothed in dirty jeans and tee shirt, his shoelaces untied and dangling. Heavy heat hung in the room.

He pulled off his lab coat. "Warm in here. I'll get the orderly to bring you a fan."

John pulled his gaze from the floor only to fix on the wall. "Thanks, but it's okay. There was one in here, but they needed it for the recovery room." He finally locked eyes. "I don't need to stay anyway, do I? I'm ready to get sprung if you're ready to get rid of me."

By the looks of the bandage sticking out of his shoe, someone had done a good job rewrapping the wound. If it checked out clean there was no reason for John to stay. He glanced at the wall clock. "Let's take a quick look at the bandage and I want to make sure you don't have a fever. I had planned to keep you till at least tomorrow, remember? And besides, it's kind of late in the day."

He thrust a thermometer in John's mouth. Exhaustion crept up from his feet to his fuzzy head. He couldn't imagine how tired John must be, yet there was a certain strength in his demeanor.

He pulled the thermometer from John's pursed lips. "Hmm. Normal." He surveyed John's face and posture. "You would probably rest better at your place. I'll let you go if you will lay low tomorrow. Deal?"

"Deal."

Neil was glad to see him go. Between the two of them, they had caused enough trouble for Hana.

He scribbled on the clipboard papers and tucked it under his arm. "Free to go."

John eased off the bed, favoring his good foot. "Thanks."

Doctor Bennett followed him to the door. John stopped and turned, his eyes filled with regret.

"I messed it all up today. I only meant to stop George. I wish you would have punched me and dragged me back here." He looked up to the ceiling.

"So do I. Guess we both messed up."

John looked toward the door and then back at Neil. His eyes seemed to stare right through him. "I've seen the way you are around Hana. I want you to know I don't think you're right for her." John waited as if hoping for affirmation.

Where had this come from? One minute they were talking about punching and messing up and the next John was warning him to stay away from Hana. He resisted the urge to tell him off.

He felt his neck and ears heat up. "I don't think Hana needs either of us at the moment." He clenched his hands behind his back. John stood still, his eyes fixed on Neil. The Katos would be waiting to see Chiko. "Gotta go." He squeezed passed John and hurried away. The sound of John's awkward clop echoed down the hall until Neil neared the recovery room. He stopped before going in.

John has you pegged. He should heed the subtle warning, but it was too soon to decide his feelings. He liked Hana more than any woman before her. John's insinuation was premature, yet Doctor Davidson had seen it too, enough to turn him in. He could still take care of her and the family as their doctor now. They needed him.

Didn't they?

"Fraternization." He had dismissed it before. Now the word seized his heart. Scandal would only serve to derail any future plans he had, with or without Hana.

"The war department couldn't possibly care about a no account doctor and an imprisoned Japanese nurse." He shook his head. "Let's wait and see, Bennett. One step at a time."

Michael's words soothed like a balm to Hana's anxiety. "She'll be out of recovery soon. I'll have the nurse come and tell you when you can see her. It's getting late and you won't be able to stay long—just for a minute. Then come back in the morning and I think you will see an improvement in the swelling."

She studied his eyes as he spoke, wondering why a man with such good bedside manner and compassion would leave the medical profession behind. Hana smiled. "Thank you for all you've done, Doctor Okada."

"Please, call me Michael from now on. I'm going back into hiding you might say." He tossed his white lab coat on the chair and pulled off the band that held his long hair. "John will know where to find me if Chiko has any complications. But she's my last patient in this formidable hospital." He scanned the room with a look in his eyes Hana couldn't decipher. Something between disgust and longing.

Hana ushered her mother toward the door. "Mama-san, you go ahead. I'll be there in a minute." She hung back with hopes of speaking to this cloak-and-dagger physician. He could disappear any time and she needed to ask him something.

Mama squinted and nudged Hana with her elbow. "You come soon."

"Yes. I will."

Michael raised his brow. "What can I do for you, Miss Kato?"

"Call me Hana."

"What can I do for you, Hana?" His smile lifted her spirits. She felt strangely vulnerable, yet safe in his presence.

Her cheeks warmed. "May I ask why you don't practice medicine anymore? If it's too personal, you don't have to answer. I have a reason for asking." He motioned for her to sit and he leaned against the empty bed.

He shifted from one foot to the other. "I won't go into detail, however, I will tell you that I found my profession to be lacking when it came to truly helping people. I have my convictions about treating the whole man, and it's not well received in the medical community."

"That's it? You gave up doing surgery for that?" She hoped her tone wasn't disrespectful. It seemed like a small thing—not a good enough reason to quit. Her reason was justified compared to that.

He raised his brows. "No. When I tried to save someone with my alternative methods—someone who wasn't a good candidate for surgery—the hospital board refused to let me treat them. They insisted on doing a surgical procedure, and I could do nothing but stand by and hope for the best."

His face paled and for the first time since she met him, his eyes saddened. She regretted asking, and now she didn't want to hear the rest of the story, sensing it would have a tragic end. "You don't have to tell me the rest. I see why this would make you question traditional medicine." Internally she poised to leave, hoping he wouldn't express the pain she could see on his face.

"I don't mind. I think you need to know—for future reference in your career and difficult decisions." He paused. Hana held her breath, too late to recant her question.

"The patient died on the operating table, just as I had predicted. The surgeons didn't care. They could have saved her. Their pride stood in the way." He hung his head. She had one more question before she guessed what the end of his story would be.

She mustered her courage. "Why didn't you operate? You are a renowned surgeon. Couldn't you have saved her?"

"I couldn't operate. You see, the patient was my wife."

It was as if lightning struck close to her. This wasn't what she guessed. She had no words to say to this man now. She should never have broached the topic. Her heart bled for him, even though he seemed at peace with it.

He stood up straight. "I couldn't go on with the farce of practicing medicine when my world fell apart. A world that wasn't ready to accept what I had to offer."

She swallowed hard. "I'm so sorry. I shouldn't have prodded you for information. I can't imagine your pain."

"I hope that imagining is all you will have to do in the near future. Death is a test for the living. Remember that." He strolled toward the door and turned to give her a half wave, half salute.

She waved back and locked eyes with his. "Good-bye. Thank you."

The fear that held her back from nursing seemed silly now. The experience at Pearl Harbor that left her emotionally crippled seemed more like an excuse than a good reason to quit. Poor Michael lost his precious wife because others wouldn't listen. In a way it resembled a kind of prejudice, just not like what she had tasted.

"Chiko." She had forgotten to join Mama. She made her way down the hallway to find her. She quickened her steps as she neared Recovery. Mama stood by Chiko's bed stroking her slender arm.

"Mama-san? How is she?"

Without looking up she started singing in a whispered tone. The Japanese lullaby pricked Hana's mind with memories of her childhood when Mama would sing it to her. If anything could soothe Chiko, Mama's lullaby could.

"She looks so small lying here all bandaged up. The swelling will go down tomorrow, like Michael promised."

Mama kept singing and reached up to tuck away a strand of Chiko's hair that had fallen on her face. Her skin was already bruised along the edge of her face. Chills crawled up Hana's back to consider how Chiko must look under the bandage. She remembered what Chiko had said about wanting to look Caucasian. What an irony she nearly lost her Asian beauty.

She stood on the other side of the bed for a while listening to the tune until Mama stopped and began to pray. The same words had been whispered by Mama many times. The missionaries who ministered to Mama and Papa years ago taught them how to pray. Hana learned just by observation, and later came to realize that God would speak back to her if she paid attention.

Where had that practice gone? How did God get lost in the chaos of her life? She didn't want the same for Chiko. Her sister must follow Mama's example and save herself the heartache of losing communion with God.

"Time to go." A nurse stood in the doorway motioning for them to leave. Mama's eyes begged Hana to let her stay.

"Mama-san, she'll be all right. They'll take good care of her. We'll come early in the morning."

Mama's arm tensed as Hana led her away from Chiko's bed. Her heart must be breaking for her little one. How much could one mother take? A son off to war and now her beautiful daughter injured and scarred for life.

They trudged down the hall and out the door of the hospital toward Block 15. The cool night air took Hana by surprise. The long day now took its toll as she felt her legs weaken. Tomorrow had to be better. Nurse Potter would be back and could help take care of Chiko. She would let Mama sleep in.

Mama stopped and leaned in to look in Hana's eyes. "You okay?" The moonlight held just enough illumination to give her a good look at Hana's expression. She smiled to cover it up.

"Sure, Mama-san. Just tired. We both need rest."

The next few days would be filled with a vigil around Chiko's bed. Somehow she would have to find time to move forward with securing Papa's release. One thing after another stood in her way. Papa counted on her. She would send for John and make him help. Maybe Michael could suggest something they hadn't thought of. He seemed the compassionate and resourceful type.

The possibilities whirled in her head all the way back to the barrack. They slipped quietly into their room. Mama pulled the curtain around her cot to undress, but weariness took over for Hana. Slipping off her shoes and arranging her pillow took the last of her strength.

John has to help me. I can't do this alone. If only I had Michael's peace of mind.

Sleep fell over her like a heavy blanket. Michael's face faded as the last picture in her mind. In her dream, he rode away on a white horse.

Chapter 10

Doctor Davidson's long lost son stood toe to toe with his father. "Son, you can't be serious," he croaked. The horror on the poor young man's face broke Neil's heart. The reunion off to a bad start, he wanted to be anywhere but here, watching Doctor Davidson ruin his first meeting with a son he thought dead.

The young man took a step back. "Of course I am. She's my wife and you'd better get used to it. Why are you acting this way? What's happened to you?"

"She's only your wife by Japanese tradition, not by America's. It's disgusting."

"Why don't I let you two talk alone." He crept toward the door wishing he were invisible.

"No, Doctor Bennett. Please stay and explain to me why my father has changed." Tom crossed his arms and stood firm against his father's equally aggressive stance. Perspiration dripped from Doctor Davidson's forehead.

Had Tom not known about his father's feelings toward Japanese? Neil stifled a sad chuckle—the son of a Japanese hater had just announced he had a Japanese wife.

"Yes, please stay and explain to my son how we have received reports of the Japs treating our soldiers like animals."

The tension thickened so much Neil had the urge to brush it away with his hand. He wished at this moment he had better peacemaking talents. Anything he said would sound as if he were taking sides. Before he could think of something intelligent to say, Doctor Davidson continued.

"Are you forgetting what happened at Pearl Harbor? They killed your uncle. How can you marry one of them?"

Tom softened a bit. "Because I love her, and her family played an important role in my life. You don't know what happened to me. I didn't tell you everything in my letters."

"You hardly ever wrote." Doctor Davidson wasn't bending to Tom's pleading words. "I spent my days worrying if you had been captured or killed by those devils. Now you come home to tell me you have a Jap wife."

Tom leaned in. "I don't care if you are my father, if you say Jap one more time, I'll belt you. It's derogatory and I won't listen to it." His chest puffed under his uniform, and his brow sprouted beads of sweat as he talked. Neil guessed he would make good on his threat. There were many times he wanted to do the same.

"You can accept my wife when she is able to join me or you'll not see me again. The choice is yours, Dad." He huffed out a sigh. "I know you're shocked, but hatred toward someone you don't even know is not how you taught me to be. Miko didn't kill Uncle Daniel."

Tom's deep blue eyes stared daggers at his father. As long as they weren't in a fist fight, Neil saw no reason to intervene. He checked the clock on the wall and willed his feet to inch toward the door.

Tom's shoulders relaxed a little as he let his arms hang to his side. His eyes turned sad and teary—his voice wavered and cracked. "What would mother have thought about your reaction? You know exactly how she would feel. She would be happy for me. She knew how to love her son. You obviously don't. You only care about your bigotry and grief."

Neil's stomach tied in a knot waiting to see what those words would do, break Doctor Davidson or enrage him. He glanced to the door to make sure no one was eavesdropping. This was not the kind of conversation he wanted anyone to hear.

Doctor Davidson's eyes widened. "Your mother would—"

"Would what, Dad? You know what she would say. She'd be ashamed of you."

Neil braced himself, ready to block a punch he knew would come now. But Doctor Davidson slumped into a chair and covered his face in his hands, sobbing. Every muscle in Neil's body twitched. He couldn't believe his eyes. The hard, insolate man who had been filled with so much darkness of spirit now wept before him. All the ill feelings toward his colleague melted.

Tom glanced at Neil before stepping close to his father. "Dad. Miko and her father saved my life. I would have died on Saipan had it not been for them. I was injured and they dragged me into the cave they were hiding in until the fighting was over. I can't tell you all about it right now, I'm still horrified by the whole bloody battle. But she's the best thing that ever happened to me. Don't throw us away because she has Japanese blood."

Doctor Davidson dried his tears. His resolve seemed to be smashed in a million pieces. Neil had never seen such brokenness. Especially not from this doctor who had never shown any weakness. But mountains under pressure have to release it or explode.

Tell them now. He shook his head. He had heard this voice before and he knew to obey. Yet everything in him wanted to leave and not get involved.

Tell them about forgiveness.

No, Lord. He tried to ignore the vortex pulling him in. If he ran now, he would miss something special. He pushed that voice away once before, and didn't keep his parents from leaving home the day they died. He could have possibly saved them. Yes, he knew better and he had to decide. Did he want to be a missionary for Doctor Davidson, or a doctor for Chiko and his other patients who waited for him? There could be only one answer, but it might include both.

Yes, Lord.

"Gentlemen. May I ask you both to sit for a minute? I'd like to tell you a story. Please." He pointed to the chairs and motioned for Doctor Davidson and his son to circle their chairs around his. He planted himself, waiting for them to oblige.

Doctor Davidson straightened in his chair while Tom and Neil sat. "I don't think you have any business—"

"Dad. If it will help you change your mind I want to hear what he has to say." They both stared up at him.

Hands shaking, he eased into the remaining chair. "Let's get it over with then." His face was red and dark circles had formed under his eyes.

Neil sighed hard and leaned forward, clasping his hands. Doctor Davidson had to surrender his heart. *God help me. Help him.*

"This is hard for me to admit. I know the hatred you have felt, Doctor Davidson. I hated for a long time after my parents died. I was supposed to drive the jeep behind them as they went to minister to people just after the bombing at Pearl. I hated myself and the people they went to help. I should have made them stay home that day, or at least gone with them."

Doctor Davidson fixed his eyes on Neil and frowned. The young man slid back in his seat, eyes wide.

Doctor Bennett pushed down the sorrowful memories and the tears that threatened to rise up.

Doctor Davidson stuffed his hands in his lab coat.

"This isn't the same. I have a right to hate the Japanese."

Neil glared at him. "No. You're wrong. None of us has the right. My parents taught me that God wants us to forgive our enemies. Hatred and revenge in our hearts hurts us and everyone who needs our love. Your son needs your love. You thought you gave it by hating the people you declared to be his enemy. That's not love. Forgiveness is a true expression of love. If you don't forgive, you will lose your son."

The heavy spirit that had dominated the room lifted. It was as if he could breathe deep again. Doctor Davidson's lip quivered. Neil glanced at the young man beside him who wiped away tears streaming down his face. He nodded. "Please, go on."

"Well, I just wanted to tell you that God will help you forgive, just as He has shown me how to have compassion and mercy for the people here." He hesitated to embrace the conclusion. It had been so long since he prayed with someone. "I can pray for you, but you have to want His help. You don't need to feel forgiveness, you just need to do it." He waited, praying silently. Doctor Davidson could jump up at any moment and storm out of the room. He had done it before, and over much less provocation.

A stillness blanketed the room like a heavy snowfall silencing the night. Resistance lifted and Neil relaxed knowing he had been obedient. The rest was up to God. Just speaking those words aloud confirmed in his heart that healing, even for him, had taken place. He had some forgiving to do too, for he still felt shadows of blame hanging over him from time to time. His parents would have hated that.

"Dad, I forgive you. Sounds like you need to forgive yourself and move on."

"I'm sorry, son. I've been so angry. I never used to be this intolerant. I never used to hate anyone. It's been building, and since your mother and you weren't here to help me make sense of it, well—there's no excuse, really." He paused and rubbed his chin.

Tom leaned over and rested his shaking hand on his father's knee. "Mom's looking down now, and would be so happy to see you whole again. Doctor Bennett's right, you know."

A long silence pushed Neil's patience until Doctor Davidson at last turned to him. "I'm sorry I turned you in for fraternization. I can't take it back. I would if I could. I see now it was all just hatred. I should have been busy being a doctor and not acting like judge and jury." He hung his head. Tears dripped onto the floor. The whole scene seemed unreal. To see Doctor Davidson, menacing doctor, fall apart before his eyes was surreal. Only God could do this.

"Dad, would you mind if he prayed for us? I did a lot of praying while I was gone. It helped me. It might help us now."

Doctor Davidson leaned back in his chair. He shrugged and cleared his throat. "I suppose it couldn't hurt, but don't expect me to become some sort of religious nut."

Neil laughed and patted him on the back. He had followed his heart and God's leading. His parents would be proud. "No expectations."

He bowed his head, saying a quick silent prayer for the right words to say for his colleague. He felt impressed to keep it short and simple.

"Dear Lord, thank you for bringing Tom home to his father. Restore their relationship and restore Doctor Davidson's heart to wholeness. Speak to all of us each day about your ways and help us to live by them. We receive your daily gift of love and grace. Amen."

It was good to sense God's presence in the room. He stood and patted Doctor Davidson on the shoulder. "I have to go see Chiko Kato now. Bandages need to come off to check for infection and see the wound. I don't particularly like this part of our job."

Doctor Davidson stood, wiping his eyes. "Want me to—well, I don't suppose they would want to see me after how I've treated them. I'll apologize later. Let me know how she's doing."

Before him stood a different man than thirty minutes ago. "I will."

He traipsed down the hall toward Chiko's room wondering what God was doing. Everything had changed in a day.

Hana and Mama stood in the doorway of Chiko's room, listening. The collective effort for today would be to comfort this scared young girl. Nurse Potter led the way. She tucked the sheet tight over Chiko as she rambled on about the day she spent with the little orphan girl, Charlie. "Poor thing seemed so lost at first. Then she warmed up to me when I baked her some of my famous cinnamon cookies. She's spending time with a neighbor until I'm done here."

Mama smiled as Nurse Potter talked. She looked up and waved them into the room. "She's doing fine. Come see for yourself." Her smile broadened across a bright face. Charlie obviously had a youthful effect on her. Her cheerfulness relieved some of the burden hovering for the last twenty-four hours. Hana's knotted stomach wouldn't be satisfied until Chiko smiled. They approached with trepidation, each moving to a side of the bed.

Chiko did smile, but with tears rolling onto the pillow. "Hi, Mama-san." Her gravelly voice was to be expected after surgery. She hated hearing it and eyed Mama to make sure it didn't alarm her.

"You look good today. How you feel?" Mama stroked the part of her head void of bandages. Hana slipped her hand into Chiko's and squeezed, her urge to cry nearly choking her.

Chiko's shoulders shook as she sobbed. "I'm scared. Nurse Potter said Doctor Bennett will be in soon to check my in…incision. What if I'm ugly?"

Nurse Potter scooted close to Hana and leaned down. "Remember what we talked about? You must let yourself heal and crying will only add to the swelling." She patted Chiko's arm with one hand while reaching the other around Hana's back to pull her in a sort of hug. "We're all here with you and you'll be fine. I hear you had the very best surgeon."

Hana casually examined Chiko's face. The bruises showed worse than she had prepared for. The swelling had diminished, but she could imagine Chiko's devastation at the sight of her once lovely face. She swallowed down pity so it wouldn't show.

Hana brightened her tone. "She's right. You just take a deep breath and let Doctor Bennett do his job. Did they tell you who operated?"

Chiko sniffled and nodded. "Somebody named Doctor O…Okada?"

"Uh huh. He's John's friend. He said he was very pleased with the surgery. He's a kind and caring man." Hana could say more about Michael, but it would sound as if she liked him too much. She couldn't deny she was drawn to him.

Chiko wiped her face with her free hand. "Can I meet him?"

"Maybe. He isn't usually around the hospital. Perhaps he'll want to check on you since you are a special case." She grabbed Chiko's toes and wiggled them.

A tentative smile peeked through Chiko's bandage. Perspiration formed on her forehead. Hana adjusted the fan to blow in her direction. The stifling heat of the summer had wafted into the hospital like someone turning up the thermostat.

Nurse Potter motioned to the hall. "Hana, would you help me set up for Doctor Bennett?" It appeared she wanted Hana alone. "Mama will keep her company." Her smile filled the room, making it seem void of all worry. Hana's shoulders relaxed in the new realization of her lifted mood. She studied her straight posture and quick steps, and pushed down the urge to press her about her source of confidence. This whole event was bearable in part because of her.

"I'll be right back." Chiko squeezed her hand when she tried to let go. "It's all right. Mama will sing, won't you, Mama-san?" She winked at Mama who took her cue to start the lullaby again. The melody floated on the air and followed them down the hall.

"Here." Nurse Potter handed her a sterile wrapped instrument pack marked *post op*. "You take these and I'll get the gauze and topical medicines." Her crisp skirt rustled as she bustled around the room. All of this was second nature to her, proven by her precise movements and ability to hone in on the exact location of everything they needed.

"Nurse Potter…Alice, why have you been so kind to Chiko…and me?"

As the words left her mouth she realized how offensive they could be, but Nurse Potter had done a turnaround in her attitude since Hana first arrived. She remembered the cold stares and curt conversations. And the first day she had walked through the hospital doors and been scared to death of this formidable woman.

Nurse Potter stopped her fussing and freed her hands, setting all her supplies on the counter. She looked to the floor, her face flushed. It occurred to Hana she had made her mad.

Instead, her eyes filled with tears. "I know I was mean when you first got here. I'm sorry for that. Your sister grabbed my heart the first time I saw her. I'll tell you why." She ran her finger along the edge of the counter, still not looking up.

"She reminds me of my daughter. Her mannerisms and personality. I found myself drawn to her and then realized what a nice family yours is." Her eyes finally searched Hana's. "My daughter ran away several years ago and I haven't seen her since. She's twenty now and I doubt she'll ever come home."

Her explanation shook lose what was left of Hana's reservations about her. How terrible that she had to live with the uncertainty of whether or not her child was alive or well. At least all of the Katos were still together, even if only in their hearts for now. One more irony of life bred in this camp.

Hana wanted to put her at ease. What could she say that would express her sympathy? "I'm so sorry. You must worry all the time about her."

"I used to. Now I'm sort of numb to caring about her choice. But I do care about Chiko. She's at that tender age when looks are everything. This will be hard on her. I don't know anything about this mystery doctor. I hope he did his best work on our little girl."

Hana's stomach fluttered. "Oh, he's the best, and so kind. I'm sure you'll meet him and then your mind will be at ease."

"Sounds like a miracle he was there to operate." She reached over and scooped up all the supplies and marched toward the door. Hana followed, clutching the instrument pouch.

"Yes, a miracle."

Nurse Potter talked over her shoulder. "Kind of like the miracle of Charlie crossing our path." She raised her brows. "I'm going to try to adopt her."

Hana stopped short. "What? Can…can you do that? I mean, it's wonderful." Her face heated as she stammered. Nurse Potter had come full circle in a short time. If only Doctor Davidson could straighten up, what time she had left working at the hospital would be easy.

Back in Chiko's room, Doctor Bennett hovered over Chiko's face shining a little light into each eye. Hana imagined everyone's heart to be fluttering as much as hers. The defining moment had arrived and soon they would all find out just how much of Chiko's face had been sewn up. Her eyes darted around to each face. Doctor Bennett intense, Mama's eyes closed to pray, Alice smiling, and if she were to guess, her own face was pale.

The events of two days ago flashed through her mind. Remembering Chiko fall and hit the edge of the mess hall table made her shudder. She closed her eyes tight to make the images stop. At this moment she was a nurse, not Chiko's sister. How nice it would be to truly turn her emotions on and off, but her stomach still churned.

"Thank you, Nurse Potter. Miss Kato, I'll take those."

Doctor Bennett's stern voice made her realize how nervous he must be. This wasn't his work he was about to reveal, and he couldn't really speak to what lay under the bandages. He held a pair of bandage scissors in his steady hand close to Chiko's head. Mama slid over to Hana's side. She could feel her trembling.

"Wait." Chiko leaned away from him. "I'm scared."

Nurse Potter took her hand. Her soothing voice eased Hana's nerves. If she could do the same for Chiko, she would be impressed—and grateful. She leaned down to whisper. "It's all right, Chiko. Remember what we talked about earlier? It will be swollen and red and it may take another surgery to make it look better. I think you're strong enough to handle this. We're all here to support you. You are a beautiful girl, no matter what the mirror might show. And I know what I'm talking about." She winked at her and wiped an escaping tear from Chiko's cheek.

"Ready now?" Doctor Bennett smiled and held the scissors low until Chiko nodded.

Mama squeezed Hana's hand so tight she felt the ends of her fingers tingle. Each snipping sound of the scissors on the bandages was like a punch in her stomach. She had to have a good result. Poor kid was an innocent bystander and for that had to endure the torture of waiting to see her damaged face.

God, please don't leave her badly scarred.

One last clip and Doctor Bennett dropped the scissors into a metal tray on the bed. He looked Chiko in the eye.

His hands still steady, he slowly lifted the ball of gauze from her face. Hana and Mama moved a step back in unison. As he pulled the last bit of bandage from her skin, Hana squeezed Mama's hand. The left side of Chiko's face was swollen and black and blue and red. Mama made a soft grunt sound. Hana pulled her arm in close to silence her.

Doctor Bennett took her chin in his hands and pulled her to face him. "Do you want a mirror, Chiko? It's not so bad, pretty one."

Chiko shook her head first and then nodded. "I have to see it eventually."

Doctor Bennett blew hot breath on it and cleaned a small mirror with his coat cloth. "Take my hand." He handed her the mirror and grabbed her other hand in his.

Chiko inched the mirror up her chest and then back down. She searched Hana's face.

Hana mustered a smile. "You are a brave one, little sister." Hana wasn't so sure she would be as courageous.

The mirror shook in Chiko's hand. Mama let go of Hana and crept close to Chiko. She peered into the mirror with her daughter and smiled.

Mama broke the thick silence. "It not so bad, huh, Sachiko?"

All eyes scanned Chiko's face, her whole body, waiting for some movement or sound. It seemed to Hana that time stood still. If it were her in that bed, she would have screamed.

A voice from behind them made Chiko look up from the mirror. "Well, Sachiko? Tell us what you think."

Doctor Bennett turned. "Doctor Okada. Hello."

❧

"John, Michael." John heard Hana's voice and tensed. It had occurred to him she might not want him here, but Michael asked him to come. Michael stayed in the doorway, so he followed suit.

Michael's soothing tone eased the anxiety hanging over Chiko's bed. "Sachiko? May we come in?"

Chiko glanced at Hana and shrugged her shoulders. "Chiko, this is Doctor Michael Okada, your surgeon."

Chiko brightened and she attempted to raise up on her elbows.

"Oh. Please come in, and John too. Hi, John."

John's inner fluttering stopped at her invitation. "Hi, Chiko."

He watched Hana's dark tired eyes, wishing he could comfort her too. Instead, Michael received the smile he longed to get.

Michael leaned in close to Chiko's face and took the tip of her chin in his hand, turning her face so the incision was to the front. The room fell silent. Michael had everyone tongue-tied, waiting for his approval.

Michael let go of her chin. "You haven't told us what you think, Sachiko."

"My name is Chiko. Only Mama-san calls me by my full first name." She stared at him for a second and then smiled to one side. "But it sounds grown-up coming from you."

"And?" Michael tipped his head.

Chiko straightened her posture. "And I don't think it's as bad as I thought it would be. Will it get better?"

"Much better. The scar will fade in time. You will learn in time to accept it as a symbol of your life experience, Sachiko. Always remember that outward appearance is not the source of our beauty. When you find yourself feeling bad, concentrate on the other qualities you have that make you unique. Then you'll always be beautiful."

Chiko kept her eyes on Michael and nodded once, and everyone seemed to hold their breath to see if she understood. Her half-smile turned to a grin, releasing the unspoken relief.

Mama's tears ran like a river down her face. "You do good, Doctor Okada. We thank you so much to help our Sachiko."

Doctor Bennett thanked Michael, shaking his hand. Hana did the same. Michael returned to Chiko's side. "You will be fine now. I'm glad to have met you. Maybe next time stay out of the fight, all right little one?"

Chiko grabbed his arm and pulled him close to her in a tender embrace. "Thank you."

Michael bowed to Mama and Hana. "Good-bye."

Just before going through the door, he paused and turned back to his patient. "You know what Sachiko means?"

Chiko shrugged.

"It means happy girl child. That's what you will be, always." With that he hurried away.

Following Michael out into the foyer, John couldn't shake off the feeling something significant had just happened. Once outside he walked beside his friend, not knowing their destination. The sun pressed hot air down on him.

Michael talked as he kept his fast pace. "Will you stop by my place, John? I have something for you."

"Sure, but I thought you were supposed to stay away from me. I don't want any more rocks smashing through your window." He stopped when Michael halted in front of him.

"I don't think our little friend George Saito will be instigating any riots today. I heard his family is leaving soon. He won't want to spoil that." He plodded up the stairs and opened the door of his apartment.

Something seemed different. There wasn't usually a lot of things in his room, but today the space nearly echoed from emptiness.

"What's going on? Where are all your belongings?" John's heart sank at the presumption filling his head.

"I'm leaving Grand Peak, John. Tomorrow."

Tomorrow. His only friend in the world would be gone in twenty-four hours.

"What? How? Where are you going?"

"I suppose you could say a great thing has happened. I'm going back into practicing medicine. I need to get out there and find a position." He reached down and picked up a brown wooden box. "I want to give you something before I go."

"How did you get permission? Not everyone can just up and leave yet you know." He grasped at any excuse to keep Michael here. He needed him.

"Never mind about that. I'm good to go." He handed John the box. "I was going to take it with me, that's why it's boxed, but I think it will do you good to tend it."

John took the box and held it up. "What is it?"

"Open it and see."

The flimsy box top was easy to pry open. He reached in and pulled out a bonsai tree about ten inches high. Its shape and exquisitely trimmed green leaves in perfect form. John had never seen one quite this well-manicured.

"It's lovely. Thanks. How do I take care of it?"

Michael handed him a pair of tiny scissors. "With these."

John turned them over in his fingers, fumbling to open them. "I don't think I can work these things."

"You will learn. This little tree will teach you some important lessons about life and about yourself."

"A tree? Teach me?" Michael was as strange as anyone he had ever met.

"You can learn from anything if you try. This tree is living and growing, just like you. Don't give up on it like you have yourself."

His words hit like flames against John's skin. Is that what he had done—given up on himself? He could get mad, but he knew Michael had his best interest at heart. Leave it to Michael to believe a tree would teach his wayward friend a lesson in life.

"I'll do my best. And just how do I find myself again? What will happen to me when I leave here? If you could just wait for a couple weeks, I might be able to get out and go with you." He felt his suggestion fall to the floor and flounder. It was weak and stupid. Happily, Michael ignored it.

Michael knelt on the large pillow laying on the floor. "You have spent your time here searching for somewhere to belong. You went about it the wrong way. A person must give to receive. You are afraid to give, to help others reach for their dreams. This is what we are put on earth to do, John. Most religions teach that. Especially the Katos' religion."

John looked away. "I've seen it, but thought it would be a sign of weakness to go around like Santa Claus all the time." He set the box on the floor by his feet and moved to the side. The sun glared through the window into his eyes.

"There are so many needy people in this world. You don't need to save them all, just open your heart and you'll know where your place is." He smiled. "Be prepared. You might be surprised what awaits you."

"But what about *my* dreams?"

"What dreams? Do you have any? You've never spoken of any." Michael's brows knit together.

John stared at the floor. It was true. He had no dreams. "Yeah, you're right."

Michael held up his hand. "Good-bye, my friend."

John grasped it and held it tight. "Good-bye."

Outside the hot sun hid behind a band of dark clouds. Thunder rumbled behind the mountain. The first storm of the season would soon be upon them. He searched the entire sky. Yes, there would be rain today—a much needed rain. Water to make things green and help the tiny gardens around the camp grow tall.

He passed Block 12 on the way to his place. He would ditch the little tree there and get to the mess hall for whatever slop they cooked up for lunch. His stomach rumbled along with the distant storm.

Out of a barrack on Block 13 a family emerged with suitcases and satchels in hand. From the hunched over old man to the twin toddlers toting dolls and other toys, they each had the same look of cautious optimism. He stopped to watch them count heads and then move in a long row toward the hill leading to the administration building.

The old man lagged behind carrying a gunnysack slung over his shoulder. After a few labored steps the sack broke loose from his grip and fell to the ground. The man scratched his head and bent to pick up what had spilled out.

John ran to aide him in recovering what he thought would be some valuable belongings. "Let me help you." He stopped short when he saw a pile of rocks.

"These for my rock garden back home."

John's mouth hung open. Was this old man crazy?

"May I ask why you are dragging them from here to your home?

Aren't there rocks where you're going?"

"Oh, yes. These rocks special. I take them to remind me of our time at Grand Peak. I gave up my garden here, but these rocks remind me to never give up."

The old man's explanation sounded like something Michael would say. John set his tree box on the ground and filled the sack again. The old man bowed and John returned the gesture. He swung the bundle over his shoulder and shuffled off to catch up to the others. Another lucky family leaving camp forever.

Time to contemplate leaving himself. How strange to think of living anywhere else, living on the outside again. Michael's summation had been correct. He had given up on his life and lost his dreams. Maybe he never had any. He turned to see the family disappear down the hill. At least the old man had his rocks to bring him some happiness. He had something to go home to. A new garden. A new challenge.

With no place to call home John would still be alone. Without his friend to guide him, he'd be lost. One more abandonment to add to his list. Now Michael wanted him to reach out to others.

It would only mean more pain, especially if Hana kept her distance.

Chapter 11

Thunder cracked just as Neil handed Hana a bundle of supplies. She jumped at the booming clap.

"You'll need these to change her bandage, but feel free to bring her here. We'll fix her up anytime." He secretly wished she would do the latter, just so he could see her while she took time off to care for Chiko. For now he would settle for helping in some small way, so she knew he cared. After a week of seeing her work her duties and slip in and out of Chiko's room, he wondered why she wasn't totally exhausted.

"Thanks. I'll likely keep her home. It will give me a chance to catch up on my research and letter writing to get Papa home. My first round of letters went unanswered. And I have to assume his physical condition is still not good, although we haven't heard from the prison for a while."

Another thunder crack. Closer this time. Hana jumped again and looked out the window.

She rested her head on the pane. "Two days in a row. Let's hope this storm brings rain. The six sprinkles from yesterday dried up fast. My father would be out watching the sky on days like this. Rain meant everything to him."

"I'm so sorry I wasn't able to help with his release. I'll keep a look out for any opportunities though, and let you know if something comes up." He would do anything for her. If he could only tell her how much he admired and liked her, but the fraternization mess hung over his head. Pushing the boundaries again would mean certain dismissal.

"I appreciate that. Well, I'll go get a wheelchair and pick up Chiko."

She smiled and left him standing there admiring her grace. Doctor Davidson swung around the corner and nearly bumped into her. Neil sucked in a breath. Hana and he had not spoken since Doctor Davidson's change of heart. His imagination whirled at the possible scenarios about to happen. Why couldn't they—

"Excuse me, Miss Kato. I wasn't watching."

Her eyes darted to Neil and then back to Doctor Davidson. "It's all right." She took one step back and stared at him, then turned to leave.

Doctor Davidson piped up. "How is your sister? I, I heard the surgery went well and she's had an uneventful week of recuperation."

Neil shuddered to hear him stumble over his words. The man had a long way to go before he would be comfortable chatting casually with a person of Japanese descent. At least he had a start now, even if he bungled it.

Hana looked at Neil. He hoped his smile would reassure her this wasn't some sort of trick.

She edged toward the hall. "Um, she's well enough to leave the hospital this morning. Her spirits are fairly good—considering." She inched away, confusion written on her face.

If only she knew what had transpired last week with Tom, she wouldn't have the anxiety she must feel at this moment, waiting for Doctor Davidson to pounce with a cutting remark. But he believed the man's transformation to be genuine. Hana would see in time. The right circumstance, the right chance for Doctor Davidson to prove himself once and for all could be just around the corner.

Doctor Davidson cleared his throat and glanced down. "Well, I'm glad. If there's anything I can do, please tell me." He turned to Neil.

Hana bit her lower lip and backed away, nearly faltering on her first step.

Neil chimed in. "See you later. Tell Chiko chin up."

He knew her head must be spinning with questions about Doctor Davidson's attitude. Neil moved close to him and patted his back. "Well done. I'm impressed with your act of kindness."

Doctor Davidson hung his head. "Here I thought I could be a father figure to you—to teach you the ways of the world. It seems that role has been reversed." He rolled his eyes and chuckled. Neil had never heard him laugh.

"You're the one who is teaching me that anyone can change, so don't feel bad."

He sauntered to the doorway and gazed down the empty hallway. The hospital functioned quietly these days with less patients and less staff. As the internees made their way home, the whole camp took on a strange, foreboding atmosphere. Hana would be leaving soon if they could get word about Mr. Kato. Selfishly, he hoped for a delay, but that would mean more heartache for Hana.

Doctor Davidson nudged his arm and broke his inner thoughts. "Hey, where are you?"

"I was just thinking about how hard it must be for the Katos to sit and wait, hoping each day Mr. Kato will be released by some miracle."

Doctor Davidson's brows flinched. "Released from where? I never really paid attention to what happened to him." Doctor Davidson checked his watch. They both blinked when a flash of lightning burst outside the window. More thunder rolled through the thick hot air.

"Leavenworth Prison. He's very ill and needs to be with his family. Hana has been hoping to get him a medical release. I tried to help, but my connection passed away a while ago." He shook his head. "I feel for her—them."

Doctor Davidson squinted and looked away. "It's all right for you to talk about Hana. I know you like her, and now I see it was none of my business to stop that. I feel terrible about turning you in. I wish I could take it back or do something to make things better. We can only hope nothing comes of the complaint."

Neil's thoughts whirled with everything Doctor Davidson said. He appreciated rules, and if the authorities thought he stepped over the bounds, he'd pay the price. Hana had done nothing wrong and her family needed help.

Crack! The storm felt as though it hovered on top of them. The lights flickered once, and then again.

He pulled back the curtain, half blocking the window. "It's too late to help me, but if you can think of any way to help the Katos, you would be a hero—my hero."

Doctor Davidson's face brightened. "Did you say Leavenworth? The chief medical officer at the Leavenworth Prison hospital was my brother's best friend in college. I haven't spoken with him since Daniel was killed. I think he would remember me."

Bells rang in Neil's head. This could be the connection to make something happen. He laughed out loud and Doctor Davidson's brows knit together above wide eyes.

"Why is it funny?"

Should he say it? He hated Christian clichés, but Doctor Davidson wouldn't know the difference. He placed his hand on Doctor Davidson's shoulder.

"Because God works in very mysterious ways."

Crack!

Doctor Davidson laughed again. "It would appear He's awake this morning."

How ironic that God would use a bigot to help the people who had been the target of his hatred. Neil recalled all the times in Hawaii his parents told him stories of this same nature. He would rejoice with them, but never knew the real joy of sharing in the miracle. Until now. *If* it worked.

"Doctor Davidson, let's go find a phone. You have a call to make."

Doctor Davidson shrugged. They strolled into Neil's office. Another flash of lightning and crash of thunder, and the lights flickered and then went out. Both of them froze, waiting for the lights to resume glowing. The morning had been dark with clouds and Neil had two lights on in his office. Now nothing. Just gray noisy sky outside.

"Doctor Bennett." Nurse Potter popped her head in the doorway. "The electricity is out all over camp. Phones too. Thank God none of the patients are on oxygen."

Phones! Not now, not when Doctor Davidson could make the call to rescue poor Hana from more pain and suffering. He kicked the chair in front of his desk.

Doctor Davidson held up his hand. "Hold on. It might be temporary."

Neil shook his head. If this was a test of his faith, God certainly picked the right time and place. He slumped in his chair.

Doctor Davidson squinted. "This is really important to you, huh?"

Important. More so than he knew till now. He didn't like being told no. It felt like God was teasing him. *Don't be childish, Bennett.*

"Yeah, I know it will happen all in God's time."

Doctor Davidson sat across from him. He scratched his head and smirked. "I sure have a lot to learn, don't I?"

After all that had gone on the last few weeks, Neil thought he would never say it.

He looked Doctor Davidson in the eye and pushed out the words. "I'll help you if I can."

Great. Just what he didn't have time for.

It wasn't that she had no faith, she just had doubts that God heard all their pleas for Papa's return. Mama's hand clasped around hers so tight her knuckles whitened. While Doctor Bennett chattered on about the anxious wait for another day for the electricity to come back on, finally getting phone connections, and so on, Hana gazed out on the yard from her vantage point on top of the barrack steps. The news seemed impossible.

Mama's voice broke through Hana's wandering thoughts. "Hana? You hear?"

She jerked her numb hand away. "Are you sure he talked to someone in authority? Could this just be a mean joke?" She hated her suspicious mind. She still couldn't trust Caucasians, except for maybe Doctor Bennett and Nurse Potter. And for sure not Doctor Davidson.

"I heard it myself. I stood right next to him when he finally got through to Doctor Winter. The man is genuine, Hana. He has changed and would never play such a trick. I hope you believe I would never be a part of something like that."

Shame crept up her chest to her hot face. Of course Doctor Bennett would never be cruel. Dare she hope for a glimpse of a miracle—and by way of Doctor Davidson of all people?

"All right. Mama-san, you stay here, and I'll go back with him and talk to Doctor Davidson. Don't say anything to Chiko yet or put anything in your letter to Martin."

Mama mumbled, standing with one hand on the barrack door lever. "She will wonder why we out here so long." Her face wrinkled with a frown.

"Just tell her, um, tell her Doctor Bennett came to get me for an emergency. I don't know. Think of something, Mama-san."

Doctor Bennett grabbed Hana's hand and helped her down the steps. She didn't realize she hadn't let go until she felt his grip tighten. She pulled her hand out of his and picked up the pace toward the hospital. How silly they must have looked, and how easily something like that could get them into trouble. She had heard of the fraternization rules.

At the hospital steps, Doctor Bennett took them two at a time to open the door for her. She scooted in and smiled at Alice sitting at the front desk. "What's the big hurry? An emergency?" She shot up from her chair, but he shook his head.

He nodded her to sit as he passed by. "No, I'll explain later."

Hana stopped at Doctor Davidson's office door which was slightly ajar. She glanced at Doctor Bennett who crowded in ahead of her, tapping as he pushed it open. Doctor Davidson waved them in and continued a conversation on the phone. Hana remembered the other times she had been in his office. Unpleasant memories. Perhaps that had all changed. The next few minutes would tell.

"I understand. So you'll call me when you get a date and time." Doctor Davidson spoke and then paused, listening to the person on the other end of the line. His gaze traveled between Hana and Doctor Bennett, but his face remained solemn.

She pushed down any real hope that this man would or could help. Unlike Mama, she learned long ago to expect the worst from providence. She unclenched her jaw when Doctor Davidson hung up the phone. He rubbed the back of his neck and leaned back in his chair. He looked as though he had just finished a debate to save his life.

Doctor Bennett pulled a chair close to Hana. "I've explained the situation. Have you any more word?"

Doctor Davidson's voice rang with a hint of optimism. He looked straight into her eyes. "I just spoke to Doctor Winter again personally. He had to do some investigating regarding your father, Miss Kato. But he did call me back as soon as he ascertained the condition of Mr. Kato's health."

Hana's confusion grew as she tried to process his new attitude. This couldn't really be happening.

Doctor Bennett stood next to Hana's chair and sounded more anxious than her. "What's the decision about releasing him?"

She tilted her head to marvel at his interest and determination.

Doctor Davidson smiled at Hana, the first genuine happy expression she had ever seen on his face. "I don't want to get your hopes up, but it looks positive."

His words slowly sank into her mind. Could it be that Papa would be with them soon? All her hopes, fears, and anxiety melted into a wall of numbing fog. She closed her eyes to focus on what to say. The doctors must have sensed her emotion—they stayed silent, much to her relief.

"I have so many questions. Tell me, Doctor Davidson, what would be the one thing that could prevent this from happening? I need to know so I can prepare myself and my family."

Doctor Davidson leaned on the desktop. "Two things could stand in the way. One, if his personal record proved he was a danger to the camp community. Second, that he was deemed not to be seriously ill. Doctor Winter says that a mild heart attack may not satisfy the board that your father is indeed better off at Grand Peak than he is in Leavenworth."

She looked into Doctor Davidson's face. "So they aren't so concerned with him putting in his time as they are his health and disposition. Correct?" Her mind spun with other questions, but this seemed important and would determine what other details she needed to know. She held on tight to the bit of clarity she had.

Doctor Davidson sat back. "Well, yes. You're correct. It's only because the Alien Enemy Emergency is over. Even though he is a convicted man, the war seems to be nearing a close, according to rumors, and life will have to get back to normal."

Back to normal. He might have had a change of heart in some areas, however he still showed his ignorance of the current and future suffering for the Japanese Americans in this country. If Papa could join them here, life would be somewhat normal. When they left here, they would have to make a new life.

"So, what's next?" Doctor Bennett piped up.

"I should know by the end of tomorrow if and when he can be released. The word is that if he is let go for medical reasons, they would want him on a train very soon." Doctor Davidson stood and rested his hands on the desk top. He spoke softly, almost tenderly. "I think you have reason to be hopeful, Miss Kato. I'll let you know as soon as the call comes in."

"Thank you. I appreciate all you have done." She wasn't sure why he took the time and trouble for Papa. Especially in light of his former bitterness. She would withhold final judgment on this man until Papa was home safe, packing up the family to leave Grand Peak forever. Even then, she would struggle to trust him.

Doctor Bennett opened the office door for her. They stood in the hall for a few moments. "May I go home and talk to Mama and Chiko before my shift? Chiko is doing well and shouldn't need me to stay at home anymore. I need to keep busy. It will drive me crazy to wait in our barrack."

He grinned. He seemed to be as relieved as she. "I'll tell Nurse Potter you'll be back. She's waiting too. Still hasn't received final approval to adopt Charlie." He leaned back to peer around the corner. "She's not at the front desk. I'll find her and fill her in if that's okay with you."

Hana nodded slowly and wandered through the foyer and outside. Her thoughts whirled with ways to tell Mama and Chiko about the news. Hoping for the best, but preparing for the worst would have to be their plan. Just entertaining the thought of Papa coming home after all these weeks pushed her to the edge of joy. She had to hold back from complete excitement until it was final. Soon she might be able to relinquish her job of keeping the family together and move on with making plans for herself. If the authorities didn't refuse his release. If—

The possibility had to be faced. Papa may never return to them.

God, please bring him back to us.

June 1945

The mess hall resounded with clapping and voices raised. John could hear a man's voice booming through a loud speaker. His breath quickened. Oh, no, not another protester trying to rile up some unsuspecting internees to riot. Hadn't they all learned their lesson?

Between Michael leaving and the possibility of Mr. Kato's eventual return, his place in the camp floated in limbo. George Saito's family had taken the bus home this morning, he had left his dark influence on some young men in camp. There could still be trouble at any time. If only Mr. Kato would come back, he could settle things down—settle *him* down.

Then what would his purpose be? The only thing left for him was to find a place to go and request permission to leave. If he could convince the camp director he had a job and place to live, he would be a free man. Free. Whatever that meant.

Another voice carried out from the hall. He took the steps by two and rushed through the door just as another cheer rose from the two or three dozen men and women sitting in the far end of the hall, most of them women, fanning themselves with small homemade fans. The gentleman causing all the ruckus stood in front, facing John, with a microphone from a small public address system in his hand.

He bellowed over the crowd rumble. "There are many anti-Japanese organizations out there right now…"

Oh boy, here it comes.

The man's tone softened. "But there are just as many pro-Japanese organizations fighting for our rights. People do care. People do want to help us. We are not alone."

The crowd erupted in applause again. John inched toward a chair and slipped into the seat. He had to hear more of this. There would certainly be a punch line soon—a catch that none of these poor people would see coming.

"The Council of Churches has already been assisting families just like yours. Many of us are leaving the camps as permission is given. The president has proclaimed an end to the war emergency where we are concerned, but we must still regain our place in society."

A young man shouted from the other side of the room. "That will never happen. No one out there cares about us. We need to come together all right…come together and fight for our rights."

Some nodded and some mumbled to their neighbor. The man up front seemed to ignore the heckler. "The effort to help us relocate to our homes is gaining strength thanks to the prayers and kindness of members of organizations like the Council of Churches." He slipped off his jacket and held up a pamphlet. "I have information for you to take so that when you are ready to leave here, you have the contact numbers you need."

An older Issei stood and raised his hand. "What about those of us who don't have a home to go back to? Many of us had our property and belongings taken from us." His last few words muffled in an emotional warble.

The troublemaker yelled louder this time. "He's right, and we have to get back what belongs to us...through force if necessary. Let's form a group that is willing to set things straight. It's time to make things happen."

The mumbling rolled over the crowd. John's hands instinctively balled into fists. There was going to be trouble here.

The man with the microphone dropped it to his side and hung his head. After a few moments of women trying to shush the men, the room fell silent with tension. Some of the women pulled out hankies and sniffled into them, a few Issei men walked out, fear painted on their faces. John thought his heart would crack in two.

Then the speaker pulled the microphone to his mouth again. "It's not time to fight. It's time to be smart. I hear that man's burden." He pointed to the older man who spoke up earlier. "This is the story I have heard over and over." His voice cracked as he continued. "It grieves me to hear it. I know many of you have lost everything. I do know there is a God who cares, and people who care. All we can offer you is our best efforts. We cannot solve all your problems, but we will be there for you, standing with you to build a new life. You'll have to fight for your rights in creative ways."

It seemed to John no one spoke or even breathed for a long moment. Then from the row in front of him came a snap of two hands coming together. Slowly first, and singular. Then another joined in and another, until the room was filled with respectful acknowledgment for the man with the mic. The troublemaker made a noisy exit, followed by only two other men.

One by one, people filed to the front to pick up a pamphlet. John stayed until the last guest had exited the building. The speaker sat on a chair in the front row, his head bowed. John stood and put his hand on his chest. Something stirred inside that was unfamiliar to him, yet compelling.

The man up front talked aloud. "God help these people."

John gradually made his way to him and stood at the end of the line of chairs. The man held his hands to his face, crying. John wiped his sweaty palms on his jeans. The room suddenly seemed very small and the man sitting there very big.

He could barely croak out the words. "Excuse me."

The man looked up and smiled. He sat up straight and reached on the chair next to him for a pamphlet, handing it to John. "Here you go, young man."

John held up his hand to reject the paper. "No. No thanks. I just wanted to ask you a few questions. If you don't mind."

"Sure. Have a seat."

John eased into a chair, scooting it to face the man. His heart and mind raced to digest the words he had heard him speak, words he had heard before. Promises not kept seemed like old friends to him, but something was different now. Something he couldn't understand, couldn't pinpoint.

He held in his emotions. "You almost had a riot on your hands. Are you just trying to stir up support for some organization, or are you sincere when you say there is a group of churches wanting to help us? I mean, it all sounds funny to me."

"Nope. It's for real, uh…"

"John. John Yamata."

The man stuck out his hand. "Simon Nishiya."

John pushed to get answers "Well, it's just that I've never heard of churches that wanted to help the Japanese Americans. What kind of churches? Buddhist? Hindu?"

Simon smiled broad and leaned back in his chair, his cheeks still wet from his tears.

"Well, I'm sure there are many other religions helping out. The ones I mention are Christian churches. A few different denominations. I know it might sound strange to many of you who have only had bad experiences with Christians. We aren't all bad, you know. Many Japanese have become Christians. Like me."

John studied his face. He looked like a nice guy, no contradiction in his eyes. Still, he had to be sure, and he had to know why Christians, Caucasian or Japanese, would help. "What's in it for them?"

"Nothing. We're just trying to follow the teachings of Jesus and extend love and a helping hand to our neighbors. It's what He would do, Jesus I mean." He turned in his seat and leaned in closer. John itched to get up and leave, but he was compelled to hear more, as if stuck to his chair.

"So it's because you are required to do this to be a Christian. You're just doing what the head guy says to do."

Simon tipped his head back and chuckled. "Well, you could say that, in a way. It's not because we have to. It's our choice. We just want to please God and make a difference for our fellow man. Simple as that. It's something you want to do when you know the Lord. You just want to do what's right in His sight."

The burning in John's stomach inched up his spine. Who was this Jesus? He had heard he was the Son of God, but it sounded like something different as Simon explained it.

He remembered all the things Hana's mother had said about Jesus, and how Hana had seemed somewhat reluctant to buy it 100 percent. Perhaps he should consider the man's words.

What was it Michael had said about doing good for others?

"So you're telling me that because these churches are followers of Jesus' ways, they are helping our people get a new start. Do they understand how things have been for us? Do they know what a fight they will have on their hands? We're not exactly desirable citizens, you know."

Simon held up one hand. "Let me answer your questions one by one. First, yes, they are followers of Jesus and that's mainly why they do what they do. Second, yes. Many of them have visited the camps and talked to Japanese Americans who have nothing. Just like this Issei man who stood just a while ago. Next, the fight is not against flesh and blood, John. They know prayer will be a big part in making things happen. There are other ways to bring about change than force."

Demonstrations and riots were the only ways John knew to make things change. It hadn't always turned out well. He grew weary of fighting, but felt lost without it. What else was there to live for? He didn't belong to anyone or anything.

"I don't know if I understand it all. I wish I could believe. I don't even know where I'm going when I get out of here. I have no skills and no family. All I've accomplished in the last year is to help lead a group that failed." He stood, embarrassed for sharing so much. This man was a stranger. Perhaps that's what made it easy to spill his story.

"I can help you, and you can help me, John. Our organization needs leaders. Let me tell you more about our—my beliefs. It sounds like you need a place to belong."

The battle that raged inside him was none like he had ever known. Every muscle turned to stone, yet his heart seemed to be melting at the same time. There was nothing left to do but stay and hear the man out.

"Alright, Simon. What can you and this Jesus do for me?"

Chapter 12

Dear Mr. and Mrs. Kato,

I am the lead physician in the surgical department at Fort Sam Houston Convalescent Hospital in San Antonio, Texas. I am writing you concerning your son, Martin Kato. He has informed me you are unaware of his recent injury during a training exercise with his boot camp unit.

First, let me tell you he is in stable condition and has no life-threatening injuries. Apparently, he has not written you about his accident because he is afraid to upset you. I understand your situation in the internment camp must be difficult, but I felt you should know about your son's condition. I did not receive permission from Martin to contact you, I am in hopes he will not be too angry.

I have come to know Martin since his accident and surgery a week ago. He is a fine young man and, you will be proud to know, a hero. He saved the life of several of his fellow recruits when a live grenade landed close to them. He pushed the men out of the way and kicked the grenade to get it away from them. Unfortunately it exploded just after contact and severed his leg. The amputation is just below his knee. He is otherwise in good health with some minor injury to his other leg, but he is very discouraged.

Martin will remain here at the hospital for another two weeks. Then he will be free to join you either at Grand Peak, or your home.

I hope you will call me if you have any questions. My contact information is included in this letter, along with information about our hospital, to put your mind at ease.

Sincerely,

Dr. James A. Robert

Hana slumped into a chair in the exam room. For the first time today, she could take a breath and gather her muddled thoughts. It had been two weeks since Doctor Davidson's call to Leavenworth Hospital. She knew Doctor Bennett grew weary of her asking day after day, but she would rather pester him than keep an ongoing banter with Doctor Davidson.

She and Nurse Potter had worked non-stop for two days, clearing out three whole wards and packing up extra equipment and supplies to be shipped who knows where. As the families left camp, the number of patients dwindled and emergencies only trickled in occasionally.

"This room finished?" Nurse Potter bounced in the room and threw a white towel over her shoulder. Her smile dropped when Hana looked up at her. "You look like you're in bad shape. Why don't you go home, young lady? I can finish up here. Besides, your mama needs you. She's probably beside herself with worry about your brother." She stepped in front of Hana and held out her hand. "Up you go."

Once on her feet, the fatigue she fought all day hit her square in the face. She closed her eyes to stop the room from spinning her to the floor. "Since the letter came about Martin, I've tried to stuff my emotions for Mama's sake. I'm just afraid when I face my feelings I'll break. Do you think that's wrong?"

"Don't know about that. Sometimes it's a good thing, sometimes not. I do know that you've had no time to bemoan Martin's heartbreaking condition. A strong active young man like Martin is bound to be devastated. You falling apart won't help that."

Hana groaned. "When will all this get better?" She rubbed her sore shoulders.

"Let's go." She marched Hana out to the foyer. "Can you get home without help? It's rather warm again today."

Hana turned and crossed her arms. "Nurse Potter, you would have made a great drill sergeant."

"It's Alice. And don't think you're the first person to tell me that." She threw her head back and laughed from her belly.

At that moment, Hana felt more affection for her than she thought she could possibly feel for a Caucasian. She would miss her when all this was over. How sad to think she might never see her again. "You've been so kind. I like you, Alice."

Nurse Potter stopped chuckling and stood very still. Her lip quivered and she placed her hand on Hana's arm. "I like you too. I'm sorry we had to meet in this place."

Hana's heart cracked like a broken vase. She had to leave before she made a scene of tears. "See you tomorrow."

Down the steps and out into the yard that led to the barracks, Hana mindlessly put one foot in front of the other, numb and tired. The sun bore down and cast a long forlorn shadow on the side of the buildings. She approached the recreation hall and reached into her pocket. One dime and one nickel. The nickel would get her a cold Coca Cola out of the cooler. She could get an extra one and take it home to Chiko.

Just inside the door, John sat at a table scribbling on a pad of paper. She hadn't seen him around much in the last week. Did he even know about Martin?

He caught sight of her and smiled, motioning her over to the table.

"Hi, John." Her heart skipped when she looked into his face. She had missed him more than she realized.

"Hey, Hana. Good to see you. How are you?"

She slipped into the bench on the other side of the table. His hair was combed back and his tee shirt and jeans were as tidy as she'd ever seen them. She had to break the news. "I don't suppose you heard about Martin."

His smile disappeared and he sat up rigid. "No. What?"

"He lost his leg in a training accident at boot camp." It still stung to say the words.

John closed his eyes tight. "No. Not Martin." His eyes popped open again and he blurted out the question she knew he would ask. "Can he walk?"

"Yes."

His demeanor changed completely from just a moment ago. She hated telling him—hated the pain of explaining about Martin. Not too many people cared anyway. She knew John would.

John threw down the pencil. It rolled toward Hana. "I'm so sorry. Your family has had just about enough, don't you think?" She caught the pencil and tapped it on his pad.

She felt the fatigue pulling her down. "It wouldn't have happened if he hadn't been drafted. That's what happens when Caucasians make the decisions for all of us."

"Hana, I've never heard you talk like that. You know there's a God that cares and holds Martin in his hands."

She pulled back and tossed the pencil onto the table. "Well, I've never heard *you* talk like *that.* Have you been spending time with Mama while I'm at work?" Something clicked inside—a certain recognition or connection to something familiar. When had he changed? Since when did his countenance include that peaceful expression Mama always wore?

"I'm just seeing things differently these days. Hana, you've always talked about your mother's faith as truth, but you never seem to be all for it. Why is that?"

Hana stared at him. He couldn't be serious. They had never discussed faith on a personal level before. She did believe in God and in miracles and in His love, but something blocked her love for Him.

Her fingers tapped on the table. "Really? Is this what we're going to talk about?" She glanced at her watch. No use trying to say that she had to go. She didn't. Maybe it was time to tell him how God had let her down.

John rolled the pencil back and forth. "Not if you don't want to.

I know if you're going to help Martin or even your father when they come home, you need to be free from your pain. I know my pain came from all my anger. Just thought it might be the same for you." He picked up his pencil again and pulled the pad in front of him.

Hana surveyed the hall. Only a few other internees off in the corner shared the room with them. If she spilled her guts, it would be to John alone. It seemed safe enough.

"All right. You want to hear about it, I'll tell you. But this is the last time I'm going to talk about it and my family is never to know. Got it?"

He nodded. Looking into his eyes, she saw the young man that stole her heart those first few weeks here. From the start, they talked comfortably together, as if they had always been friends. Then the group got in the way. The look in his eyes now told her she could tell him everything. She needed to tell him.

"You know I was at Pearl Harbor during the bombing, right?"

"Yeah."

"The morning Pearl was bombed, I was sitting at a coffee shop with my nurse friends. We had just finished our night shift and I was going to have breakfast and go home to bed. All of a sudden we heard planes roaring overhead. One of them flew directly over the top of our quarters in the next block." Hana's eyes darted up to the ceiling.

"Go on."

"We thought at first it was flyboys from Hickam Field. Then we heard the bombing and ran to the window. It looked like the whole harbor was on fire. Black smoke everywhere. Someone in the street screamed that they were Japanese planes."

John pulled his hands from his lap and folded them on top of the table. His eyes never left her gaze, and he didn't interrupt. He had always been a good listener.

"I knew I had to get to the hospital if this was a real attack. They would need all personnel. So I left the shop and dashed across the street, through a shrapnel shower. I was so scared, and I ran as fast as I could. The streets filled with people running—women and children, soldiers. I just kept dodging flying debris and moved toward the hospital. Then something hot and hard hit the back of my head. I fell and everything around me started spinning. I could smell hot metal and smoke. The sky over the harbor was almost totally black."

"Were you hurt bad?" She had John's attention for sure. He reached over for her hand, but she pulled away.

"I passed out for a little while. When I woke up someone was tugging at my arms, pulling me. I heard voices. 'Dirty Jap, leave her. There are real Americans to help. Let her die.' It was a Caucasian seaman. I'll never forget those words."

Her heartbeat thumped in her temples, heating her ears. She had to go on with the story.

"He kicked me in the side. I coiled up and he came after me again and grabbed me by the hair and spit in my face. The other seaman followed suit and kicked me in the back. Then they left me there, bleeding from my head and hardly able to move." Her throat clogged with tears so she swallowed hard. Hearing it out loud brought back sights and smells she had tried so hard to forget.

John slapped his palm on the table. "I can't believe it. What kind of men would do that?"

Hana couldn't quit now. "I laid there until the bombing stopped. I don't know how long it was, maybe an hour, I don't remember. Then I crawled across the street and up the steps of our quarters. I heard footsteps running toward me. I was so afraid it was the men coming back. I pulled myself up on the porch and hid behind the railing. Then I blacked out. I woke up screaming in a hospital bed. I don't know how I got there." She sighed long and hard to clear her voice and relax her queasy stomach. So many others never made it through that day. She was grateful for surviving.

"I didn't sleep without nightmares for months. Not about the bombing, but about the beating I got from Caucasian soldiers. My head injury healed and the bruises on the outside went away. I've just never trusted another white person again. Sometimes I think I hate all of them. They took something from me, not just my freedom, but my dignity."

"Hana, you're going to go home soon. Doesn't that help?"

"What home? Do you think it's going to be easy out there? They still hate us, John. I've been able to come to like Alice, you know, Nurse Potter…and Doctor Bennett, but the rest of them I can't forgive."

There it was in a nutshell. She heard it from her own lips and knew how it went against everything she heard in Sunday school—everything her parents had taught her. She used to believe in forgiveness. That was before Pearl.

She stood. "Anyway, I guess you know why I'm struggling to trust God these days."

John's face paled. "I'm more sorry than I can say. My heart hurts for you. Makes my problems seem pretty small, my mountains not so tall. I guess we both need God to help us."

There was God again. What was it with his new religious thinking? She looked at her watch. Now she really was out of time. She put the nickel back in her pocket. The craving for soda had disappeared.

John stood. "Hana, you know how I feel—"

She couldn't let him go there. "Don't, John. I have to go. I'll let you know when we hear about Martin coming home. I hope it's before Papa gets here, but, well, I'll find you."

She bolted out the door and down the steps, tears streaming off her face. Partly relieved and partly stirred up she made her way toward her barrack. There would be so much to do to prepare for both the Kato men to come back. She'd have to push down all the emotions again and keep Mama and Chiko strong and busy.

They would look to her for strength, and she would have to pretend she had some left over.

"Chiko, he'll be home in a week. Why don't you wait and say it all in person?" Hana grabbed another piece of clean clothing from the basket. Mama had insisted on washing all of Martin's clothes before he arrived. Without knowing what the status of his leg was, or even which leg was missing, she wouldn't cut off any pant legs. They wanted to be ready for Martin's homecoming, and Papa's too if they could just know when it would be. There had been no news after three weeks and Hana had almost given up hope it would happen.

Chiko frowned. "I think he needs to get a letter now. He must be very sad and I know how he feels—well, sort of."

Hana left her pile and sat next to Chiko on her cot. "Are you still sad about your scar?" Hana's stomach panged with guilt. She had neglected to make sure her sister had healed emotionally. With their lives in turmoil most of the time, she couldn't keep track of everyone. She hadn't reached out to Chiko like she should have.

"Sometimes. I forget that it's there and then I look in the mirror and want to cry. But not all the time. Michael stitched it up so nice and tight, it really doesn't show that much." She leaned forward to see where Mama was in the room, then whispered in Hana's ear.

"I wish Mama would let me wear some makeup to help cover it."

Hana shook her head and gave Chiko a squeeze around the shoulders. "Maybe I could talk to her. She just might have changed her mind since Doctor Okada mentioned it."

The whispering over, Hana resumed her chore. "When you're done with the letter, would you let me add a note at the end?"

"Me too." Mama raised her hand, still sorting through all the old letters that came rejecting Papa's release. It would be better if she put them away, but there was no convincing her. They only needed to know when Papa would travel back to Grand Peak.

Chiko chewed the end of her pencil and then looked up from her letter. "I'll read it to you and then you can write something."

Hana rolled her eyes. The last thing she wanted to concentrate on tonight was the rambling letter of a teenager. She finished folding the last tee shirt and plopped onto a chair. Mama stilled her hands.

"Okay, go."

After clearing her throat several times, as if getting ready to sing an aria, Chiko read aloud.

Dear Martin,

I was very sorry to hear about your accident. I hope your leg is much better now and that you are learning to walk just as good as before. You are so lucky to be alive and I am too. I know you don't know about my accident. We didn't want to worry you. I fell and hit my head on a table. It knocked me out and cut my head real bad and my face too. Doctor Bennett and another man named Michael rushed me to the hospital but there was no one there to do a good surgery for me. We found out Michael was a face surgeon before the war and he operated on me.

I have a scar on my face. It's not too bad. I just didn't want you to be scared when you saw me. Like I said, you and I are lucky. I know you might think you can't do the things you used to. I thought I would never be pretty again. It makes me sad sometimes.

If you get sad, just remember how God saved you from dying so you could save those other guys.

I miss you and can't wait to see you again. We will all be together when Papa comes home and it will make everything all right.

See you soon. I love you.

Chiko

She put the paper in her lap and looked up at them. Hana could barely speak after such tender words. Leave it to a selfish little teenager to come up with encouraging, healing sentiments. Now if only Martin received them well.

Mama cried and cried. Chiko jumped up and ran to wrap her arms around her mother. "Isn't it okay? I tried to make it sound good. I hope I said the right things."

"It beautiful, like you, my Sachiko." Mama wiped her tears and returned to her paperwork.

Hana stood and gave Chiko a warm hug. Pride for a sister emerging as a young woman, with charm and wisdom, had eluded her until now. It seemed that this place muddled everything she saw and heard. Her filter had broken and she hated it. So many people turning from caterpillars to butterflies lately. Doctor Davidson, John, and now Chiko.

"Great letter, sis. I don't want to add a thing. I should have had you writing letters to get Papa out. They'd have let him go sooner." It was for sure now, but it would be a few more weeks before they would see him walk off that train. A few more weeks until the Katos would be together again.

Someone knocked at the door. She answered to find John. He still carried himself in his newfound posture. "Hi, John."

"Hi. I hope it's not too late to visit. I need to talk to you and your mother if it's okay."

She swung the door open and he stepped inside, checking his shoes first. After their talk in the recreation hall a few days ago, she had seen him only in the distance as he walked to and from another building. No doubt she had driven him away with the candid account of her Pearl Harbor experience. She thought he cared more than that.

Right now his usual shyness had been replaced by a cheerful attitude. "How are all of you tonight?" He winked at Chiko, who giggled and returned to address her envelope for Martin's letter.

"Please sit." Mama pointed to a chair. "You want tea? I have pot on stove."

"Oh, no thanks. It's still too hot this evening for tea."

"At least not hot like June last year. July just around corner, then very hot."

Mama was chatty tonight. Hana marveled at how John could bring out the conversationalist in everyone these days.

He scooted to the edge of the chair. "I'll get right to the point. I'd like to throw a party for Martin when he comes home, and I need to know if you have anyone you'd like invited. I mean besides the guys he hung out with." His eyes moved between Mama and Hana.

As soon as the words sunk in, Hana felt her breath catch in her chest. Party? He couldn't be serious. By all indications Martin's spirits were not high, and the fact that he didn't even write to his family about his injury created a red flag about his emotional state.

She hated to be blunt, but this idea had to be squashed. "No party."

John's smile disappeared. "Excuse me?"

"I said no party. Martin is likely in no mood to celebrate his lost leg." Her chest hurt to have this discussion. John should have known better.

"Hana." Mama flashed her typical look of disapproval.

"I'm sorry, Mama-san. We have to consider Martin's state of mind. He didn't even want to tell us about his leg, and the doctor said he was discouraged. He needs time to adjust."

John stood and shook his head. "I think you're wrong. A party wouldn't be about his loss, it would be about our gain that he isn't worse off. Martin would understand and enjoy it."

She had never seen him stand up to her before. He seemed to know what he wanted and stood tall with conviction. He just didn't understand Martin as well as she did. She grew up with him and knew how his pride would take precedence.

Chiko jumped up and stood between John and Hana. "I think a party would be perfect."

John nudged her and returned his attention to the argument. "I would make sure it was tastefully done." He paused and glanced at Mama. "But if you are against it, of course I won't do it."

Mama didn't speak up, so the decision defaulted to Hana. There couldn't be any other answer. The risk of offending Martin wouldn't be worth satisfying John's need to throw him a party.

"I say no. It's too risky. If Martin is in trouble emotionally, we have to be careful to support him the way he needs to be supported. I'm sorry, John. I know you mean well and we're grateful for your friendship. I hope you understand."

He nodded and moved toward the door. With his hand on the knob he turned to her. "I think you're wrong, but I suppose we shouldn't risk hurting him. We can always plan one later when we see how he is, right?"

"Right!" Chiko's enthusiasm made John laugh. Hana felt bad for putting her foot down, but someone had to. But then there was Mama's silence.

When John left, Hana kept a close eye on Mama, feeling a certain tension surrounding her. Mama always had an opinion, and often kept it to herself. This time it seemed to be on the tip of her tongue. The evening wouldn't finish on a good note unless Mama spoke her mind.

"Mama? Are you upset about not having the party?"

"It could be right thing to do. We need to think some more." She pulled out her Bible from under her pillow and curled up on her cot. "We talk tomorrow."

The push and pull of opinions had Hana second guessing her decision. Preparing for Martin's return had turned into a battle of wills. Mama would pray about it, but sleeping on it seemed more reasonable.

Chiko would side with Mama and John. Maybe she was wrong, maybe this would be good for Martin. She just didn't want to make a mistake. The best thing that could happen would be if Papa made it home before Martin. It seemed now it wasn't meant to be.

The uncertainty had gone on long enough. Even Mama was waning under the long wait. This week she would approach Doctor Davidson and see if he could speed up the process. Her doubts followed her to bed and when heavy eyelids made for sleep, she wished for relief from the responsibility Papa had given her.

He had to come home soon. She didn't know how much longer she could last.

Chapter 13

Since the day he prayed with Simon, John's life had centered and started to make sense. A new feeling. He pulled the pamphlet from his top drawer and read the first page of Council of Churches information. No more foggy thinking, no more chasing after other people's ideas of right and wrong. He had some ideas of his own, but he needed to talk to someone like Simon to confirm his plans.

He folded the paper and tucked it in his jeans pocket. He had to find a phone and call the number printed on the back of the pamphlet. As he made his way to the administration building, he marveled at all the people leaving Grand Peak. Even though so many had already taken their chance to leave, the head count in camp stood at around 9,000. Only 2,000, give or take, had finally found the freedom they deserved.

"They give us twenty-five dollars and a train ticket, and say good-bye," an old Issei had told him yesterday. "How we supposed to go home with that? And what home is left?"

John's heart broke for him and all the others he had been interviewing over the last few weeks. Keeping busy felt liberating, and this time there would be a good outcome.

He nearly slid as he stumbled down the hard packed dirt hill. Stopping to secure his footing, he shaded his eyes against the scorching sun. From here the barracks seemed to stretch on forever, almost reaching the base of the mountain. Thankfully, it was only an illusion, or else he would have run away and lost himself on its slopes forever. Instead, the vast scablands surrounding the outside of the fence made a buffer of dry wasteland. Only the small acres of agriculture provided a relief from the view.

"Hey."

Doctor Bennett plodded up the hill in his direction. John resumed his descent and met up with him half way. He wondered if this man would see a difference in him, a change showing on his face. The perfect Doctor Bennett would surely relate to him now that he had decided to trust in God. The closer he got to him the more absurd the idea sounded.

He gave a subtle wave. "Hello."

Doctor Bennett looked down to the ground to avoid the blaring sunlight. "How are you, John? How's the foot?"

John moved to the side so both could look at each other without squinting. "Good. Almost back to normal. I don't notice it anymore. Thanks for fixing me up. I'm just sorry about what happened to Chiko because I had trouble with George. I should have waited until I felt better."

Doctor Bennett adjusted his stance. "I should have pulled you out of there before things got out of hand. I've never been good at confrontation." He held his hand to his brow. "Where you headed?"

"Admin."

"Just came from there. Had a little trouble of my own to straighten out. The big wig from Billings was here to—well, anyway, I hope I'm free and clear."

Doctor Bennett in trouble? John doubted it could be anything serious. The accolades from the Kato family and hospital staff made it sound like he was as important as Roosevelt.

"You're not in trouble again, are you?" Doctor Bennett smiled and tipped his head toward the building below.

Right. His reputation still followed him. "Just need to use the phone. Brought my nickels." He jingled the change in his pocket. The reason for his call would remain his business.

"You can use the phone in my office if you want. It's free if you keep it quiet. Only supposed to be for medical business, but I don't much care about rules. I don't think you're calling the Japanese Mafia or anything sinister. Are you?"

John wasn't sure whether to take offense or laugh. Still, he was tired of standing there in the heat, and would just as soon save his nickels. He would take Doctor Bennett up on his offer and see what developed. Maybe some questions about Hana might spark a debate. He pushed away thoughts of competing for her affection with the good doctor. "Sure, I'd like that. You headed there now?"

"Yep, let's go." Doctor Bennett took off up the hill and to their right. The dust beneath his feet flew up in the breeze so John caught up with him.

He couldn't resist prodding. "Hana doing okay with her nursing duties?"

Doctor Bennett didn't answer. John didn't expect he would. They trudged through the field, taking the short cut to the hospital side door. Although Doctor Bennett could be a foot taller, he didn't have a knack for dodging large rocks. He stumbled over one and John caught his arm, sparking an answer. "Thanks. She's always done great. She's a wonderful nurse and a very nice person. Why do you ask?"

Why *did* he ask? Deep inside he knew why. He loved Hana. Period. End of story. And he didn't want anyone to get in the way, so he had to know if this Caucasian man could be a threat to his plan to win Hana. Was it ridiculous to imagine her falling for the great doctor? He wouldn't take the chance.

"Just curious. I know how much she loves nursing and that she wasted so much time being fearful to go back to it—with good reason." He hoped his words pushed the conversation in the direction he needed.

"Hmm. I guess I don't know the story. I'm just glad she came to us. Both for the hospital and me personally."

Bingo. He had hit a nerve. Now to get to the meat of the issue. They stepped in sync up the steps to the door of the hospital. He followed Doctor Bennett to the office marked with his name. C.O.S.

He didn't even know what that meant, but it didn't matter what title he held, he couldn't have Hana without a fight.

Doctor Bennett waved his arm toward the corner. "Please, sit behind the desk. The phone is probably under a pile of paperwork, you'll find it. Before you make the call I think we should talk." He flopped into one chair and propped his legs up on one opposite.

John felt his jaw clench. He'd started it and now had a full blown confrontation on his hands. He would admit the man was intuitive—and gutsy. He turned the chair to face him, his stomach rolling. Maybe that was Doctor Bennett's plan.

John sat hard on the chair. "Okay, that's fine with me. I'll tell you up front that I have loved Hana since the day I first saw her three years ago. She's Japanese American, so am I. You're not. You can't possibly understand her and what she's been through. I can. It's really that simple, and if you care for her, you will not pursue her." He caught his breath after the long tirade and sat up straight in the chair, his hands firmly folded in his lap. His eyes remained locked on Doctor Bennett's face.

Doctor Bennett leaned his head against the back of the chair. After a long silence he pulled his legs to the floor and leaned forward.

"I can tell you've thought this through. My words will be more spontaneous, so bear with me." He paused and rubbed his forehead. John almost wished he hadn't goaded him into this. Had his words really sounded so scripted? The educated man could probably talk him down in two sentences.

"I'll be straightforward too. I have deep affection for Hana. It could be love and I'm fully aware of what that could mean if she returned my feelings. So far she hasn't. But I believe she might if given a chance. If she did, I would gladly embrace a relationship. If you want to consider this a challenge, go ahead. I happen to think that God will show her and me if we are to be together."

He leaned back and John waited for him to say more.

Doctor Bennett scratched at the stubble on his chin. "I know you don't understand this. I pray about my life, and if Hana is to be a part of it, I'll know."

Prayer. The word felt like a rock thrown at him. He would throw it right back.

"I know about praying. I've become a Christian, and though I have much to learn, I too believe God will show Hana the way. If it's a challenge you want, we will have to fight with prayer. I still believe she would be better off with someone who has been through what she has."

Doctor Bennett's eyes widened. Perhaps his declaration had shocked him. "Fair enough. I'll leave you to your call." He rose and grabbed the doorknob, turning to look John square in the eyes. "Congratulations, and welcome to the family of God." He tipped his head and smiled.

John knew he meant it sincerely. Despite everything between them, he liked the doctor, but he could never agree with God if Doctor Bennett won Hana. If God took Hana, he would have no one. The thought made his chest ache. It could be a long wait, and God just might test him through it all.

Shoving papers away he found the phone. Lifting the receiver he dialed zero and waited for the operator to come on.

"Yes, operator, I need long distance. I have the number. The call is for Mr. Simon Nishiya."

As he waited God nudged him.

Leave her to Me.

July 1, 1945

The waves of heat rippled across the air like a butterfly searching for a place to land. The men and women sitting on crates and suitcases at the train station found what they could to fan themselves. The odor of perspiration struck Hana as she walked through the yard looking for a sliver of shade for Mama and Chiko to wait. She tried to imagine where everyone was going and what kind of future lie ahead for all of them. As much as the last three-plus years had dragged on, it seemed impossible that their suffering was drawing to an end. Or was it?

Mama and Chiko huddled under the eve of the terminal building. Chiko had dressed up for Martin, using her new found skills at applying makeup. Hana chuckled over Mama's lost battle, surrendering to Hana's convincing argument for Chiko to wear ever so little.

"Are you cooler sitting here, Mama-san?"

Mama nodded and craned her neck every time she heard a loud noise. They should have waited until closer to the train's arrival to come to meet it, but Mama's nerves couldn't handle staying at home another minute, no matter what the temperature. "We go now." She had declared.

In the distance the low roar of a train engine echoed through the thin hot air. A small crowd stood and moved toward the tracks, staring and pointing. Hana didn't want to move. Any energy expended in this heat took as much strength as running a mile. Her heart thumped when she felt the rumble of the train rising from the ground. Martin would be home. Not the same as he left, but home.

"Hana, come here with us." Mama circled her arm in the air and smiled. Chiko fussed with her skirt and tucked loose strands of hair back up in her comb. Hana handed both of them a tissue to dab their wet brows. They must all look fresh and presentable for Martin.

She inched closer to them while watching the dusty train cars creep to a long halt. The train fit the slow motion of life, taking people away and bringing them back. Soon Papa would be on another train pulling into the station.

"Martin!" Chiko hollered next to Hana.

"Shh. Don't embarrass him."

"Oh, he won't mind." She jumped up and down waving both arms.

Hana turned and put her face inches from Chiko's. She took Chiko's hands in hers. "Martin is a proud man. This may be difficult for him to see us for the first time since his amputation. Don't overdo it, please."

Chiko's eyes filled with tears and she hung her head. She didn't want to scold, but Martin's feelings were more important at the moment. She squeezed Chiko's hands. "But we need to be cheerful, okay? No tears. You're a doll. Martin will be happy to see you look so pretty."

The teen managed a smile and composed herself.

Tears dried, the three of them linked arms. Servicemen and local Caucasians jumped from the train steps. One by one Hana counted the seconds, then minutes. Just when it seemed there was no one left to disembark, Martin appeared at the end of the passenger car to their right. He propped a crutch under each arm and a soldier beside him threw a duffle bag to the ground in front of them. The bag had the stamped name of Kato on one side.

Martin leaned on the young man for a second until he looked straight at Hana. Then pushing away, he braced himself on the crutches and placed them down one step. Mama gasped, and Hana held her arm to keep her still.

"Let him try, Mama-san," she whispered over the bustle of voices and shuffling shoes.

Her stomach turned to knots as she watched him make another step on his own, wavering back and forth on the crutches. She grabbed Mama's hand and took a few steps toward him through a crowd of onlookers slowly dispersing. Each step he maneuvered must have been like walking in quick sand. Poor Martin. She would get closer in case he fell, enough to catch him if she could get past two ladies wearing large straw hats. Against her compulsion to push past them, she waited for them to move.

She peered around one women in time to see Martin attempt the last step. In horror she watched the crutch slip out from under his grip. He grimaced as his footing gave way and his arm flailed, flinging one of the crutches. His body coiled in a tumble. She watched the slow motion action, frozen and tense.

Chiko screamed behind her. Just before he reached the ground, someone came from nowhere, stepped in to break his fall and hold him up. She squeezed between the two ladies to see what was happening.

Doctor Bennett.

"Easy." He spoke calmly to Martin's red face.

Hana forgot about her grip on Mama's hand. Her arm extended to the end of its reach, she let go of Mama and hurried to Martin's side. She grabbed one of his arms and Doctor Bennett pulled on the other until Martin was upright, although unsteady and wobbling nearly out of control.

"I'm fine. Just get me out of here. Everyone is staring." Martin growled at Hana. She wanted to cry, imagining his anguish and frustration. She held it in for his sake. If only Papa had come home before Martin.

She held his arm close and struggled to straighten his crutches. She glanced at Doctor Bennett whose eyes darted between her and Martin. Mama and Chiko stood clutching each other, Chiko's eyes wide and her face streaked with tears. Hana had an unsettling urge to laugh at Chiko's ruined make up. Mama smiled and took a few shuffled steps, leaving Chiko behind.

Martin finally looked up and grinned at Mama. Hana wondered if he would realize who propped up his left side. He never had the admiration for Doctor Bennett the rest of the family did. There were times when he seemed almost hostile. Recollections of his sarcasm about the "white doctors" resonated in her ears now.

Doctor Bennett spoke up. "Careful, there's a step." Martin jerked his head toward his helper. The grin disappeared.

After a few more labored paces, Martin stopped short of Mama's embrace. He pulled his arm away from Doctor Bennett and stared at him.

His eyes turned cold and his mouth twitched. "Thanks, but I don't need your help. *We* don't need your help." Mama took the last few steps in his direction and hugged him around the neck. Chiko joined in, taking Doctor Bennett's place under Martin's arm.

Hana's throat tightened when he backed away, sympathy written on his face. Again she felt like crying. Martin had been rude and she wanted so much to rebuke him, but couldn't in these circumstances. His attitude had only worsened about Doctor Bennett. Why? The questions would have to wait for another time, when she could observe Martin's state of mind.

Martin leaned into Mama. "It's good to see you, Mama-san. I'm sorry it's like this." He looked down to his leg. His eyes had lost their sparkle and Hana knew Mama's heart must be breaking for her son. She would have gladly taken his burden from him. Yet, Mama would be the first to say his injury could all be part of God's plan. So much faith in such a little person.

When she looked back, Doctor Bennett was gone. She ached to thank him and explain about Martin. She would be sure to find him at the hospital tomorrow. His appearance at the station today confirmed his kind heart. He lived up to the Christian name, unlike so many others—even of their own kind. Surely Martin would see that in time. If there was enough time. She sighed to think of not working with Doctor Bennett anymore.

Mama patted Martin's arm. "We have good food prepared for you. Someone sneak into camp special things. We take you home now. You rest." Hana slipped away from his side. Mama hooked his arm and the three went ahead of her. She hung back hoping to see Doctor Bennett. Her eyes scanned the yard, but only Japanese faces looked back at her.

"Coming, Hana?" Martin had turned around. He stood his ground, frowning, until she caught up with them. She clenched her teeth. He had no right to be so cold. *Grace, I must extend grace.*

Martin gripped the rails and looked up at Mr. Hahn, the bus driver. Mama stepped close to him, reaching to assist him up the steps.

"Welcome back, Martin. We are proud of you," Mr. Hahn said as he left his seat and extended a hand down to him.

Martin took hold and hopped up one step at a time, each hop making a thud against the metal steps and jarring the bus. Hana cringed to think of the pressure on his foot and the humiliation he must feel. Her impatience at his attitude seemed trivial now.

Mama and Chiko followed Martin onto the bus. Hana took one last look around. At the other end of the yard Doctor Bennett jumped into the front seat of the rusted old hospital van. How strange he was there to come to Martin's rescue.

She could hear Chiko chattering through the open windows. Martin would get a good dose of what he had missed all these months. She would have to whisper to little sister to hush.

The only empty seat left on the bus was next to a young Japanese woman who sat staring out the window, handkerchief to her nose. Hana waved to Mama and slid in next to the crying female. Between her compulsion to comfort the woman, and her smoldering emotions about Martin, she would have a long trip back to camp.

"Are you all right?" Hana whispered to her companion.

"Yes, well no. I just saw my husband off on the train. He's headed overseas. Army. He's been home on leave for a week." She sniffled into her handkerchief. "I may never see him again."

"Oh, I'm sure he'll come back. Most do, you know. The odds are in his favor." Hana wasn't sure her facts rang true. She only wanted to give a glimmer of hope to the sad girl.

"I hope so. He was lucky to be able to be here with me on leave. They could have made him stay out." She tucked her hanky in her pocketbook.

"Why would they keep him out of camp? Doesn't he live there with you?"

Hana thought of all the other young men from camp who had obeyed the government's call to join the fighting. Her feelings were still mixed on the topic. Why would they want to fight for a government that imprisoned them? Papa had asked that question a dozen times before he was arrested.

"He has only visited sometimes. He's not Japanese. He's Caucasian." She returned her gaze to the window, her small frame jolted by the bouncing bus.

It was as though electricity had jolted her heart, boring deeper into a wound she fought so hard to seal over. The world had changed. Bit by little bit, and still changing. Her emotions meshed into a jumble of questions reverberating in her mind. A Japanese woman had been married to a white man in war time, throwing off fear to face it together. It reminded her of how she was once so brave. Stretching her courage to go to Pearl Harbor, far away from her family and nursing buddies. It seemed so right, yet had turned so bad.

How would this family ever survive the new world out there? What if Chiko fell in love with a white man? No. She wouldn't think of it now. Besides, it was unthinkable—for either of them. At least until the pain and division of the war died away.

She caught a glimpse out the window of Doctor Bennett's van moving in front of the bus. Her heart warmed to think he had been there for Martin, or tried to be. Even John wasn't there. He should have been.

After three days of watching Hana drag herself into work, dark circles under her eyes and without her usual pleasantries, Neil couldn't resist speaking to her about it any longer. He left word with Nurse Potter, who had expressed equal concern, for Hana to come to his office as soon as she reported for duty.

If she needed rest, he would give her time off. If she needed a friend to talk to, he prayed she would open up to him. After his conversation with John about her, he knew he would have to follow his heart or prepare to leave Grand Peak. Doctor Davidson could handle the remainder of the year as long as the other Japanese doctors didn't leave too soon.

"Doctor Bennett, I was told you wanted to see me." Hana's dark eyes drooped a bit and her shoulders slumped ever so slightly. Her voice scratched like sandpaper.

He stood, thinking over his words carefully. Go easy. "Come in and have a seat." She shuffled to a chair and raised her brows. He longed for her to smile.

"How's Martin? I bet the family is happy to have him home."

She nodded and looked past him out the window. He squinted to see a pool of tears form in her eyes; her big brown eyes that rarely sparkled anymore.

She zeroed in on his face and edged to the front of the chair. "Is there something you needed to talk to me about?"

There was just no way to circle around the issue. "I'm worried about you. You seem exhausted, distracted, and not your usual self. Can you tell me what's going on? Do you need time off?"

Each question seemed to bombard her like bullets and her composure slowly crumbled, along with the dam holding back her tears. He stood and inched around the desk to lean on the front of it. Her shoulders shook with silent sobs.

"Hana, please talk to me."

She looked up, her eyes red and sad. "It's Martin. He's…he's not the same. He's bitter and angry and won't do anything for himself. He sits around, expecting Mama and Chiko to fetch for him. He won't talk unless he has to, and at night he has nightmares that keep us all awake." Her words tumbled out of her in a landslide. Then she took a deep breath.

She wiped tears with her sleeve. It confirmed what he suspected. He sensed Martin's attitude when he helped him off the train that day. At this moment he would like to get his hands around Martin's neck and choke some sense into him. She deserved better treatment, even from a wounded soul. Self-pity was an unacceptable attitude in this situation.

"I sit up with him for hours so I don't get much sleep. I worry all day wondering if he is running Mama ragged. The only time he leaves our place is to go to the latrine. I don't know what to do."

Neil bit his lip for a moment and handed her his handkerchief. Think. Something had to be done to make this better.

"Wasn't he sent home with orders for rehab? I've seen it help more than just a patient's mobility. It helps their morale too." He paused. "I'm sorry, but it sounds like Martin needs a kick in the rear." He walked to the window, wondering how they would ever get him to come to the hospital for a prosthesis and physical therapy. Hana wasn't in any shape to drag him here.

He turned to her. "Who would he listen to?" She blew her nose and nestled into the chair and shook her head. "If we could just get him here, we could start with exercises to strengthen, and then order his prosthesis."

"He won't listen to anyone. He's too angry." She hung her head for a moment. "I know what that's like. He's a man and that makes it worse. I worry for Mama's sake." She fiddled with the handkerchief, folding it into a small square, then unfolding it.

Neil held out his arms toward the door. "Then we might have to go to him. But we'd need an excuse."

A voice boomed from just outside the door. "You've got one."

They both jerked their heads toward Doctor Davidson who stood with arms folded, grinning like Neil had never seen before. Hana straightened up at the sight of her adversary.

He cleared his throat, keeping Hana in his peripheral. "Doctor Davidson, come in."

Her face turned red. She stood and moved toward the door, glaring at Neil. It dawned on him she had misinterpreted Doctor Davidson's demeanor and comment.

"Miss Kato, wait." Doctor Davidson spoke softly. "I didn't mean to sound so flippant and I'm sorry to eavesdrop. I heard just enough to know that my news might help. Please sit. Let me explain."

She first looked at Neil and relented when he nodded. Doctor Davidson had nearly botched a good chance to win her over.

He felt strands of hair sticking to his forehead. This better be good. "Tell us what you mean."

Doctor Davidson settled into a more relaxed posture, leaning near Hana. "If Martin needs incentive to get back on his feet, I think his father coming home would do it, don't you?" He stared into her face, not moving a muscle.

"You've heard something." She stared back with sparks flying from her eyes.

One side of his mouth curled up. "Yes. I just got the call to say he'll arrive on the train at Center City on July 20th. They are making a special stop there for internees leaving and arriving to join their families here. He'll be on that train. You won't have far to go to pick him up. Of course he'll be guarded until released into your mother's custody."

Neil held his breath waiting for her to speak or acknowledge the information. This is what Hana had been waiting for, working so hard to make happen. Now his heart wrenched to think how strange it would be to see the end of this struggle.

"Are you sure? This time it's for certain? What is his condition and why did it take so long?" She rattled off questions faster than Doctor Davidson could answer them. He patiently waited for her to finish.

"Wait, one at a time." Doctor Davidson leaned back. "I'm sure this time it's for real. As for his condition, he's not been well, but the doctor I spoke to didn't see any reason for him not to travel. It took so long because of the usual government red tape. I had to send in a recommendation, and Doctor Bennett did too." Her gaze shifted to Neil, then back to Doctor Davidson. "Then my friend at that facility had to do some fancy talking to convince the authorities your father needed to be released to join his family—that imprisonment for his case served no purpose and would only endanger his health."

"So, will he be free to leave Grand Peak with us?" The spark had come back in her eyes and the strength back in her silky voice. Neil quietly heaved a sigh.

"That will depend on if the camp director will vouch for him. He would have to sign a release since your father was under his jurisdiction at the time of his arrest."

He saw in Hana's face the same thing he was thinking. It might never happen. The camp director had been resistant to granting any favors in his time here.

He broke in. "That's going to be a problem. He's not an accommodating person. I've dealt with him on hospital personnel matters." As uncooperative as the man had been with small issues, he couldn't imagine a sudden change of heart about Mr. Kato, or any of the resistance group. He studied Hana's reaction.

She waved her hand in the air, defeat hanging over her. "He'll never agree. I remember seeing him there when Papa left. He's not very nice."

Doctor Davidson cleared his throat. "That's where I come in. Bet you didn't know I have a secret against Mr. Camp Director. Been waiting for just the right time to use it."

He turned to Hana, whose eyes roamed the expanse of the camp outside the window. Her hands folded neatly in her lap, her solemnness ripping at his heart. Her only hope was the man in front of her now. How ironic it should come to this—enemy becomes ally—no, savior.

"What secret?" She mumbled, turning to frown at Doctor Davidson.

"Nothing you need to know. What's important is that I know."

The room seemed to cool even though the heat of the day had raised the temperature considerably over the last hour, like an oven pre-heating for a bake fest. Hana stood and held out her hand to Doctor Davidson. Neil's mouth fell open, but no one noticed. Something significant had just happened and he felt as though he had been a part—almost like his father would have done. Perhaps he could follow in his parent's footsteps and still be a doctor. It seemed at this moment that God could use anyone at any time.

Either way, he wanted Hana by his side. His feelings had intensified toward her, and as soon as her father came home he would make her aware of them. He remembered how his parents had loved each other. He welcomed the memories, they filled him up and right now spilled over like pouring hope from a bottle.

"Thank you, both of you."

Neil walked her to the door. "Don't forget about our plan for Martin. I think he'll want to be in better shape for your father." He wasn't sure at all his plan would work. Martin's pride and anger could stand in the way of all their efforts—Papa or no Papa. The task would not be an easy one.

"I'll take you up on the offer to take time off, if you can do without me this afternoon."

He nodded.

Doctor Davidson called after her. "I'll let you know if I hear anything." He stood to leave.

"Doctor Davidson, before you go I need to tell you something."

"Sure." He sat again.

"I've been cleared of fraternizing charges."

Doctor Davidson jumped up. "Really? How?"

"With things winding down around here, they didn't think I was a threat to the rule. I didn't volunteer any information. I think they are just short handed in this department, you know?" He rubbed his aching shoulder. "So you are free to stop feeling guilty."

Doctor Davidson stood and leaned against the desk. "I can't tell you how sorry—"

"It's okay. Let's forget it. I'll be okay if I stay out of trouble. They left it on my record."

"Be careful, my friend. At least until you're out of this place." Doctor Davidson slipped out the door.

The thought of leaving here carried so many questions. Questions that would make him search his heart and mind about two things; where did he want to go, and would he have someone to go with him? He knew the latter took precedence, but was the least likely to turn out the way he wished.

Chapter 14

Simon held out his hand to John. He looked older than John remembered, and this time his suit had been replaced by jeans and a short sleeved plaid shirt. John broke into a wide smile and shook the man's hand.

"Good to see you again, Simon. Thanks for coming all the way out here to see me."

Simon set his small beat up suitcase on the ground and pulled a blue bandana out of his back pocket. "I wasn't that far away really when I got the message you called. Just up in Billings." He whistled as he wiped his brow and neck. "Is it always this hot here?"

"Sometimes hotter. Winters can be brutal with freezing temps and blowing snow." John picked up the suitcase and motioned for Simon to follow him. "Most of the internees didn't even have long sleeved shirts or even coats when they arrived that first winter. The old ones still tell the stories of how it was the coldest winter on record for the area."

Simon trudged alongside John as they made their way up the hill and around the first block of barracks. The air was still and suffocating, but the smell of rice cooking still permeated as they passed a mess hall. John felt a pang of remorse for asking Simon to come, but he needed his help to accomplish his mission. He had no one else to turn to and Simon had been willing, even eager.

John nodded in the direction of the block he had called home for so long. "My place is just down the way."

They both tipped their heads to the neighbors standing in the shade of the buildings and laughed at the children pushing tumbleweeds with sticks—a form of amusement concocted early on in their internment. The guards would yell at them if they ventured too close to the fence to collect a fresh, round tumbleweed. John did his best to sneak one from the far side of the administration building whenever he got the chance.

Simon's smile faded into pursed lips. "Amazing what children will do to have some fun."

John knew what must be rolling around in Simon's mind. He too often pushed down anger at the thought of all the innocent ones forced to live in this place.

"Here we are." He opened the door for his guest and set the suitcase on the only cot in the room. "You'll have to bunk with me I'm afraid."

Simon surveyed the twelve-by-sixteen-foot room and then cocked his head. "And where is my sleeping mat? I'll not take your cot."

John laughed. "I have a mat to sleep on, and you most certainly will take my cot. I insist." He patted Simon on the shoulder. "Don't worry about me. I've been on my own since I was seventeen."

Simon sat on the edge of the cot and attempted a bounce. He smiled. "Which reminds me—I don't know your story. I mean, what your life was like before you hit the jack pot with an invitation to live here." His smile remained. John was tentative about smiling too. He realized joking about it might ease the pain.

"Yeah. Well, I don't want to bore you with my sad song." John pulled up a crate and straddled it, facing Simon. He would rather get right to the issue—helping these people get back home, or find a home for them now that they could leave. His heart had been heavy as he took in the looks of confusion and worry on the faces in camp. Internment was one thing—homelessness was another.

"I really want to know, John. It would help me know you better and know your heart is in the right place. No offense, I need to be certain you have nothing to gain by your plan, whatever it is." His smile disappeared, replaced by raised brows.

John bowed his head. "Okay. I'll tell you about me. Then we talk about something else, right?"

"Right." Simon settled his back against the wall and crossed his legs on the cot.

John leaned against the opposite wall and began to tell him the same story he had only told one other person; Martin Kato. He shared how his parents had been deported and how he ran away from the friends they left him with. The tale took about fifteen minutes to tell, and when he was finished, Simon shook his head.

"Sorry, man. That's rough. But you have come through it by the grace of God. I hope you can see He has a plan for you."

John shrugged, his feelings shifting from one place to another now. "Well, I suppose what I'm about to propose to you could be just what He had in mind all along. Who would have thought loser John Yamada would amount to something?"

Simon chuckled and held his hand up as if to protest. "Sounds like something Moses would have said."

"I just want to be useful to my people. So many of them have no place to go, and I need help to figure out the best way to help them. Can we talk about that, and do you have any ideas?"

John's hands shook. Simon would think him crazy. Maybe he wasn't ready for this kind of service. Simon probably wanted him to grow up some more first. It would crush him to hear that kind of answer. After a few moments of contemplation, Simon spoke up.

"You'll have opposition. You'll hit brick walls. You'll be rejected. Can you handle it?"

John reflected on something he had read in the Bible. It rang true now, more meaningful than he thought possible. Simon would understand.

John swallowed hard. He had to prove to Simon he could do this. "If what I read about Jesus' life is true, He had to face the same thing. I know I'm not God's Son, but I think I can do this. I know I can. It's the first time I've had a purpose, and I'm determined not to ruin it."

"I agree. I think you can do it too. I just want you to be aware that your first obstacle will be the administration right here at Grand Peak. The camp director is difficult and uncooperative. You'll have to claw your way over him to make the inroads you need to help these people."

Why hadn't he considered that? He had only dealt with the codger a few times. "I didn't realize he would be such a problem about this. You'd think he'd want us all out of here as smoothly as possible. Can we side-step him?"

"Sometimes, but he has the earthly power to make it hard on the internees, even just for spite. You just have to remember you have a Higher Power to trump his."

John's confidence waned a bit as he considered the hurdles he would have to jump. Seeds of doubt fluttered in his mind.

Simon slapped John's shoe. "Hey. Don't fade on me. Don't let anything deter you from what you know is right. You're pleasing God, not man. If He is for you, who can be against you?" Simon opened his case and took out a notebook. "Okay, let's get down to business. Tell me how many are left here and where most of them are from."

The rest of the afternoon flew by. John's vision dimmed occasionally, but Simon helped him work through his questions, and by nightfall they had scribbled page after page of notes and information.

The two of them agreed. Everything had to be done by the new John. The old one would only mess things up. He had to fight, but God's way this time.

Then there was Hana. He'd prove himself to her too.

"I suppose you think I'm pushy."

Doctor Davidson and Neil walked down the path to the nearest mess hall. The hospital mess was only open a few days a week now. Neil peeled off his lab jacket and squinted up at the sky. Another clear day, hot and dry. The mess hall wouldn't be much cooler. At least it would be shade and away from listening ears. He dreaded this conversation and had spent quite a bit of energy on avoiding Doctor Davidson's invitation to chat.

Yet, this time seemed different. Doctor Davidson was different. Maybe everything would be better from now on. Even Hana had changed, working less hours than ever before. He couldn't reach her anymore, and life for the Katos had grown more complicated. He missed her.

"No, not pushy, just persistent." He patted Doctor Davidson's back as they climbed the steps to the mess. They stopped just inside the door. "I appreciate you asking me to join you in practice once we are done here. It's just not what I thought I'd be doing. I hoped to be a missionary, but it seems that God may have another plan. Every time I go to fill out the application papers, I get checked inside. I just don't know for sure what that plan is." He pointed to a group of tables. "We can talk about it if you still want to."

Doctor Davidson nodded and grinned. "I do. You're not the only one who has had a change of plans." He grinned. "I know things with a certain someone haven't gone as you hoped."

Neil winced at the thought of Doctor Davidson knowing about his feelings for Hana. Deep in his inner desires, he continued to hold on to hopes that Hana would come to care for him too.

They chose a table close to the door. "I'll grab two cups."

Neil settled onto the bench. "Thanks."

The smells of a boiled chicken lunch barely lingered—a blessing as far as he was concerned. He ate outside the hospital mess only when absolutely necessary since the food was generally better there. A cup of coffee couldn't hurt, or so he hoped.

The clinking of silverware coming from the kitchen echoed off the walls. The once new picnic tables dotted the hall, now worn and coming apart. Only three other people remained in the room, each sitting alone, their backs to him.

He sat and pulled his fingers through his hair and then down the back of his sticky neck. With fewer doctors and nurses at the hospital, work hours seemed longer. His feet ached as did his head. The room echoed with occasional laughter from the kitchen help. He wished he could be that happy about his toil these days.

Doctor Davidson came toward him with two white steaming mugs. It dawned on him how foolish it was to drink hot coffee on a day such as this. As he reached up to take the cup he caught a glimpse of one of the young men sitting at a table. He turned his head to the door, then at his watch, then back at the door.

"Hey, isn't that Martin Kato over there?" Neil pushed his forehead in the general direction of Martin's table.

"I don't think I've ever seen him." Doctor Davidson smirked and turned red. "You were probably expecting me to say they all look alike to me. To be honest, I have said that more than once."

"I suppose most of us have. Anyway, that's him. I haven't seen him since the day he came home. Remember me asking you to order his prosthesis? He never came by for it, even after the news about his father coming home. That little plan flopped." Neil shook his head wondering why a vibrant young man wouldn't want to walk without help from crutches or someone to lean on. Hana told him Martin's pride would get in the way. She obviously knew her brother well.

Doctor Davidson scowled. "It's a shame. It's still in a box in my office. What can we do to get him to the hospital? If wanting to be better before his father came home didn't do the trick, what will?"

"I don't—"

"Doctor Davidson."

Nurse Potter stood at the door with hands on hips, half scowling, half smiling.

"Uh, oh. You're in trouble again." Neil chuckled and sipped his coffee. It slid down his throat, bitter and thick. He nearly gagged, but Alice distracted him as she approached.

She puffed out a long breath through her cheeks. "You got away without signing this discharge order for Mrs. Hito. Lucky for me I saw you come in here. Been chasing you for five minutes."

"Well, you'll need to get used to chasing now that you have a little girl to corral." Doctor Davidson took the paper from Nurse Potter, who grinned wide. Neil knew she would make a great mother for Charlie.

She cocked her head. "I guess you're right. Thanks to you two vouching for my impeccable character, I'm a new adoptive parent." She snatched the paper from Doctor Davidson and turned slightly. She stared in Martin's direction. "Is that Martin?" Her voice softened. She folded the paper and stuffed it in her skirt pocket.

Neil set his mug down and pushed the acidic brown water away from him. "Yes. He looks nervous about something. Hana says his disposition is pretty bad and hard on her and the mother." His blood boiled just to think about the hardship Martin had caused her.

"He needs his prosthetic and therapy. Why hasn't Hana brought him by?" Her brows knit across her face. She took a step back and then stopped, staring at Martin.

He eyed Doctor Davidson who eyed Nurse Potter. "Won't cooperate. He's full of—"

"Self-pity." She finished his sentence just as she took one step in the march toward Martin.

Doctor Davidson nodded toward Martin, a smile spread across his face. "Now look who's in trouble."

"Better go referee." Neil jumped to his feet. "This could be ugly in a fun sort of way." He stumbled as he ran after Alice who clipped along as if she had a mission. He had no doubt she was about to accomplish it. He watched her closely.

She came up behind Martin and gently laid her hand on his shoulder. He jumped and swiveled on the bench to look at her. Neil couldn't see her expression, but Martin's did not exactly brighten at the sight of her face. As he shuffled around to see both of them, Nurse Potter spoke.

"Remember me, Martin? I'm Nurse Potter from the hospital. We've been hoping you would come by and get fitted for your new leg. Why don't you come on with us now and we can get you started?"

Neil choked down the tension, wincing at her words. Martin's lips trembled and perspiration dripped from his temples. He braced for the worst, knowing she didn't take well to rudeness, no matter what the situation. His answer made his position on the matter clear as a starry night.

"Look, lady. I don't want a—" He cupped his fingers in a quotation mark motion. "—new leg. Why don't you mind your own business?"

Neil took a step forward to intervene, but Nurse Potter held up her palm for him to stop. She stood up straight. The whole room seemed to be heavy with stagnant air—the powers that be awaiting her response.

She raised her voice one level. "Well, now. Why don't *you* stop feeling sorry for yourself and be a real man for a change, instead of leaning on your poor little mother and gracious sisters? They have better things to do than to be your babysitter and tote you here and there like some overgrown baby."

Oh, no! "Nurse Potter!" Neil tried to stop her. He leaned back to summon Doctor Davidson for help, but Doctor Davidson shook his head and smiled. He would be no help. He had to soften her hard persona before things got out of hand. "Maybe Martin—"

She broke in with a sarcastic tone he hadn't heard in some time. "Maybe Martin is too scared to try."

Martin's face turned the shade of a ripe cherry. Neil expected him to explode at any minute. He inched closer to her in case Martin lost it all together and lashed out at her from where he sat. The kitchen crew rushed out and mingled, whispering at a distance.

Martin's red face now blossomed with perspiration. "Get out of my face. You have no right to speak to me that way." His voice raised in pitch with each sentence. "I lost this leg training to fight for this wonderful country that has my family in this place and my father in prison. What could someone like you possibly know about what I'm going through? Go away." He shot Neil a sneering command to get this meddling woman out of his sight.

Neil's stomach knotted as she persisted. "You don't scare me, and you don't know anything about my pain. You're just another runaway like my daughter. No guts to face life as it is, so you have to make someone else feel as miserable as you feel. Maybe I wasn't a great mom, but I didn't deserve my daughter's treatment. I happen to know your mother is the best. She doesn't deserve a coward for a son."

She paused, tears brimming and about to spill. Neil's eyes darted between her and Martin, waiting for the next round of nasty banter. Finally, Martin opened his mouth to speak. Nothing came out. He hung his head and closed his eyes. A tear escaped and dripped down his cheek. The room fell silent and the kitchen help slinked back into their space behind the serving counter, some shaking their heads, some frowning.

"I can't." Martin's voice quivered.

"Can't, or won't?" Her rebuff made Neil recoil. It could be she had gone too far.

Before Martin could answer, she sat next to him and took his hand. "Martin, we only want what's best for you. Hobbling around on one leg the rest of your life isn't the best thing. It doesn't have to be that way. You were brave enough to join the fight. Now be brave enough to finish it and make one last walk to the hospital."

Martin choked down a sob. Neil's taught muscles relaxed to know the last bell had sounded on this bout. Martin's brow softened and he nodded once.

She patted his hand. He pulled it away. "We can go right now if you want. Might be good to get it over with, you know?" Martin slapped the table top, not with malice or anger, but with what seemed to be resolve. He looked up at the ceiling and sighed hard, then sat up straight.

His eyes met Neil's. "You helped me once before, at the station. You willing to do it again?"

The clog of emotion in his throat cleared just in time to accept. "Sure. Let's do it."

Doctor Davidson appeared by his side. "Can I be of service?"

Neil cringed. This might be another round in the ring. Martin surely knew the old Doctor Davidson, and he wouldn't blame him for resisting his help. Words of prejudice are not easily forgotten for anyone.

The seconds ticked by as Martin stared at the floor. Was he remembering some snide remark or rude comment from the old Doctor Davidson? There was every chance that Hana's opinion of Caucasians had influenced him.

The champion nurse chimed in. "I think we can handle it, but thank you." She always knew what to say. "We'll need that box from your office though, if you don't mind getting it ready."

"Sure. I'll have everything ready by the time you get there." He took a step back and bumped into Hana.

Neil's stomach lurched. Hana stood firm and despite tear stained cheeks, she managed a wide smile.

No one had seen her come in, and she must have heard enough to know what had taken place. She sidestepped Doctor Davidson and stood next to Nurse Potter. Worry seemed to fall from her like shackles. He said a silent prayer that with Martin's surrender and Papa's return, life for the Katos would mend a bit.

"Hey, sis. You're just in time. I'm going to get a new leg today."

Dust swirled around the Kato's room. Not from a dust storm, although one had rolled through two days ago, leaving silt on every roof and window sill in camp. No, this little storm was Mama's doing. She had busied herself cleaning and sorting since the day Hana brought home the news of Papa's long awaited return. Despite Hana's words of caution, Mama flitted around with a positive attitude all week.

"Something could always go wrong," she had told Mama.

"It all work out. You see." Mama then declared to Hana as she pulled out Papa's box of clothes. She had made two trips to the sundries store to pick up thread and a new sewing needle to take in Papa's pants. A letter from him yesterday sparked energy in her Hana hadn't seen for so long.

Dear family,

I am coming back to you. It is a miracle. I am most eager to see you all again and hear all about camp and our friends.

Mama-san, I have lost weight and will need you to work your magic on my clothes. No need to worry, I am feeling stronger just knowing I'll be joining you all in a few weeks. You can fatten me up when we return to Washington.

Martin, my heart aches for your loss, but we will get through it together. I am proud of my son, no matter our differences. We can find work back home and build a new life.

Hana and Chiko, help your mother to prepare to leave Grand Peak. As soon as I have permission from the government, we will find our way home.

I must go now. One more doctor's examination before they let me go. I am most grateful for the efforts of those who made this possible.

Your loving,

Papa

The realization that Papa might not look the same or even be healthy enough to leave Grand Peak any time soon hit Hana as she re-read the letter each night. Could this really be the beginning of the end for them and all the others in camp? She dared not get hopes too high. Their luck had been bad before now. Still, it appeared as if luck might be coming around to their side, if there was such a thing. Mama would say no.

There was no time to earn the extra money they would need to depart. God would have to provide, just like Mama always said.

"You hear me?" Mama shouted from just outside their door.

Hana perked up. "Oh, yes, Mama-san?" She stood from her perch on the cot and hurried to where Mama stood with a basket of clothes in her arms.

"I say I go to latrine to wash these. Be back soon. Then we go help Martin back from hospital."

"Martin should be able to walk himself home. After a week of therapy, he's doing well. He's so stubborn, but that has helped him get better faster."

Mama shut the door behind her. Hana stood still in the hazy room of filtered dust. Tiny particles danced in the sun's rays that streamed through the window. She could taste the dryness.

Standing alone in the middle of the room she remembered the scene from the movie she had seen while in nurses training. Scarlet O'Hara stood with hand raised to the sunset, making a vow never to go hungry again. That's how it was now.

Someone knocked. Jumping back, she caught her breath. She opened the door a sliver to see John and another man smiling at her.

"Hi. I brought a friend to meet you." John's tone was bright. More cheerful than she had seen him in a long time.

She opened the door wide. "Come in."

She motioned toward the chairs around the table and they both sat after she pulled one up for herself. Her stomach fluttered to see John after barely talking to him for weeks.

John rattled on like a boy with a secret. "This is Simon. Simon, this is Hana Kato. We've been friends for a long time, right, Hana?"

She nodded at John and then at Simon. "Nice to meet you." It wasn't like John to make friends, especially with respectable looking ones like Simon. She had never seen him in camp before. Her chest tightened when she wondered if he were here to bring bad news about Papa. The thought stung her.

John continued. "Simon is here to help me put together a plan for the remaining internees."

Whew. Her shoulders unwound and she smiled at last. "Oh? What plan?" She glanced between the two, hoping John wasn't mixed up in some scam.

John glanced at Simon who nodded and sat back as if to give John room to speak. "Our people need help to leave here and find places to live and work on the outside. You know that well, Hana. I've had this idea on my heart for a while now and I asked Simon to help me. He's part of the Council of Churches that help Japanese Americans get back on their feet. Pretty great, huh?"

Council of Churches? On his heart? Whatever was going on here certainly didn't sound like the old John. He sounded more like Doctor Bennett than himself. Her fingers numbed until she relaxed her grip on her hands in her lap. John's eyes blazed with something. Anticipation? Excitement?

What should she say? "Uh, yes. Great. What is your plan, and who is helping you?" She had a million questions. This would be a good place to start. She glanced at the door, wondering when Mama would walk in on them.

John surveyed the room. "Where is Mama-san? I'd like her to hear what we have to say. This will affect her too as head of the house."

Obviously John hadn't heard about Papa coming home. Mama burst through the open door, wild eyed and toting her basket. "I no head of house."

The two men joined Hana in jumping up from their chairs. Mama tossed the basket on the table and pointed a finger at John. He backed away one step. "Hana's Papa head of house and he be here soon to run you off."

"Mama-san!" Hana's cheeks flared and she reached for Mama's arm. "They are friends."

Mama could not be consoled. Something had set her off and she continued her rebuke. "What you want from us?"

Hana tried to pull Mama down to sit in her chair, but felt her arm jerk away.

"Mama-san, they are here to help. John didn't know Papa's coming home. Please calm down." She spoke close to Mama's ear, soft and slow.

Both men turned solemn. "We'll go now." Simon turned to Mama-san and bowed. "I am very sorry we disturbed you, Mrs. Kato. We meant no harm."

Hana stared at John's frozen face. He looked hurt and stunned.

John stuffed his hands in his pockets. "I'm sorry, Mrs. Kato," was all he could manage to say. Her heart stung to see his happy countenance dashed.

Hana nodded toward the door and they shuffled out like two little boys who had been caught smoking behind the barn. Now to figure out what set Mama off and why.

"Mama-san? Are you all right?"

This time Mama let her guide her to the chair. All at once her spunk left her and was replaced by a crumpled woman in tears. Hana had never seen her cry like this. Even when they got word of her grandparents' death in Japan she didn't break down this way. Sobs racked her narrow shoulders. Hana pulled her chair close and watched her shaking for a moment.

The debris that dammed up layers of emotion finally broke loose in a torrent of cries mixed with giggles. The tower of strength had her breaking point—something Hana had never even considered.

She glanced at her watch. Martin would be wondering about them. She couldn't leave Mama alone in this state to go get her brother. She grabbed a tissue and tucked it under Mama's bowed head. Chiko would have to bring Martin home by herself.

"M … Martin. He waiting." Mama choked out the words, now rocking herself.

"Martin will be fine. Chiko's with him. He's not helpless anymore, Mama-san." She sat next to Mama but didn't touch her. Time to just sit and be there for as long as necessary.

She watched her mother rock and gradually gain composure. It was better that she let all this out now. To do it in front of Papa would have been devastating to him.

Just hang on Mama.

Chapter 15

July 20

She just wanted her knees to hold her up and her heart to stop racing. The realities of Papa's return were close enough to touch, and at this moment she hoped, no prayed, nothing else could harm the Kato family. With Papa joining them and Martin back on two feet, they could plan their departure from Grand Peak. Papa would know just what to do and where to go.

Hana pushed Mama out in front of their little family crowd. Martin stood next to her as if guarding her. "Mama-san, tell me if you get too warm standing here." She nodded and her eyes continued to search back and forth. She clenched the edge of her tunic—the same one she wore that terrible day he left. It was as if that piece of clothing had become her good luck charm, something from the past and a symbol of a future for her and Papa. How sweet she looked as she waited on the edge of the top step of the station building.

Chiko had even convinced her to dab on just a touch of pink rouge. "Mama-san, you look so young with pink cheeks." Hana thought Mama would probably agree to anything today.

A few dried brown leaves fluttered on the two lone trees just past the station. The town of Fillmore wasn't exactly a thriving metropolis or lush with gardens and big houses like back home. The scent of hollyhock wafted so strong Hana could almost taste it. The beautiful flower climbing up the fence seemed to be the only one they could grow here, not like the azaleas and lilies that flourished on the coast of Washington. Soon Papa would be fussing over new starts of the flowering plants he loved so much.

"I think I hear the train." Chiko stopped biting her fingernails long enough to lean forward and tune her ear to the distance. Her eyes brightened and she nodded to Hana in affirmation. "It's coming."

Hana placed her palm on her abdomen. Papa would see her excitement and mistake it for anxiety if she couldn't stop shaking. Had she done a good job with her brother and sister like she promised? Would he be pleased?

"Come on, Mama-san." Chiko tugged at her sleeve. Mama didn't budge. Her mother wouldn't be one of those women to make a scene or bring attention to their situation by rushing Papa.

"I wait here for minute. You and Martin go." She waved Chiko on as she scanned the windows of the train cars whirling by them.

Hana held a deep breath to settle herself. The shuffling of feet caused plumes of dust to rise from the ground. She closed her eyes as the train jerked and then stopped, sputtering and spewing gravel from underneath it. The sound of men's voices raised caught her attention—angry voices hurling through an open window.

Several MPs pushed through the waiting crowd. Through voices loud enough for everyone to hear, Hana recognized one of them as Papa's. She glanced at Mama whose face was locked in a worried scowl. A few passengers hurried off the train, looking back over their shoulders to see the two men fighting through the dirty train car window. Mama must have seen the men's faces because she stepped down and inched her way through the crowd as if no one was there.

Hana stepped forward to catch the corner of Mama's tunic. She felt the silky material slip through her fingers as Mama forged through the obstacles. The voices stopped suddenly. The MPs hopped up on the platform of the car and burst through the open iron door.

A woman screamed from inside the car. Hana's heart jumped to her throat. She reached for Mama again and held tight this time to pull her back. Chiko ran to their side, her eyes wide and full of fear.

She cowered between Hana and Mama. "What's going on?"

Martin limped his way close to them. "Did you hear Papa's voice a minute ago?"

Mama stood up straight and pulled Chiko close to her. Mama's eyes blinked against the dust as she stared at the window where Papa had been standing. Now the only visible reflections were of a young man and an MP. Hana could barely see, but the younger man stared at the floor of the train car. It looked as though an MP held both of his arms from behind. Hana trembled uncontrollably.

"I'm going to see what the problem is." Martin took one step before Hana could speak. She grabbed his arm and motioned with a nod toward Mama. He glanced at their mother and then stepped back.

Hana searched their faces. "You all stay here." If something had happened to Papa, she would be the one to find out. How inconceivable that anything could go wrong now. So close to his embrace—so close to regaining a whole family again.

She pulled in her elbows and tried not to breathe in the stench of body odor coming from the small gathering of people crowding near the train car. The heat of the morning made a steam bath of humanity with everyone huddled so close. She brushed up against a small child clinging to his mother, who wasn't paying any attention to his cries.

She bent down for a few seconds. "I'm sorry, little one. Are you all right?"

The child sniffed and wiped his face. Dust like powder left stains on his chubby cheeks. She patted his head and frowned at the mother.

No one had left this train car since the first group. Hana's stomach churned wondering why Papa hadn't appeared. She fidgeted with her watch, ready to jump aboard if nothing happened in the next few moments. She rocked back and forth on each aching foot, wishing she had worn her nurse's shoes.

One of the MPs jumped off the train steps "Out of the way. Get back!" He pushed the crowd back, waving his arms. He ran to the station door and squawked orders at the station master, who picked up the receiver of his phone.

Hana took a step forward. The MP came back and pulled at her arm to get in front of her, then turned to the crowd. "Is there a doctor or a nurse here?"

Looking back at Mama first, she prepared herself to speak up. Not knowing if there was a Caucasian or Japanese person in need, any medical person was likely to keep their mouth shut, even ignoring their oath to heal.

"I'm a nurse." Hana barked from behind the man. She glanced back at Martin who was teetering on a wood crate to see above the heads of the crowd. He nodded—she supposed in agreement with her brave admission. At least this could get her aboard to see if Papa was there.

He turned to look her over. "You're a nurse?"

Indignation wiggled up from her gut. She stuck her chin out and answered in her best authoritative voice.

"Yes, sir. I am. Can I help?"

Her eyes stole a quick look at her white short sleeved blouse and navy blue slacks, Papa's favorite look for her. Perhaps she didn't look professional. It shouldn't matter. She just identified herself as a nurse. No one else had spoken up, so she would be his only choice.

"Come with me." His tone warmed a bit and she took one step to follow him.

Another MP emerged with the young man she had seen in the window. The handcuffs around his wrists glistened in the sun. The flashback of seeing Papa in cuffs when he was arrested left her legs wobbling. It was the thing that set their miserable year in motion. The rest of the crowd parted to let them pass.

Her guide stood by the door and let her enter first. A few Caucasian men hovered over someone lying on the floor.

He pointed to the patient. "He's unconscious. See what you can do until the doctor from the camp gets here." He stepped back for her to go ahead of him, but her feet seemed to have a mind of their own and didn't wish to move.

A doctor coming from camp could only mean Doctor Bennett or Doctor Davidson. The Japanese American doctors would likely never be called away for an emergency. Stepping into the aisle, the others moved to the side. The conductor checked his watch and shook his head before moving to give her a clear view.

Papa.

Her already shaking knees buckled and she sank to the floor as gracefully as she could. It seemed no one else noticed her shock and horror. Papa's head rested on an article of clothing, a sweater maybe. The right side of his gaunt face revealed streaks of blood. She wanted to reach out and touch him. Her ice cold hands wouldn't move.

"I need … more room." Her voice squeaked through her tears. "Can you … carry him to the end of the car?" Her gaze froze on the writing on his blood stained shirt.

FORT LEAVENWORTH PRISON.

Papa had his freedom now, but would he live to be free? Would he live at all?

The conductor wiped the sweat from his brow. "You'll have to get him off the train as soon as possible. We have a schedule to meet." His face puffy and red, he looked ready to explode.

The men carefully nestled Papa into the empty floor space at the back of the car. Forcing her legs to function, she knelt beside him and cradled his wrist between her fingers.

"Pulse slow and irregular."

A woman dressed in her Sunday best slid beside her, holding a bundle of gauze. "This is all I could find. And here's a wet towel. It's clean."

Hana unfolded one and wiped Papa's brow to find the source of the bleeding. A gash at least three inches long parted his hair, running along the crown of his head. Blood trickled from the open wound. Worse than that, he hadn't regained consciousness. She glanced behind her. The dressed-up woman stood waiting, silent and calm. Whoever she was, Hana needed her help.

"Can you check to see if the doctor is on his way?"

The woman's slender face and curly brunette hair complemented her graceful manner. "Sure. Is there anything else I can get for you?"

"No. We just need to get him to the hospital, but I don't think he should be moved till the doctor sees him."

Once again the conductor pulled his watch from his pocket and stared at it. "Can't you just move him to the station office? I'm sure he'll be fine there."

The woman glared at him and turned to Hana. "Don't worry, I'll find out."

Hana watched her hurry away, her pink skirt swishing past the seat backs. Papa groaned, jostling her attention. Her heart leapt. She leaned in to his face to whisper.

"Papa? Can you hear me?"

His left eyelid fluttered. She touched his cold cheek with the back of her hand. "Papa. Open your eyes." She dabbed his wound with fresh gauze, the bleeding less than a trickle now. She stroked Papa's head, pulling back the strands of hair stuck to the blood. She didn't remember his hair being so gray.

"Time to wake up. Please wake up." If he knew how desperately they needed him, he would rise and take over as he always did. Even if he and Martin still fought, even if he continued with the resistance, she welcomed any sign he would re-join the living.

He groaned again. The oven-like heat in the car suffocated her. She used one of the pieces of gauze to wipe her forehead. Someone tapped her shoulder.

"I'll take over."

When she heard Doctor Bennett's voice she scooted to the other side of her father. All the burden pressing on her shoulders lifted.

The conductor bustled through the compartment door to the car in front of them. "At last, someone who can get this man off my train." Hana wanted to lock the door behind him. If he returned, she wouldn't hesitate to punch him in the head. She had already resisted the urge to trip him as he walked by.

Hana couldn't stop her teeth from chattering as she reported Papa's status. "He's starting to stir. Pulse slow and irregular. The bleeding has decreased. I—I"

Doctor Bennett touched her hand and whispered to her. "Slow down, Hana. You're going to hyperventilate if you aren't careful. Breathe." He turned his attention to the wound. "I've never seen you so shook up about a patient. Are you all right?"

She risked breaking the dam of tears to look at him. He had to know.

"This is my father."

Doctor Bennett stared at her, his mouth open. "Your father?" He pulled the stethoscope away from Papa's chest. "I'm sorry."

The tears wouldn't hold back any longer. "I don't even know what happened to him. They didn't tell me. Mama and Chiko are out there with Martin. I need to tell them Papa's hurt." The tears flowed as she blinked to clear her vision. The train car felt like it moved, but she knew it was her unsteady mind.

Doctor Bennett opened his bag and crushed an ampule of smelling salts. "The MP who brought me here said two men argued and one of them knocked the other down. He hit his head hard." He waved it under Papa's nose and waited.

Hana grabbed the side of the nearest seat post. "It must have been the man they led away in handcuffs."

Doctor Bennett nodded and leaned close to Papa's ear. "Mr. Kato. Can you hear me?"

Hana's mind whirled with all the puzzle pieces. "That man was Japanese."

"Yes, it must have been him." He tried the salts again. No response.

She placed her hand on Papa's chest. A Japanese man had hurt her father. Her fortress crumbled, her safe haven of the Japanese American community suddenly waved a danger flag.

Papa rocked his head from side to side, coughing and groaning. His eyelids fluttered again and his cloudy gaze landed on Hana's eyes. She held his face in her hands.

"Papa-san?"

"Hana." His voice a wisp of a whisper.

"You'll be all right Papa-san. Just lie still and we'll get you to the hospital." Her eyes darted to Doctor Bennett.

"Mr. Kato, can you see how many fingers I'm holding up?"

"F—Four."

Doctor Bennett eyed Hana and pulled in the two fingers he held in front of Papa's face. Two orderlies tromped up the isle with a folded cot. Hana stood and stumbled aside. Now was her chance to find Mama and the others.

Doctor Bennett must have read her mind. "They were sitting on a bench outside the station. I saw Mama's red face and escorted her inside and sent Martin to get them all some water. She needs your attention. I'll handle your father. You can come to the hospital once you make sure they're okay." He looked deep in her eyes, not moving, as if waiting for her to acknowledge him.

"Thank you."

She labored over the walk from the back of the car to the steps outside. She had forgotten how hot it was in the car, until a warm breeze hit her face. Very warm, but cooler than the steam bath she just left. A few onlookers still remained, some grumbling that they couldn't board yet. She could see on their faces the desperation to leave this place behind. Tired eyes searched the windows and shaking hands clutched precious small bags. They didn't understand their good fortune at being able to leave. She turned her head, refusing to give in to angry thoughts and questions for God about why and when.

Once inside the station waiting room she spied Mama and Chiko huddled together in two chairs in the corner, next to a window stained and fogged. Martin stood guard over them, his watchful eyes darting between the window and the station office. Chiko jumped from her chair and ran to her. Her arms wrapped around Hana so tight she nearly lost her breath. Hana held her while she sobbed.

"Where is Papa? Someone said a man died on the train. It's Papa isn't it?"

Hana grabbed her shoulders and held her at arm's length. "Look at me. Papa is not dead. He's hurt, and we're taking him to the hospital. Doctor Bennett is with him now." She snatched her sister's sweaty hand and pulled her over to Mama, who sat staring at the window. Hana's heart sank to think of what was flowing through her thoughts. She must be imagining the worst had happened on the other side of the fogged glass.

Hana tenderly touched her shoulder. "Mama-san?"

Without moving her eyes from the window she spoke softly.

"Will he live?"

"I don't know. We will know more when we get to the hospital. Are you all right?"

A slow nod and then she stood and shuffled toward the door, her soft flat shoes scuffing along the dusty wood floor.

Martin's voice steadied her. "What can I do?"

"Take Mama to the hospital. She won't want to go home."

Martin limped along beside Mama, keeping close. There wasn't anything more Hana could say to make them feel better. Words of hope eluded her. She should tell Mama a Japanese man hurt Papa.

No. No need to compound her pain. For now, she had to go to him and make sure Papa received the best of care—time to be in charge as he would want. She couldn't fail him, not after all that had happened over the last several months. She didn't want him to feel the way she did now.

Betrayed.

The sun that hovered like a fire ball all day now lay cradled by the top of the mountain, casting low shadows on the hills below. Any minute darkness would settle over the flat land and cover the sea of tarpapered buildings. From her perch on the front steps of the hospital Hana watched the windows in each barrack light up one by one, twinkling in unison.

She tried to collect her emotions and tie them up tight, but it was her stomach that balled in knots. Mama would walk through the doors soon and she would need Hana's strength. She closed her eyes to concentrate. Drowning out Doctor Davidson's words would take noise she couldn't produce on her own.

"I'm sorry, Mrs. Kato. His heart was too damaged. We couldn't save him."

Couldn't save him. Did they try hard enough—did they let the Jap-hater treat him? She should have been in the room as they worked on Papa instead of letting Alice talk her into staying outside the door. Maybe they just didn't do all they could for a dying Issei.

She covered her face with shaking hands, fatigue and sorrow smothering her. "Don't be ridiculous, Hana. You're imagining things."

The sun disappeared just as Mama stepped out to stand beside her, her beautiful tunic dusty and wrinkled. Her silence crushed against Hana's chest. It wouldn't do just to spit out useless words of comfort. Mama deserved more than that. She slipped her hand into her mother's and squeezed.

Mama squeezed back, but kept her eyes straight ahead into the darkness. The light hanging from a broken fixture on the outside of the whitewashed hospital flickered on. Hana saw Alice out of the corner of her eye, standing in the window. She nodded at Hana and smiled a knowing smile, then moved away from the glass.

"We go home now. Chiko and Martin worry."

Hana dreaded walking through the door of their residence without Papa. This was to have been the day of reunion, not separation. Chiko would probably have cried herself to sleep and Martin would be quietly sitting at the table. The calm summer night would leave not a breath of air to circulate in their room. This more than any night, they needed a cool breeze to soothe tired hearts.

"Are you all right, Mama-san?" Hana strained to say the words without crying.

Mama nodded and took the first step toward home. Hana let go of her hand and followed, glad they would make it all the way before the search lights came on. There was no point of a curfew now. Half the internees had already left the camp. What punishment could rule-breakers receive now? They had no home to lose, no assets to freeze, no more men to send to war.

And Papa was dead. Of all the bad things that could happen, there was nothing left to hurt the Kato family.

They reached the steps to the barrack. Someone called out from down the yard.

"Hana!"

Mama didn't even turn around, but stepped through the door, leaving her alone under the dim light of the rising moon. Doctor Bennett jogged toward her. She looked around to make sure he didn't attract attention. She waved and then held her finger to her trembling lips.

She stepped down and walked a few yards to meet him.

"What do you want?" She looked up at the guard tower and then into his eyes. "Don't make any trouble, please."

He came close. His face reflected the moonlight, showing his tired eyes. "It's all right." He stopped to catch his breath. "The guards know I make calls at night. I had to check on you. You left before I could talk—"

She held up her hand. "What more is there to say? You sent Doctor Davidson out to tell us the bad news. Papa's gone. We'll be leaving here without him." She didn't want to take her pain out on him, but couldn't stop herself.

She saw the harshness of her words ripple across his face. He shook his head and mumbled something she couldn't hear. As still as the night was, she couldn't hear anything. Just the pounding against her chest. How could a broken heart beat so loud?

"I went to make out the death certificate and then you were gone. I had to tell you how sorry I am. We tried everything in our power to save your father." He looked to the moon now dominating the sky, then back to her eyes. "I know how hard it is to lose a parent. Mine both died unexpectedly, and in the confusion after the attack on Pearl, I didn't have much time to grieve. I just wanted to tell you not to come to work for as long as you need."

Hana let her crossed arms fall to her side. She had forgotten about his parents' death. He really did know the pain of loss. She should have been more understanding instead of jumping to the conclusion he didn't care.

"I'm sorry I got angry. I know you've experienced this too. I'm so tired I can't think straight. I'll stay home tomorrow and then see what happens after that."

She turned to go back. He reached out and touched her arm. "Take your time and let me know if there is anything I can do. Anything."

She stopped but couldn't look at him. "Thanks. We will be fine. You don't need to worry about us. Goodnight."

Just inside the barrack she leaned against the wall. The sounds of cheerful voices down the hall made her cringe. Laughter and chatter like that wouldn't be heard in the Kato cubicle. They would deal with Papa's death alone and in silence.

Their door creaked as she eased it open. As she predicted, Chiko slept soundly and Martin sat sulking at the table with Mama sitting opposite him. The hot heavy air indeed had no breeze to stir it. She tiptoed to the window close to Chiko's cot and jerked it open a crack.

Martin whispered across the room. "It won't help."

Mama spoke out, patting the chair next to her. "You come sit."

Hana glanced at Chiko, wondering if she would wake at Mama's voice. Lying with her back to the room, her shoulder rose and fell with deep breaths.

"Poor thing, she didn't even take off her shoes. Mama-san, remember the nights when I would fall asleep on the parlor sofa, waiting for Papa to come home from a community meeting?"

Mama smiled as a tear slipped down her face.

"I would wake the next morning in my own bed with my shoes on the floor. Papa had carried me upstairs and tucked me in, clothes and all." It still warmed her heart to think of it.

There would be no comfort in waking tomorrow for Chiko, or herself. Papa would not be there to carry them ever again.

She slid into the seat beside Mama and folded her hands in her lap. Her gaze shifted from Martin to Mama. Something more than grief hung between them. The tension hinted they had exchanged words before she came in.

"Mama-san says no funeral." Martin blurted out the words and then leaned back hard against his chair. "I told her I disagree. We could put something together."

Hana studied Mama's tired face. Even in the low light, the darkness under her eyes and the deep wrinkles over her brow revealed weariness unutterable. Despite opening the window, the air stifled her. She reached over to help Mama out of her tunic. She must have been sweltering in the quilted satin garment.

Mama let her pull it from her, then straightened the white blouse she had been wearing underneath.

She leaned toward her son. "We cannot do Japanese funeral. Papa not want us to put something together. He deserve real funeral with real ceremony or nothing at all. He was proud man and even though he American, he honor his ancestors with traditional funeral."

Martin jumped up and wobbled as if he had forgotten about his new leg. Hana braced herself with feet flat on the floor to catch him if he fell. He teetered back and forth before grabbing the edge of the table. "We have to do something. It's not right to just forget him. Mama-san, you can't do that."

Mama stood to face him. "You don't tell me what to do. Papa is my business. I his wife. I know what he want."

Hana put a finger to her lips and pointed to the sleeping Chiko. "I'm sorry, Mama-san. Why don't we sleep on it and we can talk about it when we're rested. We're all exhausted."

Martin hung his head and inched away from the table, using his hands to steady himself. "You're right. I'm sorry too, Mama-san." He shuffled to his cot and pulled the curtain around it.

Mama shuffled to her cot. "We go to bed. Talk tomorrow or next day."

Mama would stand her ground. Without the means to have the Japanese funeral, she would protest against any ceremony at all. Especially without friends and family around. Even John hadn't shown his face in support.

She couldn't blame him. She hadn't been exactly open to refreshing their previous relationship. The strain of her life had limited their interactions, and she hadn't seen him since the day

Mama chased him from this room. She missed him and wished he were here to talk to. He must have heard the news by now. Word traveled fast in camp. Especially bad news.

She curled up on her cot, too tired to get undressed. She closed her eyes and envisioned Doctor Bennett's hurt face from earlier. She had thought he cared for her at one time, but when she needed him most, he wasn't there. Hana wished he had been the one to tell the family Papa had died instead of the insensitive Doctor Davidson. Had she expected too much of him, and John?

It was time to go home.

It wouldn't really be home without Papa.

Dreams turned to nightmares each time Hana dozed off during the long night. The darkness had finally given way to the sun peeking through the small cracks where the wall met the ceiling. Martin's attempt a few months ago to stuff the holes with wet paper had failed during the last dust storm. She smiled as she remembered how she had teased him. That was before he went to basic training—before he lost his leg.

Before Papa died.

She had risen early and sat on the stoop outside, praying the last twenty-four hours hadn't really happened. Mama came to find her and then put all her children to work. Hana knew it was an attempt to keep their minds off Papa. Cleaning and scrubbing wouldn't help. Nothing would.

The morning dragged on in silence and slipped into afternoon without fanfare. They exchanged few words. No one knocked at the door or came by to share their condolences. Mama made Martin take Chiko to lunch at the mess hall. They had come directly home, shaken from the stares of curious folks from the block.

Chiko sniffled as she relayed the story. "One old man stopped by our table and bowed. He looked so sad, Mama-san. Do you suppose he knew Papa?"

Hana's broken heart threatened to make her physically ill, but she choked back rolling bile to stay strong for Mama. She cringed at the thought of being stuck in this room, trying not to cry. There would be no point in taking more days off. She needed something to occupy her mind until Mama recovered enough to make plans to leave Grand Peak for good.

Chapter 16

"God often comes through the back door to surprise us." Simon patted John on the back, laughing. "I should have warned you about His creativity when it comes to persuading us to do His will."

John shook his head. "Never in my wildest dreams did I think I would be doing God any favors. Why would he choose a rabble-rouser like me?"

"You aren't the first rabble-rouser God picked to help His people. The Bible is full of stories. Well, you'll read them sometime, and then you'll know what I mean."

He had just begun to read the Bible. He could never quite get the meaning of books and had trouble maintaining good grades in school. He dreaded bringing home report cards, knowing that his father would belittle him. He saw the shame in his eyes. That God would choose him to be anything but a loser seemed impossible.

Simon reached in his briefcase, pulled out a small book and handed it to John. "You'll need this."

John's hands shook as he held it—a brand new Bible. This was it. He wouldn't ever turn back now. Simon believed in him enough to give him such a gift. He had felt bad about himself all his life, but this was different. Humility was something he knew little about, but this must be what it meant to be humbled, in a good way.

"John, you'll have doubts after I leave. Pray and read God's word. He'll guide you back. I know you'll be fine." He shook John's hand.

"Until we meet again, my friend.

"I can't thank you enough for reaching out to me that day. My life will never be the same." John pulled Simon into an embrace. "See you in a few months."

John waved as the bus pulled away with Simon smiling through the back window. He should be excited about the plans they made and the contacts gained thanks to Simon's help. His fledgling organization was now prepared for the large task of guiding the remainder of the internees out of the barbed wire and into the cruel world. The burden loomed over him, but he knew he wasn't alone in the job. If only everyone else had the same heart of faith he now felt.

He turned when the bus was no more than a speck and felt something on his arm. He looked to see a drop of water, then up to see the sun had disappeared behind a dark cloud. Another drop tickled his nose and then another. His eyes scanned the sky. Rainclouds formed, ready to burst.

"We sure need this rain to cut the heat. Let's hope it's a good one." The station master called from his open window, craning to see the sky from his vantage point.

The dust on the ground blew soft puffs each time a drop hit the dry path. Before he could reach the overhang of the building, the cloud exploded in thunder and the deluge began. Soon the smells of wet dirt and clean wood filled his nose. It had been several weeks since the last meager rain, and he had forgotten how sweet it smelled. He watched it from a dry spot on the porch, but the urge to stand in it overwhelmed him.

The old man called out to him. "She's comin' down now! That should wash the dust off everything."

John chuckled. The old man was absolutely giddy. He felt somewhat giddy himself, standing in the rain and feeling it soak through his clothes. He closed his eyes and let the drops flow over his face. His mind wandered back to his childhood. Rainy days were his favorite kind of weather—thunder an extra bonus.

After several minutes the drops stopped and John dropped his arms. The sun popped out again in all its glory, shining off the small puddles in the dirt. He jumped up on the porch and nodded to the old man. "That was nice."

"Yep. Just too short. It'll dry up in no time." He tipped his head and motioned for John to approach. "You headed up to the barracks?"

"Yeah."

"I have some letters here I need delivered to some folks up there. If you know any of 'em would you take these?" He waved the envelopes in the air.

John stepped close to the window. "Sure. Who are they for?"

"Well, let me see. Thomas Hito, Shannon Okawa or John Yamada. Know any of 'em?"

"I know Thomas Hito, and John Yamada is me." He smiled and took the two letters. "I'll stop by Thomas' on my way. Thanks."

He tucked his letter under his arm while he stuffed the other in his pocket. Who would be sending him a letter? He had no close relatives and they wouldn't know where he was anyway. Trudging up the hill, he stared at the writing on the envelope. His heart trembled as he recognized his mother's handwriting. He stopped walking. His hand shook violently as he ripped open the letter. He held it to his chest before reading it. It was a miracle.

July 2, 1945
Dear Son,

I have at last discovered where you are interned. I have been searching since we heard of the evacuation over three years ago. I hope this note finds you well.

I wanted you to know your father and I have been moving from place to place over western Japan. We have been working where we can find jobs. Life is not the same here since we are at war. Jobs are plentiful but don't pay much. But at last your father has a good job waiting for us in Hiroshima. I will send you our new address as soon as we are settled.

Perhaps someday you will want to join us here in Japan. I know you must be angry with us, but we thought we were doing the best thing for you. Please forgive us.

Write to tell me if you are leaving and have a new address. We hear rumors that Japanese are mistreated and I worry. When will they let you go?

Your loving mother.

He looked at the date again. Three weeks ago. They must be settled by now. Another letter would come soon if he knew his mother.

"Mother."

He strained his mind to remember what she looked like. Her soft black hair framed her round face and deep eyes. He always wondered why such a pretty woman would marry a homely man like his father.

His mouth dried up, but his palms remained sweaty. Was this really happening? His parents sent him a letter after all this time.

"Yes, Mother. I'm angry. But who wouldn't be?" The feelings of hurt and abandonment rose from the place in his heart he had buried them. Yet, how could he not forgive them now that he had been forgiven by God. It would be wrong to hate his parents.

He stared at the envelope. As soon as she sent a new address he would write and tell them about his new mission here in camp. His steps lightened as he dodged through the barracks, cutting across to Block 10. Thomas would leave camp soon along with the rest of the younger internees. John's heart quivered thinking of all the ones who would need his help.

The one person he wanted most to help had drifted from his life over the last few weeks, and now she was grieving a loss even he couldn't relate to. Especially now with the letter in his hand telling him his parents would be there for him someday. He had longed to approach her, but the last encounter at her barrack drew a picture plain enough for him to see he wasn't welcome in her life. But she might need him now. He could only hope she would accept him back.

"How can I help, Lord?" He folded the envelope and slid it into his pocket. "What can I do?"

Hana held the door latch in her hand, dreading going inside their room. Another long day of trying not to break down over losing Papa. Packing Papa's things, writing to friends and relatives, all stamped his death on her heart. The trousers, socks and hankies she had lovingly packed for him had all been returned in a plain brown box. His prison laundered clothes smelled of bluing, just what he hated. Mama had poked her fingers through the holes in the socks, shaking her head. Hana watched in disbelief one evening as Mama quietly darned them and placed them back in the box.

Hana's mind wandered more than ever these days. Before long she would be useless if she continued on this emotional merry-go-round. If only there could be closure for all the unhappy events of the last few weeks, the last few years. Only anguish remained in her heart, and a nagging static confusion about her future.

Chiko stood behind her. "Are you going in?"

"Oh, yes. Where did you come from?" Hana pushed the door open and let Chiko go in first.

"I just came through the other door and saw you standing there."

"Why are you home so late? I didn't see you at the library. I thought you were going to meet me there after I finished work."

"Had something else to do and then…well, you'll never guess where else I've been." She strolled over to Mama and hugged her. Mama shooed her away and continued folding this week's laundry. Mundane and routine tasks seemed to comfort her these days.

"I bet you'll tell us." Hana flopped onto her cot and fell back against her pillows. She kept a close eye on Mama, who seemed lost in another world.

"I just went to hear a lady talk about entering beauty school when I get out of here and finish high school. I think it's something I could do and I like what she had to say. Mama, do you think we would have money to send me?"

"Maybe."

Hana wanted to jump up and choke her sister for her frivolous attitude. How could she even think about money for beauty school when uncertainties mounted in front of them? Mama winked at Hana, a small sign of hopefulness. Even in the light of all their tragedies, Mama held out hope, even for beauty school.

Life outside would be a rude awakening for both of them. She had heard the stories of heartbreak of young Nisei trying to get education or jobs since leaving the camps. She kept the worst of it from Mama, but it might be time to explain the realities. She glanced at Papa's urn sitting on his chair in the corner. At least they had that. Most of the internees who passed away lay in the camp cemetery. No funeral for Papa, no remembrance, no one to care he was gone except his wife and children. He deserved so much more. She should have seen to it.

Hana pulled the curtain and slipped out of her uniform. "Are we going to the mess hall together tonight, Mama? And where is Martin?"

Martin shut the door and threw a couple newspapers on the table. "I'm here. Checking the papers for news about home. Not many jobs up there. We gonna go eat?"

"We can't go yet." Chiko's high pitched voice made everyone turn.

Hana plopped down on her cot. "Why not? You want to wait until the line gets too long?" It wasn't like Chiko to put off a meal, even when she was sad. There had to be an ulterior motive.

Chiko glanced at her watch and stood to look out the window. "No, I'm just not very hungry yet. Can we wait just a little while, Mama?"

Hana jerked back her curtain. "Why?"

Mama stacked a pile of clean folded shirts and jeans on the chair. "I wait with you. Hana you and Martin go if you want." Mama was the one who needed to have dinner. She had lost weight in the weeks since Papa's imprisonment.

The door shook from someone pounding. Hana tucked in her blouse just in time.

Chiko pushed her way past Mama to the door. "I'll get it."

Hana scowled at her sister's unexplained enthusiasm. "Good grief, Chiko." She slipped on her loafers as fast as she could. Mama stood and ran her hand through her hair. They never had visitors, except for special Japanese holidays, and few since Martin returned.

Chiko smiled and waved in a crowd of people with John in the forefront. He bowed and said hello in Japanese. Hana glanced at Mama who stood frozen with her hand over her mouth. John stepped aside and one by one several Issei filed into the small space, each holding something in their hands. Doctor Bennett brought up the rear of the procession carrying a small table which he placed in front of Mama, who stood nearly against the wall with her mouth open.

No one spoke and Hana realized she had held her breath as she watched the silent ceremony. Chiko left the door open and squeezed her way through everyone to stand with Mama and Hana. Martin made his way to them.

Mr. Hito, dressed in what must have been his Sunday best, bowed to Mama. "We are here to honor the life of Eiichi Kato, with your permission, Mrs. Kato." He bowed again, his chin dipping to his chest. Hana's heart swelled as she read the faces of all present. Although they stood shoulder to shoulder in a sweltering room, no one flinched. She could taste the perspiration on her upper lip. She ran her tongue between it and her teeth to ease the dryness in her mouth.

Mrs. Hito stepped up to place a hand-painted cloth on the table, her delicate hands carefully smoothing out the corners. She directed a trembling smile Mama's way. Another Issei woman arranged a small vase with a stick of burning incense on top of the cloth. They both bowed again and stepped back.

Mama bowed to all of them. "I thank you. You are most welcome in our home. Please continue."

The remainder of the visitors came forward one by one, holding offerings of food and small gifts to lay on the table. Hana picked up Papa's urn and placed it in the center. Mama reached behind her and pulled a small photo in a folded cardboard cover from under her pillow and placed it next to the urn.

Without prompting, the older ones began singing an old Japanese song, softly at first, then with more confidence. Hana had never heard that particular tune, but as she listened tears brimmed in her eyes—the tears she had pushed back for so many days. The melody filled the empty place inside she had hidden for months, even years.

Her knees weakening, she backed up to Papa's cot and rested on the edge. Her gaze wandered to each person and finally landed on John's dark eyes fixed on her. His hands clasped in front of him, he stood proud, swaying with the rhythm of the song. She stayed with him until the song was done, then broke away to survey the faces of the other guests. All eyes focused on Mama, except for Doctor Bennett's. He stared at her, but then lowered his head.

Another neighbor stepped forward and bowed. She laid an envelope tied with a little black and white ribbon on the small table next to the incense. Hana knew from another wake she had attended that it was a money gift from the mourners. Gratitude overwhelmed her—not for the money gift, but for the kind acts of remembrance to her family. She thought no one cared and she felt shame for doubting God's people.

Chiko leaned to her mother. "Mama-san, I asked Doctor Bennett to come and say a few words. The Christian ministers aren't around and, well, he knows our family and was with Papa-san when—when—" Her voice trailed off and Martin wrapped his arm around her, pulling her close enough to bury her nose in his chest.

Hana suddenly realized Chiko had arranged the entire event. She must have persuaded the others to come. The crowd shuffled as one more person slipped through the partially opened door. Doctor Davidson. Hana froze in fear—her heart skipping. But there he stood with his hands clasped in front of him and head bowed.

She caught Doctor Bennett's eye and he nodded slowly to her. His smile reassured her. Still, what was Doctor Davidson doing here? Had he honestly changed that much?

Mama's face glowed as she nodded to Doctor Bennett. "We honored to have you speak."

Hana nestled close to Mama and pulled out a chair from their table, guiding her to sit. Doctor Bennett cleared his throat and held a piece of paper. The top of it fluttered in his trembling hands. "I have a poem to read." He cleared his throat.

"Autumn wind of eve,
Blow away the clouds that mass
Over the moon's pure light
And the mists that cloud our mind,
Do thou sweep away as well.
Now we disappear,
Well, what must we think of it?
From the sky we came.
Now we may go back again.
That's at least one point of view."

No one moved or even shifted from their stance. He had read with lyrical clarity. The incense burned a sweet fragrance.

He continued. "I didn't know Mr. Kato, but I do know the quality of the family he leaves behind. A loving dutiful wife and three gifted children. God works in ways we don't always understand, but we learn to trust in His love and mercy, knowing it comes in His way and His time. We offer thanks to God tonight for the life of Eiichi Kato and the legacy of dignity he leaves to the Japanese community. May God grant you all freedom from this place, but most importantly, freedom in your hearts to love and be loved, and to move forward in courage."

Hana's face grew hot. She absorbed his words, partly afraid to heed them. She had abandoned her faith in God, questioning why he would make them suffer so much indignity. Yet, Mama had not wavered from her faith, and she had endured much more heartache. Papa's example of courage and justice came from a solid faith in the God he felt led him on his path.

A fire burned in her chest as she watched the visitors file past Mama and give a word of hope before they left. The last to come through was Doctor Davidson, with Doctor Bennett standing beside him. Hana shook inside as they approached her first. Doctor

Davidson's face showed no sadness or anger for a change. His eyes were soft as he looked deep into hers.

His voice shook. "Please forgive me for my cruelty to you. I've been wrong and I want to assure you I don't wish to be your enemy. Neil Bennett and my son have helped me see I need to change. I'll do my best to be a better doctor and, well, a better human being. With God's help." He turned to walk away.

The wall around Hana's heart cracked and began to crumble. As if the mourners and Doctor Bennett wasn't enough, this hard-hearted man finished the job of breaking her stubborn lack of faith in mankind—and maybe in her Heavenly Father.

She touched his elbow to stop him and held out her hand. "Thank you, Doctor Davidson."

He met her gaze, tears shining. Taking her hand in his, he smiled. She smiled back, disbelieving the altered exchange between both of them. He released her hand and nodded to Mama.

Mama bowed and he brushed by Doctor Bennett to follow the rest of the guests. A cool breeze blew through the open door, relieving the stagnant air. Hana's knees shook as he held out his hand to her. She sighed and almost laughed out the words. "I'm so grateful for your speech."

"My pleasure." He turned to Mama, who still sat straight postured in the chair.

"We thank you, Doctor Bennett."

Martin stuck out his hand and he grasped it in his, giving it a few pumps.

Chiko reached up on her tip toes to hug him, making his face turn red. He turned to leave. "See you tomorrow."

All at once the room was empty except for Mama and her children. Hana's head spun and she realized John had left without a good-bye again. It had become his specialty.

"That was good thing." Mama looked happier than she had seen her in many days. Martin and Chiko sat together on his cot, talking about the old ones who had come.

It seemed as if the whole world and everyone in it had been altered.

Mama stood in front of her, head cocked and brows raised. "You all right? You look funny."

"I'm fine, Mama-san. How about you? Are you happy about tonight?"

Mama nodded and then disappeared behind her curtain. "I go to bed now. We make some plans in the morning."

Martin left Chiko reading a book on her bed and grabbed a towel. "I'll be back. Just leave the window curtain open so I can maneuver by moonlight. Okay?"

Hana shrugged. "Sure." She could have sworn his limp had all but disappeared as he walked out the door. She closed the window down to a crack and stared at the moon. It must be the same moon that was shining right now over Bainbridge Island. The moon had always been there, sometimes invisible, but shining tonight when they needed reminding of its presence. Just like God. He had always been there, she just couldn't see Him until His light shone so bright in this room tonight.

She whispered low. "What kind of plans, Mama? How will we make it without Papa? Who will take care of us?"

She knew the answer as soon as the question left her lips. How could she have been so hardened? If Doctor Davidson could learn to trust God, so could she. Whatever was going to happen to them, she would give it to God. She would no longer resist His leading—wherever it may take them.

❧

"We're going home."

Martin's declaration startled Hana. Without considering Mama's feelings he had just now decided to become the head of the household with a dramatic announcement.

Hana stood up, her palms sweating. "You don't decide for all of us, Martin."

She felt Mama's hand grab her arm and pulled her down to the chair. "You wait. Martin explain."

Chiko leaned into Hana's face. "I want to go home. Where else would we go?"

Mama put her finger to her lips.

Martin grabbed the back of the chair he stood behind. "Anyway, Mama and I talked about this some time ago. I've made some inquiries to the old neighbors on the island. There is work to be found after all, even on the old farm. Of course, it's owned by Caucasians and more automation than Papa was used to. But I've heard most of the owners are sympathetic."

How could he possibly know for sure? Most of the word back from the outside was that Caucasians resented the Japanese Americans coming back into their communities. Her skin crawled to think of exposing her family to ridicule or even danger. Still, she had decided to trust God, however scary.

She turned to Mama. "You two discussed this without me?" She felt heat rise on her neck. "How could you do that? Papa wanted me to help you make the decisions. Don't you remember?"

She heard her words come back to her. They sounded disrespectful, but Mama should know how important it was to Papa. Trusting Martin with such a big decision seemed a bit premature. Even if she needed to let go, was this the time? "I'm sorry, Mama-san, but—"

Mama took Hana's hand. She turned to her until their knees touched. "Papa would want this. You hear him talk about home."

Martin softened his authoritative tone. "I know it will be hard to go back without Papa, but we can make it work. I think you want to go too. You're just afraid to face everyone. You've been gone a long time—since before Pearl Harbor. We can do this together."

Mama chimed in. "With God's help."

The prickle in Hana's heart told her it must be right. But she needed to be sure.

"I need to think about this. Do we have to decide today?"

Martin looked down but Mama shook her head. The room closed in and she had to find better air outside.

She stood and patted Mama's shoulder. "I'm going for a walk. I need to absorb this."

No one tried to stop her, although she heard the faint rumble of complaint from Chiko as she bounded down the steps onto the hot, packed dirt. Where should she go? No hospital duties today and the monotonous paths between the barracks had no appeal. Her feet had walked every inch of this camp, and she hated it.

She eased herself onto the bottom step. It could be the last chance she would have to just sit. From now on her time would be taken up with packing up the hospital, finishing out her duties, and saying her good-byes. Leaving the camp would be easy, but leaving the people she had come to care about wouldn't.

Alice Potter, Doctor Bennett, the other nurses, and even Doctor Davidson held a special place in her life's experience. And John. She clenched her hands together. How could she say good-bye to him? She denied her feelings for him over and over, mistrusting his every move, but she had to change that somehow. And what would she do with the flutters in her stomach whenever Neil Bennett came near? She had denied that too.

She had to bury all those feelings forever. He had moved on and she would be leaving.

Mama touched her shoulder. "Hana."

"Yes, Mama-san."

"I want you to read letter. It from Papa."

Hana's heart jumped. What letter?

She scooted in next to Hana on the step and handed her the wrinkled homemade envelope. "He write it before he go to prison and I save it for him."

She didn't want to take it. It would be too hard to read it now. But Mama knew best about these things, and Papa must have wanted it read. She swallowed hard and opened the envelope.

My dearest wife and children,

If you are reading this, then I am no longer with you, but in the arms of Jesus. How blessed I am that those missionaries so long ago showed me the way to eternity. I will wait for you to join me, and pray you keep the faith until we are together again.

Chiko, you have been a joy to your mother and me. I know you will grow into a beautiful and respectful young woman, and continue to be a blessing to your mother.

Martin, despite our differences, I am proud of you, my son. You will lead our family back to wholeness and safety once internment is over. I know you will face the hardships with dignity and wisdom. Take care of your mother and sisters.

Hana, you have been our strength and right hand, but there will come a time when you must let Martin lead the family. I pray you will continue to serve others, whether through nursing or whatever path God takes you on. Learn to trust Him with your whole heart, and move beyond your past hurts. With Him, you will find your way.

My sweet wife. Your love and companionship has been a prize far above jewels. May God protect and prosper you as you love our children and serve Him. The memories of our years together are forever burned in my heart.

I am in a better place. Do not mourn too long. There is much work to be done in our family and our community. Do not neglect to help those in need.

Love and peace to you.

Your husband and father.

Through pools of tears, she saw in her mother's face the peace her father wrote about. The peace that had eluded her for so long.

"Mama-san, I'm sorry I lost my faith. Papa must have known my struggle to forgive the people of my past. He knew I was afraid to embrace my fellow man—whether Japanese or Caucasian."

"He know."

If her parents could persevere, so could she. If Martin could walk again, she could surely run. If Chiko could be brave enough to go back home, how could she not be her example of courage?

"Papa want us to keep going. He never stop. We cannot. He tell me before he go to prison that he think he not come back. I hold fear in for long time. Till just before funeral when I mean to John.

But I know Papa in better place. I think he knew. I let it go."

The weight of sorrow and hiding from life lifted as she sat with Mama on the step. No words exchanged, yet monumental freedom of spirit bonded them there, gluing them tightly together. A new life was about to begin. She wouldn't fail Mama—or God.

Chapter 17

August 5, 1945

The woman's scream penetrated the walls, jarring John out of a sound sleep. Voices and radio noises echoed down the hallway of the barrack. Outside, footsteps pounded the path as if someone was running by. Then more voices and crying from outside prodded John to pull on his jeans, grab a shirt, and run to his door.

In the hall a man held his wife in his arms just outside their door. He eyed John. "Have you heard?"

"Heard what? What's happened?"

"A giant bomb was dropped on Hiroshima." He patted his wife's back and pushed her into the open door of their room.

"Giant bomb? What are you talking about?" John buttoned his shirt, missing a hole here and there. There had to be some mistake—a rumor with great exaggeration.

The man left his doorway and stepped closer to John. "They called it an atomic bomb." He rubbed his forehead. "Hiroshima. My wife's family lives there. She's worried sick."

The name rang in his head. No. The letter, where was the letter from Mother?

"I gotta go calm my wife down. We have a radio if you want to come hear about it." He backed away and disappeared through the door.

John couldn't move. He squeezed his eyes shut and tried to remember. "Hiroshima. It can't be the same city. Maybe I didn't read it right."

Once inside the room, he pulled open the small drawer in his homemade bed table. The letter rested on top of the new Bible that Simon had left with him. His fingers fumbled to pick up the envelope. What if it were true? His parents could be injured, or dead.

His hands shook as he pulled the lone piece of paper out and unfolded it. *Please don't let it be Hiroshima. Please, God.*

He scanned her handwriting until he saw it.

...a good job waiting for us in...Hiroshima.

"No!" He fell to the floor and leaned against the cot. The name resounded in his head, bouncing around in an echo. Perhaps they never got to Hiroshima, or might be in the part of the city not bombed.

"How do I find out?" He rose to stand on shaking legs. "I have to find out if they are dead."

He slipped on his shoes. The door slammed against the wall as he pulled it open. No bother shutting or locking it. Surely someone out there would know what was going on. He reached the bottom of the stairs. Hana ran toward him.

She waved, but with panic seared across her face. He wanted to feel bad for her. She also had family in Japan. Even though she had lost her father, she still had Mama. He looked past her to see only a few internees wandering in the yard. No chaos. Up in the guard tower, three guards huddled together, slapping each other on the back. Their laughter stabbed at his heart.

Hana stood before him. "I'm on my way to the hospital, but wanted to make sure you heard the horrible news."

He clutched the letter in his fist. What did it matter if he wrinkled it? He'd be better off if he hadn't received it. He studied Hana's face—full of worry. She had a beautiful face. He recalled the first time he saw her. She had smiled at him and his heart beat out of his chest. There was no smile now.

"Yes, I heard. What do you know?"

She touched his arm. "Are you all right? Do you have family in Hiroshima?"

He shuffled to the shade between the barracks. She followed him and positioned herself directly in front of him. The scent of soap from her skin filled his nose. Why did she have to stand so close? He wanted her to comfort him, tell him his parents were alive.

He looked to the blue sky. "I do. At least I think I do.

She moved around him to lean against the building. "I don't understand. Who?"

He held out the letter. She stared at it for a moment and then slipped it from his grip. He blew out a long deep breath as she read it. She likely wouldn't care. She hadn't cared about him for some time. Maybe he should have explained to her sooner about his conversion, his partnership with Simon, and the group he would soon lead. He could have earned her approval once and for all. The approval he would have no chance to earn from his father now.

He glanced at her face, watching her eyes scan the page over and over. How wonderful it would have been to belong to someone such as her. His blood rushed to his feet as he leaned against the building.

She dropped her arms to her side. "I'm so sorry, John. I didn't know." She folded the paper and handed it to him. "What are you going to do?"

"Wait."

She nodded. "I'll help you in any way possible. There'll be information circulating soon, I bet. We can find someone who has a radio and listen in. The BBC always has good news broadcasts."

He wanted to laugh at her enthusiasm, as if she were planning a party. She meant well, he knew that. Her eyes told him she did care after all, a look that would sustain him through any horrible news.

She pushed a lock of hair from her forehead, but the wind blew it back in her face. "Look, I have to go change and get to the hospital. Why don't you come by tonight and we'll go next door. The Hitos have a radio."

He used his finger to flip back the strand of unruly hair resting on her forehead. "Sure, thanks." His parents would have liked her.

He choked back thickness in his throat.

Her face flushed and she smiled before running off. His eyes followed her until she was out of sight. He might have lost his parents, but he might have gained back a friend. If only he could hope for more than friendship. It all depended on her and—

"And Doctor Bennett." He mumbled as he stomped up the steps. "Doctor Bennett who can do no wrong." Just inside the doorway he tossed the letter on the cot. "Jealousy doesn't become you, John. How can you be jealous at a time like this?" His heart ached with mixed emotions.

Exhaustion set in as the horror of the situation gripped him. His hard bed comforted him as he rolled into the center of it and closed his eyes. Hana's face drifted in and out of his mind's eye. She did seem closer today than she had in so long. He'd give anything to know her heart at this moment. He'd give anything to know if his parents survived the bomb.

"If it's your will, Father, save them."

If it's meant to be with Hana it will be—Doctor Bennett or no Doctor Bennett.

⁂

The last time she met with the two of them in the same room, she hated one of them. Now as she stood in the doorway of Doctor Bennett's office, she felt the peace of reconciliation flow over her like a soothing balm. How good it was not to be tied up with fear and accusations when facing Doctor Davidson. Perhaps he felt the same about her.

She pulled in a breath to push out the words. "Good morning, doctors." There. She could be pleasant to him—even sympathetic. Doctor Davidson had been through a lot and so had she. This they had in common.

Doctor Bennett's face brightened when he saw her. He rushed around his desk to pull a chair out. "Please, join us."

"Thanks. I suppose I know what you're talking about. It's a

terrible thing." She crossed her legs and pulled her skirt over her knee.

Doctor Davidson sat opposite her and seemed to search her face for approval. "A couple months ago, I would have been overjoyed that someone had dropped a bomb." He hung his head. "Now, I can't believe I ever felt that way. How could I have been so mean?"

Doctor Bennett perched himself on the edge of his desk. "Doctor Davidson, don't be so hard on yourself. You're no different than a lot of folks who lost loved ones at Pearl. At least you've had a change of heart. Besides, President Truman said doing this will save more lives than will be lost."

Hana had to break in. She couldn't just accept it so easily. "That's *if* Japan surrenders. If they don't, I'm not so sure. I know the President is trying to help us make sense of this, but it's too early to tell. Many of us have relatives still in Japan. We're scared for them." Her stomach felt wound up tight. She wondered if they could understand.

Doctor Davidson looked up. "I know how you feel. My son's wife and her family are over there. They could be dead."

His tone broke Hana's heart. She had forgotten all about his son. "I'm so sorry. I know you must be worried."

Doctor Bennett stood and put one hand on her shoulder and one on Doctor Davidson's. "I'm sorry for all of us. Let's just pray it all works together for the good of this country and Japan."

Hana felt the warmth of his touch on her shoulder. His caring manner had always impressed her, but now he seemed so close. Too close. She ignored the butterflies dancing in her stomach.

"Well, doctors, I need to report to Nurse Potter. She'll have my hide if I'm gone too long." She turned to leave.

Doctor Bennett called after her. "Did you know she's leaving tomorrow?"

Her heart jumped. No. Not yet. She wasn't ready to be without Alice here in this place. She spun around and shook her head. "I didn't know. I'll miss her."

Doctor Bennett's voice shook ever so slightly "We all will."

Doctor Davidson nodded.

She stood and hurried to the door. "See you both later." She wanted to run down the hall and confront Alice—talk her into staying a while longer. At least until—

She stopped half way to Alice's desk. "Don't be so selfish, Hana Kato." If anyone deserved to leave here, it was Alice Potter. She had her adopted little girl, Charlie, to think of now. She never had to be here in the first place. Like Doctor Bennett and Doctor Davidson, she took the job voluntarily. When most others would have quit long ago, they all stayed. Especially Alice, who had been there longer than both doctors.

Alice stood at the end of the hall with hands on hips, smiling. "I'd like to talk to you, Nurse Kato." She motioned for Hana to come.

Hana swallowed back tears and marched over to the woman she had come to love and admire. The entire Kato family had benefitted from her competent care and bossy demeanor. She smiled to think how scared she was that first day of this burly nurse with her hair in a bun. Now, she would say good-bye to her and wish her well.

She led Hana to the front desk and plopped down in her chair. "I'm horrified at the news this morning. Are you worried about family over there?"

"Yes, my mother and father both have relatives there. Not close ones, but still, it's very upsetting. I wish we knew more about how bad it was." She tapped her fingernails on the counter.

Alice placed her hand on Hana's. "It's in God's hands now. We have to trust Him, don't we? That's what Mama-san would say, right?" A tear slipped from her eye, but Hana knew it was because of something more than Japan. She braced herself for what Alice was about to say.

Alice sighed hard and leaned back. "I'm leaving here tomorrow."

Hana looked away. "I heard." She bit her lip and straightened. "I'll miss you, Alice. You've been a good friend."

When Alice looked back, her face was soaked with tears. Hana reached into her skirt pocket and pulled out her handkerchief. "Here, blow your nose and let's have a good day."

Alice's belly shook as she laughed. "Yes, Ma'am. You'll have to take over for me as head bossy nurse."

"I will."

Chiko bolted through the door and threw her arms around Hana. Alice darted around the desk.

Hana lifted her sister's chin. "What's wrong? Are you still upset over the bombing?"

Chiko nodded and wiped her cheeks with her hand. Alice handed her Hana's hankie and hugged her around the shoulders. "You can tag along with me today, and we'll keep our mind off the rest of the world for a while. How's that sound?"

Chiko leaned into Alice. "Sure."

Alice patted Chiko's head. "Someday Charlie will be as tall as you. I wish we could live close by so you could babysit her."

It was best Chiko didn't understand this would be her last day with her friend. She was confident Alice would break it to her gently.

The two strolled arm in arm out of the foyer and around the corner. Every conceivable emotion rolled over Hana in waves. Her feet wouldn't move, so the only thing to do was wait until she had control.

She imagined the entire camp must be feeling this way. Like the sand on the beach at home. As a child she would pat the wet sand with her hands until water bubbled up, changing it from solid to liquid. It was like that now. Nothing solid to hang on to.

Except God.

Neil buried his head in his hands. The front desk was in such disarray he barely knew where to start looking for the paperwork he needed.

"Nurse Potter! Come back."

Only three days and it seemed as if the hospital had fallen apart. Hana had done her best to pick up the slack; he didn't know what he would have done without her. He had shut down another two wings due to lack of patients. More families left every day. Soon he would be saying good-bye to Hana. His chest ached to think of it. Especially without her knowing how he felt.

Hana slid through the front door and quickly shut it. "It's already hot out there." She looked over at the open window behind the desk and scowled at him. "Shut that window. Do you want all that hot air to rush in here?"

"Yes, Ma'am." He slammed it shut and turned to salute her. "It's like having Alice back."

He hoped she would smile, but instead she waved a piece of paper in the air. "Casualties. Thousands of them. This is the first of reports coming out of Japan about the dead and injured." She dropped her arms and stared at him. His heart wrenched to see her so upset.

He eased his way around the counter. "It's terrible. I can't imagine the suffering. We need to press our government to send relief. I've already talked to a government official I know."

Hana folded the paper and stuffed it in a tote. He'd never seen her carry one before. "New bag?"

She pulled it over her shoulder and looked down. "Yes. I thought I should take home some things out of my locker."

He knew what was coming. "Your family is leaving soon, aren't they?"

"Yes."

"Oh, I see. Well, uh, be sure to let me know the day you want to be your last and I'll put in the paperwork for your final pay." He sounded as though his mouth was full of gravel.

She nodded and left him standing there.

"No, it's time to tell her. Don't let her go."

"What?" Hana's voice rang in his ears. He clasped his hand to his mouth. *You spoke aloud!* She heard him. She must think him a fool. Now what?

He turned his head to face her. "I said, I'd like to have a chat with you when you have a moment." He felt the heat rise up his neck and prickle his ears. She would catch on if he didn't get control.

She tipped her head. "I have time right now, if you do."

Now? He wasn't prepared. Perhaps that was best. He could speak his heart without rehearsal. "Sure, let's step into Alice's office. I think there are two chairs left in there."

A Japanese doctor and nurse hurried past Hana. She turned to peer after them, but then followed him into the office. He held the door open for her, swallowing what small amount of spit he had left. The office still smelled of Alice's perfume—the same perfume he had told her repeatedly was against regulations to wear on duty. Now he was glad to have it linger.

Hana dropped the tote on the floor and wiggled into the rickety chair. "Do I need to fill out some forms or something in order to leave my position here?"

He thought better of shutting the door and swung it open. "Well, yes, but that's not what I want to talk about."

His feet felt like they were cast in cement, but he trudged to the other chair and sat on the edge, leaning toward her. "Miss Kato…Hana, I need to be blunt. There isn't much time left and I have to say what's in my heart."

He saw the panic on her face, but didn't care. At least she let him call her Hana, and this was something he had to do. He would never forgive himself if he didn't try. "You must know I have great affection for you. I haven't always been good at hiding it." He paused, hoping for a smile.

Her face flushed, but she still locked her gaze on him. He grasped his hands together and squeezed hard. Nervous shaking was not what he needed now. What he needed was a response. She only raised her brows.

He filled the silence. "I know we are very different people—a different race and creed. But we both love God and medicine. That could be enough to sustain us as a couple, don't you think?"

Was he crazy? He had just proposed to someone who had no clue he was in love with her. He imagined she would end the conversation and walk out, never to return.

She blinked. "Go on."

His heart pounded so hard, he thought she must hear it. "Well, I guess what I want to know is if you feel anything for me, or if you think we could have a future together. I know this is sudden and shocking, but in times like these, formalities are a waste of time. Do you agree?"

Her gaze moved to the floor. She was as still as the stagnant air in the room. He felt the trickles of perspiration run down his temples. If there had been a clock in the room, it would have ticked away what seemed to be hours.

She leaned to rest her elbows on her knees and folded her arms across them. "I don't know quite what to say. I'm not going to lie and say I didn't sense you had feelings for me. But I never expected this." She shifted her gaze to the window.

He pushed down the hope that rose up in his belly. "I'm sorry to be so abrupt." She really hadn't said anything to encourage him—yet.

She stood and paced in front of him for a few seconds, then stopped and slipped her hands in her pockets. "I admire you, Doctor Bennett, and I have to admit I like you very much. More than I should. We come from two different worlds. I think it would be impossible for me to marry a Caucasian man. It's too hard, even illegal in some states. Would you really want the kind of life having a Japanese wife would bring?"

He stood to face her and pulled her right hand from her pocket, holding it tight. "First, I think you can call me Neil now, at least in private. And I'm used to hardship. I was a missionary kid, remember? The world will change. We could make it. Hana, I love you. Don't leave with your family. Come with me to start a new life. We could go east where they don't care so much."

She looked down at their joined hands. "I don't think so. Neil, I don't know if I care enough for you to make a life together. I have other—other people in my life."

He dropped her hand. "You mean John?"

She nodded.

"Just because he's Japanese doesn't mean he's right for you." He placed his hands on his shoulders. "Will you think about it? We could do a lot of good as a medical team, and lifelong partners. Hmm?"

She took one step back and sighed. After another minute she gave him a half smile. "I'll think about it—Neil. No promises. No commitments. Just thinking about it. Can you live with that for a week?"

A week. An eternity.

Chapter 18

August 31, 1945

He had to face being orphaned for real this time. The posting on the message board said it all. A distant relative from Japan had telegrammed all the internment camps to share with anyone with the last name of Yamada or Kobe a list of family casualties at Hiroshima. John couldn't read the information written in Japanese, but he knew his parents' name when he saw them. Both of them gone—burned to death in the initial blast of the bomb.

And now, Nagasaki had been hit. More carnage of people he didn't know—more orphans created. Yet, how many more would have died because of a Japanese military prepared to fight until every person in Japan was gone?

"Poor Mother and Father. I almost had you back."

"John?" Hana's soft voice called to him, like from a dream. He had been wishing for her company and here she was, standing beside him in the mess hall.

He patted the bench next to him. She slid close, their shoulders touching. He wanted to rest his head next to hers, but could only stare at the board. He wiped the perspiration from his upper lip. "My parents are dead. Someone from Japan sent a telegram. I might have searched for years if I hadn't seen this list. God must have led me here this morning."

She pressed her shoulder into his. "I'm sorry. I know how hard it is and how hurt you must feel. It's a pity you couldn't have seen them one more time." Her voice soothed his sorrow a bit, and her presence completed him somehow. She was all he wanted now. He had a job to do and he wanted her with him forever.

He shook his head. "It's just such a terrible way to die. I've heard rumors of how horrible it was for the people there. Do you think they suffered?"

"I don't know, John. From the talk I've heard at the hospital, it's pretty bad. No one knows how to deal with this kind of thing." She looked to the floor. "Let's just believe they went quickly."

The tears stinging his eyes wouldn't be stopped. Hana wouldn't mind if he showed emotion, she was too kind to deny him that. "How come God allows wars and bombs and bad things? Even though I have faith in Him now, I still don't understand."

She slipped her hand into his. "I asked Mama the same question this morning. She closed her eyes tight and smiled. Then she said that God's heart was broken too. He gave man free will and we must live with the choices some make."

The tears found their way to his chin and onto his shirt. "I suppose we might never really understand."

"Mama says that's what true faith is. I'm learning to trust God again, but I have a long way to go. I'm thankful for Mama."

"I could use a mother like her." He squeezed her hand. "Thanks for being here. I need you today."

She smiled and nudged him. "I'm here. At least for a few more days."

He felt the blow to his chest as if someone had hit him. "You're leaving here, aren't you?"

"Yes, in three days. Martin has everything arranged. He's the man of the house now. Even though I had a hard time giving him control, I'm very proud of him. He's taking us home to Bainbridge Island and will look for work in the strawberry fields just like Papa."

He didn't care about Martin, the fields, or anything except that she would be gone. There was no time to woo her. The words choking him had to be expressed. "Don't go home. Stay with me."

She pulled her hands away and folded them in her lap. "What do you mean?"

"You know what I mean. I love you. I need you. I have a job to do here and I want us to do it together." He grabbed her hands again and held them tight in his. "We belong together. I feel it's right."

Hana closed her eyes. A tear slid down her cheek. Was this a happy tear or a sad one? It didn't matter. Chances to snatch a happy future could slip right through his fingers if he didn't seize the moment.

"Hana?"

"I heard you." She seemed to hold her breath, but finally opened her eyes and looked square into his. "I think I love you too, but there are many things to consider. My family needs me too, now more than ever. I can't abandon them."

He opened his mouth to protest but she shook her head.

She raised her perfectly shaped brows. "What is this job you want me to do with you?"

"I'll tell you about it later. What's more important is us, forever. I'm sorry to pressure you, but we're running out of time. I feel like I've been waiting for so long."

She looked away, face red. He held his breath. She could have another reason to hesitate—a worthy adversary. Doctor Bennett. What use would it be to ignore it now? Time to bring it out in the open and help her see the doctor could never be right for her. There were a million reasons he could give her.

Leave her to Me.

Every muscle in his body relaxed at the sound of God's prompting. This is what true peace was—how many times had he prayed for it? He would have to fight every selfish impulse now.

But God, I need to show her the way.

Leave her to Me.

Hana stared at him. "Can we talk about this later? I need to get to the hospital." She stood and he grasped her hand tight.

"May I come by tonight? If your family is leaving, I need to say good-bye." In truth, he just wanted to see her. He could say his good-byes to the family another day, but he had to see her face again soon, to see what was in her eyes.

She brushed off the back of her skirt. "Sure, you can come by." She backed away from him. "I hope your heart isn't too broken."

He tilted his head. Was she telling him no?

She stopped. "I mean about your parents. I'm really sorry."

He sighed hard. "Thanks."

Her steps quickened and she disappeared. The pounding in his chest subsided. He shouldn't hold on so tightly. God had it under control. Wasn't there a tale about holding a bird so tight you crush it? His heart would break if he crushed what they had, even if he had to settle for status quo. She hadn't said yes, but she didn't say no. Michael would have told him to let life unfold—something new for him.

He didn't like it one bit, and something, or someone, nagged at his gut.

Neil Bennett's words had her mind spinning. Thinking over his proposal overnight hadn't helped her make a decision. How could he declare his love and expect her to return it so readily when they were just friends? She had guessed some time ago he had feelings for her. It was clear now that ignoring him and those hints of affection didn't deter him.

She thought back to all the times he stood close and her heart thumped. Denying it now was useless.

And now John's declaration of love. He needed her. She felt drawn to him more than ever, but that wasn't enough. She had to know for sure, but how could she decide when they were leaving so soon? All the way up the walk to the hospital she rubbed her temples to clear her fuzzy thoughts.

"You're cleaning the laundry room out today, so stay hidden and forget about both of them." Her own words didn't convince her.

The coast was clear as far as she could tell when she peeked around the corner and down the hospital hallway. She had a straight shot to the end and into the steaming, smelly laundry room.

She dodged carts and an occasional orderly to make it all the way in one charge. Safely inside the double doors she sighed with relief. She could hide in here all day, ignoring her confusion—or figure out how to resist the urge to love them both. Sun streamed through the only window on the outside wall and reflected off the metal tables used to fold sheets and towels.

"Hello? I'm here for laundry duty." She hollered past the fog of steam to the man standing back by the boiler that heated the water. He kicked pipes and twisted the metal handles. Each time he turned one, steam rolled out onto the floor. She could barely see him, but heard him calling the boiler nasty names.

She walked through the fog and bumped into a long metal table. "Ouch."

The man turned. When she saw his face she gasped. Neil.

He came close and leaned over to see her rubbing her thigh. "Are you all right?" He looked into her eyes and then down again, wiping the perspiration from his brow.

She felt like laughing and crying at the same time. Her leg throbbed, her pride stung, and standing here was the one person she had tried so hard to avoid. She pointed to the boiler. "Never mind about me. Just go ahead and finish your job with the…stupid piece of junk, I believe you called it."

He frowned and then a half laugh escaped his lips. Hana couldn't contain her emotions anymore and let the nervous energy come out in bursts of giggles. She held her stomach as the joy of humor rolled from her heart. It was an amazing feeling, one long overdue. Before Pearl Harbor, before her injury, she laughed a lot.

Neil leaned back on the table and it rolled away from him. She reached out to catch him and missed. His leg flew up and she tumbled after him. Landing hip first on the floor beside him, pain squelched her laughter. They had landed on the hard floor at the same time, elbows touching. She had never been this close to him.

She could smell the bleach in his white lab coat. Her heart pounded so hard she couldn't hear anything. She had to get up. He was too close. She didn't want to be this near to him.

He pushed himself up on his elbows. "You okay?"

She nodded and felt something warm drip down her forehead. He reached over and touched his finger between her eyes.

He squinted at her. "You're bleeding, but it's just a nick."

When he shifted position, his hand landed on hers. Her breath left her and she sat still, unable to move. She could hear him breathing next to her and wanted him to move away. No. She didn't. As the steam floated away, so did her resolve.

"I have to get up." The weakness in her voice wouldn't fool him. She still couldn't move and he made no indication he was going to stand.

"Hana."

He leaned in, his nose to her nose. She closed her eyes just as his warm lips pressed ever so lightly on hers. He pulled away slowly and then crouched on his knees. She opened her eyes. This was against everything she thought she wanted.

"Let's go take care of that cut." His voice was like music, soothing and melodic, yet almost a whisper.

"Yes." She took his hand and he pulled her up from the floor. He was close again. She wanted to run, but wanted to stay there, breathing in his smell.

"Let me turn off the, uh, stupid piece of junk, and we'll find an exam room."

No. She had to stop this now. Her heart had been divided, complicating everything, just when she needed clarity.

She backed away from him. "Really, I can do this myself. It just needs cleaning up."

"I'm the doctor. You'll do as I say." He smiled at her and resistance faded again.

They crossed the hall into an empty exam room. He pointed to a chair by the counter. She walked as if in a daze and sat. She should have been more careful. This was a mistake and he must know that.

It was all wrong—a relationship between a Japanese and a Caucasian.

God, what am I going to do?

He rummaged through a box, pulling out a bottle of mercurochrome. If someone walked through the door right now they would surely see the look on her face and see her attraction. Could it be she loved him too? What about John?

She had to dispel the heavy emotion in the air. "Since when do you work in the hospital laundry room? You're the Chief of Staff around here. Where's the mechanic?" Even though she tried to change the subject, it wouldn't be enough to calm her raging nerves. He would see her hands shaking if she didn't tuck them under her knees.

He pulled back her hair and pressed something onto the wound. "Practically the whole laundry crew is out with colds. I've fixed the thing before, so when there was no one else to do it, I came to the rescue. Guess I didn't do so well for you. Let me see that cut."

The stinging made her jump. "Ow. I hate that stuff."

"Just a tiny adhesive bandage and you're done." He smoothed the bandage on her forehead and then stepped back. "Beautiful." His stare moved from her brow to her eyes.

She looked away and stood, smoothing out her skirt. She glanced in the mirror. No one would even see the wound. "This place seems to be dangerous for me."

His smile was boyish and hopeful. "I'm hoping you mean the head injuries and not me."

"Well, I guess it would apply to both. Neil, we can't do this." She headed for the door. "I have to get to work before someone comes looking for me."

He shrugged and turned to throw the gauze in the trash. "I think we can, do this I mean."

There was no time to debate with him. She wanted to work and put it all out of her mind. The kiss was a mistake. She would forget all about it and stay out of his way. Then she would give him his answer tomorrow. Really, she knew the answer.

It had to be no. Didn't it?

Chapter 19

Even his eyes had changed. Before, they were dull and gray. Now a sparkle of excitement and wonder she had never seen glistened as he spoke. Hana smiled as Doctor Davidson rambled on like a child anticipating a field trip to the zoo.

"I'll be learning a lot about Japanese customs and the language before I go. The small team I'm with has been patient with me so far. I'll admit it's not been easy. You people speak a hard language to learn, one of the hardest I'm told."

His demeanor, his verbiage had all transformed to fit his new life of faith. She had been skeptical at first, but the man standing before her jabbering away was anything but the bigoted doctor of a few months ago.

He raised his brows. "Maybe you could teach me a few Japanese words that would be helpful when I go over there."

She felt her face flush. "I don't speak Japanese, Doctor Davidson. I only know a few words myself. I was born in America and my parents spoke English most of the time."

It had likely never occurred to him that she didn't speak the language of Japan, just like Neil had assumed at first. The poor man was in for a long road of arduous instruction on the subject. She doubted he would be able to master speaking Japanese in the near future.

He shook his head and turned beet red. "I should have figured that out. I'm sorry. Anyway, I should go. I've packing to do." He held out his hand. "I hope you will forgive me for all the trouble I gave you. You're a good nurse. Any hospital would be lucky to get you. Call on me as a reference if you need one."

She felt the warmth of his hand and wondered how she could ever have disliked him so. Never did she dream she would be on the receiving end of a Caucasian's good will. Perhaps the world would accept her and her family someday soon.

Doctor Davidson disappeared out the front door of the hospital. She would probably never see him once they were all gone from here. Or Alice, or Michael, or any of the others who had made a mark on her life here in camp.

She unpinned her cap and folded it to fit into her skirt pocket. The air outside smelled of vegetables. The hot sun had ripened the fields, but few Japanese laborers were left to harvest them. Next spring the dirt would go dormant with no one to plant. Come next planting season, her family would be home. Martin would be following in Papa's footsteps at a large farm and Chiko would be itching to finish her junior year of high school.

She followed the fence line, no longer afraid of the guards. They didn't care anymore if the buffer zone was breached.

She stared up at the mountain. "And what will you be doing, Hana Kato?" If only God lived there and would look down on her, giving her the answers she longed for. "Will you be working in a white hospital? Helping Mama do laundry for the rich ladies in town?" Her voice drifted off on the hot breeze as she neared her block. "Or will you choose John or Neil, and start a new life with one of them?"

She reached the steps to the barrack and eased herself down. The sun had begun its journey to the horizon, leaving her a spot of shade to cool in, to think in. When would the answers come? Everyone seemed confident about leaving except her. Martin busied himself making arrangements, Mama packed and cleaned, and Chiko wrote letters to her old friends. They had no doubts. But they didn't have the choices she had.

Chiko sauntered around the corner and stood at the bottom of the steps. "Whatcha doing?"

Hana marveled at how the scar on Chiko's face had faded. Doctor Okada had done a wonderful job. Her little sister would be a beauty in no time, grown and on her own. She wouldn't need her big sister so much anymore. Not once they got home and she bounced back into life.

She reached up to straighten the collar on Chiko's blouse. "Thinking."

Chiko squeezed in next to her. "About what?"

"Oh, just some important decisions to make. Nothing you need to worry over." She pulled her cap out of her pocket and fanned herself with it. "What are you doing out here? Don't you need to help Mama with packing?"

Chiko grinned and picked at her fingernail. "She's got plenty of help in there."

"Don't tell me. Martin has decided to take charge of that too." She smirked while Chiko shook her head.

Teasing was not a welcome activity at the moment. Fatigue had set in and she had to get ready for dinner at the mess hall. John would be by and she wanted to freshen up. "Chiko, what are you not saying?"

Chiko jumped up from her perch and giggled her way through the barrack door. Hana followed, hearing strange voices coming from inside. Men's voices. Her muscles tensed as she recognized Neil Bennett's laugh. She turned her back to the wall next to the door and leaned against it. The last thing she wanted was to see him. The only thing worse could be—

"Here, let me lift that, Mrs. Kato."

No! John's voice bellowed through the open door. Feeling like a trapped rat, she inched further from the doorway. The only way of escape was past the opening. She might be seen, and besides, Chiko would tell them any minute that she was home.

"Agh." She whispered and then held her breath.

Chiko leaned through the doorway. "Are you coming in?"

"No."

Martin was next to poke his head over the top of Chiko's. "You have company, sis."

Closing her eyes tight didn't make the situation go away. There was only one thing to do.

Hana, it's time to face the music, swallow the pill, bite the bullet.

She straightened up as her siblings let her pass. The room fell silent as she marched to the table and sat in the only available chair. "Well, Mama. It seems you have excellent help tonight. How did you round up these fine gentlemen?"

Mama giggled and pointed to John, and then Neil. "They show up just in time."

Hana shifted her gaze back and forth between the now blushing men. "Did you—come together?"

Neil chimed in with his usual wit. "He followed me here. So I guess I had the idea first."

Martin propped his good leg up on his cot. "Ha. Good one, Doctor Bennett."

Her slicing glare didn't seem to faze Martin. He continued to chuckle at the expense of everyone's discomfort.

"They good help." Mama nodded as she placed a small stack of old books into the corner of a box. "But we done now. Time to go to dinner."

"I'm starved." Chiko skipped out the door ahead of Mama.

Martin pushed himself up. "You boys coming?"

Despite her ears feeling as though they were on fire, Hana managed to speak calmly. "Yes, why don't you go to dinner with Martin? I'll be there soon."

Why were neither of them speaking? John and Neil both stood their ground, even as Martin slipped out the door.

She stood and waved them on. "Really, go eat."

John pulled out the chair vacated by Mama and sat firmly on the seat. Neil also nabbed a chair and did the same, his arms crossed. Hana held her stomach in tight at the sight of the two men sparring with body language.

She slithered back into her chair and tapped the table with her fingers. "So, no dinner? What would you like to do then? We could play cards, charades?" Her smile reflected in their eyes, but still, neither one flinched.

The moments ticked by so slowly, she thought time had stood still. This could go on all night. Her stomach growled. Surely they were hungry too.

John broke the awkward silence. "I think we both want the same thing. A moment of your time alone."

Neil nodded, but captured her gaze with the gleam in his eye. "I think the first one here should talk to you first."

John leaned in Neil's direction. "Let's let Hana decide."

"It's only fair for me to speak to her now. I'm still her boss, you know." Neil's back was rigid now. His handsome face stern.

John's square jaw clenched. "I've known her longer and we have things to discuss."

"So do we. Her and me, I mean." Neil's voice cracked. He scooted to the edge of his chair.

John's stare looked as though it would bore straight through Neil. "You can talk to her tomorrow at the hospital."

"We already had a long talk at the hospital, didn't we, Hana?" Neil's eyes pleaded with her to validate him.

He wouldn't expose their little moment of weakness this morning, would he? Yes, yes he would. It was time to make a move. She slapped both palms on the table. "I'm going to dinner. You two stay here and duke it out if you want."

As she closed the door behind her she thought she heard arguing. It was clear to her now. Neither John Yamada nor Neil Bennett was the man for her.

September 1, 1945

It had to rain today of all days. For weeks the skies taunted the dry ground with dark clouds that never produced a drop of rain. The acres around the camp browned under the sun, waiting for the heavens to open up. But today as the station buzzed with internees toting suitcases and boxes, the downpour soaked everyone and left bogs of mud where hardened dirt once was.

Martin ushered his mother to a dry spot under the station building eves. "Stay here where it's dry, Mama-san. I'll find out which bus we get on." He turned to Hana. "Make sure Chiko doesn't wander off."

She had given up long ago trying to corral Chiko. Besides, her heavy eyelids kept her from focusing on anything at the moment. Barely two hours of sleep weren't enough to fill her empty patience. At least the night had brought resolution to many things. Papa was right—prayer works. Not only did the answers come, she had been bathed in the peace he always talked about.

She huddled close to Mama and talked over the rumbling crowd. "Mama, you're shivering. Are you warm enough? Where's your sweater?"

Mama clutched her pocketbook. "I fine. No worry. Just want to go home, you know?" Hana hated seeing her so anxious. Then a smile graced her mother's face. She pointed to John in the distance. "He doing good job." Her eyes followed him as he moved from one Issei to the next. "He so much like Papa." She turned to Hana. "You think so too?"

Not waiting for an answer, Mama sat down on her suitcase and rifled through a small bag.

The first bus plowed through the mud and stopped in front of the crowd. A uniformed man stepped off and hollered a destination. Several groups of internees worked their way to the front and boarded. Children clung to their parents, jumping and squealing at the prospect of taking a ride. Faces of the older folks revealed various emotions—fear, anticipation, relief.

Chiko came alongside Mama. "Look, there go the Hitos." She waved wildly, but the Hito family looked straight ahead, as if afraid they would lose their place on the bus—lose their chance to go home.

Hana searched the perimeter of the yard until she saw him. John stood surrounded by a group of older internees. He handed out flyers and spoke to each one individually. They nodded and picked up their luggage to join the group boarding another bus that just arrived.

She caught his eye. He smiled and waved, then moved on to the next group of waiting travelers. How comfortable he looked taking charge and even comforting some of the timid older women.

Mama spied a neighbor and hurried over to say her good-byes.

Neil was suddenly at Hana's side. "Looks like this is it, Miss Hana Kato."

His eyes bore dark circles much like hers. She must have caused it. He had certainly been the source of her sleepless night. And John.

She pretended to be looking for someone. "Good morning. Yes, this is a day of great significance for all of us." She looked down at the mud puddle in front of them. "I don't know whether to be happy or sad."

He stood so close she felt the warmth of his elbow touching hers. "I know what would make me happy."

Hana pulled in a long breath as he leaned into her. How could she resist such a man? Yes, he was Caucasian. But he was also strong, confident, intelligent, and a leader. She glanced John's way, knowing she could say the same about him.

"I'm sorry I left you and John so abruptly last night. If I had known we were to leave this morning instead of tomorrow, I wouldn't have been so flippant. It wasn't until we got to the mess hall that they made the announcement."

Neil cleared his throat. "Hana, I still want you to come with me. It's not too late and I've been awake all night thinking about us. We can make this work. I know you have feelings for me. I don't want to leave without you."

The rain had changed to a light drizzle. Another bus rolled into the yard, but no one got off to announce its destination. Martin came and stood next to Hana. "Hey, Doc. You getting on one of these busses?"

"Yes."

Martin glanced back and forth between her and Neil. His brows knit into one, then a look of understanding crossed his face. "Well, good luck then." He thrust his hand out and Neil shook it. Martin squinted at Hana. "Stay close to Mama, okay?"

Hana nodded and pointed at their mother, chattering away in Japanese with her friend.

Martin never would approve of her being with a Caucasian. Even though he liked Neil as a doctor, he would protest a marriage with his sister. It would be a hard road to travel for a mixed race couple right now. Neil had to know that, but he must love her enough to try.

"Neil, I prayed all night. I had to know what God wanted for me. For us. I—"

"Hey you two." Doctor Davidson hopped onto the porch. "Time to go our separate ways. I wish you both the best." He patted Neil's shoulder. "Sorry to bail on my invitation to join you in private practice. This is my only chance to help my son find his wife's family." He handed Neil a slip of paper. "This is the name of the agency I'll be with. If you want to join us, we could use a good doctor and nurse to come to Japan with us." He winked at Neil and shook his hand, then held it out to Hana.

The impulse was too great to ignore. She reached up and kissed his cheek. "Good-bye, Doctor Davidson. I'll never forget you."

A tear replaced his smile. He took one step back and stared into her eyes. "Nor I, you. Good-bye, Hana." He tipped his head toward Neil. "Take care of my friend there."

Heat filled her face as Doctor Davidson hustled off toward a group of Issei men. She frowned at Neil. What had he told Doctor Davidson?

"Doctor Bennett?" Someone waved at him and pointed to an old woman perched on her suitcase, her head in her hands.

He grabbed her arm. "I'll be right back. Don't move."

She nodded. She had no intention of moving.

He weaved his way through the now diminished crowd. She would wait, and try to calm her fluttering stomach before giving him her answer. She caught sight of John headed for her. Martin stopped him and they embraced. John whispered something in Martin's ear and they both glanced her way. Martin patted John's shoulder, but neither of them smiled.

Hana scanned the yard for Chiko and Mama. Martin wouldn't be happy if she lost track of them. They stood together talking to another family. Suddenly John was next to her, his clip board tucked under his arm. He looked up to the sky. "Rain stopped. That's good."

She could read something in his eyes. Something she had never seen before. Happiness? No, more than that. Contentment and satisfaction—not about her or their relationship—it ran much deeper. He had found himself. It wouldn't matter if she stayed with him. He would be complete without her, so it seemed.

She glanced at Neil tending the old woman. She never thought before that *he* might need someone. But now, she sensed he was the one who should have someone by his side.

She turned her attention to John. "How are you doing with all this? You seem very organized."

He stuck his hands in his jeans pockets. "I'm doing my best. I know it's what I'm supposed to do. It's a good feeling to be executing God's plan for a change. I'm sorry it took me so long to see it." He stepped up to stand next to her.

She was proud of him. "I'm so glad. You'll be great, and these people need you."

He placed the clip board on top of her suitcase and slipped his hand into hers. "Hana, I think you know what God's plan is for you too. I can see in your tired eyes you've been up all night. Me too. I won't tell you what He told me. You have to decide and do what God puts on your heart. Either way, I'll love you and keep you in my prayers."

His lips brushed her cheek. She knew what to do. It would be hard, but someone had to be disappointed. John snatched his clip board and rushed off to another group. His muscular frame radiated confidence. He worked the crowd—his tender smile extending grace to his fellow Japanese Americans.

She woke from her daydream to see Martin standing before her. "You're not going to Washington with us, are you?" Tears rolled down his cheeks. "I've sensed it for days. Then when you were talking to Doctor Bennett, I saw it in your eyes." He touched her arm. "Don't do anything you'll regret. We need you at home." He limped away from her, just in time for Mama to take his place.

She frowned at Hana. "You okay?"

"Yes, Mama-san. I'm okay. But I won't be going home with you." She choked back tears and willed her knees to stop shaking.

"I know. I see it in your eyes, and God tell me." Mama tenderly took Hana's face in her hands. "You good daughter. You go with him. Be happy."

Hana placed her hands on top of Mama's. "But how—"

The camp siren wound up and blared above them. Everyone looked up and around. Confusion and fear slithered through the crowd until a guard jumped on top of a crate and waved his arms.

"Japan has surrendered! The war is over! The war is over!" He jumped down and ran into the building, leaving everyone standing still, with only the wailing siren as noise.

It finally stopped and an eerie silence hung over the people. No cheers or applause, no laughing. Only faces full of apprehension and maybe pain. It was as if an ocean wave had snuck up on them and knocked them off balance. What would this mean for all of them? Hana wanted to hug them all and tell them it would be okay. But she wasn't sure herself.

A guard shouted from the steps of a loaded bus. "The last of you will board the bus coming down the road now!"

Martin and Chiko came to stand by Mama. Chiko's sobbing told Hana Martin had told her they would leave without her. No words were necessary. One by one Hana embraced her family. She held Chiko for a long time, feeling her shake with emotion. She would be all right, as would Mama and Martin. They had each other. Her heart ached for them as they shuffled away from her and boarded the bus. Chiko wiped away a circle of dust from the glass and waved through the window, still sobbing.

Hana staggered at the sight, but waved back. "Good-bye, little lady."

The bus pulled away and slid through the mud to the main road. Hana watched till it was out of sight—just like the day Papa left. She would see them again someday, though.

"You didn't leave." Neil bounded up the step and hugged her.

She let him embrace her, but then pushed him away. His smile faded. His shoulders dropped as she looked into his eyes. "Neil, I have great affection and admiration for you. But I don't love you. I can't go with you. We don't belong together. I was tempted, but that's not enough to build a life on."

"But you didn't go with your family. I thought—" He looked past her.

She turned to see John standing nearby. Still and alone. Waiting.

"I see." He backed away and gave her a half smile. "I guess this is good-bye then." She watched his Adam's apple go up and down. "You'll always be in my heart." He turned and spotted Doctor Davidson hopping into a large white van. "Doctor Davidson! Wait up!" He grabbed her hand and kissed the back of it. She squeezed his hand before he let go.

She watched him stand at the van door, obviously asking Doctor Davidson to wait for him. He turned and blew her a kiss before running off toward his cottage. She nodded and felt the warmth of John behind her. She leaned into him and waved to Neil, feeling the tingle of John's kiss behind her ear.

The war had ended for the world, and for her personal struggles, but not for the Japanese Americans still facing the fight to regain their property, dignity and sense of community. She surveyed the acres in front of her. The yard was empty except for a few internees who had come to bid farewells, their fate yet to be discovered. Uncertainty hung in the air even now. But not in her heart.

"Ready?" John took her hand. "There's lots of work to be done here."

She wiped her wet face. "Funny. I thought I was so clever not to fall for a rabble-rouser."

"I'll always be one. You'll learn to live with it."

November 1945

Overnight the wind had turned to an icy knife, penetrating Hana's coat and stinging her ears. The memories of late summer and all of fall were blurred together in a cloud of names and faces of those who had lastly and finally left Grand Peak. It was over. Not just the war and incarceration, but the men, women, and children's lives, as they once knew them, were over.

She shivered and flipped her coat collar around her neck as she approached the top of the hill above the administration buildings. John waved from below and dipped his head into the wind.

"Hurry up, I'm freezing." Her voice followed the breeze. He picked up his pace toward her and reached her in one last giant step.

"Whew. There's a bite to the air this morning." He slipped a Dodger's baseball cap from his pocket and pulled it tight over his head. "You packed?"

She nodded, examining his features. His face had grown older somehow over the last three months. Or was it just the look of fatigue and little sleep? Her chest welled at the recollection of his hours of sacrifice and dedication to facilitate the exit of the last of the internees. He had turned into a man she would be proud to marry, if only he would ask her.

He wrapped his arm around her shoulders and pulled her in close. Her shivering stopped as she snuggled in. They stepped in tandem toward the barrack. Once inside, John stoked the small embers in the stove with the last of the scrap lumber pile.

"Simon should be here in less than an hour. We can wait here for a while, then take our things back down to meet him." He held his hands close to the stove pipe while Hana pushed her bags to the door.

The room looked similar to the day they arrived—mostly empty, with only cots and the stove. Her stomach clenched to remember the look on Mama's face when she first stepped through the doorway.

Even though Hana sensed her pain, Mama never spoke one negative word about their new place. How many buckets of sand and dirt had Mama swept from the floors over the years, and how many pictures had she hung to make the dismal place more like a home?

Home.

Who could call this home? And where would her home be now? John had yet to answer her questions about their future, and in this moment she prayed again for God to give her peace and drive out all fear knocking at her heart.

The silence in the room broke when John cleared his throat. She jumped out of her thoughts and turned to him. His smile was as enticing as ever.

"Are you ready? In your heart, I mean."

"Ready for what? I don't know what to expect once we step out of this barrack. It's all so strange." She shuffled to the window. "What are we supposed to do with all the memories? I don't know how to process the consequences of the last four years. Do you?"

She felt his arms slip around her as she scanned the empty camp yard. The mountain stood as the sentinel it always had been, now topped with snow.

"Let it happen over time. We'll process it together, and with all the others we'll connect with when we get where we're going." He hugged her tight.

"And where is that, John. You haven't told me."

"Home."

"What home?"

"Isn't there a saying that home is where your heart is? Well, in this case I should say home is where your Mama-san is." He loosened his hold on her.

She spun around and grabbed his arms. Her heart pounded in her ears. She searched his eyes for signs that he was serious. Yes. He was.

"Home to Bainbridge Island?" Her whole body shook and she grasped him tighter. "Are you sure?"

"Where else would we go? They're expecting us. Simon has been in touch with them and it's all arranged."

She leaned her head on his chest. The tears and shaking wouldn't stop. Papa would be happy that John was taking her home. The family would be together again, but without him. She wiped her wet face and nodded to John. "You'll have to fill some big shoes in our family, young man."

"No. Martin can do that."

He bent down to pick up his satchel. "Besides, I hope to be the head of *our* home. Yours and mine. If you'll have me."

"I'll consider it." She grinned as she gathered up her own bags and stood up straight. "You'll have to behave."

"Deal."

The trek down the hill seemed to last forever. Hana thought of all the feet that had trod the path, heading out of injustice and toward the unknown. So many had died here, and so many had been born here. The essence of their lives walked like ghosts with Hana as she kept pace with John all the way to the waiting car.

Simon greeted them with a hearty embrace. "Ready?"

Hana's feet seemed frozen to the ground. The sight of the open gate turned her stomach.

"Hana?" John called from the car.

She turned to face the mountain, wanting to gasp for the breath that she couldn't calm. What was wrong?

Get going, Hana.

Her legs remained stubborn and still. It had been too long since she first made her way through that gate. She wasn't the same broken woman, but could she face the hardships that lie ahead? The wind bit at her face, but it refreshed the heat in her cheeks.

It's time to go. I am with you. This time the voice was not her own. Not John's, or Mama's, or Papa's. It was the voice she had come to recognize again after four years of separating herself from it—the voice she had barricaded behind her own barbed wire protective fence. Just as the camp was being torn down, so were the walls between her and God.

Papa had tried to tell her. "God's light will penetrate any fear, if you let it in."

She felt the warmth of light now, unsticking her feet from the ground she had hated for so long. Freedom, emancipation, called to her. Even the memories of Pearl Harbor couldn't seize her now.

More familiar ground waited for her, but she could take the lingering spirit of all those who touched her life here. Dr. Bennett, Dr. Davidson, Alice, and Michael. All of them, in their own way, had helped her find her way back. She lifted her head, nodding to the mountain.

"Good-bye."

As Simon drove, no one spoke. Tiny jagged flakes of snow fell against the window and quickly melted. The pain of the past would soon melt too, and her purpose would be clear again. She closed her eyes to imagine the healing that was to come, for her and for the Japanese American community. She would be cooperative with God from now on, letting Him take the reins of her life, and John's.

It was true, what Mama always said; "God take care. You see."

About the Author

Jan Cline is the author of *A Heart Out of Hiding, The Greatest of These is Love* (devotional), and contributing author for many anthologies. She lives with her husband in the Pacific Northwest and enjoys golfing and spending time at their little cottage on one of the beautiful lakes in the area.

Her love for history started as a child. Her father took her and her sister to museums, historical places, and stopped at every historical roadside marker in the western U.S.! Combining that with a love for writing was only natural.

Please visit her website at www.jancline.net, and join her on Facebook, Twitter, and Pinterest.

If you enjoyed *Emancipated Heart*, please leave a review on Amazon.com or your favorited review site.

Discussion Questions
Emancipated Heart

1) If you had 48 hours to pack and move to an unknown place, taking only what you could carry, what would you choose to bring?

2) What is "due process", and what does the constitution of the United States have to say about it?

3) What were the various reactions to internment for the characters in the Kato family, and why were they different?

4) What was Hana's biggest fear? At what point did she overcome it?

5) What did the characters of John and Neil learn from their diverse experiences at the camp? How much did their difference in race contribute to their thought process?

6) How did the characters feel about going home, and why? What was the reaction to the end of the war for the internees, and why?

7) How is the world different today in regard to racial fear and political engagement of alien Americans? Or is it different?

8) What, if anything, would you do differently if you were one of the internees?

References and Resources

Other books of interest on internment:

Looking Like the Enemy by Mary Matsuda, Gruenewald, NewSage Press (April 16, 2005)

Only What We Could Carry by Lawson Fusao Inada, Heyday; First Edition (August 1, 2000)

Hotel on the Corner of Bitter and Sweet, a novel by Jamie Ford, Ballantine Books (January 27, 2009)

Death poem read by Doctor Bennett: Hōjō Ujimasa (1538 – August 10, 1590)

Densho website: http://www.densho.org/

Heart Mountain Internment Camp Interpretive Center, Wyoming: http://www.heartmountain.org/

The Legacy of Heart Mountain, documentary by David Ono & Jeff MacIntyre, ©2014

Days of Waiting, All We Could Carry, documentary films by Steven Okazaki, ©Farallon Films

The History Channel online

Farewell to Manzanar, by Jeanne Wakatsuki Houston & James D. Houston, ©1973

54066916R00161

Made in the USA
Charleston, SC
23 March 2016